Five terrific, exciting and festive
romances to heat up the holidays!

Happy Christmas Love

MILLS & BOON®

Featuring
Bestselling Authors

Helen Bianchin
Sharon Kendrick
Susan Stephens
Lucy Gordon
Linda Turner

D0227397

Happy Christmas Love

MILLS & BOON

Helen Bianchin
Sharon Kendrick
Susan Stephens
Lucy Gordon
Linda Turner

Harlequin Mills & Boon Limited, Eton House,
18-24 Paradise Road, Richmond, Surrey TW9 1SR

HAPPY CHRISTMAS LOVE MILLS & BOON
© Harlequin Enterprises II B.V./S.à.r.l. 2010

A Christmas Marriage Ultimatum © Helen Bianchin 2004
Yuletide Reunion © Sharon Kendrick 1998
The Sultan's Seduction © Susan Stephens 2004
The Millionaire's Christmas Wish © Lucy Gordon 2004
A Wild West Christmas © Linda Turner 1996

ISBN: 978 0 263 88829 4

024-1110

Harlequin Mills & Boon policy is to use papers that are
natural, renewable and recyclable products and made from
wood grown in sustainable forests. The logging and
manufacturing processes conform to the legal environmental
regulations of the country of origin.

Printed and bound in the UK by
CPI Mackays, Chatham ME5 8TD

A Christmas Marriage Ultimatum

Helen Bianchin

Helen Bianchin was born in New Zealand and travelled to Australia before marrying her Italian-born husband. After three years they moved, returned to New Zealand with their daughter, had two sons, then resettled in Australia. Encouraged by friends to recount anecdotes of her years as a tobacco sharefarmer's wife living in an Italian community, Helen began setting words on paper and her first novel was published in 1975. An animal lover, she says her terrier and Persian cat regard her study as much theirs as hers.

Helen Bianchin's most recent novel,
***Public Marriage, Private Secrets*, is available**
now from Modern™ Romance.

CHAPTER ONE

CHANTELLE transferred the last bag of groceries into the boot and closed it, then she returned the shopping trolley to a nearby bay. Minutes later she eased her mother's Lexus out from the car park and joined the flow of traffic heading north.

Handling left-hand drive after a four-year absence didn't pose any problems at all, and she slid her sunglasses down to shade her eyes from the glare of the midsummer sun as she headed towards Sovereign Islands, a top-end luxury residential estate on Queensland's Gold Coast, comprising numerous waterways where boats and cruisers lay moored adjacent waterfront homes.

It was an idyllic setting, and she approved of her parents' move from their frenetic Sydney lifestyle. Mother and stepfather, she mentally corrected, although Jean-Paul had taken on the role of father when she'd been nine years old. Too long ago for her to regard him as anything other than a much-loved parent.

The past few years had wrought several changes, she reflected musingly.

Who would have thought at twenty-four she'd have thrown up a position as pharmacist in an exclusive Sydney pharmacy, a modern apartment, family, friends...for a small villa owned by her parents in northern France?

Yet four years ago it had seemed the perfect place to escape to following an end to a brief, passionate affair.

A month after her arrival, she'd discovered she was pregnant. So she'd stayed, gaining work in the local *pharmacie*, and had the baby, a beautiful dark-haired, dark-eyed boy she'd named Samuel. It had become a matter of pride to be self-supportive, and her parents visited twice a year.

Now, after a four-year absence, she'd brought Samuel to Australia for him to sample his first southern-hemispheric Christmas.

'No snow,' she'd explained when the jet touched down in Brisbane two days ago, and rejoiced in her son's wonderment at the switch in climates as he embraced his grandparents.

How simplistic life was to a child, Chantelle mused as she traversed the first of three bridges leading to Anouk and Jean-Paul Patric's home on one of seven islands linked to form the suburban Sovereign Islands estate.

Children responded to love and affection, and her son was no exception. Bilingual, he was equally conversant in French and English. Tall for his tender years, thick dark hair, beautiful dark eyes, with a melting smile, he was his father in miniature.

Chantelle shook off the whisper of ice slithering down her spine at the thought of the man who'd fathered her child.

Dimitri Cristopoulis. Undeniably Greek, American educated, tall, dark and attractive, an entrepreneur in his mid-thirties who dealt in the buying and selling of hotels and apartment buildings in several major cities worldwide.

Even now, his image was as vivid as it had been four years ago. Broad sculpted facial features, olive textured skin, dark gleaming eyes, and a mouth to die for.

Sexy, sensual and incredibly lethal, she'd mentally accorded when she'd first caught his gaze in a Sydney city restaurant.

She hadn't been wrong. He was all three, and more…much more. She, who was incredibly selective in sharing her body, had gifted hers willingly after one night.

For one month they'd enjoyed life and each other with a passion that captured her heart. Only to have it torn apart with the arrival of an actress claiming to be his fiancée.

Confrontation involved accusations and argument, and Chantelle had walked away…out of his life, her own, invoking her parents' promise not to divulge information as to her whereabouts. In a bid for a new life, a new identity, she had reverted to her legal birth-name of Chantelle *Leone*.

Now Chantelle turned into the boulevard housing

the elegant home her parents had retired to last year from their mansion in Sydney, used the remote modem to open the gates, and garaged the car.

Jean-Paul appeared as she opened the boot, and together they caught up the grocery bags and took them indoors.

'Maman, Maman!'

Chantelle deposited the bags on the kitchen table and opened her arms wide to scoop up her son. 'Hello, *mon ange*. Have you been good for Grandmère?'

'*Excellent,*' Samuel assured as he wrapped his arms around her neck. 'Tonight we're having a party.' He pressed kisses to her cheek. 'Grandmère says I am an important guest.'

'Very important,' she confirmed, hugging him close. He was the most precious person in her life, and she never failed to ensure he knew just how much he was loved. 'After lunch you must have a long nap, hmm? So you will be at your best, and everyone will think you totally adorable.'

'Totally.'

Chantelle chuckled and buried her lips into the curve of his sweet neck. He was developing a delightful sense of humour, and his smile…it bore the promise of having the same devastating effect as the man who'd fathered him.

Which tore at her heartstrings more than she cared to admit. Already, the likeness between child and father was fast becoming apparent. Too apparent, she perceived, making it difficult to dismiss Dimitri Cristopoulis from her mind.

A silent derisive laugh rose and died in her throat. As if that was going to happen any time soon. His image was just as powerful now as it had been four years ago.

Worse, he invaded her dreams...teasing, taunting, enticing in a way that brought her awake heated, restless and *wanting*.

'We'll have an early lunch,' Anouk relayed as she began unloading the grocery bags. 'Then we begin preparations, *oui*?'

It proved to be a busy afternoon, and Chantelle stood with Anouk and Jean-Paul for a final inspection before they retreated upstairs to dress.

The large terrace looked festive with a tracery of coloured lights, lanterns and potted flowers gracing the area. Holly and mistletoe, a tall Christmas tree festooned with decorative ornaments, with wrapped gifts for the guests. Bottles of wine for the men, and handmade chocolates for the women which Anouk and Jean-Paul would hand out at the evening's close.

A kindly protestation not to go over the top fell on deaf ears, for Anouk had merely smiled, patted her daughter's hand, bestowed a fleeting kiss to one cheek, and assured it was just an informal gathering of friends.

Given her mother's penchant for entertaining, and the many formal social events Anouk had hosted in Sydney over the years, Chantelle conceded with musing humour that tonight's soirée fell into *informal* by comparison.

Samuel's delighted enchantment with everything

was sufficient reward for the requisite part she was expected to play.

Consequently she selected a stunning black evening trouser suit, draped a long red silk wrap across her shoulders, added minimum jewellery, and went with subtle make-up before leading Samuel downstairs.

Jean-Paul greeted guests in the main foyer, directed them through to the terrace, whereupon Anouk ensured they mixed and mingled seamlessly while hired staff offered liquid refreshment and proffered trays of hors d'oeuvres.

Anouk was a charming hostess, and Chantelle joined her mother as they moved effortlessly from one guest to another, pausing while Anouk exchanged a few words, a smile as she introduced her daughter and grandson.

Everyone seemed pleasant, and Chantelle silently commended her parents' circle of friends.

Samuel was in his element, and determined to illustrate his good manners as he formally offered his hand at each introduction.

He was a hit, she acknowledged with maternal bemusement, exuding the charm of a child twice his age.

Just like his father.

Where did that come from? A hollow laugh rose and died in her throat.

Not a day went by when she wasn't reminded of the man who'd fathered him.

Chantelle was aware of her mother's voice as she effected yet another introduction, and she summoned a smile as she greeted the guest.

'Andreas recently moved to the Coast,' Anouk explained. 'And purchased a mansion in a neighbouring Sovereign Islands boulevard.'

There was something about the man's stance, the way he held his head that drew her attention.

'Your parents very kindly included me in this evening's festivities,' he informed in a voice that held a faint accent that was difficult to place.

Andreas… The name was of Greek origin.

'We have something in common,' he offered. 'My son is also visiting for Christmas. He's in the car finishing a call on his cellphone.'

She envisioned with some scepticism a high-powered entrepreneur digitally available twenty-four by seven, negotiating and closing deals worldwide.

'I'm sure you'll enjoy his visit,' Chantelle conceded politely, aware of a momentary intentness evident as the man's attention focused on her son.

Was it her imagination, or did she glimpse conjecture before it was quickly masked?

Then the moment was gone as Anouk steered her towards a young couple who spent several minutes enthusing about their recent trip to Paris.

Chantelle enjoyed their praise of a city she adored, and they lingered together awhile.

'If you'll excuse us?' Anouk inclined with a warm smile. 'Another guest has arrived.'

The last, surely? Chantelle mused as she followed her mother's line of vision to a tall, broad-framed man whose stance portrayed an animalistic sense of power.

Even from a distance he managed to exude a physical magnetism most men would covet.

The set of his shoulders beneath their superb tailoring held a certain familiarity, and she fought against the rising sense of panic, tempering it with rationale.

How many times had she caught sight of a male figure whose stature bore a close resemblance to that of Samuel's father, only to discover his facial features were those of a stranger?

As it would prove on this occasion, she mentally assured as she saw Andreas move towards him.

Father and son. Had to be, she registered as the two men greeted each other with familial ease.

Seconds later they both turned at Anouk's approach, and Chantelle froze, locked into speechless immobility in recognition of a man she'd hoped never to see again in this lifetime.

Dimitri Cristopoulis.

What was he doing here? Here, specifically in her parents' home?

Dimitri's family resided in New York…didn't they?

He'd never said, and she hadn't asked. She choked back a hollow laugh. Had she even given it a thought?

In seeming slow motion Chantelle witnessed the introduction process, aware of Dimitri's calculating gaze as it encompassed first her, then her son, before settling with ruthless intensity on her own.

'Chantelle.'

The sound of his voice sent shivers scudding the length of her spine. How could so much be conveyed in a single word?

No. The silent scream rose and died in her throat at what she glimpsed in those dark eyes before it was masked.

With mounting consternation she watched as he sank down onto his haunches and extended his hand to her son.

'Samuel.'

The similarity between man and child was indisputable. Her son, but undeniably *his.*

Everything faded to the periphery of her vision, and she was conscious only of Dimitri and Samuel. Her hand closed over her son's shoulder in a protective, reassuring gesture.

'Pleased to meet you,' Samuel offered with childlike politeness.

Dear heaven, this was the culmination of her worst nightmare. Instinct screamed for her to scoop Samuel into her arms…and run as fast and as far away as she could.

Except Dimitri would follow. She could sense it, *knew* it in the depths of her soul. This time there would be no escape…no place she could hide where he wouldn't find her.

Chantelle was dimly aware of her mother's voice, although the words failed to register.

Did anyone guess she was a total mess? Every nerve in her body seemed to shred and sever, changing her into a trembling wreck.

Dimitri rose to his full height, and she caught sight of the veiled anger apparent in those dark eyes an instant before he masked it.

There were questions…several, she sensed he would demand answers to. Yet the most telling one was startlingly obvious.

Fear closed like an icy fist around her heart. He couldn't take Samuel away from her…could he?

Was it her imagination, or did the air fizz with tension? For a wild moment she felt if she so much as moved a muscle, she'd be struck down by its invisible force.

'Maman, may I be excused?' A small voice penetrated the immediate silence, and brought Chantelle's undivided attention.

'Naturellement, petit.' She offered a polite smile, then she turned and led Samuel towards the staircase.

A reprieve. One she badly needed. It would allow her time to recoup her severely shaken composure, and prepare for whatever the evening held in store.

For the next hour she could legitimately use Samuel as a shield. But the time would come when she'd have to face Dimitri alone. What then?

She felt the slight tug of Samuel's hand and realised she retained too tight a hold on it. A self-derisory sound choked in her throat at such carelessness, and she lifted him into her arms, then buried her lips against the sweet curve of his neck.

'Maman, who is that man?'

Bathroom duty complete, he studiously dried his hands, his dark eyes solemn as he posed the query.

Your father. Two simple words which couldn't be uttered without an accompanying explanation to his level of understanding.

'Someone I met a long time ago,' she said gently.

'Before I was born?'

Chantelle bent down and brushed her lips to his forehead. 'Uh-huh.'

'He's very big. Bigger than Grandpère.' Solemn dark eyes locked with hers. 'Do you like him?'

Oh, my. 'Grandpère?' she teased. 'Of course. Grandpère is the best, *non*?'

'*Oui*. And Grandmère,' Samuel added. 'But the man is scary.'

Scary covered a multitude of meanings to a child whose vocabulary was beginning to broaden. 'He would never hurt you.' She could give such reassurance unequivocally.

'No,' Samuel dismissed. 'He had a scary face when he looked at you.'

Out of the mouths of babes. 'Maybe it was because we had a disagreement.' A mild description for the blazing row they'd shared.

Her son absorbed the words, then offered with childlike simplicity, 'Didn't he say sorry?'

'No.' But then, neither had she. 'Shall we go downstairs to the party? Grandmère will wonder where we are.'

To remain absent for too long would be impolite.

Besides, she adored her mother and refused to allow Dimitri's presence to mar the evening.

It took considerable effort to act out a part, but act she did...smiling, laughing as she mixed and mingled, conversing with what she hoped was admirable panache.

Exclusive schooling and a year being 'finished' paid off in spades, and she defied anyone to criticise her performance.

She was supremely conscious of Dimitri's presence, and he made no effort to disguise his interest. It was only by adroit manipulation that she managed to avoid him during the ensuing hour.

Samuel held most of her attention, and it was with a sense of suspended apprehension she signalled it time for him to bid the guests 'good night.'

Preparations for bed and the reading of a story took a while, and she watched as his eyelids began to droop, saw him fight sleep, then succumb to it.

Chantelle switched off the bedlamp, leaving only the glow of a night-light to provide faint illumination. Five minutes, she allowed, enjoying the time to study his face in repose.

He was growing so quickly, developing a sensitive, caring nature she hoped would remain despite the trials life might hold for him.

An errant lock of hair lay against his forehead, and she gently smoothed it back before exiting the room.

As he was a sound sleeper who rarely woke during the night, she was confident he wouldn't stir. However, she intended to check on him at regular intervals, just in case the excitement of travel, a strange house and a party atmosphere disturbed his usual sleep pattern.

A degree of misgiving caused her stomach to tighten as she re-entered the lounge. Most of the guests had converged on the adjoining terrace, and she caught up a flute of champagne from a proffered tray as she moved outdoors.

The string of electric lanterns provided a colourful glow. The sky had darkened to a deep indigo, and there was a tracery of stars evident, offering the promise of another warm summer's day.

Anouk and Jean-Paul worked the terrace, ensuring their guests were content, replete with food and wine. It was a practised art, and one they'd long perfected.

Chantelle followed their example, pausing to chat to one couple or another, genuinely interested in their chosen career, the merits of the Gold Coast, relaying details of her plans during the length of her stay.

Invitations were offered, and she graciously deferred accepting any without first conferring with her mother.

Dimitri was *there*...a dangerous, primitive force. She was supremely conscious of his attention. The waiting, watching quality evident...like a predator stalking for a kill.

If he wanted her on edge, he was succeeding, she perceived, aware of the cracks beginning to appear in her social façade.

'Chantelle.'

The sound of his deep drawl shredded her nerves. All evening she'd prepared for this moment. Yet still he'd managed to surprise her.

'Dimitri,' she acknowledged, forgoing the polite smile.

He wasn't standing close enough to invade her personal space, yet all it would take was another step forward.

'We need to talk.'

She arched a deliberate eyebrow. 'I'm not aware we have anything to discuss.'

'No? You want I should spell it out?'

It wasn't easy to maintain a distant, albeit polite façade. 'Please do.'

Dimitri didn't move, yet it appeared as if he had, and she forced herself to stand absolutely still.

'Samuel.'

Chantelle felt fear gnaw at her nerve-ends. 'What about him?'

A muscle bunched at the edge of his jaw. 'The Cristopoulis resemblance is uncanny.'

'Consequently you've put two and two together and come to the conclusion he might be yours?' How could she sound so calm, or inject the slight musing element into her voice, when inside she was shaking?

'You deny the possibility?'

'I'm under no obligation to you, or anyone, to reveal his father's identity.'

'You want me to go the distance with this?' Dimitri queried in a voice that was dangerously soft. 'Seek legal counsel, access his birth certificate, request DNA?'

Ice slithered the length of her spine. 'Is that a threat?'

'A statement of intention,' he corrected.

'I could deny your request for DNA.' The need to consult a lawyer seemed imperative.

His mouth formed a cynical smile, although there was no humour apparent in those dark eyes. 'Try it.'

Her stomach performed a slow, painful somersault. 'You possess an outsize ego. What makes you think you were my only lover?'

'I was *there*,' Dimitri reminded with deceptive quietness. Leashed savagery lay just beneath the surface of his control, and he gained some satisfaction as soft colour tinged her cheeks.

Was his memory of what they'd shared as startlingly vivid as her own? They'd spent every night together, never seeming to be able to satisfy a mutual hunger for each other.

Possession on every level. An all-consuming passion that had known no bounds.

She had lived for the moment she could be with him, resenting each minute they were apart. The sun had never shone more brightly, nor the senses become so defined. If hearts sang, hers had played a soaring rhapsody in full orchestra.

As for the sex... Intimacy, she corrected, at its most intense...highly sensual, libidinous, *magic*.

'There was no one else for either of us,' Dimitri pursued in a silkily soft voice that speared her heart.

Chantelle drew in a deep breath, then slowly released it. 'Aren't you forgetting Daniella?' Even now, it hurt her to say the actress's name.

A muscle bunched at the edge of his jaw. 'We dealt with that four years ago.'

'No,' she corrected with incredible politeness. 'We had a blazing row over the disparity between *her* account of your relationship, and *yours*.'

'At which time you chose to believe her version, rather than mine.'

Even now, the scene rose up to taunt her…the harsh words, the invective. 'She conveyed telling evidence.'

'Cleverly relayed to achieve the desired outcome,' Dimitri attested. 'Daniella is a scheming manipulator, and an extremely clever actress.'

'So you said at the time,' Chantelle declared bitterly. 'Yet you still walked.'

Her trust in him, what she'd thought they had together, had been destroyed. 'I couldn't stay.' He hadn't tried to stop her. Nor had he called.

To be fair, neither had she.

'Shall we begin again?'

'There is nothing to discuss.'

'We can do it here, now. Or we can share dinner tomorrow night.' He waited a beat. 'Your choice.'

'No.'

One eyebrow slanted. 'You want to play hardball?'

'I don't want to *play* at all!'

His features assumed a hard mask. 'I deserve to know if Samuel is my son.'

'What if I tell you he's not?'

His gaze pierced hers, indomitable and frighteningly inflexible. 'I want proof, one way or another.'

Bravado rose to the fore as she held his gaze. 'You don't have the right.'

'Yes, I do. Seven, tomorrow evening. I'll collect you.'

She didn't want him here. In fact, she didn't want to see him *anywhere*, period!

'You want to do this with a degree of civility?' Dimitri queried. 'Or—?'

'I'll meet you.' She named the first restaurant that came to mind. 'Seven.'

Without a further word she moved away from him, seeking another guest...*anyone* with whom she could converse and therefore escape Dimitri Cristopoulis' damning presence.

CHAPTER TWO

'YOU look charming, *chérie*,' Anouk complimented the following evening as Chantelle collected the keys to her mother's car.

'Thank you.' She'd chosen a slim-fitting dress in black with a black lace overlay, short sleeves and a square neckline. Black stiletto-heeled sandals lent her petite frame added height, and she'd swept hair the colour of sable high into a careless knot.

'It's nice of Andreas' son to invite you to dine with him.'

Nice wasn't a description she'd accord Dimitri… or his motives behind the invitation. If Anouk knew the real reason there would be concern, not pleasure, evident.

However, not even her mother knew the identity of Samuel's father. Her parents had been absent from Sydney at the time of Chantelle's affair with Dimitri, and afterwards, when told of her pregnancy, they'd counselled informing the child's father…advice she'd chosen to discount.

She crouched down to give Samuel a hug. 'Be good for Grandmère, hmm?'

'*Oui, Maman.*'

Such solemn brown eyes, she mused, kissing each childish cheek in turn.

'Thanks,' she said lightly as Anouk gathered Samuel close. 'I won't be late.'

For the past eighteen hours she'd derived countless reasons why she should opt out of tonight. Only the knowledge Dimitri was capable of forcing a confrontation in her parents' home prevented her from employing any one of them.

It took twenty minutes to reach the glamorous hotel situated on the Spit at Main Beach. Chantelle chose valet parking, and stepped into the marble foyer.

Expansive with glorious oriental rugs, comfortable sofas, it stretched out to a double staircase leading to a lower floor, beyond which lay a wide decorative pool, an island bar and, in the distance, the ocean.

It was spectacular, and a waterfall added to the tropical overtone.

Chantelle admired the view for numerous seconds, then she turned towards the restaurant.

'Punctual, as always.'

The sound of that familiar, faintly accented male voice caused the knot in her stomach to tighten.

Get a grip, she remonstrated silently. She needed to be in control, and nervous tension didn't form part of the evening's agenda.

She turned slightly and met Dimitri's steady gaze.

'It's one of my virtues.'

'Would you prefer a drink in the lounge, or shall we go straight in?'

She even managed a slight smile. Amazing, when the butterflies in her stomach were beating a faint tattoo.

'Why don't we cut the social niceties?' Cool, but neither calm nor collected.

Damn him. He'd always had this effect on her equilibrium. The sight of him sent her pulse racing to a crazy beat. It was the whole male package, his choice of cologne, the freshly laundered clothes… the faint male scent that was uniquely his.

All it took was one look, and her system went out of control. Even now, when she told herself she hated him, heat pooled deep inside, and the pulse at her throat felt as if it jumped beneath her skin.

Could he sense it? *See* it? Dear heaven, she hoped not.

The *maître d'* issued a greeting and led them to their table, where he summoned a drinks waiter, performed an introduction, then graciously retreated.

Dimitri ordered a crisp chardonnay, requested bottled water, and then he settled back comfortably in his chair.

There were a hundred places she'd rather be than *here, now*. Yet what choice did she have? Her parents could cope with anything life threw at them, but Samuel was too young, too vulnerable, and she'd go to the ends of the earth to protect him from harm…physical, mental, emotional.

Take control, an inner voice urged as she reached for her glass and sipped chilled water.

'Let's not pretend this is anything other than what it is,' Chantelle opined coolly, and saw one eyebrow slant in silent query.

'Perhaps we should order?' Dimitri suggested as the waiter presented the menu.

Food? The thought of calmly forking artistically presented morsels in his company killed what little appetite she had.

Nevertheless, it was necessary to order something, and she settled on a starter and skipped the main course.

'Not hungry?'

'Is my appetite an issue?'

His gaze remained steady, and had the effect of unnerving her...which was undoubtedly deliberate.

'Relax.'

Oh, sure, and that was easy, given he inevitably had a bundle of legal tricks up his sleeve ready to heap on her unsuspecting head.

'I'm here at your insistence,' Chantelle reminded. 'Sharing a meal I don't particularly want in the company of someone I'd prefer never to have to see again in this lifetime.'

'Pity.'

Her eyes flashed dark fire. 'What do you mean... *pity*?'

'If Samuel is my son,' Dimitri voiced with dangerous softness, 'you'll have to get used to me being part of your life.'

'The hell I will!'

Something moved in his eyes, and she felt a chill slither down the length of her spine. 'Take it as a given, Chantelle.'

The words were hard, inflexible, and seared her heart. 'You don't have that right.'

The arrival of the waiter brought a welcome break, and she viewed the contents of her plate with misgiving, sure the smallest mouthful would stick in her throat.

'Eat,' Dimitri bade, and she did, managing to do justice to the food. He wasn't to know her taste-buds had gone on strike.

Conversation had never been so difficult to summon, and anything she thought to offer seemed inane.

It irked her unbearably he was able to affect her this way. *Act*, she chastised silently. Adopt a practised façade, and pretend Dimitri Cristopoulis is just a man like any other male.

Oh, sure…chance would be a fine thing! She had only to look at him and every nerve-end tingled into vibrant life.

Four years hadn't made the slightest difference. It was as if her soul recognised his on some base level and sought recognition.

Damn him. Damn coincidence for putting them both in this part of the world at the same time! Fate was playing a cruel hand, intent on causing emotional havoc before the game was over.

Who would win? a silent imp taunted.

Dimitri replaced his cutlery, then he picked up his

wineglass and leaned back in his chair. 'Do you want to begin, or shall I?'

Chantelle lifted a hand in a negligent gesture. 'Oh, please. Be my guest.'

For a few seemingly long seconds he didn't speak, and she could tell nothing from his expression.

'Samuel's birth certificate records June one as the day he was born.'

How could he know that?

Dimitri's mouth moved to form a wry smile. 'I called in a favour.' All he'd had to do was make a few phone calls, and he had the information he needed within hours.

'Nine and a half months after we began our relationship,' he pursued, watching her expressive features through a narrowed gaze. Anger had been just one of the emotions he'd experienced at the confirmation. Resentment had followed with the knowledge she'd chosen not to reveal her pregnancy. There was also a mixture of pride and joy at the thought he had a child…a son.

As to the child's mother…he'd deal with her. But not easily.

'So,' he continued silkily. 'Shall we move on?'

'Samuel is *mine*,' Chantelle reiterated fiercely. 'I could have had an abortion.' She'd never considered it as an option. Hadn't, even from the onset, thought of a child…Dimitri's child, but indisputably *hers*… as an encumbrance.

'Yet you didn't.'

She remembered the birth, when she'd cursed

Dimitri a hundred times…and she thought of the moment the nurse had placed Samuel in her arms. The indescribable joy that transcended all else, and the fierce protectiveness for the tiny life.

'No.'

He wanted to reach across the table and shake her. For denying him the opportunity to be there, to care for her, and to claim the child as his own.

'Tell me,' he pursued silkily. 'Did you ever intend for me to know I had a child?'

'Not if I could help it.'

'Your body, your responsibility?'

'*Yes.*'

'Allowing some other man to take my place? Raise my son as his own? Give him his name?'

Chantelle could sense the anger beneath his control, *feel* it emanate from his body as a tangible entity.

'Samuel is registered as Samuel *Leone.*'

'Something that can easily be changed.'

'To what purpose?' she demanded. Anger rose to the fore, darkening her eyes. 'I live in France, you reside in New York.'

'Samuel is a Cristopoulis. He has a heritage,' Dimitri endorsed with quiet savagery. 'I intend to ensure he claims it.'

'With you?' She was like a runaway train, unable to stop. 'What are you going to do, Dimitri? Engage a nanny during Samuel's visits? Maybe look in on him as he sleeps when you leave your apartment in the morning, and again when you return long after his bedtime?' She picked up her napkin and thrust it on the table. 'Is that your idea of parental visitation rights?' She rose to her feet and gathered her purse. 'Hell will freeze over before I'll allow it.'

He watched her with interest, admiring the fire, the sheer will beneath her fury. A mother defending and protecting her own, he mused.

The waiter chose that moment to deliver the main course, only to stand poised as he sensed the onset of a scene.

Chantelle turned away from the table, only to have her escape forestalled as Dimitri's hand closed over her wrist.

She tried to wrench her hand free, and failed miserably. Fury pitched her voice low. 'Let me go.'

'Sit down.' He waited a few seconds, then cautioned with chilling softness, 'We're not done yet.'

'I'll have the *maître d'* call Security.'

'Go ahead.' His voice was a hateful drawl.

'There's nothing further you can say that I want to hear.'

He didn't move, but something about him changed, hardened. 'If you prefer negotiations to share custody of our son be dealt with through the legal system...so be it.' He released her wrist, and regarded her steadily.

Why did she feel like a butterfly whose wings had been pinned to a wall?

'Sit down, Chantelle. Please,' he added.

'Following the manner in which we parted, anything amicable between us is impossible.'

'Daniella fed you a tissue of lies, which you chose to believe.'

'You walked out,' Chantelle accused.

His gaze speared hers. 'What did you expect?'

'You should have told me about her.' Even now, she could feel the anger surge at the memory of that awful scene.

'Daniella was never in the picture.'

'So you told me at the time. Perhaps you should also have told *her*.'

'I did.'

'That's not what she said.'

'It wouldn't have served her purpose to tell the truth.'

'Her purpose being?'

'To send you running as far away as possible.' He waited a beat. 'She succeeded.'

'And you know that *because*?'

'You'd already left your apartment when I rang. The phone number I had for you was disconnected. Ditto your cellphone.'

Pain spiralled through her body. 'That's easy to say *now*.'

'You'd left the pharmacy,' he continued. 'No one had any idea where you were.'

Anouk and Jean-Paul had been absent, enjoying a European vacation, and Chantelle had begged both employer and work colleagues to disavow any knowledge of her whereabouts. 'I took leave to visit relatives in France,' she revealed. 'Within weeks I was offered a job, so I found lodgings, began work…' She paused fractionally. 'And discovered I was pregnant.'

'With my child.'

There seemed no point in further denial. 'Yes.'

'You refused to consider I might choose to support you?'

'I didn't need your support.'

'Therefore you imagined I had no right to know you'd conceived my child?'

She looked at him carefully. 'Imagined?' A wry smile tugged the edge of her mouth. 'I didn't think there was *anything* left to the imagination, given the way we parted.' Her shoulders lifted in a negligible shrug. 'At that stage neither you nor I wanted anything to do with each other, ever again.'

'And now?'

'What do you mean—*now*?' Her stomach took a dive. 'Nothing has changed.'

One eyebrow slanted. 'No?'

'In three weeks Samuel and I return to France. You'll depart for New York, and we'll probably never see each other again.'

'Wrong.'

'Excuse me?'

'Think again.'

'Samuel doesn't need a father,' Chantelle said fiercely. 'He especially doesn't need *you*.'

'I intend being part of his life,' Dimitri reiterated silkily. 'With or without your permission.'

'Something you'll never have.'

'You'd prefer a legal fight rather than a cordial agreement?'

'I'd prefer,' she managed with a degree of vehemence, 'never to see you again.'

'That's not going to happen,' he asserted in dry, mocking tones. 'By virtue of the interest we have in our son.'

'A son you knew nothing about until twenty-four hours ago!'

'But now I do,' Dimitri said smoothly.

'I won't share Samuel with you.'

'The law courts will have a different view.'

The waiter appeared and presented Dimitri's main course, and she watched as he made no attempt to pick up his cutlery.

Instead, his eyes were dark, almost still as he regarded her.

'I don't want Samuel to be pushed and pulled between two parents who don't like each other,' she said quietly.

'You consider us as enemies?'

Oh, God. 'We're not exactly friends.'

A faint smile tugged the corner of his mouth. 'Yet we were lovers.'

Dear heaven, just thinking about what they'd shared sent pain shafting through her body. She'd lived, breathed for the moment she could see him, be with him. Just the sound of his voice on the phone was enough to send her pulse racing and have heat pool deep within. She'd loved him, *loved*, she cried silently, with all her heart. Her soul. Everything. Only to have it shatter into a thousand pieces.

'That was years ago,' she managed carefully, hoping her voice didn't convey her shredding nerves. She wanted to ask why he'd tried to make contact after that fateful day.

'Not so many,' he reminded. 'And it feels like yesterday.'

Don't, she wanted to protest. Please don't go there.

'You should eat,' Chantelle encouraged in a bid to change the conversation.

'Concern for my digestive system?'

'Why not admit we've reached a verbal impasse?' she countered. 'We oppose each other on every issue regarding my son.'

'Our son,' he corrected.

'If I hadn't—'

'Visited your parents? If I hadn't chosen this particular year to spend the festive season with Andreas?' His regard was unwavering. 'Yet we did.'

'And now we have to deal with it?' As soon as the query left her lips, the knowledge hit that it was *she* who would have to deal with the changes. Dimitri would insist on playing a part in Samuel's life, and he was powerful enough to enforce his legal right to do so.

His eyes never left hers, and she struggled to diminish the impact he had on her senses.

'Perhaps we should take advantage of fate, and redress the day we walked out of each other's life.'

A cold fist closed round her heart. 'Rehashing the past won't achieve anything.'

'It might, however, give credence to our reactions.'

She didn't want to do this. It evoked too many painful memories.

'You're not curious as to why I tried to contact you after I returned to New York?'

'Guilt?'

He recalled that day with disturbing clarity, aware it ranked high among those numbered as the worst in his life.

To Chantelle's credit, she had no idea, and he took in her expressive features, the slight tilt of her chin, the pain in those beautiful dark eyes.

'An hour before I arrived at your apartment I'd had a call from New York to say my mother was in hospital on life support following an horrific car accident.' The food on his plate remained untouched. 'I'd spent time organising a flight, delegating work to colleagues. Leaving was the hardest thing I had to do. There were words I wanted to say,' he continued. 'Except I didn't have the time or the opportunity.'

Chantelle held a vivid recollection of the phone call she'd received from Daniella, and Dimitri's appearance soon after. The actress's allegations had succeeded in filling her mind with doubt and resultant anger. Anger she'd levelled at him within minutes of his arrival at her apartment.

She recalled his denial, his reassurance…and his anger when she'd refused to accept his word as truth. One thing had led to another, and when he'd said he had to leave, she'd vowed if he walked out the door she wouldn't allow him back in.

'The food is not to your liking?'

Chantelle heard the words and registered the waiter's appearance at their table.

'I'm sure it's fine,' Dimitri offered, and brushed aside an offer to bring a fresh serving, qualifying, 'Thank you. No.'

His mother had been critically injured? He'd had to return immediately to New York?

The words reverberated inside her brain with alarming confusion. 'You should have told me,' she managed quietly, regretful she hadn't given him the chance.

'She remained in a coma for several weeks. Andreas and I took it in turns to sit with her. In the end we had to accept she had no hope of recovery.'

She was silent for several long seconds, unable to utter a word. 'I'm sorry,' she offered at last. 'I wish I'd known,' she said quietly as she attempted to come to grips with the words she'd flung at him in anger…testing his control, and breaking it.

With devastating result…for both of them.

'Andreas took a long holiday with his sister in Sydney and decided to make the city his base, handing control of the corporation to me.'

Chantelle closed her eyes, then opened them again. Like a long-unfinished puzzle, some of the missing pieces were falling into place.

It explained much, yet left an aching void for what might have been.

To continue sharing his table, his company, was more than she could bear.

'If you don't mind, I'd like to leave.'

His gaze never left hers. 'We're far from finished.'

Emotion welled up inside, making her feel physi-

cally ill. 'For tonight, we are.' She stood to her feet
and extracted a note from her evening purse.

'Don't even think about it,' Dimitri cautioned in
chilling warning as he signalled the waiter for the bill.

'There's no need for you to leave,' Chantelle protested stiffly.

'Yes, there is.'

She moved ahead of him, aware he followed close
behind her as she crossed the marble-tiled reception
lounge to the concierge.

'I'll ring tomorrow and arrange a suitable time to
spend a few hours with Samuel.'

No. 'I'm unsure what my parents have planned.'
The words tumbled from her lips in quick succession,
and incurred his steady gaze.

'Naturally you'll accompany him.'

Oh, God. 'I don't think—'

'A few hours, Chantelle.'

'He has a nap in the afternoon,' she offered in
desperation.

'In that case, we'll organise a morning.'

The Lexus drew in ahead of Dimitri's hire car, and
Chantelle was unprepared for his actions as he
cupped her face and brushed her lips with his own.

It was a light, almost fleeting touch, but it wreaked
havoc with her fragile emotions.

For a moment she could only look at him, her
eyes wide and vulnerable until she successfully
masked their expression.

Her mouth parted, then closed again, and without
a further word she turned and slid in behind the

wheel, engaged the gear, then she sent the vehicle down the incline to street level.

It was a scene she replayed again and again as she lay unable to sleep.

His scent, his touch evoked feelings she thought she'd dealt with.

Fat chance, she muttered inaudibly as she tossed and turned for the umpteenth time.

The question was…where did they go from here?

Where did she want to go?

A few days ago her life had been secure on a path of her choice. Now confusion reigned, and she didn't like it at all.

CHAPTER THREE

CHANTELLE stood at the kitchen sink and watched Samuel play with Jean-Paul. Her son, even at three and a half, was beginning to show a flair for kicking a ball.

'This morning it appeared you slept badly, and you've been troubled all day,' Anouk ventured gently. 'Is there something you want to tell me, *chérie*?'

Maternal instinct was acute, Chantelle admitted ruefully as she shook excess water from the salad greens she was preparing for their midday meal.

'Your date with Andreas' son last night did not go well?'

'It was OK.' Making light of it didn't fool Anouk, who teased,

'You were home early.'

Chantelle effected a faint shrug. 'We ate, talked a little.'

'You will see him again, *oui*?'

If only you knew! 'You share the same social circle as his father. The festive season usually involves a few parties. I imagine it's inevitable.'

Anouk placed a baguette into the oven to warm, then she crossed to the refrigerator, removed the cooked chicken and began carving.

'One senses the chemistry. It is almost as if you have met before.'

There was never going to be a more appropriate moment. 'Dimitri is Samuel's father.' It was done.

To give her mother credit, she never missed a beat as she continued carving poultry. 'I wondered as much. So what are you going to do?'

Ever practical, Chantelle mused. 'You just took a quantum leap of four years.'

Her mother began loading slices of chicken onto a serving plate, and paused long enough to shoot Chantelle a telling glance. 'It was your choice to keep private Samuel's father's identity.'

'You never queried my decision. Weren't you curious?'

'Of course. What mother would not be?'

'And now, you have no questions as to the why and how of it?'

'*Chérie*, I know you well. You do not gift your body easily. For you to do so, the man has to be special, someone you deeply love. If that were not true, you would not have had his child.'

Emotion brought a lump to her throat. 'Thank you.'

'So,' Anouk reiterated with prosaic gentleness. 'What are you going to do?'

Chantelle began layering a bowl with lettuce and sweet, succulent tomatoes. 'He wants to spend time with Samuel,' she offered slowly.

'Of course. But you are afraid, *oui*?'

'He wants to share custody.'

'And you do not want this.'

'I don't want anything to upset or confuse Samuel.'

'And you, *chérie*?' She carried the platter to the table, then turned to regard her daughter. 'What about you, hmm?'

'I feel as if my life is slipping out of control. If only Dimitri's visit hadn't coincided with mine!'

'But it has,' Anouk offered gently. 'And now you must deal with it as best you can.'

But what was *best*? And for whom? Samuel? Herself?

Sadly they were not the same. Her son would be captivated by Dimitri's presence in his life. Whereas she was beset by a host of ambivalent emotions.

Lunch was a convivial meal eaten alfresco on the terrace overlooking the pool. Samuel delighted in displaying his burgeoning vocabulary, both in French and English, and Chantelle had just settled him for his afternoon nap when she heard the distant peal of the phone.

'Dimitri,' Jean-Paul relayed as he informed the call was for her, and he gave her shoulder a light squeeze as she took the receiver.

'Is this a good time?' Dimitri's slightly accented drawl did strange things to her composure, and she resisted the impulse to press a hand to her churning stomach.

'I guess so.'

'Such enthusiasm,' he chided with mockery, and she stifled a sigh of frustration.

'What is it you want, Dimitri?'

'If you don't have plans for tomorrow, I'd like to spend time with Samuel.'

'And if I do?'

'The following day, Chantelle, or the day after that.'

She didn't want to do this. Given a choice, she'd prefer Dimitri to fade into the woodwork for the duration of his stay. But that wasn't going to happen.

'Tomorrow morning will be fine.' Capitulation was the wisest course, given she couldn't keep putting it off.

'If you name the place and give me a time, we'll meet you there.'

'Pack swimming gear. I'll collect you at nine.' His voice was firm, and he cut the connection before she had the chance to argue.

Damn the man! Anger simmered just beneath the surface of her control for what remained of the day, disturbing her sleep, and priming her determination to say exactly what she thought of his high-handedness at the first available opportunity.

Chantelle woke to a day bright with the promise of brilliant sunshine, together with the heat and humidity of a subtropical summer.

Samuel's excitement was a tangible thing as she filled a backpack with every conceivable item needed for whatever occasion Dimitri had in mind.

'When are we going?' and 'Where are we going?'

tumbled from her son's lips in five-minute intervals soon after she had relayed the morning's outing.

'Ah, *petit*,' Anouk protested fondly. 'Soon, *mon ange*.'

The faint *clunk* of a car door closing brought a mixture of relief and trepidation as Chantelle waited for Dimitri to ring the doorbell.

'Maman, Maman, the man is here.'

'Dimitri, sweetheart,' she corrected as Anouk moved to answer the door, only to reappear less than a minute later with Dimitri at her side.

Attired in designer jeans, a navy polo shirt and wearing joggers, he resembled the epitome of the businessman bent on leisure. The soft denim hugged his hips, emphasising the muscular length of his legs, and the polo shirt moulded his breadth of shoulder like a second skin.

Chantelle felt her stomach flip at the sight of him, and deliberately summoned a smile as she greeted him, watching as he solemnly extended his hand to her son.

'Samuel,' he offered warmly. 'Nice to see you again.'

The smile, she accorded silently, was for Samuel's sake, and she was all too aware of her own restraint. Four years ago she would have almost run to him, lit with the joyful anticipation of his touch, the feel of him as he pulled her close and ravaged her mouth with his own.

Now she simply caught Samuel's hand in her own, brushed a kiss to her mother's cheek, then she collected the backpack and slung the strap over one shoulder.

'Let me take that.' He reached for the backpack, and their fingers touched for a few seconds.

Liquid heat sped through her veins, igniting her senses, and she silently cursed her reaction.

Samuel, who'd been so excited only moments before, now fell silent, seemingly in awe of the man whose company he was going to share for the following few hours.

'We'll be back around midday, Maman,' Chantelle said as they walked out to the car.

'After an early lunch,' Dimitri added, and incurred Chantelle's swift denial.

'Samuel has a nap after lunch.'

'I'll have you home in time to settle him down.' He collected the junior safety seat and set it in place on the rear seat of his car, then he stood back as she lifted Samuel into it and secured the safety strap.

'I'll sit beside Samuel,' she declared as she straightened, only to have Dimitri indicate the front seat.

'*Chérie,*' Anouk intervened gently, 'he'll be fine.'

Maternal chastisement…or was Anouk bent on some subtle arrangement of her own?

Anouk couldn't help but be aware of her daughter's reticence, and God help him…Dimitri had to know she didn't favour spending several hours in his company.

Chantelle flashed each of them a stunning smile. She could do *gracious*…she just had to remember she was doing it for Samuel.

'Andreas suggested the water theme park at Coomera as a fun place for children,' Dimitri offered.

'There's lots of water. We got wet. Maman too,'

Samuel endorsed with childish enthusiasm, and Dimitri chuckled.

'I gather he's already been there?'

'Once,' Chantelle admitted, unwilling to offer it was his favourite place.

'In that case, we're guaranteed he'll enjoy himself.'

We…there's no *we*, she wanted to deny, and almost did, except Samuel's immediate presence stopped her. Later, she promised herself, she'd correct Dimitri's assumption.

The theme park was well-patronised, given it was the long midsummer school break and there was a host of visiting tourists to the area.

'Maman, we can go up there, *oui*? Please.'

Up there meant exchanging her jeans and top for a swimsuit. An action she normally wouldn't think about twice, if Dimitri hadn't been there.

She was acutely conscious of him, aware of his slightest touch, the warmth of his smile. Hell, he knew how to work it! Charm, he had it in spades. Four years ago she'd have believed it genuine. Now she wasn't so sure.

'Why don't I take him?'

Chantelle felt all her protective instincts rise to the fore. 'I don't think—'

'Dimitri,' Samuel sanctioned without a care in the world, and lifted his arms to be picked up, surprising her.

'Are you sure?' she queried dubiously, and gained an affirmative nod in response.

'Sure.'

'OK, champ, let's get rid of some clothes and go test the water.'

Her son's almost unconditional acceptance made her wonder if there was any truth in some deep recognition of shared genes.

Dimitri turned towards her. 'Why not join us?'

'Next time.' It would give her valuable minutes to steel herself to strip down to a swimsuit. Which was ridiculous.

Samuel was in his element as he took to the junior water slide, returning again and again as he delighted in the ride.

Chantelle almost convinced herself she was only watching her son, but it was the man catching him after each downward slide that held her attention longer than it should.

'Can we go up there?' Samuel begged as they returned to her side. 'Dimitri said I must have your permission.'

Oh, he did, did he? Well, she could hardly say *no*, when only a few days ago she'd taken Samuel *up there* herself.

It was a much larger slide with curves and covered sections, rushing water, and children under a certain age were only permitted to take the ride with the supervision of an adult.

They placed their outer clothes in lockers, then joined the queue for the more advanced ride.

When it became their turn Dimitri went in first and Chantelle followed with Samuel positioned closely between her thighs.

It was fun, and when they reached the end Dimitri rose lithely to his feet and caught Samuel, extending a hand to help Chantelle to her feet.

'Can we do it again, please?'

How easy it was to please a child. And how innocent Samuel appeared to be to the undercurrents between the two adults accompanying him.

As Chantelle looked at both child and man, the physical likeness between them was striking, and she glimpsed a vision of what the child would look like when he grew into a man.

Did Samuel possess any of her physical qualities? It was difficult to tell as the facial bone structure underwent a gradual change during the formative years. The dark hair perhaps, but then Dimitri's hair was equally dark.

This time out, Chantelle headed the downward ride, with Samuel held firmly in Dimitri's grasp, and afterwards they took a break for drinks and a snack.

There could be little doubt Samuel was having a ball, and neither his energy nor his enthusiasm lagged as Chantelle and Dimitri indulged him with several of the rides the theme park had to offer.

To his credit he didn't protest when it came time to change into dry clothes and leave. He remembered without prompting to thank Dimitri for bringing him to visit.

'I have a picnic hamper in the car,' Dimitri relayed as they made their way to the parking area. 'There's a picnic reserve at Paradise Point where we can eat.'

Casual, laid-back, it was a relaxed way to end the morning.

Except Chantelle was the antithesis of relaxed! She'd found it difficult when they'd been amongst a number of people, but isolated into an intimate group of three on the sandy foreshore at the picnic reserve only heightened her emotional tension.

Samuel ate well, and when he finished he drifted the few feet to the sand, where he became industriously immersed in collecting shells.

'Has it been such a hardship?'

She sipped the chilled mineral water as Dimitri packed what remained of the food into the cooler.

'Samuel had a great time.'

'And you?'

Chantelle looked at him. 'What do you want me to say?' He was close, much too close. 'I appreciate you're bent on turning my personal world upside-down? Thank the universe for throwing us together at the same place at the same time?' She was on a roll, and went with it. 'Thank you for forming an empathy with my son? An empathy I'll have to explain can only be rekindled at intervals we agree upon, or, failing that, as the law courts decree?'

'Why not take it one day at a time?'

'Whichever way I take it,' she declared with soft vehemence, 'the end result will be the same.'

'Will it?' He regarded her steadily, and the depth of his gaze tested the fragile tenure of her control. 'You can't perceive there might be a solution?'

'Maman.'

Suddenly Samuel was there, his hands cupped as he held a collection of shells, and Chantelle rose quickly to her feet and went to help him, infinitely relieved at his interruption.

'We will take them back for Grandmère, *oui*?'

'Indeed. She will treasure them.' She reached into her backpack and retrieved a plastic bag. 'We'll wash them when we get home.'

Within minutes she brushed the sand from his feet, slid on his joggers and cleaned his hands, aware that Dimitri replaced the cooler into the car, then followed it with the rug.

They were only five minutes from Sovereign Islands, and Samuel's eyes were drooping as Dimitri pulled into her parents' driveway.

Retreating was relatively easy as she slid from the car, collected her backpack, and moved to retrieve Samuel from his junior car seat.

'I'll take him.'

'It's OK.' Please, just let me get him and leave.

She badly needed to subside into her own space, as far away as possible from his. The morning had been a success, as far as Samuel was concerned. For her, it had dented the protective wall she'd built up around herself four years ago when survival of self had become paramount in her life.

'I'll be in touch.'

Was that a threat or a promise? She felt too disturbed to examine the ramifications of either.

'Thanks.' The gratitude was a mere facsimile, and one he recognised as her return to polite formality.

'My pleasure.'

He slid in behind the wheel, ignited the engine, and waited until she went indoors before reversing down the driveway.

CHAPTER FOUR

AN INVITATION to a mid-week cocktail party numbered the second party in five days. Which was something of a record for Chantelle, for, while she recognised the necessity for childcare during her working hours, she rarely employed a baby-sitter for anything other than an important social obligation.

Choosing what to wear didn't pose a problem, and, pre-warned by Anouk to pack evening wear, Chantelle selected black silk evening trousers, added a matching camisole and a black chiffon silk wrap threaded with gold. Stiletto heels, minimum jewellery, understated make-up, her hair swept into a smooth twist, and the overall look completed an image that met with her approval.

'We're going to another party?' Samuel queried as she brushed his hair, then straightened his shirt.

'Yes. Grandmère has many friends, and you, *mon enfant*, are her only grandchild. She wants to show you off.' She dropped a kiss on top of his head, then drew him close for a hug. 'There will be other children there, and you'll have fun, I promise,' she reassured.

'OK.'

His smile was matched by her own. 'Let's go.'

Would Dimitri be a fellow guest? She hoped not. She didn't want to cope with his disturbing presence.

Half an hour later she entered the opulent lounge in their host's luxurious home, after being greeted and introduced to the host's nanny and ensuring Samuel was comfortably settled in the downstairs playroom with six other young children.

Dimitri was unmistakable, standing on the far side of the room, not so much for his height and breadth of shoulder, the sculpted facial structure, or the expensive cut of his clothes.

It went deeper than that, combining a raw sexuality with electrifying passion; the inherent knowledge of how to pleasure a woman. A quality women recognised and many sought in a discreet bid for his attention. And there were the not-so-discreet few...of whom Daniella Fabrizi topped the list!

Damn. Why did the actress's name have to enter the equation?

Almost as if Dimitri sensed her presence he turned, and his dark, gleaming gaze locked with hers, held, as she offered a polite smile in acknowledgement of his presence before turning away.

He was something else. She cursed a vivid memory of how it felt to be in his arms, the sensations he was able to evoke in her without any effort at all. She was the instrument, he the master virtuoso, creating a sensual music that was uniquely theirs as they became lost in each other. Primitive, intensely passionate, he'd aroused emotions she hadn't known existed. And afterwards the degree of *tendresse* he displayed in the aftermath of a wildly erotic lovemaking always undid her.

Even now, she was intensely aware of him. The feel and touch of him, the satiny textured skin, the rough hairs on his chest arrowing down to the nest couching his manhood.

There had been no one else since him. No man of her acquaintance had aroused the slightest spark of sexual interest.

Introspection could become a dangerous pastime, and with deliberate ease Chantelle mixed and mingled with fellow guests, exerting her social skills without seeming effort as she greeted people she'd met at the party Anouk and Jean-Paul had hosted a few evenings ago.

'Let me get you another drink,' a familiar voice drawled close by, and her heart-rate went into overdrive as she turned to meet Dimitri's musing gaze.

'Not at the moment, thanks,' she said politely, aware of the faint aroma of his exclusive cologne. He was close, much too close, and she shifted slightly, gaining a much-needed inch or two of personal space.

'Samuel is downstairs?'

She was nervous, and that fascinated him. The tiny pulse at the base of her throat throbbed at an increased beat, and he resisted the temptation to soothe it.

'Yes.'

'Relax, *pedhaki mou*,' he bade gently, and saw those beautiful eyes flash momentary anger. 'Save the indignation for when we're alone.'

The affectionate 'little one' got to her, for it brought back too many memories...of love, laughter, and exquisite sex.

'Now, there's the thing,' Chantelle responded coolly. 'I have no intention of being alone with you.'

'You don't envisage a truce?'

'What did you expect? That a rehashing of the day we parted would magically wipe the slate clean?' She kept her voice low. 'If you dare suggest the necessity is *for Samuel's sake*, I'll hit you.'

Something moved in those dark eyes, something she couldn't define, and sudden apprehension slithered the length of her spine.

'Be aware of the consequences of such an action,' Dimitri cautioned with chilling softness.

'You're all charm.'

A slow smile curved his generous mouth. 'And you're a piece of work.'

'How nice we understand each other.' She held out her glass. 'Perhaps I will have another drink.' Her smile was a mere facsimile. 'It's a spritzer.'

Chantelle waited until he turned towards the bar before slipping from the lounge to check on Samuel. The happy laughter echoing from the playroom provided reassurance, and she watched unobserved as the children interacted together.

He looked so relaxed and content, and her heart went into meltdown. Nothing, she promised silently, and no one could be permitted to upset his secure world.

At that moment he lifted his head and saw her framed in the doorway.

'Maman!' He ran towards her, and his pleasure stirred her heartstrings. 'We are leaving?'

For a moment she sensed his disappointment, and hid a smile. He was a very sociable little boy. 'Not yet.'

'Good. I'm having fun.' He caught hold of her hand, his face a study of round-eyed excitement. 'Damian and Joshua are going to the park tomorrow to see the dolphins.'

'We will go to watch the dolphins one day, too.'

'We will? When, Maman?'

'Perhaps we could make it tomorrow,' Dimitri suggested from close behind her. 'If that suits your mother.'

He possessed the stealthy tread of a cat, for she hadn't heard a sound, and she steeled herself against his close proximity.

'Please say we can, Maman,' Samuel pleaded. 'I do so much want to see the sea lions too. Damian says they bark, and wave. And the dolphins jump out of the water.'

Chantelle didn't want to disappoint him, but the thought of spending several hours in Dimitri's company didn't appeal. 'Perhaps,' she qualified. 'But first we must check with Grandmère. We are her guests, *oui*?'

Hope, patience, resignation passed fleetingly over his features. *'Oui, Maman.'* For an instant his expression brightened. 'Grandmère and Jean-Paul can come too.' He turned towards Dimitri. 'Can't they?'

'Of course.' His smile was genuinely warm as he hunkered down to Samuel's eye level. 'But first, Maman must ensure there are no other plans for tomorrow, hmm?'

'*Oui.*' He looked up at his mother. 'May I go play now?'

'Enjoy, *mon petit*. I'll come collect you when we're ready to leave.'

She watched him rejoin the other children, then she turned and made her way to the stairs, uncaring whether Dimitri followed or not.

'You could have consulted me first,' Chantelle said in an angry undertone as he joined her.

'Only for you to refuse?'

His indolent drawl raised her anger level a notch. 'Look—'

'We agreed I should spend time with Samuel.'

Chantelle paused and turned to face him. 'It was more like you issued an ultimatum.'

'You want difficult, Chantelle? I can give you difficult.'

She could see the purpose evident, the dangerous inflexibility apparent. He had the wealth and the power to command top-flight lawyers to produce suitable documentation with breakneck speed.

'I want what's best for my son.'

'Then we're in total agreement.'

He was the limit, and she told him so. 'I wish—'

'I hadn't chosen to spend this Christmas with Andreas?'

'Yes! Damn you,' she vented, hating him.

He looked at her long and hard. 'Are you done?'

Her head tilted and her eyes sparked brilliant fire. 'For now.'

'Good.'

She was unprepared for the way his head lowered down to hers, and before she could move his mouth closed over hers in an evocative kiss.

His hands cupped her face as he went in deep, savoured, then he slid a hand down her spine and pulled her in close against him.

Oh, dear God. She couldn't think, didn't want to, as all her senses went every which way but loose and she began to respond.

In the recess of her mind she knew she should resist, but it felt so good. Dear heaven, how she'd missed his touch, the feel of him.

His arousal was a potent force, and she gave a sigh in protest as he began to retreat, gentling his mouth until his lips lingered briefly before he lifted his head.

For a moment she was lost, unaware of where she was, only that she was with *him*. Then reality descended, and confusion clouded her eyes, leaving them vulnerable for a few seconds before she managed to mask their expression.

'That was unforgivable.'

Dimitri pressed a finger to her slightly swollen mouth.

'I hate you.'

'No,' he said gently. 'You don't.' He traced a finger over her lower lip. 'You hate having to admit even to yourself that what we once shared together is as strong now as it was four years ago.'

Oh, dear heaven, why did he have to be so right?

Yet she'd known the instant she set eyes on him again the emotions she'd harboured for him had never lessened.

Acknowledging it didn't mean she had to like it. And nothing, she determined, *nothing* would allow her to run a repeat. That way lay heartache and despair. She'd been there, done that, and had no intention of doing it again.

Chantelle closed her eyes for a few seconds, unaware Dimitri watched the fleeting emotions play across her expressive features, then she opened them again. 'I think we should return to the lounge.'

His mouth curved to form a generous smile. 'Before we do, I suggest you renew your lipstick.'

For a few seconds her eyes widened and she looked intensely vulnerable, then she masked her expression and reached into her evening purse and applied colour to her lips.

Without a further word she turned and ascended the stairs, aware he was following close behind her.

As soon as she reached the lounge she checked Anouk's location, then began threading her way across the room.

'Samuel is fine,' she assured. 'He's made two new friends, and heard first-hand accounts of the dolphins and sea lions at the marine park.'

'I suggested we might take him there tomorrow if you have no plans for the day,' Dimitri drawled from behind her, and she felt her stomach curl at his close proximity.

'Why not make it a family day?' she said quickly. Too quickly, for she glimpsed her mother's faint surprise.

'Darling, thank you, but no,' Anouk declined with a gentle smile, wondering why her daughter's composure appeared distinctly ruffled. 'You and Dimitri go ahead. Samuel will have a wonderful time.'

Without doubt, Chantelle admitted. But what about her?

'Jean-Paul is keen to take the cruiser out on Sunday,' Anouk ventured conversationally. 'Perhaps Dimitri and Andreas would care to join us?'

Maman...no. Don't do this!

'We thought we might spend a few hours at Couran Cove. It's a delightful resort.'

'You must let me take you all to lunch.'

Anouk waved a dismissive hand. 'Chantelle and I will assemble a picnic basket.' She offered a stunning smile. 'All that's required is your presence. I'll confer with Jean-Paul and ring Andreas with a time.'

Dammit, what was Anouk doing, for heaven's sake? Exhibiting a naturally kind heart, or playing matchmaker?

A relaxed cruise of the bay, a picnic on a tourist island had all the promise of being fraught with tension...*hers*.

Dimitri inclined his head. 'Thank you.'

Chantelle felt a desperate need to put some space between them, for he loomed too large and too close for her peace of mind. If she'd been aware of him before, *now* her body was a finely tuned instrument almost vibrating with need for his touch.

It wasn't fair…nothing about Dimitri Cristopoulis was *fair*.

He had no right to re-enter her life and try to command it…even for the duration of a family visit.

If she could, she'd take Samuel, organise the next flight to Paris and return to the place she'd called home for the past four years.

Yet such an action would amount to running away. Besides, it would upset Anouk and Jean-Paul…not to mention Samuel, who adored his grandparents. And how could she explain such a sudden change in plan to a little boy who was so looking forward to a Christmas far different from any he'd experienced in his short life?

No, she was doomed to get through the next few weeks as best she could. Dammit, she was an adult, and in charge of her own destiny. No one, especially not Dimitri, could change that.

So why did she have such a strong instinctive feeling she was slowly losing control?

'If you'll excuse me?' Dimitri inclined, wondering if she was aware he could read her expressive features.

'Yes, of course,' she said quickly, and glimpsed the faint mocking amusement apparent.

It was another hour before the guests slowly began to dissipate, and Chantelle breathed a sigh of relief when Anouk suggested they should leave.

Samuel was fading fast when she collected him from the playroom, and she lifted him high as she reached the stairs.

'Tired, *mon ange*, hmm?' she queried gently, and felt her heart turn over as his arms encircled her neck. He was such an affectionate child, and she pressed a kiss to his temple. It was something she hoped would never change.

Chantelle reached the top of the stairs and found Anouk and Jean-Paul waiting for them. Dimitri's presence sent the blood pumping a little faster through her veins, and she looked at him in silent askance as she joined them.

Dimitri met her gaze and held it. Then something moved in the depths of his eyes. This was the woman he'd loved and lost. The child she held in her arms was his own.

The bond between them was a tangible entity, and one he had no intention of losing.

'Let me take him.'

'He's fine,' Chantelle said quickly, unwilling to re-linquish Samuel.

For a moment she thought Dimitri was about to argue, and she hurriedly added, 'He's almost asleep.'

It took a few minutes to thank their host, and make their way to the entrance lobby.

Dimitri walked at her side as if it was his God-given right, and she threw him a veiled glare.

'Nine-thirty tomorrow morning?' he queried as they paused in the doorway.

The marine park. In Anouk and Jean-Paul's presence, what else could she say except 'Thank you. We'll be ready'?

CHAPTER FIVE

THE Gold Coast was the home of theme parks, and it was almost *de rigueur* for holidaymakers with children to visit most, if not all of them.

At ten the parking area adjacent the marine park was well-filled, and with the sun shining brightly in a cloudless sky, the day promised heat, humidity and, if they were lucky, a fresh temperate sea breeze.

Chantelle had come well-prepared, with hats, sunscreen cream, bottled water, change of clothes for Samuel, each packed into her backpack. A portable stroller would prove useful when Samuel began to tire. Every eventuality covered, she mused as she slid sunglasses in place.

Casual wear was the order of the day, and she'd chosen a denim skirt, cotton shirt, and wore trainers on her feet.

As to Dimitri, even cargo trousers and a T-shirt did little to disguise his dynamic aura of power. Designer sunglasses and the NY-monogrammed cap added to the overall look of a corporate executive on holiday.

Chantelle had prepared in advance for the ticket box, and she extracted a high-denominational note.

'What do you think you're doing?' His indolent drawl held a degree of musing tolerance.

'I don't expect you to pay for us.'

'You want to begin an argument at this hour of the morning?'

It was impossible to tell anything from his expression, so she didn't even try. 'Please.' Independence was important to her, and she didn't want to owe anyone anything. Especially not Dimitri.

'No.'

Apart from initiating a tussle, there was little she could do but acquiesce and throw him an eloquent glare.

Once through the gates she focused on Samuel's delight as they viewed the underground marine world with sharks, stingrays and various large fish held in massive glass tanks.

There was a programme to observe, and first up was the dolphin show. Dimitri secured their seats, and Chantelle very quickly positioned Samuel between them. An action which drew an amused smile.

The accompanying commentary proved to be a show almost on its own, and Samuel clapped as each dolphin performed its trained act, laughing with sheer delight as the wonderful sea mammals dived and leapt on command.

'We can watch them again?' he queried eagerly as the show concluded, and he made no protest as Dimitri swept him up to sit astride his shoulders.

'Of course,' Dimitri promised. 'Later.'

'Dimitri said we can, Maman,' he assured, blissfully happy at the prospect. 'Later.'

They exited the area, and chose time out for refreshments.

Man and child seemed perfectly at ease with each other, and there was a tiny part of her that envied the simplicity of a child's trust.

A small seed of doubt rose to the fore. Had she been wrong in keeping Samuel's existence from Dimitri? Yet she knew unequivocally that if he'd known, life as she'd known it for the past four years would have been vastly different.

He would have insisted on sharing custody. Something she hadn't been ready for then, any more than she was ready for it now.

Yet how could she deny her son? Nerves tightened into a painful ball in her stomach at the thought of explaining Dimitri was Samuel's biological father.

Surely he was too young to harbour any resentment against her?

'All done?'

Dimitri's voice broke into her thoughts, and she spared him a quick glance as she secured Samuel's hat and reapplied sunscreen.

'Where to next?' she managed brightly, and saw Samuel's attention was held by the distant monorail.

'Can we go on that ride? Please,' he added quickly, offering Dimitri an appealing smile.

'Don't see why not.' Dimitri held out his hand. 'Do you want a skyscraper view?'

As if he needed to ask! Riding a man's shoulders was a new experience, and, judging by Samuel's willingness, one he couldn't wait to repeat.

There was no doubt her son loved every minute of the day's outing. He was almost too excited to eat lunch, and following the sea lion show he began to visibly wilt.

'I'll carry him,' Dimitri said quietly when Chantelle suggested the stroller, and he simply lifted Samuel to rest against his chest, with his head curved into one shoulder. Within seconds the little boy's eyes drooped closed.

'He's already asleep,' she said quietly. 'Perhaps we should leave.'

'There's a shady spot over by those trees. Let's go sit down awhile.'

There were a few jetskis on the lake, together with a small powerboat towing a clown-suited man on waterskis.

Tricks, thrills and orchestrated spills that had the audience gasping, and she watched with pretended interest as her son slept peacefully against his father's chest.

Anyone observing them would immediately assume they were a close family unit. But that was far from reality.

'Is Daniella still on the scene?' It was a stark query, but one she felt impelled to ask.

Dimitri's gaze narrowed. 'We share mutual friends.'

An advantage Daniella had used without scruples

in the past. 'Uh-huh. So you see each other from time to time?'

'Occasionally.'

Well-orchestrated occasions, seemingly innocent, yet deliberately planned by an actress who knew how to play the game.

'How remarkably—' she paused fractionally '—convenient.'

'Her purported relationship with me was nothing more than a figment of her imagination.'

That wasn't how Daniella figured it. 'So you said at the time.'

'Something you didn't believe then,' Dimitri discounted silkily. 'Any more than you do now.'

She shot him a look that lost much of its effect given he was unable to detect her expression beneath the shaded lenses. 'Perceptive of you.'

'We've done this already.'

So they had. If he was telling the truth, Daniella Fabrizi had a lot to answer for.

Samuel napped for a while, and woke to the sound of the park ranger announcing the afternoon sea lion show on the speaker system.

Their attendance capped Samuel's day, and on arrival home he clung as Dimitri released him from the car seat. 'Thank you for taking me to see the dolphins, and the sea lions,' he added, then planted an impulsive kiss on his father's cheek.

Chantelle stood transfixed for a few seconds as Dimitri returned the affectionate gesture.

'I like you,' Samuel said with childish candour.

'Thank you,' Dimitri responded solemnly. 'I like you, too.'

'Will you come and see us again?'

'You can count on it.'

'We're going to see the fireworks tomorrow night.'

Chantelle's heart ached with emotion. Samuel—stop, she wanted to urge, only the word remained locked in her throat.

Fireworks and Christmas decorative-light displays formed part of the lead-up to Christmas, and Anouk had elicited information on all the activities available for children.

'You can come too,' Samuel invited earnestly, and she intercepted quickly,

'Maybe next time. Dimitri has a busy schedule.' She summoned a smile as she met his gaze. 'Thanks for giving Samuel such a lovely day.'

Dimitri let her make her escape. For now.

'We're going to see pretty lights,' Samuel declared as she selected his clothes. 'There will be lots of bangs.'

Chantelle held out her hand, and experienced a warm tide of affection as he wrapped his arms around her legs.

It had been another hot day, and the temperature hadn't cooled with the onset of evening.

Chantelle stepped into cotton fatigue trousers and a singlet top, slid her feet into trainers, and scooped the length of her hair into a ponytail, then she helped Samuel don shorts and a T-shirt, added sandals and a cap.

'We're having lots of fun, Maman.' He lifted his head and gave her an infectious grin. 'I love it here. And I love Grandmère and Jean-Paul.' He looked thoughtful for a few seconds. 'I like Dimitri, too.'

Oh, my. 'That's nice.' What else could she say? Least said, the better! 'Shall we go join Grandmère and Jean-Paul?'

Tonight's adventure took in a massive fireworks display at one of the Coast's major shopping complexes, timed to begin at nightfall.

A twenty-minute drive, time out for parking and gaining a position among the gathering crowds of people meant little spare time before the display began.

Jean-Paul hoisted Samuel on top of his shoulders, whereupon Samuel emitted a blissful sigh. 'I can see everything. But Jean-Paul is not as big as Dimitri.'

Chantelle met her mother's gaze, saw the faintly raised eyebrow, and revealed quietly, 'Dimitri carried him on his shoulders while we were at the marine park.'

'Uh-huh.'

'Don't,' she swiftly cautioned, and Anouk offered a musing smile.

'*Chérie*, I'm merely doing the maths.'

'It won't do you any good.'

Anouk's smile broadened into a fulsome curve. 'We shall see.'

'Maman—'

The warning went unheeded as a brilliant series of skyrockets exploded in myriad sprays of vivid colour.

Samuel laughed and clapped his hands in delight.

'Dimitri. Dimitri's here.'

She wanted to vent her frustration, and almost did, except Dimitri moved in close and she made do with lancing him with a telling glare.

'Dimitri,' Anouk greeted warmly. 'How nice you could join us.'

With Samuel perched high on Jean-Paul's shoulders, it wouldn't have taken Dimitri long to pinpoint them among the assembled crowd.

His presence had an unsettling effect, and she hated the familiar curling sensation deep inside. Unbidden, her pulse-rate picked up, and she felt its thudding beat at the base of her throat.

Could he see it in this dim light? She hoped not.

He made no attempt to touch her, but it was enough that he was *there*, positioned mere inches from where she stood.

Samuel was in his element, laughing and clapping with delight at each bang and subsequent burst of colour. The designs were many and varied, and lasted a while.

'Dimitri, look!' He twisted towards Dimitri and pointed to one spectacular star-burst.

Jean-Paul had a firm grip on his legs, and he appeared to have no sense of fear as he called, 'Look, Maman, isn't it magnificent?'

'Magnificent,' Chantelle agreed. His delight was catching, and Anouk turned towards her.

'He's a beautiful little boy. Such innocence, so much heart.'

'Indeed,' Dimitri drawled in agreement.

All too soon the display concluded, and the crowds began to disperse.

Samuel made a sweeping gesture with his arms. 'They're all gone.'

'But it was wonderful while it lasted,' Chantelle offered gently as Jean-Paul swung the little boy down onto his feet.

'*Oui, Maman.*'

She leant down and ruffled his hair. 'And now we must go home. Tomorrow is another big day.'

'We're going out on the boat.' He looked up at Dimitri. 'Jean-Paul's boat.'

'Yes, I know.' Dimitri picked him up and held him in the crook of one arm. 'Would you like it if I came along too?'

'Yes.'

There you go, Chantelle muttered beneath her breath. Male bonding achieved in record time. A few hours a few days apart, and her son had reached an almost instant rapport with Dimitri.

She should be grateful. She assured herself she didn't mind sharing Samuel…she just didn't want to share him with Dimitri.

Together they began wending their way towards the vast parking area, and Chantelle turned towards Dimitri as they reached the base of the steps. Anouk and Jean-Paul were walking ahead of them.

'I'll take him.'

'My car's not far from here.'

Within minutes they reached Anouk's Lexus, and Chantelle began settling Samuel into his safety seat.

'We'll take Samuel home, *chérie*,' Anouk offered. 'We can detour past a few of the houses displaying Christmas lights. It's still relatively early. Why don't you join Dimitri for a coffee?' She turned towards Dimitri. 'There's a delightful area at Main Beach filled with trendy cafés. Chantelle will give you directions.' Her gaze swung back to her daughter. 'You so rarely go out, and it's such a pleasure to baby-sit my grandson.'

'Grandmère will read me a story,' Samuel declared, oblivious to his mother's growing tension.

'I don't think—'

'Darling, you think too much,' Anouk chided. She crossed round the car and slid into the passenger seat, whilst Jean-Paul, the traitor, took his position behind the wheel.

She'd been neatly shanghaied, and with an adroitness part of her could only admire. But then, Anouk was an expert at subtle manipulation.

So where did that leave her? With Dimitri, and reliant on him for a ride home. She watched the Lexus reverse out and purr towards the marked exit before she turned towards the man at her side.

'If I thought for one minute you had a hand in this, I'd hit you!'

'Now, there's an interesting thought.'

His indolent drawl almost undid her, and she speared him a dark glare. 'You can skip the coffee.' She was on a roll. 'In fact, you can skip taking me anywhere. I'll take a cab.'

'And disappoint Anouk?' he queried mildly.

'Besides, we need an opportunity to discuss arrangements for sharing custody of Samuel.'

For a few seconds she was rendered speechless, then the impact of his words hit with cold reality.

'Coffee,' Chantelle capitulated, and earned his wry amusement.

He gestured towards a line of parked cars to his right. 'My car is over there.'

She didn't want to do this. Dear heaven, if she had her way Dimitri would disappear in a puff of smoke. But given that unlikelihood, she had to face facts.

A discussion. Well, there was no harm in conducting a discussion. It didn't mean she had to agree to anything.

'I assume you're aware how to reach Main Beach?' she queried stiffly as Dimitri eased the car through the exit and branched off to connect with the main road leading through the heart of Surfer's Paradise.

'I acquainted myself with a map.'

Chantelle settled for silence unless spoken to, and it was only when they neared the traffic-controlled intersection adjacent Main Beach that she offered directions.

Trendy cafés lined the attractive boulevard, and it irked a little when he slid the car into a recently vacated parking spot.

'Do you want to choose, or shall I?' Dimitri queried as he locked the car and joined her on the pavement.

She gave a faint shrug. 'Coffee is coffee.' It was a popular area, with patrons filling most of the outdoor tables.

They wandered the southern end of the boulevard, and secured the first empty table available.

The waitress was efficient, and appeared within minutes to take their order.

'You've done an excellent job rearing Samuel.'

Chantelle looked at him carefully. 'Let's not play games, Dimitri.'

'Just cut straight to the chase?'

The waitress returned with bottled water and two glasses, then crossed to another table.

'It's a wasted exercise, because I doubt there's anything you suggest that I'll agree to.'

'Because you fear the effect on Samuel.'

'Yes.' She drew in a deep breath and expelled it slowly. She held up a hand, and began ticking off opposing points on each finger. 'He's too young to travel without an accompanying adult. I wouldn't want to entrust him to the care of anyone other than myself. I'm not in a position to take several leaves of absence from work.' She paused beneath his intense interest, and endeavoured not to allow him to diminish her in any way. 'You travel extensively. When would you be able to fit Samuel into your current lifestyle?' She lifted a hand, then let it drop to the table. 'Oh, dammit, none of this is easy!'

The waitress delivered their coffee, and Chantelle watched as Dimitri added sugar to his, then took an appreciative sip.

'What if I was to offer a solution?' He replaced the cup down onto its saucer and spared her an enigmatic look.

'Such as?'

'We could marry.'

Shock widened her eyes, and her face paled. 'Excuse me?'

'Samuel gains the security of a two-parent household,' he elaborated. 'If you choose to continue working, that's your prerogative.'

Chantelle viewed him steadily, unsure whether to laugh or cry. 'You perceive that as a neat package. Loose ends tied, you get to have your son full-time on a permanent basis.' Anger rose and threatened to burst the surface of her control. 'What's my part in all of this?'

She couldn't stop the words. 'Do I get to play whore in the bedroom, and social hostess as and when required?' Her voice lowered to a heartfelt huskiness. 'Thanks, but no, thanks.'

The thought of living with him, sharing his bed…oh, lord, don't even go there!

'Would it be so bad?'

'How can you ask that?'

'Samuel needs to know he's my son. How do you think he'll feel when we tell him I'm his father?'

Her eyes blazed. 'You think I haven't agonised over that. Lost sleep over it?'

'You imagine he won't ask why we can't live together?' Dimitri pursued as he leaned back in his chair, presenting an image of unruffled composure. 'What are you going to say to him?'

'The truth,' she managed shakily. 'To his level of understanding.'

'Which you expect him to accept?'

Her coffee remained untouched, and she looked at it dispassionately, aware that if she took so much as a sip she'd be sick.

'We have a good life. Samuel is a happy, well-balanced little boy. I don't want that to change.'

'It won't.'

'How can you say that?'

'Easily.'

Don't you know I can't live with you? she wanted to scream at him. Share your bed…and not wither and die a little each time knowing Samuel is your main concern and I'm little more than the baggage that accompanies him?

'Dimitri—'

'Think about it.' He drained his cup, and looked askance as she left hers untouched. 'Would you prefer a *latte*?'

'I'd prefer to go home.'

He wanted to extend his hand and pull her close, ease her fears and promise he'd take care of her. There were other words he wanted to say, but now wasn't the time or the place.

If he could dispense with the barriers she'd erected… Patience, he cautioned. A lot could happen in two weeks, and he intended to capitalise on every opportunity.

He summoned the waitress, paid the bill, then rose to his feet.

Chantelle didn't offer so much as a word during the drive to Sovereign Islands. Instead, she gazed sightlessly at the tracery of lights reflected on the Broadwater, and she had her seat belt unbuckled as soon as Dimitri drew the car to a halt in Anouk's driveway.

She released the clasp and opened the door. 'Good night.'

'I'll see you tomorrow.'

For a moment she looked at him blankly, then she remembered Andreas and Dimitri were joining them for the day on Jean-Paul's cruiser.

She slid from the passenger seat and closed the door behind her without uttering a further word.

Indoors, she checked with Anouk that Samuel was settled in bed, then bade her mother 'good night.'

'Are you OK, *chérie*? You look pale.'

'A headache,' she invented, not wanting to begin a question-and-answer session, then immediately felt bad. Maternal love was a precious thing. 'Dimitri asked me to marry him.' She waited a beat. 'I said no.'

'Chantelle,' Anouk protested sympathetically. '*Chérie—*'

Chantelle lifted a hand. 'Please, Maman. I beg you. Not now.'

She made for the stairs, checked on Samuel, then quietly undressed and slipped into bed to lie awake until just before dawn.

CHAPTER SIX

SUNDAY provided little opportunity for Chantelle to discuss the previous evening with Anouk, as Samuel was inevitably within listening distance, and there was food to assemble for the day's outing on Jean-Paul's cruiser.

Andreas and Dimitri arrived at ten, and within half an hour Jean-Paul had eased the large cruiser away from the jetty and headed into the main waterway.

It was a beautiful day, the sun high in a clear azure sky, and Samuel became a focus as they headed for Couran Cove.

'He's a generously spontaneous child,' Andreas complimented, as Dimitri hoisted Samuel into his arms for a clearer view.

Chantelle proffered a warm smile. 'Yes, he is.'

'I am proud he is my grandson,' he said quietly.

'Thank you. I have yet to tell Samuel.'

'But you will.'

'Yes.'

Oh, lord, the telling would raise several inquisitive questions…the most obvious one being why they weren't living with his daddy…and worse, *when* would they?

There was no doubt he liked Dimitri. In fact, *liking* was rapidly becoming affection.

She should be pleased. It would make things easier.

Not. The mere thought of sharing custody, being forced to let Samuel go from her care for specified lengths of time several times a year was enough to throw her into a nervous spin.

As far as today was concerned, convention decreed she play the social game. As she had all too often during the past week.

Thankfully Anouk, Jean-Paul and Andreas were present to act as a buffer. And Samuel, who delighted them all with his enthusiasm, his non-stop chatter and numerous questions about the boat, the harbour, and when they berthed at Couran Cove there were the resort attractions to amuse him.

Dimitri was a natural in the role of father, always close by, so much a part of the inner family circle that to any onlooker they were a family.

Which, strictly speaking, they were. Yet it was a fact she neither wanted to recognise nor accept.

'He's very good with Samuel,' Anouk offered quietly when they were briefly alone.

'Yes, isn't he?'

Without doubt Dimitri had earned her mother's unqualified approval. Jean-Paul, a shrewd judge of character, appeared similarly won over. Samuel was a cinch…which left only *her*.

Was she insane to knock back the sensible solution of marriage with him? As far as the sex was concerned, it would hardly be a hardship, and his wealth would ensure she'd never have to worry about money.

But what about her own emotional heart? Could she exist in a marriage based on convenience? Live her life in Samuel's shadow solely for his benefit?

He was much too young to comprehend or understand such a sacrifice.

Besides, she had a very nice life on her own merit.

There was a well-paid job, a pleasant villa to live in, a small car, savings. She and Samuel were doing just fine.

But wouldn't it be good to have a man in your life? a wicked imp taunted silently. Someone to share the events of the day, to be taken care of, and a warm male body to curl into through the night?

What about *love*? Shouldn't that play an important part?

The imp declined to answer.

If Dimitri had an inkling of her inner struggle, he gave no sign. Although once or twice she caught his thoughtful gaze, and wondered at it. Then there were the few occasions when he stood close, and she felt the heat from his body, sensed the faint musky scent of his cologne…and silently damned her reaction.

It should have been a relaxing day. Yet acting a part and keeping a smile permanently pinned in place took its toll, and by the time they left Couran Cove for Sovereign Islands she was nursing a headache.

'Please stay for dinner.' Anouk extended the invitation to Andreas and Dimitri as they reached home. 'Just a simple meal of cold chicken, salads, with bread and fruit, a little wine.'

Maman, Chantelle protested silently. *Don't do this.*

Except she was overruled by Jean-Paul's enthusiasm and Samuel's whoops of delight.

'Only if you'll allow me to reciprocate,' Andreas agreed with a smile.

So it was done, and while the men tended to the cruiser, Chantelle bathed and settled Samuel for a short nap, then she helped Anouk in the kitchen.

'Are you going to tell me why you turned down Dimitri's marriage proposal?' Anouk deftly cut cooked chicken in portions and placed them on a large platter.

Chantelle's hands momentarily stilled in the process of washing salad greens. 'It wasn't so much a proposal as a convenient solution.'

'And a convenient solution is such a bad thing?'

'We're doing fine on our own.'

'Why are you so afraid, *chérie*?' Anouk queried gently.

Did her mother have to be so astute?

'I don't want to enter a marriage where love is one-sided or confined to mere affection.'

'But is it? The chemistry between you is apparent to anyone who cares to look.'

Chantelle began shaking excess water from the salad greens. 'Next you'll try to tell me I'm still in love with him.'

'Aren't you?'

Now, there was the thing. For a few seconds her mother's query locked the voice in her throat. 'Sexual attraction, Maman. That's all it is.' And knew she lied.

Samuel woke after an hour's nap, and joined the men on the terrace.

Chantelle set the outdoor table with plates, cutlery and napkins, added glassware, then carried out the food while Anouk cleared the kitchen.

'Sit with me,' Samuel pleaded minutes later. 'Maman here.' He patted the seat on his right. 'And Dimitri there.' The seat on his left received a pat. 'Please,' he added.

'You're the flavour of the month,' Chantelle murmured as she moved past Dimitri, and heard his faint chuckle.

He was too close.

'That bothers you?'

All she had to do was move an inch and her arm would touch his. 'Why should it?'

'Perhaps we could pursue this later?'

'I don't think so,' she responded in an undertone, only to cut the conversation as Anouk, Jean-Paul and Andreas crossed to the table.

It was a relaxed, convivial meal, although afterwards Chantelle could recall little of the conversation.

Dusk became night, and Samuel urged Dimitri to witness his prowess with a Play Station game while Chantelle and Anouk took care of the dishes.

Two male heads, Chantelle witnessed as she entered the family room to collect Samuel for bed. Both so dark, their body language so closely linked it brought a lump to her throat.

'Time for bed, *mon ange*,' she said gently, and saw him struggle with disappointment.

'Can Dimitri read me a story? Please, Maman.'

She wanted to say *no*, and almost did, except when it came to the crunch she couldn't do it. 'If it's OK with Dimitri,' she managed, aware of Dimitri's steady gaze before it shifted back to their son.

'Here's the deal. I read the story, and Maman gets to tuck you in.'

Chantelle watched Samuel lead Dimitri upstairs, and she valiantly ignored the sudden ache in the region of her heart.

They were becoming close. Too close for her peace of mind. For what would happen when it came time to say goodbye?

She allowed them twenty minutes, then she went up to Samuel's room.

Dimitri sat cross-legged on the floor close to Samuel's bed, with a picture storybook in his hand, his voice quiet as he read the words.

Samuel was trying to stay awake, but his eyelids were beginning to droop, then they flickered as he valiantly fought sleep, only to close as his breathing changed and he slept.

Dimitri rose carefully to his feet, and stood for a moment looking at the sleeping child, then he turned and preceded her from the room, pausing as she quietly closed the door behind them.

'Thank you.'

She raised slightly startled eyes to meet his.

'For today,' he said quietly. He lifted a hand and brushed gentle fingers down one cheek. 'Go take something for that headache.'

How could he know? She opened her mouth, then closed it again, and nearly died as he lowered his head down to hers and took possession of her mouth in a lingering kiss that took hold of her senses and sent them spinning out of control.

'I'll be in touch.'

There were words she wanted to say, but none came immediately to mind as they descended the stairs and joined the others in the lounge.

Within minutes Andreas signalled their intention to leave, and amid voiced thanks for a wonderful day, the two men bade Anouk, Jean-Paul and Chantelle 'good night.'

Another day, another theme park.

Chantelle struggled with her conscience as Dimitri eased the car into an empty space in the large parking area adjacent MovieWorld.

In truth, each and every theme park was on her list of places to visit with Samuel. So why should it make any difference that Dimitri accompanied them?

Except it did...in spades. His presence heightened her stress levels, and pitched her to tread a fine emotional edge that played havoc with her senses.

She only had to look at his mouth to be forcibly reminded of just how it felt possessing her own...and her own eager response.

This was a man with whom she'd shared every intimacy…the heat, the passion, the primeval, mesmeric hunger for each other…ecstasy at its zenith.

The memory kept her awake too many nights, and when she slept he frequently haunted her dreams, causing her to wake in a tangle of bedcovers, her skin damp with sensual heat…only to discover she was alone, empty and aching.

On the occasions she told herself she was dealing with it…there was Samuel, Dimitri in miniature, as a vivid permanent reminder of what had been.

'Are we really going to see how they make movies?'

Samuel's voice penetrated her wayward thoughts, and she caught hold of his hand as they joined the queue at the ticket line.

'It's more like a movie show with live acts and stunts,' she corrected, reaching for her purse. An action which incurred a dark glance from the man at her side. Worse, Dimitri covered her hand and firmly returned it to her side.

Chantelle's bid for independence both amused and irritated him. 'We've already done this.'

Samuel's pleasure increased as the day progressed, and he was delighted with the various action shows, fascinated by the stunt actors, and through the eyes of a child…the apparent realism.

It was proving to be a holiday he'd never forget, and although she'd planned it this way, she hadn't envisaged Dimitri having any part in it.

A chill shivered over the surface of her skin. Had Dimitri already sought legal counsel? Was a team of lawyers preparing custody papers ready to serve on her? Or was he hoping to persuade her marriage to him was a more satisfactory option?

Doubts swirled inside her head. Was she being selfish denying Samuel a family life? Could she marry Dimitri and be content with a *convenient* marriage? Would it be enough? Sacrifice her life for that of her son?

Dimitri had made it sound so simple, so *feasible*. So, independently, had Anouk.

Did *she* have it so wrong?

Maybe Dimitri could view the arrangement with favour…hell, why wouldn't he? A wife in his home, his *bed*…not to mention full-time custody of his son and heir.

'Dimitri.'

The feminine voice was incredibly familiar, and one Chantelle would never forget.

'Darling, what on earth are you doing *here*?'

Daniella Fabrizi. Tall, incredibly svelte, her dark auburn hair loose in a flowing mass of curls, and her make-up a work of art. Attired in a cream linen suit whose skirt hemline rested several inches above her knee, and whose jacket was slashed to a low V and revealed an enviable cleavage.

The question had to be what Daniella was doing here.

Following Dimitri? Or was the actress unaware of his plans? Chance was a fine thing, but Chantelle knew Daniella left nothing to chance. So it had to be a calculated trip from her native New York.

'Daniella.'

Dimitri's voice was an indolent drawl, and it was impossible to detect much from his expression.

'I flew in yesterday with Victor LaFarge,' the actress revealed. 'He's thinking of shooting a movie here and wanted to check out the location, the studios.'

And you just decided to tag along? Actresses didn't usually check out locations and studios...did they?

'We must get together, darling.' A slight pout of those beautifully moulded lips was a contrived gesture. 'I rang and left a message with Andreas.'

Dimitri didn't confirm or deny he'd received it, and Daniella's gaze shifted to Chantelle.

'Why, you're here, too. I thought you'd moved abroad.'

'Daniella,' she acknowledged with as much politeness as she could muster.

The actress's gaze shifted to Samuel. 'What a cute child. Your nephew?'

'Samuel is my son,' she said quietly, and saw Daniella's gaze narrow, followed by the moment comprehension dawned.

'Well, now,' the actress began with silken vehemence as she swung back to Chantelle. 'Aren't you just the cleverest little thing?'

She wanted to pick Samuel up and move away, and she almost did, except only cowards ran.

'I didn't realise this visit represented double-duty,' Daniella commented, shooting Dimitri a stunning smile. 'It won't, of course, create an obstacle.'

What in hell was the actress talking about?

Samuel's existence wouldn't cause an obstacle to *what*? Daniella's plan to cohabit with Dimitri? Maybe even marry him? An act that would catapult Daniella into the position of part-time stepmother?

Not in this lifetime, Chantelle vowed silently. She deliberately checked her watch, then turned towards Dimitri. 'Samuel and I will be at the Batman show. It's due to begin soon.' Somehow she managed a warm smile, although it failed to reach her eyes. 'Do stay and chat with Daniella.'

'I would hate to keep Dimitri from an obligation.'

She was a first-class witch. But what else was new?

'Oh, *please*,' Chantelle assured. 'Dimitri is free to do whatever he wants.' With that she took Samuel's hand and began leading him away.

Not that she got very far before Dimitri joined her.

'You had no need to run away.'

She spared him a dark look. 'Correction. I was removing myself from the line of fire.'

'Would you believe I gave her no inkling of my visit to the Coast?'

'Doubtless your secretary organised your flight.' What point subtlety? 'Daniella is a very resourceful woman.' She couldn't help herself. 'And very good at ego-stroking. You must be flattered.'

Dimitri wanted to shake her, then kiss her senseless. If Samuel hadn't been present, he'd have tossed convention to one side and opted for the latter.

Instead, he did neither.

'I don't possess an ego,' he drawled with musing humour. 'Nor do I covet flattery.' He spared her a sideways glance. 'Unless you want to offer yours?'

'Are you kidding?'

'Maman,' a small voice intercepted, 'are you angry with Dimitri?'

You have no idea, she accorded silently. *Anger* doesn't begin to cover it.

'Look,' she encouraged him, indicating the scene ahead. 'Batman.' As a distraction, it worked wonderfully well, and she didn't even protest when Dimitri took Samuel from her and hoisted him onto his shoulders.

For the remainder of the afternoon she kept up a civil front…for Samuel's benefit.

It was after four when they exited the gates and made their way to Dimitri's car. Samuel was fading fast, and she knew he'd fall asleep within minutes of the car being in motion.

Chantelle didn't offer any conversation during the drive to Sovereign Islands, and she unlatched the door as soon as Dimitri brought the car to a halt in Anouk's driveway.

'I'll take Samuel,' she said quickly. 'He might wake.'

'Will that be a disaster?'

'Of course not.' She looked askance as he crossed round to her side. 'Dimitri—'

'Chantelle?' he gently mocked.

'Don't be facetious,' she flung beneath her breath, and incurred a dark glance. She refused to be reduced to an undignified struggle, so she simply stood aside and let him unclip the restraints holding Samuel secure in the safety seat.

Which meant Dimitri got to carry Samuel indoors.

'Oh, poor *petit*,' Anouk murmured as she saw her grandson asleep in Dimitri's arms. 'Take him straight upstairs. Even if he only naps for a little while, it will be better than the short time he has already had.'

'I'll take him,' Chantelle said swiftly, and sent up a silent prayer to the deity Dimitri would hand Samuel over. She didn't want to share this indomitable man's presence in the confines of Samuel's bedroom, for Dimitri's height and breadth would swamp the room.

However, the deity wasn't listening, and she merely received a musing look as Dimitri moved past her and headed towards the stairs.

'Maman,' she protested, only to have Anouk direct her a telling glance.

'*Chérie*, you are very tense. Has it not been an enjoyable day?'

What could she say? Nothing, at least not right now. 'I'd better go check.'

Samuel rested silently on the bed, and Chantelle carefully tucked a cellular cotton blanket over him.

She turned and encountered Dimitri's dark gaze, and for one electrifying minute she was unable to move.

Then his mouth widened into a slow smile, and the spell was broken as he stood aside for her to exit the room ahead of him.

Chantelle stepped quickly from the room, and all

but ran down the stairs, supremely conscious that Dimitri followed close behind her.

'How is he?' Anouk queried. 'He didn't stir?'

'He's asleep, Maman.'

'Good.' Anouk turned towards Dimitri. 'Will you join us in a drink?'

'Thank you, but no. Another time, perhaps?'

Was he anxious to leave so he could call Daniella? She told herself she didn't care…and knew she lied.

CHAPTER SEVEN

CHANTELLE opted for a quiet day at home with Samuel instead of accompanying Anouk and Jean-Paul to a nearby shopping complex. Especially as they'd visited the day before so Samuel could see Santa with all the other children.

Parking was at a premium, the crowds many, and she didn't want Samuel becoming over-tired.

'Shall we bake a cake for Grandmère?'

'A surprise.' Samuel's eyes lit up at the thought. 'Chocolate, Maman.'

'Chocolate it is.'

She set to work, and had just popped the cake into the oven when the phone rang.

It was Anouk, sounding agitated, which was unusual. Her mother never became agitated.

'*Chérie*, I'm at the hospital. Jean-Paul tripped and fell. The stupidest thing. He was avoiding a boy riding a skateboard at speed in the car park.' She paused fractionally. 'We are waiting on X-rays. It's possible he has fractured his collarbone.'

'Are you OK?' Chantelle queried at once. 'Do you want me to come sit with you?'

'No, I'm fine. But I don't know what time we'll be home.'

Late afternoon, with Jean-Paul in obvious pain and wearing a protective sling.

He was required to rest, and the next few days were spent quietly at home. The news of his accident spread, and Dimitri called in for a visit, spent time with Samuel, and was about to leave when Anouk opened the drawer of an escritoire and retrieved two embossed tickets.

'Jean-Paul and I were to attend a charity ball to-morrow evening.' She handed them to Dimitri. 'Please, take these. You and Chantelle can attend in our place.' She turned towards her daughter. 'I'll mind Samuel. Six-thirty for seven. Black tie. It's to aid the Leukaemia Foundation.'

What if I don't want to go? Chantelle almost queried, only to be outnumbered before she had a chance to decline.

'Please,' Jean-Paul acceded. 'It's a good table, and a fund-raiser for a worthy cause. Anouk is on the committee.'

Thirty-six hours later Chantelle stood in the large lounge adjacent the hotel ballroom and glanced with interest at fellow guests assembled there.

Men attired in dark evening suits, the women in designer gowns and jewellery, real and faux.

The evening's affair was indeed an *event*. Capacity

attendance, she surmised as she sipped champagne and orange juice.

Dimitri was something else in a superbly tailored dinner suit, white shirt and black tie. He had the look, the stature that set him apart from other men. Add an aura of power, and the result was devastating.

He drew women's attention like bees sensing a honey pot. Feminine interest, blatant and discreet, but apparent none the less. Four years ago she would have smiled and silently voiced 'you can look, but I get to take him home'. Then she had known how the evening would end, with a loving that lasted through the night.

Now they'd spend the evening together as social equals, pretend they were enjoying themselves, then he'd deliver her to Anouk's door, and they'd occupy separate beds in different houses.

Did he lie awake at night aching, as she ached for him? The long, sweet loving, the passion? So intense, like twin souls transcending reality and merging into one.

Standing close to him like this, she was aware of him to an alarming degree. The musky aroma of his cologne mingling with the clean smell of freshly laundered clothes acted like an aphrodisiac, heightening her senses, and accelerating her heartbeat.

It was crazy, but she had an urge to slip her hand into his, feel the warmth and strength apparent, and have his fingers thread through her own. To have his eyes warm with sensual heat in silent promise…for her, only for her.

Oh, dear God…*get a grip*.

Conversation. Chantelle reached for it like a drowning person reaching for a life-raft.

'When do you return to New York?'

She was nervous, Dimitri observed, idly watching the throbbing pulse at the base of her throat.

'New Year.' He placed the palm of his hand between her shoulder blades and moved it gently in silent reassurance. An action that earned him a startled glance as his hand slipped to rest at her waist. 'The second of January to be precise.'

A week before she was due to return to Paris with Samuel.

'I'm surprised you were able to structure such a long break.'

'My life isn't entirely given over to business.'

The faintly accented drawl brought a tinge of colour to her cheeks. 'I didn't imagine it was.'

'No?'

There was something going on here she didn't know about. An elusive, almost mesmeric interaction she could only guess at.

Dammit, what game was he playing?

'Dimitri!'

Chantelle steeled herself to present a polite façade as she turned towards Daniella and Victor LaFarge. The likelihood of this being a chance encounter was remote.

'You should have told me you'd be here tonight.'

The actress did provocative reproach well. The faint pout, the slight tilt of her head…and a sultry gaze that exhibited blatant lust.

Overkill, definitely. But what man wouldn't react?

'Where are you seated?'

If Daniella suggested they occupy the same table, she'd *scream*. Then common sense prevailed; seating arrangements had been organised in advance.

Chantelle noticed the three sets of double doors were now open, and guests were beginning to vacate the lounge.

'Shall we go in?' Dimitri inclined.

Was it deliberate, or merely a courtesy? Chantelle wondered as he urged her towards the ballroom entrance.

His hand remained at her waist, and she could have sworn his fingers effected a soothing squeeze.

What was he doing, for heaven's sake?

Efficient organisation ensured the guests were directed to their reserved seating, and Chantelle sank gracefully into a chair at a table close to the catwalk.

'Ah, there you are.'

She could only look on with startled dismay as Daniella collected two place-names, replaced them with hers and Victor's, then quickly transferred the place-names to the table she and Victor had been assigned.

'That's better.' The actress promptly took the chair next to Dimitri.

It was? Chantelle couldn't imagine anything worse. Whatever happened to good manners? Had Daniella no shame?

Apparently not.

'Darling,' Daniella purred with feline sensuality as she placed a hand on Dimitri's arm. 'You didn't return my calls.'

With deliberate care he removed her hand. 'No.'

Oh, my. He was rejecting her advances? In public?

'It was very impolite of you, *caro*.' The pout was back, and although a smile was in evidence, her eyes were green ice.

'You think so?'

Victor seemed fascinated with their exchange, and Chantelle reached for her water glass. She needed something stronger, but the wine waiter had yet to appear at their table.

'Victor and I'll be on the Coast for another few days, then we fly down to Sydney to check out the studios there.'

'Indeed?'

Mercifully the wine waiter provided a welcome distraction…one that extended several minutes as Dimitri effected a round of introductions to the four guests sharing their table.

The MC announced the purpose of the evening, noted the charity, and introduced the chairwoman, who gave a splendid speech on the Leukaemia Foundation's goals and achievements. After which a popular singer came on and produced a stirring rendition of a familiar ballad.

Chantelle was supremely conscious of Daniella's attempts to gain Dimitri's attention. And his apparent disinclination to play *polite*.

The starter was served, and she almost died when

he forked a small shrimp from his plate and offered it to her.

What was this? He was feeding her? It had been something they did whenever they'd dined together in the past. So why *now*? Nothing had changed... had it?

She wasn't so sure of anything any more, especially not *him*.

There was a break between the starter and the main, during which time the MC showed slides of children with leukaemia and encouraged the guests to dig deep with donations and the purchase of raffle tickets.

Chantelle made a contribution, and barely contained her surprise at the high denominational bills Dimitri added to the basket being passed around their table.

'Victor, take care of it,' Daniella commanded languidly.

The waiters began serving the main course, placing alternate plates of fish and chicken...the usual practice at such events.

'Oh, please, take that away and bring me a salad,' the actress said with disdain.

Daniella Fabrizi excelled at playing the diva. Four years ago the actress had been a new kid on the block, but fame and fortune had obviously wrought changes...none of which Chantelle considered an improvement. But then, she had every reason to be biased!

'I imagine you hired a baby-sitter for...Sam, isn't it?' The actress directed the query to Chantelle.

'Samuel,' she corrected. 'My mother is looking after him.'

'How convenient for you.' Daniella's voice dripped barbed cynicism beneath the superficial smile.

'Yes,' she agreed, and watched the actress transfer her attention to Dimitri.

'We really must get together for dinner.' Her hand rested on his thigh, and her eyes glittered with suppressed anger as he calmly removed it. 'The four of us, of course,' she added quickly.

'I don't think so.'

Chantelle consciously held her breath for a few seconds, aware all conversation at their table had come to a sudden halt.

'Darling, why ever not?' Daniella pursued with a tinkling laugh. 'We've been intimate friends for a long time.'

Dimitri rested his cutlery. 'We were never intimate. Your deliberately orchestrated interference caused unutterable grief and denied me the pleasure of sharing Chantelle's pregnancy and the first three and a half years of my son's life.'

'Oh, really, how can you say that when we—?'

'Shared one date five years ago.'

The silence was electric. The muted music, the guests' chatter…it all faded into the background.

'Since then you've contrived to elicit invitations to the same functions I attend,' Dimitri continued with dangerous silkiness. 'Almost everywhere I turn, be it Athens, London or Rome…you manage to be there.'

'Don't be ridiculous.'

She was good, Chantelle complimented silently. She did injured indignation to perfection.

'It amounts to stalking, Daniella.'

'How can you say that?'

'Easily.' He waited a beat. 'If you won't desist, I'll have no option but to take out a restraining order against you.'

'I don't understand how you can be so cruel.'

Pathos was evident, and seemed incredibly genuine as the actress recoiled from what she perceived to be an unjustified attack.

'I travel extensively on location. My visit here has been at Victor's invitation.'

Victor remained silent. Integrity, or a desire to distance himself? Probably the latter.

'Your inclusion at tonight's function?' Dimitri persisted silkily.

'Publicity. It's an essential part of an actor's career.'

'I have it on authority the venue was fully booked.'

'So? Someone must have cancelled.'

'And the several messages you left on Andreas' answering machine?'

'Why shouldn't I look up an old friend?'

'We're merely social acquaintances, Daniella. Accept it and move on.'

The waiter appeared at their table and placed a delectable salad in front of the actress, who took one look, and demeaned him with attitude. 'Is this the best you can do?'

The anger simmering beneath Daniella's control threatened to erupt into an explosive scene.

The waiter apologised and requested the actress's specific requirements.

'The food is appalling. Don't bother.'

Temperament was one thing, but nothing excused bad manners.

Chantelle picked at the food on her plate, rearranging the artistic vegetable compilation, forked a morsel of fish, then reached for her wineglass.

Dimitri calmly collected his cutlery and finished the contents on his plate.

Doubtless he was accustomed to shooting people down in flames. Maybe he did it in business on a daily basis. However, she needed a temporary escape from the tense atmosphere.

With deliberate movements, she pushed her plate aside, folded her napkin, then she excused herself.

It seemed feasible to freshen up, given the main event...a fashion show...was due to begin when guests had finished the main course.

How long could she remain absent? Five minutes, ten? It didn't take long to reapply lipstick and powder her nose, but she waited ten minutes before entering the vestibule.

Only to come face-to-face with Daniella, whose transformation was something to behold.

'Don't let that little performance fool you,' the actress vented in barely controlled fury. 'Dimitri is mine, he always has been.'

Chantelle drew in a calming breath, hating the scene she knew was about to unfold. 'I don't believe you,' she said steadily, and took a backward step as Daniella moved close.

'Are you calling me a liar?'

Oh, hell. She didn't want a cat-fight, but she was damned if she'd remain quiescent. 'Did it never occur that you're delusional? Or that you possess an unhealthy obsession for a man who wants nothing to do with you?'

'*Bitch.*' Daniella's hands clenched and unclenched with rage. 'Just because you bore him a son—'

Chantelle held up a hand. 'Stop it right there,' she warned, and made to walk away, except she wasn't quick enough as Daniella's palm connected painfully with her cheek.

'Don't mess with me. I can have you taken out—' she clicked a finger and thumb together with expressive emphasis '—like that.'

'You think Dimitri wouldn't put two and two together?' Chantelle challenged, and felt the first stirring of fear as Daniella's eyes darkened to emerald.

'I can make him want me. I know tricks—'

She'd had enough. Without a further word she pushed past the actress and walked to the lift, which mercifully opened as soon as she pressed the call-button.

At Reception she had the concierge summon a cab, which appeared within seconds, and she slid into the rear passenger seat, gave the driver Anouk's address, then focused on the passing traffic, the nightscape, in an effort to dispel Daniella's vengeful image.

It didn't work, nothing worked, and she alighted

from the cab feeling as if she'd run an emotional marathon.

Anouk met her at the door, her features creased with concern.

'What is it, *amie*? Dimitri has called, not once but twice. *Merde,*' she breathed. 'What is that mark on your face?'

'Maman—don't ask.'

'But of course I will ask!' The sudden peal of the phone provided a momentary distraction. 'That will be Dimitri again.'

'I don't want to speak with him. I don't want to see him.'

'*Alors*—I must answer that.' She did, and Chantelle gathered little from her mother's end of the conversation other than she confirmed Chantelle was home.

'He is on his way here now,' Anouk revealed as she cut the connection.

'Maman, if you let him in the door, I swear I'll take the next flight out of here.' Stupid, angry tears threatened to spill, and she brushed at them in a futile gesture. 'I'm going upstairs to bed. We'll talk in the morning.' She caught the concern on her mother's features, and relented a little. 'Promise.' Then she crossed to the stairs and went to her room.

With care she removed her make-up, then slipped out of her clothes. There was a tense moment as she glimpsed the beam of reflected car-lights in the driveway, and she swiftly turned the safety lock in position.

Dimitri might get past Anouk, but she was damned if she'd face him tonight.

Within minutes there was a light tap on her bedroom door. 'Chantelle. Dimitri insists on speaking with you.'

She took a deep, calming breath. 'Whatever he has to say can wait until morning.'

It was a while before she saw car-lights switch on and his car reverse down the driveway. Then, and only then did she unlock the door and check on Samuel before retreating to her room to lie in bed staring at the shadowed ceiling.

CHAPTER EIGHT

CHANTELLE slept badly, and woke to find Samuel tugging at her arm. With automatic movements she reached forward and gave him an affectionate hug.

'Maman, wake up. Dimitri is here, and Grandmère is waiting to take me to the beach with Jean-Paul.'

What on earth was the time?

Eight, she determined with a silent groan. 'I need to shower and dress, *mon ange*. Go downstairs and wait for me. Fifteen minutes, OK?'

'OK,' he said happily. 'I've had breakfast, and Grandmère is packing a picnic.'

Ten minutes later she donned jeans and a singlet top, slid her feet into sandals, then she caught her hair into a ponytail. Make-up? Forget it.

Subterfuge was alive and well, she perceived as she entered the dining room. Dimitri stood with Samuel hoisted in his arms as they both surveyed Jean-Paul's cruiser moored at the jetty stretching out from the water's edge.

Jean-Paul, his arm in a sling, looked distinctly bemused, and Anouk was slotting bottled water and juice into the portable cooler.

Dimitri turned as he sensed her presence, and gave the appearance of being totally relaxed...until she met his gaze, and she glimpsed something she didn't care to define.

'Maman is here,' Samuel said at once, and looked at his grandmother. 'Can we go now, Grandmère?'

'Of course.' Anouk ran a quick check. 'Sunscreen, hat, insect repellent, change of clothes, swimsuit, towels...yes, that's everything.'

'Grandmère is going to show me how to catch fish.'

She is? Well, now, that has to be a first.

'We're going to eat it for dinner,' Samuel informed as Dimitri released him to stand on the floor. '*Au revoir, Dimitri. Maman.*'

'The coffee is hot,' Anouk declared. 'And there are croissants warming in the oven.'

'I'll help you with the cooler.' Dimitri crossed to where it stood and followed Anouk, Jean-Paul and Samuel out to the car.

Chantelle poured fresh juice, drank it, then filled a cup with coffee, choosing to take it black and sweet. Her nerves were in shreds, and the thought of food repelled her.

Minutes later she heard the car start, and she steeled herself for Dimitri's return. Even so, his reappearance in the kitchen surprised her and she almost spilled her coffee as he entered the kitchen.

For a moment he simply looked at her, and she met his searching gaze with fearless regard.

Soft denim jeans and a polo shirt did little to minimise his impact on her senses, and, unless she had it wrong, it didn't appear he'd slept any better than she had.

'Would you care to tell me why you walked out last night?'

His voice was silk-smooth and sent shivers scudding across the surface of her skin. 'I gather Daniella wasn't forthcoming?'

He thrust a hand into each pocket of his jeans. 'She denied speaking to you. At first.' The memory of his confrontation with Daniella still had the power to anger him, and he clenched his fists in silent frustration.

'I can take care of myself.'

He moved to stand within touching distance, then he lifted a hand and cupped her cheek. 'You have the beginnings of a bruise.' He brushed a thumb-pad gently over her cheekbone.

Beneath his touch she felt strangely helpless. 'Dimitri…'

He cupped her face and tilted it so she had to look at him. 'From the moment I met you, there has been only *you*. In the past four years no one—nothing— has come close to what we shared together.'

He lowered his head and brushed his lips to her cheek, then trailed a path to the edge of her mouth. 'I want you in my life.'

'You can't always have what you want.'

His mouth covered hers in a kiss so incredibly sweet it made her want to cry. 'Yes,' he said softly, 'I can.'

'Because of Samuel.'

He was silent for a few seconds, and she tried to wrench away from him, only to be held fast where she stood.

'That requires a *yes* and *no* qualification. Yes, because I want to be part of my son's life. And no, because *you* are more important to me than anything or anyone else. Without you, I merely exist.'

Love…what about *love*?

'You want me to spell it out?'

His gaze held hers, and she couldn't look away.

'I fell in love with you within days of when we first met. It never changed, even after we went our separate ways.'

Daniella had contrived to poison what they shared then, and now, with manipulative effect. Except this time it hadn't worked.

'I won't allow it to happen again.'

Dared she believe him? She wanted to, desperately.

He pulled her close, one hand holding fast her head while the other slid down to cup her bottom. Then his mouth closed over hers, and she became lost in the taste and feel of him.

It was magical, mesmeric…a passionate intoxication of all her senses.

When he lifted his head she could only look at him, and her bones began to melt at the raw desire apparent.

'This is one level on which we communicate,' Dimitri said in a husky groan, as he slid his hands beneath her singlet top.

Her skin was like satin, so smooth and silky, and delicately scented. He wanted to taste every inch of her in a long, slow loving that would drive them both wild, bury himself inside her and watch her spiral out of control, then join her in the ride.

'I need you. Dear heaven, you can't begin to believe how much.'

'I don't think—'

His mouth possessed hers, and any thought of resistance was lost as her hunger matched his.

She couldn't get enough of him as instinct ruled, and she made no protest when he swept her into his arms and made for the stairs.

He entered her bedroom, and she retained little recollection of dispensing with her clothes, his. There was only *now*, the heat and the passion in a fast and furious lovemaking that tore the breath from her body and left them slick with sensual sweat.

Dear heaven. She felt as if she'd been consumed by an emotional storm so intense she *burned* from it.

All her senses were on high alert, and she could feel every inch of her body…inside and out.

Dimitri cupped her chin and gently turned her head towards him. 'I love you.'

The warmth of his smile melted her bones and she offered a tremulous smile.

'Marry me, Chantelle.' He dropped a kiss at the edge of her shoulder. 'I want to share your life.' He nibbled a path across her collarbone, then slipped low to nuzzle at her breast. 'And have you share mine.'

He trailed his lips to her navel, dipped the tip of

his tongue and teased the hollow there before moving to one hip and kissing a path to her knee.

He knew where to touch, the location of each sensual pulse-beat, and he explored them all with such excruciating slowness she was almost begging when he sought to gift her the most intimate kiss of all.

She cried with the pleasure of it, and reached for him, exulting in his quickened heartbeat, the thudding of his pulse, and he entered her to indulge in a long, slow loving that left them both sated and sensually replete.

'You haven't said yes,' Dimitri ventured as he drew her in close against him and pillowed her head into the curve of his shoulder.

'Not fair. You have me at a disadvantage.'

'*Agape mou,*' he murmured against her temple, 'I plan to keep you at a disadvantage on a permanent basis.'

She lifted a hand and teased her fingers through the swirling hairs on his chest. 'You do realise it's the middle of the day?'

'And that makes a difference, because?'

'We should get up.' She made a slight effort to move, and thought better of it.

The warmth of his smile reached down and touched her soul. 'Soon, hmm?'

'Anouk and Jean-Paul—'

'Won't return until after four.'

'A conspiracy, huh?'

'Good management,' he corrected.

Chantelle lay quietly, exulting in the languid

warmth of a woman who had been thoroughly loved. This was where she wanted to be, with this man, for the rest of her life.

'Yes,' she said simply.

Dimitri stilled. 'Is that *yes*, it was good management, or have you agreed to marry me?'

A light laugh bubbled from her lips. 'Both. Besides, we've just had unprotected sex. Twice. The last time we did that, I fell pregnant. I think I should make an honest man of you.'

He tunnelled his fingers through her hair and settled his mouth over hers in a long, evocative kiss that almost made her weep.

'Soon. Very soon,' he promised. 'We'll organise a licence and get married before we leave for Paris.'

'Whoa, not so fast,' Chantelle protested. *'Paris?'*

'You need to give notice and pack everything you want to transfer to New York.'

'We? You're coming with us?'

'Pedhaki mou,' he assured with musing indulgence, 'I don't intend letting you out of my sight.'

It was an hour before they rose and shared a shower, then, dressed, they went down to the kitchen and raided the refrigerator for a late lunch, choosing to eat out on the terrace overlooking the sea.

Chantelle sat quietly as she sipped chilled white wine, and became lost in reflective thought.

If she hadn't returned home for Christmas; if Dimitri hadn't chosen this particular festive season to visit his father... They might never have met again, never had the chance to experience the joy, the passion of two people so perfectly in tune with each other.

'I love you,' she said gently, turning towards him.

'*Cristos.*' The word emerged with heartfelt warmth. 'Now you tell me.' He rose from the chair and pulled her to her feet.

'What are you doing?'

'Taking you inside.' He threaded his fingers through her own. 'I don't want to shock the neighbours.'

CHAPTER NINE

'MAMAN, we are home. Grandmère helped me catch a fish.'

There was a moment's silence as the child absorbed the scene in front of him. Slowly he turned towards his grandmother. 'Grandmère, why is Dimitri kissing Maman?'

'They are standing beneath the mistletoe, *mon ange*, are they not? It is a Christmas tradition, *oui*, for adults to kiss beneath the mistletoe.'

'Only adults?'

Dimitri lifted his head and turned towards his son.

Then he swept wide an arm as he beckoned Samuel to join them.

Samuel ran, and was lifted high into his father's arms. He wriggled a little, pressed a kiss to his mother's cheek, then impulsively gifted another to the man who held him.

'This is nice.'

'Nice enough for you to share Maman with me?'

Samuel looked thoughtful. 'Are you going to be my daddy?'

Chantelle held her breath.

'Would you like that?' Dimitri queried solemnly.

'*Oui.* Maman doesn't know how to catch fish, and she won't let me have a proper bicycle. But I'm getting big, and I won't fall off.'

Anouk smiled and caught Jean-Paul's hand. 'In this case, three isn't a crowd, but five definitely is. Let's go look at the garden for a while.'

Christmas was the season for family, with love, laughter, gifts and giving.

For Chantelle it held special meaning, for from this moment on she'd always connect the festive season with being reunited with the love of her life.

Three weeks ago she would never have imagined in her wildest dreams she'd be planning her own wedding. Or that she would reveal to her son his real father's identity.

Miracles had been worked to ensure the marriage could take place amongst family the day before their departure for France.

Returning home for Christmas had brought more than she could have ever dreamed of, and she lifted her face to meet Dimitri's warm gaze as Jean-Paul handed out gifts assembled beneath the Christmas tree.

The brief touch of his mouth on hers was a vivid reminder of what they would soon share together.

'Dimitri is kissing Maman again,' Samuel announced, and encountered his father's broad smile followed by his teasing drawl.

'You'd better get used to it.'

Samuel grinned and shrugged his shoulders. He didn't mind. His mother was happy, Dimitri was cool, and, by the number of brightly packaged gifts beneath the tree, Santa had rewarded him well.

What more could anyone want?

Yuletide Reunion

Sharon Kendrick

Sharon Kendrick started story-telling at the age of eleven and has never really stopped. She likes to write fast-paced, feel-good romances, with heroes who are so sexy they'll make your toes curl!

Born in west London, she now lives in the beautiful city of Winchester—where she can see the cathedral from her window (but only if she stands on tiptoe). She has two children, Celia and Patrick, and her passions include music, books, cooking and eating—and drifting off into wonderful daydreams while she works out new plots!

CHAPTER ONE

THE first time Clemmie saw Aleck Cutler, she knew she had to have him.

There was only one tiny obstacle in the way—he just happened to be dating someone else at the time.

Worse. He might only be eighteen years old, but apparently he was serious about the girl. Everybody said so. Very, very serious.

Clemmie didn't believe them. Not at first. People didn't get married at eighteen, for goodness' sake, so it couldn't be *that* serious, could it? Okay, people could fall in love at eighteen, but they didn't generally get *married*. What would be the point?

And anyway, Clemmie thought, staring hard at her fountain pen. He couldn't possibly be in love with Alison Fleming, even if he thought he was. Because that wasn't part of Clemmie's life plan. He was going to fall in love with *her*, just as she had fallen love with him the first time she saw him. When he had held the door open for her and said, 'Hi,' his greeny-blue eyes crinkling at the corners as he gave her the most irresistible smile imaginable.

It was like being touched by magic—there was no other way to describe it. And if Aleck hadn't realised yet what was as obvious to Clemmie as the writing on the wall—namely, that they were made for each other—well, he soon *would*!

Clemmie gave a great sigh as she glanced down at the open textbook in front of her. She was bored; that was the trouble. She had been bored for a whole month—ever since she had joined the sixth-form of Ashfield High. A month of trying to get used to a new house, a new town, new school, new stepfather...

Clemmie bit her lip and picked up her pen to write, but found herself unable to concentrate and put it down again almost immediately. She stared out of the window across the school playing fields. It wasn't as though she didn't *like* her stepfather—she did. Dan was a good man, who loved her mother, and her mother deserved that love. Clemmie's father had died when she was little, and it had been a real struggle for her mother. It was just...

Clemmie sighed once more as she retied the ribbon at the end of one thick, shiny plait. Did the two of them have to be quite so ecstatic about each other all the time, and in front of *her*?

It wasn't that they were constantly pawing at each other, or kissing, or anything like that. Just that sometimes the way her mother gazed at Dan, and the way that he gazed back at her—well, it just made

Clemmie think she shouldn't even be in the same building, let alone the same room!

The school was fine, too, if she was being honest, and much more relaxed than the city school she had been used to in London. It had a good academic reputation and it wasn't too big, though it had lots of playing fields where you could walk at lunchtime and lose your soul up into the sky. And the other girls in her year were friendly. The boys, too, thought Clemmie, wincing; some of them had been *very* friendly.

Except for Aleck Cutler, of course.

Apart from that one blinding smile on her first day, he had remained cool and polite and indifferent.

He was in the year above Clemmie, and the unrivalled star of the school. He was the kind of person you wanted to hate because he was so perfect, but ended up sighing over. He loved sport and hated books, but he had the best grades in his year. He never showed any personal vanity whatsoever—in fact, he never seemed to bother what he looked like— yet he never looked anything other than thoroughly delectable, whatever he was doing. Covered in mud and wearing a pair of short-shorts, he attracted large audiences of swooning schoolgirls who normally couldn't tell one end of a rugby ball from the other!

He lived on his parents' farm on the edge of Ashfield, and he worked there every weekend and all through the holidays—and the hard, physical work made him fitter and tougher than anyone else of his age.

He was wonderful in just about every way,

Clemmie had decided. In fact, there was only one blot on the landscape, and that was Alison Fleming, his girlfriend.

Clemmie had found out as much as she could without seeming too obvious. The facts were simple. Aleck had been going out with Alison Fleming for six months, and in that time he had not looked at another female. Worse was to follow. Alison Fleming was very beautiful, with pale, turquoise eyes and a mass of honey-coloured hair which always hung in an immaculate gleaming bell to her shoulders.

Clemmie did everything in her power to get Aleck to notice her, motivated by a deviousness she'd been unaware she possessed. She hung around unobtrusively until she saw him leave the building—with or without Alison—and then she would saunter along home on the opposite side of the road, with her long red-brown hair flying wildly and her skirt rolled over twice at the waistband so that it showed yards of long, stockinged leg.

She joined the School Debating Society, of which he was the Chairperson. The only problem being that whenever he was in the room all Clemmie's brilliantly thought-out arguments went straight out of her head, and she stared at him, totally tongue-tied. It certainly put her off a career in public speaking!

But as time went on, and the end of the year approached, Clemmie gradually began to accept that maybe the love affair she longed for just wasn't meant to be. Aleck would be leaving soon, and going off to university. And not alone either—but with

Alison. He obviously just wasn't interested in any other girl. Although sometimes, *sometimes*, Clemmie could have sworn that she had seen him giving her a hard, slanting look from beneath the dark lashes which shaded those amazing blue-green eyes of his.

It might have all died a quiet death had it not been for the night of the Summer Ball on the last night of term, which was thrown in honour of all those who were leaving the school. Clemmie didn't particularly want to go—seeing Aleck for the last time, with his arms draped around Alison, would be like subjecting herself to the most awful form of torture.

In the end, she was persuaded to go by her mother.

'You *must* go, Clemmie.' Hilary Powers frowned at her daughter. 'You're always complaining that there's nothing to do around here, and now you're turning down the opportunity to go to a really nice dance!'

Clemmie turned her mouth down. What could she *say*? That she'd fallen hook, line and sinker for a man who was besotted with someone else?

'And I'll give you money for a new dress,' smiled Dan. 'How about that?'

Clemmie couldn't win.

She bought a dress which was absolutely beautiful but left very little to the imagination. A black silk slip dress, beneath which she could wear only the briefest of black lace thongs.

'Do you like it?' she asked her mother.

Her mother screwed her face up and looked at her daughter. Pale face, too many freckles, dark hair spilling down like mahogany satin—gorgeous! But the *dress*? 'I'm not sure, darling. It's a bit revealing.'

'Gee, thanks, Mum!' scowled Clemmie. 'You do wonders for my confidence!' What *was* it with mothers, sometimes?

'Are you wearing a bra?'

'I *can't* wear a bra—it shows!'

'Then I'll lend you my black chiffon wrap,' said her mother briskly. 'You can throw that round your neck and look slightly more decent.'

Clemmie got ready with Mary Adams from her year, the two of them standing giggling and shaking with nerves as Clemmie swept unfamiliarly thick mascara onto her dark lashes. She was so nervous that she accepted a glass of wine from the cask in Mary's fridge, and then another. By the time she arrived at the dance she was floating, *floating*—and danced with every single boy who asked her.

Too giddy and too excited to eat, she glugged back a glass of the fruity punch she was given and tried not to look at Alison Fleming, who was demure and stunning in virginal white. While Aleck looked like the only real man in the room, his height and build and bearing making him seem like warm flesh and blood, while the others all looked like cardboard cut-outs.

Clemmie was on her way back from the rest room, moving slightly unsteadily along the corridor with her eyes glittering darkly against the dead-pale of her cheeks, when she saw Aleck.

He was standing with his back to her, standing

perfectly still by the window of an empty, unlit classroom. His old classroom.

Clemmie drew in a deep breath of longing. She should go straight past. He wasn't interested. He had a girlfriend.

But the wine and the punch had loosened her tongue and this was probably the last time she would ever see him.

'Hi,' she said recklessly, standing illuminated in the bright light of the corridor.

Aleck turned round slowly, his eyes flickering over her in a way she didn't quite understand. If he was surprised to see her, he didn't show it. But then, his face rarely showed anything, and it certainly didn't now.

'Hi,' he said coolly.

Clemmie gulped and walked over to stand beside him at the window, which overlooked the tennis courts and the soccer pitches beyond. She wondered what this school would be like next year, with no Aleck Cutler to gaze at, to think about, to fantasise over... It didn't really bear thinking about.

'So,' she said, and stared out into the night as her eyes grew accustomed to the darkness. 'What are you looking at?'

He gave a small laugh, then shook his head. 'Nothing.'

Clemmie felt bold. 'Yes, you were!' she teased. 'I saw you.'

He found himself smiling reluctantly. She was as exuberant as a puppy. 'Okay, then,' he admitted. 'I was just looking out at that old house. See?'

She followed the direction of his eyes but she knew which house he was talking about. The tumbledown house which dominated the town. From her bedroom window in Dan's house, Clemmie would look down at the overgrown lawns, the flowerbeds which were choked with weeds. In autumn, the fruit fell from the apple and pear trees, lying ignored and rotting on the ground. It was a sad house, she had often thought. A neglected house. 'You mean the old grey one? Isn't it supposed to be haunted?'

He shook his head. 'I don't believe in all that stuff! It's only spooky because no one's lived in it for years.'

'I wonder why?' she queried softly.

Aleck looked at her, finding her ridiculously easy to talk to and yet sensing some unknown danger in the air. 'Because it's big. And it's run-down—you'd need serious money to update it and run it. People with that kind of money don't generally want to live in a small town like Ashfield.'

'But you do?' she asked perceptively.

He shrugged. 'Maybe.'

There was silence for a moment, though Clemmie could hear her heart booming out in a muffled thud. She saw the pensive set of his profile. 'Feeling sad?' she asked softly.

He narrowed his eyes suspiciously, like a man not used to being quizzed about his feelings. 'Sad?'

'About leaving.' She noticed that he wasn't looking into her eyes any more, just staring very hard at her silky black dress, and that a tiny muscle had begun to work in one cheek.

There was a pause. 'A little. Closing a chapter of your life is always sad.' He gave a low laugh, and abruptly turned his attention away. But not for long. He looked back into her eyes then, and Clemmie felt drawn in by the magnetism of that cool, mocking gaze. 'Though maybe nostalgic would be a better word.'

'Yes.' Clemmie giddily swept her fingers back through her thick red-brown hair, so that it spilt in mahogany streams all the way down over her silk-covered breasts. Dizzy with wine and longing, she tried to think of something interesting and original to say, and failed dismally. 'Will you be sorry to leave?' She leaned back to perch her bottom on the wide window-ledge and smiled at him.

The movement distracted him as much as the invitation in her eyes, and Aleck found his eyes drawn once again to the pale gleam as her breasts thrust heavily towards him. He felt the slow, insistent throbbing of desire start to build up, felt it begin to pulse powerfully through his veins. 'Sure, I'll be sorry,' he said, in a husky voice that didn't sound like his own at all. 'There's a lot I'm going to miss.'

Drunk with the heady delight of his proximity, with the obvious appreciation in his eyes, Clemmie found herself purring like a parody of a sex-symbol. 'And what are you going to miss most?'

Aleck felt his muscles tense as she lounged back negligently on the window-ledge. She might as well have been naked for all that dress was covering her up, the two inverted vees of the bodice taut and stretched as they struggled to restrain the lush young breasts. The silk lay smoothly against her flesh, except for where he could quite clearly see the outline of some outrageously flimsy G-string. Aleck swallowed. 'Well, I'll miss seeing you,' he told her, in a throaty whisper.

Clemmie opened her dark eyes even wider, her surprise completely genuine. '*Will* you?'

'Sure, I will.'

'I didn't think you'd even noticed me,' she told him honestly.

He gave a hollow guilty laugh, as Alison's memory slipped from his mind like sand through his fingers. 'Not *notice* you?' he demanded unsteadily. 'Oh, come *on*. You'd need to be blind or pretty stupid not to notice *you*, Clemmie…'

His face gave him away.

Clemmie could see the fight that was taking place within him, yet she was too trapped by desire to heed it. Too flattered by the look on his face which must have mirrored her own. A look she had dreamed of, night after night, but never thought she would see in the flesh. Compelled by a need she did not recognise, she put her hands up behind her head to cushion her head on her palms, and the action did even more to accentuate her breasts. 'You do say the nicest things,' she smiled.

Appalled at his behaviour, and yet unwilling or unable to stop himself, Aleck took a step towards her. Why not just give her what she so obviously wanted? What *he* so obviously wanted, too. 'Do I?' he murmured. 'I don't just *say* the nicest things, Clemmie, I do them as well…'

He moved his lips towards hers, and Clemmie wondered if she had imagined the dark note of warning which had coloured the throaty whisper of his response. But then his mouth was covering hers and the effect was like lighting touchpaper.

He showed none of the finesse of the Aleck of her dreams, just pulled her into his arms and began a kiss which was so shockingly intimate and so unbelievably sensual that Clemmie felt she should have been outraged by it. Yet she found herself kissing him back as though she had been born for just this moment.

He pulled her closer, so close that her lush silken-covered breasts were crushed against his chest. God, he could feel those nipples digging into him like tight little rocks. He couldn't help himself, and just briefly brushed his fingertips over each straining mound, expecting her to slap his face. But she didn't.

She couldn't. The moment he touched her, she was lost. His. Submerged and drowning in silky-dark erotic waters. She knew that she shouldn't be letting him do this, that she should be pushing him away, insulted—but instead Clemmie nearly died with pleasure when he touched her breasts. The wine and her loneliness and the overwhelming emotion she had felt for Aleck Cutler since the moment she'd first laid eyes on him, all combined to become the most potent, sensual cocktail of her young life.

His mouth was still on hers as his thigh pushed its way insistently between hers, his fingers now straying beneath the silk of the bodice itself until they alighted on each exquisitely aroused nipple and he circled the bare skin of each painful peak with erotic triumph.

'Clemmie,' he moaned into her mouth.

'W-what?'

'God, you're so *beautiful*,' he managed to get out, from between gritted teeth.

Her head tipped back as he kissed her neck. 'No, I'm n-not...'

'Beautiful,' he contradicted, still in that dazed kind of voice. 'And I want you. Do you know that? So badly.'

'I want you, too,' she gasped in wonderment, and laced her fingers into his thick dark hair.

His hand moved to the pert curve of her bottom, cupping each silk-covered buttock with a groan, and he was just about to slide the slithery material up, so that he could touch her legs and beyond, when the brief and rapid sound of footsteps heralded a third person's arrival and the room was thrown into bright light.

Bedazzled, they sprang apart—just in time to see the Head of Science standing by the light switch, with a whole gaggle of giggling fifth-formers just behind him.

'Good evening, Cutler,' he said stonily. 'Perhaps you and Miss Powers would like to come to my office. I think that a little talk is probably long overdue. Don't you?'

Clemmie looked up into Aleck's face. For a split second their eyes connected, and in his she could read the unmistakable message of self-disgust and outraged recrimination.

And she knew then why mothers always warned their daughters about being too easy. Because Clemmie would have done anything to be able to remove that look of seething contempt from Aleck Cutler's beautiful eyes.

CHAPTER TWO

'MOM, Mom—*Mom*! Is this really, *really* our new home?'

Clemmie laughed and looked up from the packing case she was hunting through. Where *was* the wretched kettle? She smiled into the excited face of her ten-year-old daughter. 'Yes, Justine,' she smiled. 'It really, really is!'

'And did I come here when I was very little?' Justine sat back on her heels and looked up at her mother.

'Yes, you did. You wouldn't remember. It was where Grandma used to live—'

'With Grandad Dan?'

'That's right.' Clemmie lifted the bright blue kettle out of the packing case with a look of triumph. 'There—found it! Why don't you go and get your sister and bring her down, and then we'll all have a break?'

'Is there any cake?'

'Ginger cake, if you're very good!'

'Whoopee!' shrieked Justine, and scooted off to find Louella.

Clemmie looked around her at the empty room, still trying to take everything in, wondering why her life never seemed to chug along comfortably like everyone else's. Not that she was complaining. Not now. Not with this lovely house to call her own. A home at last, after a long time searching.

Clemmie sighed, remembering the man who had brought her and her mother so much happiness. *Dear* Dan. Because he'd been her stepfather she had not expected him to love her. But he *had* loved her, loved her as much as if he had been her own father. And yet...

When he died, she had somehow expected him to leave the house to one of his blood relatives, not to her. There had been a nephew somewhere, an elderly aunt somewhere else. And it wasn't as though she'd seen a lot of him. Her visits from the States had tended to be when she could afford them, which hadn't been very often. And after her mother had died she hadn't had the heart to come back to Ashfield at all.

Clemmie's mother had died six years previously, and—judging by his letters—Dan had never seemed to get over that. Yet when they'd rung Clemmie in America, to tell her that Dan himself was seriously ill, she had damned the expense, jumped on a flight and come straight over. He had died that same day, gratified that the woman he had looked on as a daughter should have been there to hold his hand while he slipped away...

Clemmie had flown back to the States—to her two beloved daughters and the realisation that she could no longer live in the small American town where her life had broken down so dramatically. Something was going to have to change…

Dan's legacy had come like a bolt out of the blue, and a welcome one. The house and enough capital to live on for a little while. A life-saver. A new beginning. A new life in England.

Clemmie's divorce had left her even more broke than she'd been before, scrubbing around to make ends meet in a country where suddenly, without her American husband, she was a foreigner. A foreigner, moreover, with foxy dark eyes and a curvy body. The kind of woman universally feared by other, not-so-happily-married women…

So she had packed the three of them up, lock, stock and barrel, and moved them back to Ashfield. Back to the town where she had spent two fractured years before going off to college, her whole view of the place coloured by her ill-advised passion for Aleck Cutler. What a gullible little fool she had been!

Part of her had wondered about coming back at all, but it had only been a small part. Women in her position had little choice about where they lived. She was happy, and grateful for Dan's legacy, and strangely drawn to Ashfield. In spite of her youthful mistakes, it was the only place where she felt some affinity with the past. And with such an uncertain future lying ahead of her, Clemmie needed to hang onto that feeling right now.

Clemmie boiled the kettle and made tea, then cut slices of dark, sticky gingerbread and laid them out in a pattern on the plate. The frantic thump, thump, thump of feet on stairs heralded the arrival of her two daughters, and as Clemmie carried the tray into the sitting room she gave them a slow smile of contentment.

They looked as fresh as daisies, she thought proudly, and not as though they'd stepped off a transatlantic flight just hours earlier. They were, quite simply, the lights of her life.

For, no matter what else she achieved in her life, she had done this—and mostly on her own, too. Produced two beautiful, intelligent and charming little girls—though she conceded that she might be a little biased! Now she had to raise them to be happy. Nothing else really mattered.

'Mummy, I've chosen my bedroom!' sighed Justine. 'It's *really* cool!'

'Why does she always get to choose first?' complained Louella, scowling.

'Because I'm ten and you're only eight!' crowed Justine.

'But it's not fair!'

Clemmie bit back the temptation to inform her younger daughter that life often *wasn't* fair—she didn't want to turn her into a cynic at such a tender age! 'Don't you like *your* bedroom, Louella?' she asked softly. 'It's the one that *I* used to have when I lived here. It isn't the biggest, but it has the best view in the house, in my opinion.'

'It's neat,' nodded Louella, so that her waist-length

brown plaits jiggled up and down. 'I can see right over the wall to that big garden at the back—the one with the swimming pool. And there was a girl there, playing on a *swing.*'

'Was there?' asked Clemmie absently, pouring out the tea.

'I waved at her—and she waved back!'

'That's nice, darling.'

'So would she be our nearest neighbour?'

'Yes, she would.' Clemmie handed over a thick slice of cake and watched while Louella took a bite. 'It's good that someone's living there at last—it was empty for years and years.' And then fragments of a long-ago conversation swam up to the surface of Clemmie's memory, and Aleck Cutler's perfect eighteen-year-old face imprinted itself there.

She shook her head, trying to get rid of it, wondering why the recollection still had the power to shake her. Because there could be nothing more pathetic than a woman of twenty-nine carrying a torch for a man who was married to someone else.

And Aleck had married Alison.

'It's not *really* like moving somewhere completely new, is it, Mom?' observed Justine slowly. 'Since I guess you must still know lots of people here?'

Clemmie shook her head. She still wore her thick, red-brown hair long, but most days, like today, she didn't have time to do any more with it than drag it back into a ponytail. 'Not really, honey,' she said softly. 'I left when I was eighteen, so I kind of lost touch. Friendships don't thrive unless you invest time

in them, and I never really had the time. I went away
to college and then—'

'Then you met Dad?' asked Louella brightly.

'That's right,' agreed Clemmie steadily, and kept
her face poker-straight. It was difficult, she had decided, to be a mature and generous human being
where her ex-husband was concerned, but she was
trying. Oh, Lord, how she was trying! She understood that it was in a child's nature to love its parents
absolutely, as Justine and Louella loved their father.
But Bill had let the girls down so many times over
the years, whittling away at that love every time he
did so, that Clemmie had to force herself to say anything positive about him.

'And once I went to the States to live with your
dad, then I didn't get to visit very often at all.'

'So you don't know very much about Ashfield,
Mom?' asked Justine thoughtfully.

'I know where the church and the shops and the
schools are—but that's about it! I'm relying on you
two to find out where all the excitement is   think
you could do that for me?'

'You bet!' grinned Justine.

The three of them sat on the floor, drinking their
tea and eating cake. Clemmie was reluctantly thinking about unpacking another case when there came
the sound of a girl's voice, calling, 'Hello?'

Justine and Louella looked at one another excitedly before springing to their feet and running into
the hall.

'Our first visitor!' smiled Clemmie, as she followed them out, and then her mouth dried as she stared at the young girl who was standing on their doorstep.

She looked about ten, the same age as Justine, but she was tall for her age, with pale hair which fell neatly to her shoulders and pale, creamy skin. But it was her eyes which made Clemmie's mouth fall open in an unconsciously shocked reaction.

Greeny-blue mesmeric eyes, fringed with thick dark lashes. There could not be another pair of eyes in the world which were that beautiful. Clemmie swallowed. This was Aleck Cutler's daughter, she realised, with a certainty which astonished her almost as much as her own heart-racing reaction.

'Hello,' said Clemmie, hoping that her voice didn't betray her shock. 'Are you our new neighbour?'

'I am,' answered the girl politely, in a remarkably grown-up voice. 'I live in the house at the back. I'm Stella Cutler.'

So she had been right! Clemmie felt her nails, concealed in the back pockets of her jeans, dig hard through the denim into the soft flesh of her buttocks, while the world threatened to sway intolerably before righting itself once more. Aleck's daughter! *Here!*

'I'm Clemmie Maxwell. I used to be Clemmie Powers. And this is my daughter, Justine.' Clemmie swallowed as she indicated both her daughters. 'And her sister Louella. Say hi, girls!'

'Hi!' the two chorused shyly.

'We were just having a tea break, Stella,' continued Clemmie, trying to behave as she would normally behave if a young neighbour came to call. 'Can you stay for a while and join us? Or do you have to get back?'

'Oh, I can stay,' said Stella quickly.

'Shouldn't you check with your parents first?' Clemmie forced herself to ask.

Stella shook her blonde head, her face curiously lacking in emotion. 'No, that's okay. I was home alone—so there's no one there to ask. But I'd *love* some tea,' she added winningly.

'Well, then, tea it is!' Clemmie led the way into the sitting room and wondered if she had suffered some kind of emotional block all those years ago. Why on earth was she feeling so disorientated just because Aleck's daughter had come to visit? He was a guy she had had a mad crush on and they had shared a kiss *twelve* years ago! Nothing more than that. So why was she making such a big deal out of it?

'Our mom makes *fantastic* cake! You should see what she does for our birthdays! She makes rainbow frosting that tastes like heaven!' Louella was confiding to Stella, her freckly face so like Clemmie's as she babbled away excitedly.

'Are you American?' asked Stella curiously.

Justine shook her head. 'Our dad was—*is*,' she corrected herself hurriedly. 'But he still lives in America, with his new girlfriend and their baby, and we live here now! But that's where we grew up, and that's why we've got accents. Do you suppose we'll get teased by the other kids?'

Stella shook her head. 'No way! All the girls will

be jealous! If you speak with an American accent everyone thinks you're a movie-star over here!'

'You're kidding?'

'No, I'm not!'

Clemmie left them chattering while she went to refill the kettle, but before it had begun to boil she heard footsteps on the stairs and Justine shouting, 'We're taking Stella upstairs to show her round. Is that okay, Mom?'

'Okay, that's fine!' Which would give her time to tackle some of these boxes…

Clemmie began to unpack the cases which were stacked haphazardly all over the kitchen floor, humming to herself as she did so. She had been torn—wanting to bring every single stick of furniture with her, mainly so that the girls would feel safe and surrounded by the familiar, but there had also been a side to her which had wanted to throw everything away. To start anew—without any objects which would remind her of Bill and the marriage she had struggled so long to sustain.

In the end she had just brought their favourite things—the good set of china which had been a wedding present, the rocking chair which Bill had carved for her in the early, happy days, and some small Shaker knick-knacks she had collected over the years. Amazing, she thought, as she pulled a jug out of the case and carefully peeled away the protective paper from it. You could spend ten years of your life in another country, and come back with very little to show for it.

Just two gorgeous daughters and a fierce determination to steer clear of men! Men were nothing but trouble and heartbreak. Men chewed you up and spat you out.

Even so, it seemed a rather cruel irony that Clemmie was now faced with the prospect of having to confront Aleck and Alison Cutler over the garden wall!

Still, she told herself briskly, as she placed a vase on the window-ledge. She had survived isolation and desertion and infidelity in a foreign country—she was damned sure that she could endure seeing her schoolgirl crush and the woman he had courted and married!

The morning seemed to fly by, so that Clemmie was able to accomplish plenty. She spent much of it wiping down the walls and the paintwork. She might think about giving each room a lick of paint once the girls had gone back to school.

Having Stella certainly helped keep them out of Clemmie's hair, and she seemed like a very self-contained child. She had organised Justine and Louella into tidying up their giant doll's house, and when Clemmie had stuck her head round the door a couple of minutes ago it had been to see three heads bent over it in industrious play!

At one-fifteen Clemmie washed her hands, put the kettle on, and was just thinking about getting some lunch for them all when there was a loud and peremptory knocking on the front door.

She stole a quick glance at herself in the mirror and grimaced at her jeans and old yellow tee-shirt, wishing that she'd made a bit more effort. She wasn't best dressed to impress any of her new neighbours! Her dusty hair could do with a wash, and her face was completely bare of make-up, which only drew attention to the freckles which spattered her nose and cheeks and which were the bane of her life.

She pulled the front door open and the welcoming smile froze on her lips as she realised the identity of the man who stood so tall and so broodingly on her doorstep. Clemmie stared up at Aleck Cutler.

Twelve years was a long time in anyone's life—particularly the years between eighteen and thirty, when adolescents became adults—but all Clemmie could think about was how the essential characteristics of the man remained unaltered.

He was even taller, yes, and he had filled out, that was for sure. The snake-hipped teenage Aleck had been transformed into a big, strong man with hard, firm flesh and shoulders so wide you felt you could have rested the world there. Just a few silver strands ran through the abundant thickness of his dark hair, but the eyes were as remarkable and as mesmerising and as vibrant as they had been all those years ago, and Clemmie felt her face suddenly grow heated…

'A-Aleck!' she stammered. 'Aleck Cutler!'

He stared at her, but made no greeting in response. Just clipped out coldly, 'So it's true. You're back.'

If his eyes hadn't been spitting unfriendly fire, Clemmie might have smiled. As it was, the hostile vibrations she was getting from him made her stiffen her shoulders defensively. 'Obviously,' she responded, her own voice chilly.

'Have you got my daughter here?'

'Y-you mean—Stella?' she managed, stung and confused by his combative air.

'Since I only have one daughter—yes, I *do* mean Stella,' he told her with icy emphasis.

Clemmie could tolerate all kinds of things, but rudeness was not one of them. Years of being insulted within a failing marriage had reinforced her determination never to let a man treat her that way again. She stared at him. So he could wipe that disdainful look off his face right now!

'Yes, she's here!' she snapped back. 'And how was I supposed to know that you only have one daughter? Telepathy isn't one of my particular talents!'

He looked at her properly then, the green-blue eyes taking their time as they slowly surveyed her from head to toes, and Clemmie was left feeling as though they had stripped her bare.

'No,' he said carefully. 'As I recall you had many talents, Clemmie, but telepathy wasn't one of them.'

'Just what are you implying?' she demanded, furious at that critical look on his face, and even more furious at the unconscious quickening of her heart when she realised that he *did* remember her name.

He gave a disparaging smile. 'Oh, you surely don't need me to spell it out for you, do you?'

'Oh, I do,' she mocked sweetly. 'I can't *stand* innuendo! So if you've got something to say, Aleck, why don't you just go right ahead and say it?'

He raised his dark brows so that they slanted in arrogant surprise. 'You mean relate the simple fact that if we hadn't been discovered, then we probably would have ended up making love—with you strad-dled over one of the classroom desks, your panties down by your ankles?'

All the heat drained from Clemmie's face—she was so shocked and horrified by his crude portrayal of what had actually happened. What a way to *put* it! 'How can you say something like that?' she whis-pered, in a hollow voice. 'How *can* you?'

He shrugged, apparently not bothered by her white face, nor her trembling mouth. 'How can I not? It's what happened, isn't it, Clemmie? Or would you prefer to define the episode as true *love*? Maybe that's how you usually justify your behaviour to yourself—I don't know.'

He managed to make the word 'love' drip with such venomous sarcasm that Clemmie stared at him in horror. 'But it was just a kiss!' she protested.

'Really?' His eyes narrowed alarmingly. 'Is that what it was? Some kiss! Do you normally let men who kiss you for the first time touch your breasts like that, Clemmie?'

She wanted to hit him. Because at least hitting him would detract from the way her body responded when he said 'touch your breasts'. How could he? How *could* he? Her fingers itched to claw at him in some frighteningly primitive way, but to do that would be to compound his opinion of her as some emotional loose cannon.

'Why are we discussing something which happened twelve years ago?' she demanded, swallowing back her lust and her anger and attempting to transform them into dignity.

'I thought that was what you wanted,' he observed. 'You were the one who persisted with the subject, weren't you? After all, I came over simply to fetch my daughter—'

'Then I'll go and find her,' said Clemmie tonelessly.

'Before you do, Clemmie…' He lifted his fingers and, annoyingly, Clemmie found herself halting in her tracks. 'Didn't it occur to you that I might be worried? Didn't you consider ringing me to say that Stella was here?'

'Of course I did!' she defended. 'And Stella *told* me that it was okay! She told me that she was home alone—'

'She was *not* alone!' he shot back repressively. 'I was working in my study, and she was probably bored and saw you arrive. She's ten years old, for God's sake—didn't it occur to you to check with me first?'

The trouble was that he was right. She *should* have checked, should have got Stella to ring her father, or should have done so herself. She hoped that he would have done the same if her girls had turned up unexpectedly at *his* house. And she wondered if she would have been so reluctant to ring if the father in question had been anyone other than Aleck Cutler…

He threw her a look that was distinctly insulting.

'Though maybe you decided that it would suit you to have her stay so long.' His eyes glinted. 'Was that it?'

'And why would I do that?' she queried steadily, her heart pounding away in her head as she began to realise just what he was getting at.

'Maybe you were hoping that I would come looking for her and…'

'And what?' she goaded, needing to hear him say the unbelievable.

'And maybe you wanted to finish off what we started all those years ago?'

Clemmie came closer to hitting someone than she had ever done in her life, but she fought the feeling as if she was fighting for her life. She was not about to start brawling like a fishwife! She managed a tight, supercilious smile. 'I don't think so, Aleck. I grew out of teenage fumblings a long time ago. Besides, even if I *was* still turned on by heavy petting—I've always made it a rule not to fool around with married men.'

His eyebrows disappeared into the thick, dark hair as he feigned surprise. 'Really? Then you *must* have changed, Clemmie, because you had no qualms about flinging yourself at me then, did you? Knowing all the while that Alison was waiting for me.'

Clemmie swallowed, acknowledging that he was speaking the truth, and yet… 'You're very good at abdicating responsibility, aren't you? You could have just said no, Aleck,' she told him coldly. '*You* were the one in a relationship—not me! And you were the one who made the first move, as I recall. You kissed *me*!'

He smiled, but his eyes were Arctic-bleak. 'So I did, but who wouldn't, in the circumstances? There are very few men who would pass up the chance of a beautiful, scantily clad girl offering herself on a plate the way you did, Clemmie.'

Clemmie finally snapped; she couldn't help it. She raised her hand and flew it at his face. But if she was fast, then Aleck was even faster, and he imprisoned her wrist with his hand, bringing her right up close to him in the process so that his eyes were a viridian haze away. They blazed fire and desire, but something else, too. Something very like animosity.

She could feel his breath on her face, warm and sweet, while her own was being sucked into her lungs in short, rapid bursts, as if she had been drowning and had suddenly found air. Just the touch of his hand where he held her wrist was enough to make her heart thunder with excitement, and Clemmie knew then that Aleck Cutler still had a unique and frightening physical dominance over her.

And she was *not* going to give in to it!

Men had tried it on again and again since her divorce, each and every one of them assuming that if she hadn't got a husband then she must be desperate for sex. So desperate for it, in fact, that she would accept a quick grope in the back of a saloon car from men whom she thought looked as though they'd landed from Mars.

But Aleck was not like that, she recognised...

Aleck was different.

Aleck was a temptation, but he was also a married man.

'Let me go,' she said quietly, and to her astonishment he did exactly that. Dropped her hand quite unashamedly, a look of mocking combat in the blue-green eyes. And Clemmie realised that it was all a game to him.

'Does your wife know you tantalise women like this?' she taunted, on a whisper. 'Your eyes promising them all kinds of alluring things? Will you rush home to finish what you started here?'

His face went deathly white, his mouth narrowing into a thin, angry line. She saw his fists whiten with tension, saw the stiffening of his powerful frame, and Clemmie suddenly felt wary, wondering what he was about to do next. And she wondered how she would respond...

'Get Stella,' he ordered in a low voice. 'Get her *now*!'

'Oh, I'll get her, don't worry,' said Clemmie, swallowing down the panic of her reaction to him and squaring up to stare at him proudly. 'And you just stay away from me in future, Aleck Cutler—do you hear?'

Their eyes met.

'Yes, I hear,' he said softly. 'But this is a small town, Clemmie, you know that. You'll be seeing me around the place—that's unavoidable. You shouldn't have come back to Ashfield if you can't stand the reality of that.'

'I can't stand the reality of married men who come

on as strong as you just did!' she snapped, and saw the light in his eyes wither contemptuously.

'I'll wait outside,' he said abruptly, his face as cold as stone.

Clemmie watched as he roughly pulled the door open, and slammed it hard behind him.

Three pairs of feet clattered down the stairs behind her. Startled out of the disturbing nature of her thoughts, Clemmie turned round to see the three girls, their faces alarmed as they jumped the last few steps to land beside her.

'Was that my father?' Stella asked, chewing anxiously on her bottom lip. 'Is he angry? Why did he storm out like that?'

'What's the matter, Mum?' asked Justine, frowning. 'Why has your face gone so pale?'

'I...I felt a little tired, th-that's all,' said Clemmie quickly, before bending down to look at Stella. 'You'd better go and find Daddy. He didn't know you were here, did he?'

Stella shook her head, close to tears. 'I didn't tell him! I thought he might not let me come.'

'Why would he not have let you come, Stella?' asked Clemmie in a low voice.

The child shook her blonde head distractedly. 'Because he swore when he heard you were coming back!'

'Oh, did he?' queried Clemmie softly.

'I should have told him that I was coming over!' babbled Stella.

'Well, yes, you should—and you always will in

future, won't you? Now go on,' said Clemmie gently, straightening up to open the front door. 'Go and sort it out with him. It'll be fine—you'll see.'

'Th-thanks,' said Stella, and ran outside to find her father.

Clemmie bit down on her lip to urge a little colour back into her face, then pinned on a bright smile before facing her daughters, hoping that she didn't look as freaked out as she felt. Explanations were the last thing she felt she could cope with right now. 'So did you have a nice time playing with Stella?'

Justine screwed her nose up, recognising that Clemmie's question was intended to change the subject and ignoring it completely. 'Mommy, why *did* Mr Cutler storm out like that?'

Louella turned her little face up, her clear blue eyes innocent and curious. 'Yes, Mummy, why did he?'

'It's—er—difficult to explain,' Clemmie hedged, as she struggled desperately to think of something suitable to tell them. 'I knew him vaguely years ago, and we didn't really get on that well then. Seems like nothing has really changed!' she finished, her face one of bright determination.

'Was he upset about his wife?' asked Justine.

Guilty colour rushed to her neck. 'His *wife*?'

'Yes,' said Louella. 'His wife died. Didn't he tell you? He hasn't got a wife, and Stella hasn't got a mummy.'

CHAPTER THREE

CLEMMIE could hardly believe what Justine and Louella had just told her. She stared at them very hard.

'Mr Cutler's wife is *dead*?' she repeated, as though saying the words aloud might make them seem more believable. 'Are you *sure*?'

Justine gave her a look which made her appear far older than her ten years. 'Mummy,' she said reprovingly, 'people don't usually lie about things like *that*, do they?'

Clemmie shook her head distractedly. 'No, no—of course they don't,' she agreed. 'It's just that it's…it's…'

'What, Mummy?' asked Louella.

'Such a shock, that's all. She must have been very young. When did she die? Did Stella say?'

Justine looked uncomfortable. 'Well, no. And we didn't like to ask—'

'Of course you didn't!' Clemmie flung her arms round both girls and hugged them both extra tightly. Poor Alison, she thought sadly. To miss out on her daughter growing up. Oh, why on earth hadn't Aleck *said* something?

Clemmie's stomach churned with embarrassment as she remembered the way she had taunted him about his wife at home. Why hadn't he told her then? Had he been too angry? Or too hurt?

She shuddered as she recalled the things she had implied, and was half tempted to run straight after him, to pour out her apologies to him now, while the wounding things she had said were still fresh. But she forced herself not to act impulsively. She was a grown woman now, not a kid of seventeen. It would only confuse her girls, and probably upset Stella into the bargain, and that was the last thing she wanted to do.

Instead, she resolved to say something quietly to Aleck when she next had the opportunity to see him on his own. She would tell him that she was genuinely sorry that Alison had died. And he could make of it what he wanted.

With a fierce determination fuelled by the need for survival, Clemmie pushed all thoughts of Aleck out of her mind while she spent the next few days settling in. In a way, it was good that there was so much to do. The phone to be connected. The post redirected. She had to sign on with the doctor and the dentist, and register the girls at the local junior school. She was fortunate that there were places for them both, and they would enrol next week, at the start of the new term.

The leaves on the trees were already beginning to turn golden, and the air held the tang of woodsmoke and the sharp bite of early autumn. Clemmie looked around the house which Dan had left her, realising just how much needed doing.

Every window in the place needed new curtains. Dan had obviously let the place go after her mother had died. It wasn't as though Clemmie wanted new curtains simply because the pattern of the old ones didn't appeal—just that they were so old and moth-eaten they didn't really serve any useful function at all! Fortunately she could sew, so all she needed was to hunt around for some cheap material.

She also needed to decide the best way to earn them some money—Bill was sending the barest minimum towards his daughters' upkeep, and Clemmie knew her ex-husband well enough not to hold her breath if it didn't arrive...

And when she had sorted out their immediate needs, she also needed to make some friends in the town—for her daughters' sakes as much as her own. As they grew older, the last thing they wanted was a lonely mother who relied on *them* for company! Clemmie winced as she remembered her encounter with Aleck. She hadn't got off to a very good start, had she?

She used the last of her savings to buy Justine and Louella their school uniforms. Clemmie thought how gorgeous they looked as they stood in the outfitters, giggling excitedly in the brand-new green and gold clothes. They had not had to wear uniforms to school in the States, and the novelty factor had a lot to do with their approval of the bottle-green pinafore dresses, the pale lemon shirts and the green and yellow striped ties.

She could have bought them second-hand, but a stubborn pride made her refuse to even consider it. The girls had enough stacked against them in any case. They were children of a broken marriage, living in a strange country and having to start a new school. The last thing Clemmie wanted was for them to stand out like sore thumbs in hand-me-down clothes. She would sooner go without herself than allow that to happen…

She was just waiting for the girls to get changed when she heard a hesitant voice behind her. 'Clemmie? Clemmie Powers?'

Clemmie turned round, frowning as she stared at the woman in front of her who had spoken. She looked about the same age as Clemmie, her face vaguely familiar through the fine lines of age.

'It *is* you! I heard you were back!' the woman said. 'You don't remember me, do you? I'm Mary Adams, and we—'

'Got ready for the end of year dance round at your house?' smiled Clemmie. 'Of course I remember you! How *are* you, Mary?'

Mary smiled. 'I'm fine. Married with a seven-year-old son who keeps growing and growing— hence all these new school clothes!' She held up several bulging carrier-bags as illustration. 'How about you?'

Clemmie kept her face cheery, despite the inevitable feelings of failure that her marriage had not

survived. But time and time again she told herself
that it was not her *fault*. She had tried her best, but
her husband had liked other women and hadn't seen
why a wife should cramp his style! For the sake of
her daughters, she had swallowed her hurt pride and
suggested counselling, but Bill had told her emphatically that counselling was for 'suckers', and that had
been the end of that.

'I have two beautiful daughters,' she told Mary
proudly. 'But no husband—he's in America and
we're divorced. I inherited my stepfather's house,
and here we are —to stay!'

Mary looked rueful. 'Well, at least you've travelled further than I have and seen a bit of the world!'
she said. 'I never moved out of Ashfield.'

'Well, there's a lot to be said for continuity,' observed Clemmie wistfully. 'And you've put down
good, solid roots.'

They looked at one another and laughed.

'We sound like a mutual admiration society!'
smiled Mary.

'Strong case of the other man's grass always being
greener?' giggled Clemmie.

'You've got it in one!'

A car drew up outside the shop front and tooted
its horn, and Mary looked over her shoulder.
'Typical! That's my husband—why do men always
turn up when you don't want them to? And there's a
double yellow line outside, so I'd better run! Listen,
why don't I give you my number?' She took paper
and pen out of her shoulder bag and scribbled down

some figures. She handed the piece of paper to Clemmie. 'Why don't you come over for a drink one evening?'

'Oh, I'd love that,' said Clemmie fervently. 'I don't really know a soul in Ashfield!' Unless you counted Aleck Cutler, of course. And Aleck didn't really count...

Clemmie dropped Justine and Louella off at school on the Monday morning. She stood at the school gate watching them go in, thinking how young and vulnerable they looked in their brand-new uniforms. But they waved their hands at her in an exaggerated fashion and she was gratified to see excitement rather than apprehension on their faces. She watched as a teacher took them off to the playground to join the others, and soon they were lost among a sea of bobbing heads. Their new life in England was beginning...

The bell rang and the noisy playground emptied, and Clemmie swallowed back the mixture of emotions she felt—the inevitable sadness and pride that her children were growing up.

But she was free! Free to do exactly as she pleased until three-thirty, when she came to pick them up again.

And yet Clemmie's heart felt heavy, and it wasn't difficult to pinpoint why. A sense of guilt hung over her like a blanket—and no matter how hard she tried she just couldn't seem to shake the feeling off. She knew that she owed Aleck an apology, yet couldn't work out how to go about it without him immediately leaping to the conclusion that she wanted to see him for all the wrong reasons.

Then her breath froze in her throat as she saw a tall, familiar figure just leaving the playground, and she blinked rapidly, wondering if her mind was playing tricks on her. Had she somehow managed to magic him up in her thoughts?

But when she opened her eyes again he was still there, dressed very casually, his long legs encased in faded jeans worn with a thick navy sweater.

Dare she face him?

He began to walk up the hill, and Clemmie watched him, lost in an agony of indecision. If she left it much longer, he would be gone, and when might she get another opportunity like this?

She began to follow him. She walked at a normal pace at first, because she didn't want to look as though she was running after him, and pretty soon he had disappeared round the corner and she had lost him.

But she knew where he was heading. To the big old house that they had stood and looked at out of his classroom window, all those years ago.

It took her about fifteen minutes to reach it, and several times she nearly lost heart and turned back, but something kept her going until she had reached the house, deserted except for a battered old Jeep which stood at the far end of the driveway.

Clemmie stared at the house properly for the first time in twelve years.

The first thing she noticed was that it didn't look as big as she remembered. Oh, it was big enough, certainly in comparison to most of the houses in Ashfield, but it wasn't the huge, sprawling mansion it had seemed to her dazzled eyes when she was a teenager.

The second thing Clemmie noticed was how the building and the land around it had been utterly transformed.

Aleck, and presumably Alison too, must have either worked day and night or spent an absolute fortune changing the tumbling-down monstrosity into the elegant building it was today. Crumbling bricks had been righted, decaying windows replaced. The lawns were smooth and weed-free, and the hedges neatly clipped. The holly-bright berries of a pyracantha blazed scarlet against the soft grey stone—and the dark, groomed elegance of Cypress trees, gave the garden a curiously Mediterranean feel.

Feeling scruffy and flustered and out of place, Clemmie smoothed a hand nervously over the crown of her head and yanked up the elastic band which held her hair back. Then, before she could change her mind, she went up to the wooden front door and knocked.

It was opened almost immediately by Aleck, his face so impassive that it occurred fleetingly to Clemmie that he might almost have been expecting her...

He said nothing at first, not a word, just stood looking at her, his blue-green eyes unreadable, and Clemmie found herself admiring and resenting his self-possession in equal measures.

'Hello, Clemmie,' he said at last, and gave an exaggerated frown. 'My memory may be growing defective, but I could have *sworn* that you told me to stay away from you.' His eyes glittered. 'Well, it's going to be pretty difficult keeping to my side of the bargain if you're going to turn up like a waif and stray on my doorstep.'

She had rehearsed several openers on her walk up here, but her nerves had blitzed them away and now, gazing into those unbelievable eyes, she found herself saying the predictable. 'Aren't you going to ask me why I've come?'

His mouth flattened. 'I presume you're about to tell me.'

Clemmie nodded, unwilling to just blurt it out, and wondered if he was going to leave her standing on the doorstep like a salesman— until he obviously took the hint and said heavily, 'I guess you'd better come in.'

'Thanks,' she said drily. 'Unless I'm keeping you from work?'

He shook his head. 'I'm an architect,' he said, as if that explained everything.

Clemmie blinked in surprise. It was the last thing she had imagined him doing. She thought of architects as pale, slender aesthetes, delicately sipping tea out of bone-china. Not rugged-looking men with ruffled hair, wearing old jeans. 'You didn't carry on with your parents' farm, then?'

He shook his head. 'The farm was sold years ago, and they bought a place in Spain; the climate suits them. Milking cows was never my idea of fun, and one of the beauties of being an architect is that you get to work from home—and you can please yourself about when you actually do it.'

'Lucky you,' she said, before biting her lip and wishing she could unsay it. He was widowed with a child, for goodness' sake—what was lucky about *that*?

His eyes narrowed as he took in her embarrassment, and when he spoke his voice sounded almost gentle. 'Come on—this way.'

She followed him along a passageway crammed with interesting things—sumptuous oils, a carved chest, a suit of armour—and Clemmie was tempted to say it was too bright and messy to be an *architect's* house.

But then he led her into a light and sterile-looking sitting room which Clemmie decided should be renamed—since it looked as though no one had ever sat in it! It was the neatest and most soulless room she had ever seen, with stark white walls and metal lamps which looked like surgical instruments. She would have bet her last penny that no one had ever sprawled here, toasting marshmallows in front of that elegant and unfriendly marble fireplace.

It was the kind of room which would have looked good in the window of a department store, but not in a *home*. It looked more like a stage set, with two pale ice-blue leather sofas facing one another.

The room was almost empty apart from the photos. Clemmie shivered. There were photos everywhere, and each one featured Alison—an eternally young and beautiful Alison.

Clemmie's heart clenched, and she thought that this was the last thing she had expected. It was all so *contained*, somehow. And this cool, watchful attitude of Aleck's—that was not what she had been expecting, either. When they had met last week there had been fireworks when he had fought with her and touched her. Today was somehow... different.

Glancing at one of the photos, Clemmie cleared a throat which suddenly felt as inhospitable as sandpaper. 'I just wanted to say how sorry I am about your wife—'

'Oh, *please*!' He shook his head impatiently.

Clemmie screwed her eyes up. 'Please, what—?'

'Please don't lie to me, Clemmie,' he interrupted her softly.

'*Lie?*' Clemmie stared at him, her mouth falling open in confusion. 'W-why would I want to lie about something like that?'

'Come on—get real.' He scowled. 'It's pretty obvious.'

'Not to me, it isn't.'

'You never cared for Alison, so why should you suddenly start professing to care now that she's dead? Alison was superfluous to you. You wanted me, Clemmie. Badly. You always wanted me. I could read it in your eyes all those years ago and I read it there again last week. And I wanted you, too...' he finished, on a bitter note of self-reproach.

Clemmie forced herself to respond logically. After all, she wasn't still a schoolgirl, flying off at the deep end when someone said something she didn't want to hear. And maybe Aleck's grief was still raw enough for him to want to lash out at other people.

But, even so, his entirely justified criticism of her behaviour made her heart sink with remorse.

'Okay, I wanted you!' she agreed, sounding more calm than she was feeling. 'But so what? It was a schoolgirl crush that got slightly out of hand, nothing more! Or do you really think that I've spent the last twelve years reliving that rather squalid little episode in the classroom, Aleck?'

His eyes flickered like the first flames of a fire. 'You mean you haven't thought about it? Not even once, Clemmie?' he quizzed softly.

Muddled by her desire to lie to him, Clemmie tried to speak, but no words came.

'Because I know damned well that I have,' he finished silkily. 'It's one of those memories which stubbornly refuses to die.'

Both thrilled and threatened by his words, Clemmie forced herself to meet his piercing gaze, feeling the betraying scrape of hardened nipples against the lace of her bra as her body instinctively responded to his powerful sexual aura. 'Why?' she questioned proudly. 'Was it so very wonderful?'

'It was left unfinished. Thwarted at its peak.' His eyes glittered. 'So it never had the chance to become destroyed by familiarity. And unfulfilled passion never leaves the memory, didn't you know? It's the sweetest fruit on earth.'

'You cynic,' she whispered.

'Cynic?' he questioned shortly. 'Or simply realistic?'

Clemmie swallowed. This kind of talk was getting

her nowhere except hot and bothered. 'I'm sorry about Alison,' she said again. 'Really, I am.' And maybe this time she got through to him, because some of the wariness left his eyes.

He nodded, then gestured rather awkwardly towards one of the powder-pale sofas, like a man unused to playing polite games in parlours. 'Why don't you sit down?'

Clemmie had planned to say her piece and go, but she was stunned by this unexpected thawing. Stunned and more than a little curious. So she perched gingerly on the very edge of one of the sofas, afraid that her denim jeans would leave some muddy mark behind! 'Thanks.'

Aleck remained standing, his back to the marble fireplace, and Clemmie suddenly thought that in *his* casual jeans and sweater he didn't seem to fit into this pale, elegant room, either. She focused her eyes on some of the silver-framed photographs behind him. Alison cradling a baby. Alison with a toddler Stella. Alison and Stella sitting in a formal studio portrait, both mother and child in elegant cream silk, their faces fixed into professional smiles. Alison misty in pearls.

Clemmie stared up at Aleck, her heart going out to him as she imagined what he must have been through. Did he want to talk about what had happened? He could easily say if he didn't. And didn't every bereaved person she'd ever spoken to always say the same thing? That people were always too embarrassed to mention the dead, so it was as if they had never lived...

'When did Alison die?'

He looked at her, his eyes widening fractionally, as if he *was* used to people pretending that it had never happened. 'Five and a half years ago now,' he said slowly.

Clemmie stared at him. 'But I thought—'

He jerked his head up to look at her, his eyes now narrowing intently. 'Yes? What exactly did you think, Clemmie?'

She wriggled her shoulders uncomfortably, feeling like a butterfly caught on a pin, unable to escape that piercing stare. 'That it had happened much more recently than that—'

'And what gave you that idea?'

'I don't know. Just the way you reacted when I…when I mentioned your wife over at my house the other day. You just looked so *raw*.' She saw him flinch and took her courage in both hands. 'What happened, Aleck?' she asked him quietly. 'How did Alison die?'

'Didn't anyone tell you?' he demanded. 'You mean, no one bothered to fill you in on the facts? Hell, local gossip must be falling short of the mark!'

'There wasn't anyone to ask,' she answered. 'Don't forget, there are very few people I know round here. I came here when I was sixteen and left again two years later. And even if there *had* been someone to ask, I'm not into tittle-tattle.'

'Aren't you?'

'No.'

He let out a long, painful sigh. 'We were in

Switzerland,' he told her baldly. 'Alison was killed by an avalanche—'

Clemmie clapped her hand over her mouth as she tried to take in the full horror of his words. 'But that's terrible, Aleck,' she whispered. 'So sudden! So cruel!'

He didn't react to her sympathy, just carried on with his story, as if telling it would diminish the first awful impact. 'We were on a skiing holiday. Alison loved skiing. It was our second to last morning, and she decided to go out with the guide. Stella was young, and not very well, so I'd stayed back at the hotel to look after her. Alison was very excited. She was a good skier—better than me, in fact—and the guide had promised to take her down one of the black runs which aren't available to your average punter. It was one of those things—they called it a freak accident. When they came to tell us, Stella took it very badly.'

'Oh, the poor, poor baby!' breathed Clemmie instinctively, and saw the sudden guarding of his expression. He did not want her pity, she realised. What good would her sorrowful words do now, years later—words that Aleck would probably regard as meaningless if they came from her? Why not stick to what was relevant?

'I just wanted to say that I'm sorry for the things I said the other day, and for the things I implied,' she told him softly. 'That's the reason I came today, Aleck, only everything came out the wrong way. I was angry and I struck out at you.'

But Aleck shook his head. 'I'm partly to blame. I said some pretty cruel things myself. I deliberately stirred you up, Clemmie. I just didn't realise how easy it would be.'

She met his darkened stare while doing her level best to resist it. What was it with her and this man? The allure he had held for her as a teenager did not seem to have diminished with the passing of the years. And refusing to acknowledge that would be immature, surely? 'You mean—you couldn't believe that I'd still behave like a complete push-over?'

'I don't know if that's how I would describe it.' He frowned. 'Let's just say that there seems to be an extremely strong chemical reaction whenever we're around one another. Even now.'

'I think it's called lust,' she answered slowly, and braved his blazing stare. 'Nothing more than that.'

'Is that all it is?' He gave a sardonic laugh. 'Oh, you *do* disappoint me, Clemmie. And here was me, rather hoping that what we were experiencing was unique.'

Unfortunately, as far as Clemmie was concerned it *was* unique. But imagine if he knew *that*, she thought grimly. He was talking about sex, and she was thinking about something entirely different. Women were always confusing sex with love—that was the biggest mistake they made in relationships. And she had vowed never to make that mistake again. 'You flatter yourself,' she told him softly.

'Do I?' he mused. 'I wonder.' And he let his eyes drift over her in a cool, unhurried look.

She *tried* to resent it, but instead Clemmie found herself dazzled by that stare, unable to move from its focus. It was like being caught in a powerful spotlight which revealed her every fault and weakness. And she found she was *glad* she had come on the spur of the moment, and not bothered getting changed, because at least he wouldn't think she had come here dressed for seduction.

Yet some stubborn, feminine side to her character wished that she *had* worn something a little more becoming. Her denims were neither old nor faded enough to be fashionable, and neither did they cling tightly to her bottom. Her sweater was a pretty shade of russet, which made the most of her shiny red-brown hair, but it was old and bobbly now from too many washings, and her blue suede moccasins were old and scuffed. In fact, she looked exactly what she was—a twenty-nine-year-old divorcee whose face was beginning to show the signs of age.

She licked her lips nervously, wondering what she was still doing here. She had said what she had set out to say, and in the process she had learnt that she was still at the whim of this most inconvenient longing for Aleck.

'What about you?' he asked suddenly. 'What brought you back to Ashfield?'

'I was left the house by my stepfather.'

'And that's the only reason?'

Clemmie threw him a scornful look. 'You think it had something to do with you being here?'

He smiled. 'Hardly. My ego may be healthy, but

it isn't insufferable.' He was watching her closely. 'So what happened to your husband?'

'Nothing happened to him. He's in America.'

'And?'

'We're divorced. And that's all you need to know, Aleck.'

'How intriguing.'

'It's nothing of the sort—it's just a common-or-garden marriage break-up story,' she said briskly, because his eyes had lightened with a luminous softness so that Clemmie found herself wanting to tell him. She, who hadn't confided in a soul, was now inexplicably gripped by a desire to pour all her troubles out. To *Aleck*, of all people! 'The sort you've heard time and time again.'

'You sound very cynical,' he observed quietly.

'Well, that's what divorce tends to do to you,' she told him bitterly, realising that if she didn't get out of here soon he'd have her blurting even more out. 'I think I'd better go, Aleck.'

'The girls are at school, aren't they?'

'You know they are.'

'Well, then? What are you rushing back to?'

'It's not what I'm rushing back *to*,' she amended wryly. 'It's what I'm running away *from*.'

'And that is?'

He knew damn well! 'You,' she answered softly.

'Why?'

She made no mention of the fact that she was tempted to reach out and touch the faint shadowing around the curve of his jaw, trace it with first her finger, then her mouth... 'Because you have trouble written across your forehead in large letters—and because I'd like to take a raincheck on trouble! I've had enough to last me a lifetime, Aleck!'

'I see!' Faint laughter lifted the corners of his mouth in the ghost of a smile. 'So there's nothing I can do to make you stay?'

It was a deliberately provocative question, and Clemmie could hear the subtle note of desire which coloured his voice. A desire which she could have all too easily matched. She became aware of the silence in the house, and of the fact that they were alone. And aware, too, that there was plenty he could do to make her stay. It seemed that her feelings for him hadn't changed very much in all these years.

But she had come back to Ashfield for a quiet life, not to lay herself wide open to having her heart broken by a man like Aleck. Because instinctively she recognised that he could inflict wounds far deeper than any Bill had made...

Reluctantly, she shook her head. 'I don't think so somehow, Aleck. I think the best thing we could do for each other would be to stay well away.'

He stared deep into her eyes. 'What a pity,' he mocked softly, and stood up. 'In that case, I'd better see you out.'

CHAPTER FOUR

SEPTEMBER blended into October, and the leaves fell in a blaze of glorious autumn colours from topaz and gold right through to copper and cinnamon. Clemmie crunched through great heaps of them on her way to dropping the girls off at school in the morning in what soon became a comforting and familiar routine.

Aleck she'd hardly spoken to—not since she had been up to his house that morning. She saw him most days in the playground, when he dropped Stella off, and he would give her a cursory nod—sometimes even say good morning, but nothing more. Clemmie felt oddly dissatisfied—she had asked him to stay away, but now that he had she found herself wishing that he wouldn't. Contrary woman that she was!

To distract herself from thinking about him, she poured all her energy into straightening up the house as best she could. The windows now gleamed as brightly as diamonds, and she had wiped every single grubby mark from the walls. In the evenings, once the children had gone to bed, Clemmie began making curtains.

To her relief, she had also managed to find herself a job, working mornings at Ashfield's general store, which sold everything from newspapers and balloons to carrots and nutty brown bread. She was hired by Mrs Humphries, the shop's owner, a rounded woman of around fifty who sucked so many sweets that Clemmie was surprised the shop made any profit at all!

True, it wasn't the most high-powered job in the world, or the best paid, but it suited Clemmie's needs since it would be only four hours a day and she could be there to drop the girls off every morning and pick them up every afternoon.

And Mrs Humphries took an instant shine to her. In fact, she seemed to have only one reservation about giving Clemmie the job.

'What about school holidays?' she asked. 'Have you thought about how you'll manage then?'

Clemmie had thought long and hard about this. 'I'm going to put a notice in the school magazine,' she told her. 'And find out if I can share childcare with someone who works in the afternoon. Lots of women with children job-share these days, so it shouldn't be difficult. But don't worry, Mrs Humphries, I'll find something.'

'Nice to be so confident.' The other woman smiled.

Clemmie shook her head. 'Needs must. And I need this job.'

She told the children about it that night, when they got home. They sat round the kitchen table, cutting out orange masks like pumpkins, in preparation for Hallowe'en, and Clemmie made them all hot chocolate and sat down at the table to drink it with them.

'You mean you're going to be working in a *shop*, Mummy?' asked Justine, askance.

'And what's wrong with working in a shop?' asked Clemmie sharply.

Justine shrugged. 'Nothing, I suppose.'

'Oh, come *on*, Justine—it must be something!'

'Just that you make fantastic cakes of your own. Why can't you sell those or something?' Justine added sulkily.

'What, from here?' laughed Clemmie, and counted off on her fingers. 'Point one—I have no capital to start up in business on my own. And point two—celebration cakes don't provide a steady income, and that's what we need right now. There are very few weddings or big parties in the autumn, darling. We can't rely on my cake-making to put food in our mouths.'

'When do you start?' asked Louella.

'No time like the present,' smiled Clemmie. 'I start tomorrow.'

Justine spread a little more bramble jelly onto her crumpet, and took a thoughtful bite. 'Stella Cutler's having a Hallowe'en party,' she said. 'She has one every year. Can we go?'

Clemmie's heart raced. 'Have you been invited?'

'Well, obviously, Mom! Or did you think we were going to just turn up?'

'What time,' Clemmie asked quickly, 'is the party?'

'Stella said her dad would ring you—'

'Why?' Clemmie questioned immediately.

'Because I said you would want him to, so you could hear all about what kind of party it would be.'

'Oh, Justine! Why did you have to do that?'

Justine looked at her mother in bemusement. 'Because that's what you're *like*!' she protested. 'You always used to check up when we were invited to parties in America. You know you did!'

'Y-yes,' said Clemmie slowly, thinking that Justine was absolutely right, and then the telephone began to ring.

She picked it up. 'Hello?'

'Clemmie?' said a deep voice.

She briefly contemplated feigning ignorance of the velvety voice on the other end, but only briefly. She had an idea that Aleck Cutler was perceptive enough to see through girlish ploys like that one! 'Hello, Aleck,' she said calmly.

'How are you?'

'Fine,' she answered stiffly. As if he cared!

There was a pause. 'Stella usually has a party for Hallowe'en—did your girls mention it?'

'About two minutes ago!'

'Well, it's on Friday night. Starts at seven—here. Would Justine and Louella like to come?'

'I'm sure they'd love to come.'

There was a pause. 'And how about you?' he asked quietly. 'Would you like to come along, too?'

'Me?' Clemmie laughed, flattered to be asked, in spite of everything. Too flattered. 'I'm a little old for apple-bobbing, Aleck!'

'I invite all the parents,' he continued doggedly. 'And at the end they just take their children home. It means that the party finishes when I want it to!'

'Smart thinking.'

'So will you come, Clemmie?'

'Do I have a choice?'

'Of course you do.'

'Well, in that case…' Clemmie glanced at herself in the hall mirror and scowled at her washed-out appearance, knowing that a sensible woman would have turned the invitation down. 'I'll come.'

'Good. See you on Friday.'

Clemmie forced herself to act as if he was just any other father inviting her to a kids' party. 'Would you like me to bring anything? Some dessert, maybe?'

'Just bring yourself,' he said, and rang off.

To Clemmie's annoyance, the days until Friday dragged like examination week. Every morning she put on the pale pink overall which Mrs Humphries gave her, tied her dark hair back neatly in a velvet bow, and went to work at Ashfield Stores. She sold newspapers and doled out little bags of boiled sweets to small children, weighed out mushrooms and cut portions of cheese from a big wedge.

As jobs went, it wasn't demanding—Clemmie felt she could have done it blindfold with her hands tied behind her back! What made it bearable was chatting to the customers, especially the elderly ones, who never seemed in too much of a hurry and were often glad to talk, if the shop was quiet. Some of them had known her mother, and Dan, and made Clemmie understand why she had leapt so eagerly at the chance of living in Ashfield again. It was the nearest she'd ever come to having a real home, she acknowledged sadly. And real roots.

Justine and Louella arrived home from school on the Friday, babbling with excitement as they dressed in the outfits which Clemmie had made for them. Louella was a ghoul, in an adapted white sheet and with her face painted to match, and Justine, resplendent in orange tee-shirt and black jeans, was dressed as a pumpkin.

'What are *you* wearing, Mummy?' asked Louella.

Clemmie shrugged, looking down at her blue denims and the bobbly russet sweater. 'I thought I'd come as I am.'

Justine frowned. 'Mummmy, you *can't*! You're *always* wearing that! You *have* to dress up! And can't you put some make-up on for a change? You never bother to wear it any more!'

'Don't I?' She smiled indulgently.

'You know you don't!'

It was true. Clemmie had grown out of the habit of putting make-up on. It seemed too much trouble to slap it on her face every morning when she was simply going to take it off again at night! And it was not—as she had told herself, time and time again— as though she was trying to attract anybody.

But Justine's words made her take a closer look

at herself. She peered in the mirror—where she saw only the blemishes on her face, the faint laughter lines around her mouth and the slight shadowing beneath her eyes.

Maybe Justine was right. Maybe a woman of twenty-nine should no longer allow her face to go bare. A bit of camouflage might be just what she needed!

'Give me ten minutes,' she told the girls.

She put on a pair of slim-fitting black jeans and a black sweater and brushed her hair out, letting it stream all the way over her shoulders and down her back in a style which she rarely wore any more since it was so impractical. She hunted around until she found her old make-up bag and applied pale foundation and lots of dark eyeshadow and mascara, so that her dark eyes looked sooty and enormous. She finished off the look with over-the-top shiny crimson lipstick and painted a large black beauty spot on one cheek.

When she walked back into the kitchen, the girls squealed with delight. 'Will I do?' she asked.

'Oooh, Mummy!' gurgled Louella. 'Are you a witch?'

'Don't be *stupid*, Lou!' said Justine witheringly. 'She's a vampire!'

'Maybe I'd better go and scrape it off!' said Clemmie, feigning alarm.

'Don't you dare!'

Bundled up in their warmest coats, the three of them walked through the wind and darkness to the Cutler house, where orange lanterns had been strung in the trees to light their way. As they neared the house, Clemmie could see a large pumpkin with a candle burning inside it in front of an uncurtained window, and black and orange balloons fluttered outside in the chill October air.

When Aleck opened the door to them Clemmie thought that he looked amazing—dressed in black jeans and a sweater very like her own. She stared up at him, her breathing almost as erratic as her heartbeat, and for a moment she despaired that she still seemed to be locked into an attraction for a man who even her worst enemy would tell her was a bad bet.

He smiled down at Justine and Louella. 'Ah! A pumpkin and a ghoul come to join us. Welcome! All the children are in the games room, getting covered in flour! Know where it is? No, of course you don't. *Stella!*' he yelled, and moments later his daughter came running up, dressed as a devil, and gave them all a wicked grin. 'Take Justine and Louella with you, sugar, and give them both a drink. I'll be along in ten minutes to check that you're behaving yourselves!'

The girls ran off, squealing with excitement, and Clemmie was left alone with Aleck, feeling oddly displaced, and wishing that she could run after them.

'I didn't know if you'd come tonight,' he said quietly.

'I said I would.'

'Yes, I know you did.' His eyes searched her face. 'But I thought that maybe I'd frightened you off last time.'

'I've been living on my own for a long while now,'

she told him quickly, wishing he wouldn't look at her like that. 'And I think I can just about deal with men who come on strong to me.'

'That's comforting,' he remarked, and Clemmie could have sworn that was mocking laughter in his eyes. And humour, she suddenly realised, could be awfully seductive.

'Here—' She awkwardly held out the tin she was holding, glad for something to do with her hands. 'I know you said not to bother bringing anything, but I made you this in any case.'

'That's sweet of you. What is it?'

'A Hallowe'en cake.'

'A *Hallowe'en* cake?' His eyes glinted as he prised the lid off and peered inside at the lavish-looking confection, which was iced to look like a spider's web. 'Mmm. Best-looking cake I've seen in a long time!'

'You'd better wait until you've tasted it before you tell me that!'

'I'm sure it won't disappoint,' he answered softly. 'Come on through and meet the others.'

The kitchen was crowded, with about twenty adults standing around chatting and drinking hot punch. Some of them Clemmie had seen up at the school; several she had chatted to while she was waiting to pick up the girls. She smiled at those she recognised and waited for Aleck to pour her a drink.

He fetched her some gluhwein and she drank the spiced punch quickly, grateful for the warmth and the instant buzz of the alcohol, which steadied her nerves a little. Aleck introduced her to several of the parents, although it took Clemmie a little by surprise to hear herself greeted as, 'Oh, hello! *You're* the woman who works in the shop, aren't you?'

Aleck flicked a quick glance at her as he led her away. 'Sorry about that.'

'What?'

'The shopgirl comment.'

'Well, it's true enough. That's what I do. I'm not ashamed of my work, Aleck,' she told him proudly. 'It may not be high-powered, but it's satisfying in a funny sort of way. I just want to earn my keep and disrupt the children as little as possible.'

'Bravo,' he whispered, and Clemmie looked at him sharply.

'Are you making fun of me?'

He shook his head. 'No, I'm not. I wouldn't dream of making fun of you.'

Her mouth gave a reluctant twitch. 'Now why do I find that difficult to believe?'

His eyes crinkled with laughter as their gazes clashed. 'Because you're a cynic?' he suggested softly.

She was grinning now, in a way she hadn't done for years. 'Oh, am I?'

She looked bloody gorgeous tonight, Aleck thought, suddenly wishing that his house wasn't full of other people. 'I'd better go and supervise the children for a while,' he said unenthusiastically. 'Check that they haven't wrecked the house. Ah! Come and meet Miss Cummings.'

A vivacious redhead with a mass of curls burst

out laughing as she heard him. 'Don't you dare call me that, Aleck Cutler!' she scolded. 'You make me sound a hundred and one, at least! Hi! My name's Maggie,' she added disarmingly to Clemmie.

Maggie Cummings was not only fun, but pretty, too. The kind of woman that Clemmie might have felt a little jealous of if she hadn't been so nice. As they chatted she told Clemmie that she had been Stella's teacher the previous year. It also became rapidly clear to Clemmie that Maggie thought Aleck Cutler was the best thing since man had landed on the Moon.

They watched in silence while he left the room, and Clemmie felt that if she *didn't* ask her question soon she would burst with curiosity. 'Have you known Aleck for very long?'

'Oh, about three years,' said Maggie, giving her a wry look. 'Which is quite long in *my* books—though I can't say how *well* I know him, even though…' Her voice tailed off and she shrugged rather helplessly in response to the question in Clemmie's eyes.

Clemmie swallowed, praying that she had misread all the signs but fearing they were deadly accurate. She drew a deep breath. 'Are you his—girlfriend?'

Maggie gave a rather hollow laugh and swallowed the last of her gluhwein. 'Heavens, no! That's far too grand and proprietorial a title—and it's one that I imagine Aleck would detest. I never felt happy about calling myself that—even when we *were* lovers.'

The word hit her like a fist in the guts, and Clemmie felt sick.

'L-lovers?' she echoed, as though she had mis-heard. 'Y-you and Aleck were lovers?'

'Uh-huh. Amazing luck, really. He fought off every single woman for ages after Alison died—but I must have done something right, because he didn't fight me.' Maggie blinked rapidly, as if trying to keep tears at bay, then picked up another glass of the punch and drank most of it in one draught. 'I kept dropping enormous hints about where our relationship was going, but it seemed that Aleck was quite happy for it not to go anywhere. I suppose that isn't surprising, really.'

'Oh?' Clemmie sipped her gluhwein, her lashes deliberately shielding her eyes, terrified that Maggie would read the envy there.

'Well, no girl can compete with a dead, beautiful wife.' She stared very hard at Clemmie. 'Can she?'

'I guess it would be stupid to try,' said Clemmie thoughtfully, picturing the sitting room, crowded with portraits of Alison.

'Did you know her?' Maggie asked suddenly. 'Alison, I mean? Didn't I hear Aleck say that you were all at the same school?'

Clemmie shook her head guiltily. 'I was only there for a year before Alison and Aleck left. I didn't... *know* her, not to speak to. Not really. I knew *of* her, of course. She was very beautiful.'

'I thought she was a cold fish,' said Maggie vehemently. 'As cold as ice.'

The last thing that Clemmie wanted to do was to get into a slanging session over her host's dead wife, so she excused herself and circulated, trying to chat to everyone in the room. And she was good at circulating. When Bill had walked out, in a place where she knew no one, it had been sink or swim, and Clemmie had quickly learnt that if she didn't go out and make friends they wouldn't necessarily come flocking to *her*.

Even so, she was glad to help hand out baked potatoes and sausages and mugs of hot tomato soup. She chewed unenthusiastically on a hot dog as the noise in the kitchen grew and grew, and then a small voice said, 'I'm tired, Mummy.'

'Now watch them all catch the sleepy bug,' laughed Clemmie to the woman she had been chatting to, and Aleck heard her and turned his head.

'Including yours?' he asked.

Clemmie shook her head, something in his eyes making her heart pound deep in her chest. 'Mine have enough stamina to keep going until dawn.'

'Stella, too,' he replied easily, and Clemmie was left feeling as though she had in some way compromised herself. Maybe he thought that a single, smouldering look from him would be enough to have her hanging around on the off-chance!

Consequently, she was determined to be among the first to leave, but fate—in the form of her two daughters—conspired against her, and by the time she found them using an ancient exercise bike in the attic everyone else had gone home. She marched them straight downstairs and into the hall.

'But, Mom, Stella's got to go around fetching all

the crisp packets and paper cups!' objected Justine. 'And me and Louella promised we'd help her.'

'Louella and *I*,' corrected Clemmie automatically, and looked down at Justine's pleading face, knowing in her heart that she wasn't being fair. Stella was the first friend that Justine had made in England and she seemed a really nice girl. And if Stella was anyone other than *Aleck's* daughter she would be delighted for her to stay and help. Clemmie shook her head, impatient with herself. When was she going to stop letting her life be governed by men?

She gave Justine her biggest smile. 'Of course you can go and help, darling. And Louella, too, but keep her with you, will you?'

'Yes! Oh, *thanks*, Mom!' And Justine ran off before her mother could change her mind.

'So,' came Aleck's deep voice from behind her. 'Since you appear to have successfully delegated all the clearing up to the children, I think you deserve a reward, don't you? Which would you prefer—wine or coffee?'

Clemmie turned round to see that he was bearing a tray containing both. 'Oh, coffee, I think.'

He raised his eyebrows. 'Sure? You haven't got work tomorrow, have you? Or school?'

'No, I haven't,' she agreed equably. 'But I do have two very noisy daughters, and I don't want to listen to them with a splitting headache.' And she had already drunk enough of his gluhwein to make her the wrong side of vulnerable.

'Then why don't we go and make ourselves comfortable?' he suggested.

It was a line which, if it had come from someone else, Clemmie might have found herself refusing. Coming as it did, from Aleck, she found that she was following him like his shadow into the sitting room.

Sitting perched once more on one of the ice-blue sofas, surrounded by the stark and harsh lighting, Clemmie again had the uneasy sensation of being on a stage-set. Or, she thought suddenly, as her eyes alighted on the silver-framed photographs of Alison which were crammed onto every available surface— in a *shrine*.

Yes, that was it—a shrine. Maggie Cummings's words came back to mock her. 'No girl can compete with a dead, beautiful wife.' Her stomach clenching, Clemmie brushed a tiny fleck of dust off the arm of her black sweater and willed herself to toughen up.

Aleck noticed the jumpy gesture, noticed the uptight way she was sitting. 'Is something wrong?'

She took the coffee he handed her, observing how big his hands looked. Big and capable. Gorgeous. She wondered if she would be able to drink her coffee without spilling it. 'I don't find this the most relaxing room in the world, if you must know.'

He nodded thoughtfully. 'Because of Alison's photos?'

'Not especially. Although—' She bit her lip.

Aleck was a powerful man in Ashfield; he had lived there all his life and done very well for himself materially, and consequently a certain mythology had grown up around the tall, handsome widower who lived up at the big house. Not many people told

Aleck Cutler what was really in their hearts. He
looked now at Clemmie with interest. 'Although
what—?' he prompted softly.

'I think you've *overdone* it on the photos a bit.
There are so many of them, Aleck, that it looks like
some kind of...' She saw the question in his eyes and
pushed the word out bravely. 'Shrine.'

He didn't deny it, or even flare up at her. Instead
he simply nodded again. 'Yes.' He expelled a breath
slowly. 'This room hasn't been touched since
Alison's death. She had just decorated it; it was the
first room in the house she had attempted. That was
her job, you see, she was an interior designer. When
she...' His voice hardened. 'After her death, when we
came home, just the two of us, Stella wanted the
room to stay exactly as it was. She brought down
every photo of her mother she could find, and I
agreed to put them in frames for her.'

Clemmie's eyes were very bright. 'I know you'll
probably think I have no right to say this to you, but
don't you think it's time that you both moved on
from that, Aleck?'

He leaned back in his chair and studied her for a
long moment, his hand resting against the side of his
face, eyes narrowed in study. 'And how do you propose I do that?' he demanded. 'Just suddenly get rid
of all the photos? Wipe out her memory? How do I
explain *that* to Stella?'

Clemmie stared at him, her mind working over-
time. Was Stella a convenient scapegoat? Maybe the
truth was simpler than he maintained—maybe *he*

was the one who was clinging onto the photographs, like a man obsessed. Perhaps the photos were a tangible warning to other women to stay away. To let them know precisely what Maggie had said: that you could never compete with a dead, beautiful wife.

'Nothing can ever wipe out Alison's memory,' she said quietly. 'She'll exist for ever in her daughter.'

'Yes.' He looked at Clemmie thoughtfully. Generous. A lot of women would have had difficulty coming to terms with that. Like Maggie. Maggie had just wanted to pretend that his other life, his married life, had never happened.

His hard, handsome face took on a fleeting trace of vulnerability, and Clemmie caught a glimpse of the teenage boy she had so adored. He settled back comfortably into the sofa and she found that a simple movement like that could drive all rational thoughts clean out of her head, to be replaced by a growing awareness of how much she wanted to physically *touch* him.

'You've tensed up again,' he commented. 'Is it me, I wonder?'

'Why? Do women often get tense around you, then, Aleck?' she queried, only half teasing.

'Not like you do,' he replied truthfully.

Clemmie forced herself to sip her coffee, wondering how truthful she dared to be. Hadn't she said enough for one day? 'Maybe that's because I still feel there is so much unfinished business between us.'

His blue-green eyes were very watchful. 'Such as?'

'Such as, I never knew whether Alison found out

about...' Her words tailed off as she wondered how best to phrase it.

'That stolen kiss?'

Put like that, it sounded absurdly romantic, and so very innocent, and yet it had been neither. Not really. One of the least innocent actions of her life, and she wasn't proud of it. Not at all. 'Yes.' Clemmie's voice was quiet.

'Oh, yes,' he said slowly. 'Alison knew all about it. Her friends made sure of that.'

'And was she angry?' Clemmie breathed, then clamped her lips together, hard. 'Gosh, that was a dumb thing to say. Of course she must have been angry. She must have been furious.'

'I guess you could say that it focused her thoughts,' he replied, in an odd kind of voice, which made Clemmie wonder whether it was just too difficult for him to think about.

He dropped two lumps of sugar into his coffee and slowly stirred it, before lifting his head to look at her, and Clemmie was caught in the full force of that blue-green gaze. 'Tell me what you did when you left Ashfield,' he said suddenly.

She was caught off-guard. Perhaps if she hadn't been she might have been less honest than he deserved, because the truth, even now, was painful. She shrugged, aiming for the kind of shrug which hinted at nonchalance, but suspecting that she'd ended up with just the opposite.

'I went away to college in London, to study catering, and it was there that I met Bill.'

'Your husband?'

'Ex-husband,' she corrected, pushing down the feeling of defeat which always rose up to haunt her whenever she thought about the father of her children. 'Yes. He was spending the long vacation "doing" Europe, and we…we…' Her words trailed off helplessly.

'You fell in love?'

She looked at him sharply. Was he mocking her? But his eyes did not ridicule her—instead, Clemmie read in them something that she had never associated with Aleck Cutler before.

Understanding.

'Yes, we fell in love—whatever love is.'

'You doubt its existence, then, do you, Clemmie?'

'At barely nineteen I think that all kinds of feelings can be mistaken for love. Anyway, we both experienced that "can't-bear-to-be-away-from-you-for-a-second" kind of feeling.'

'Heady stuff,' he commented drily.

'Yes. It came as a bit of a relief, actually—' Then she closed her mouth as she realised just what she had been about to say.

'Relief?'

A relief to discover that Aleck Cutler was not the only man who could make her feel as if she was walking on air. That was what she had meant. But she wasn't giving his ego a free massage by telling him *that*! 'Just that when you both feel like that, and you decide to make your future together, it gives you a feeling of security.'

'And your life had been pretty short on security?'

She nodded. So he could be astute as well as understanding, could he? 'My father died when I was tiny—maybe you knew that? We lived in London, and Mum had to go out to work to support us. I was the original latch-key kid,' she added self-deprecatingly. 'When Mum met Dan I was delighted for her, of course—but it meant the upheaval of moving here. And sixteen is a bad age to move. I never really settled.'

'No,' he commented, his expression thoughtful. 'I don't expect you did.' He poured them both a second cup. 'So what happened next? With Bill?'

'Oh, we got married. In secret.'

'For romantic reasons?' he queried.

Clemmie shrugged. 'Not really.' At the time it had seemed the perfect solution, but the hasty ceremony, performed in front of two unknown witnesses, had seemed shabby. As though it didn't matter. 'Because Bill's parents were in the States, and it didn't seem fair to invite my mother and Dan if Bill had no one there for *him*. Justine arrived pretty soon after that. Then we had to wait for my papers. After that we went to America.'

'Whereabouts?'

'Oh, everywhere—or it seemed like everywhere! Florida first. Then Idaho. New York for a while.' She widened her dark eyes at him. 'Want me to continue?'

Aleck watched the way that her black sweater clung to the swell of her breasts, and he was invaded by a sexual hunger which was quite alien to him in

its intensity. There was really only one thing he
wanted right now, but he didn't feel it prudent to say
so. And even if he did, he doubted whether he would
get it... 'Yeah. Finish your story, Clemmie,' he
prompted, quashing the stifling throb of desire.

'Bill had the original itchy feet. He couldn't hold
down a job once he was bored with it. And he had a
pretty low boredom threshold,' she added wryly.

'So you decided to leave him?'

Clemmie's face was rueful, her lips puckered with
resignation. 'Oh, no! Quite apart from the fact that I
was living in a strange country, we had two children
by then. I really *wanted* my marriage to work.'

'But Bill didn't?'

'Bill wanted all the things which ultimately wreck
a marriage—personal freedom to the detriment of
everyone and everything else around him.'

'And what exactly does that mean, Clemmie?'

She swallowed down the revulsion. 'It means that
Bill was a good-looking man with an eye for firm,
young flesh—the younger the better.'

'Hell—'

'*No!*' she interrupted vehemently, the word spilling
out like poison, but maybe the reason for that was that
she had never told anyone the whole story before. Not
a soul. So why choose Aleck Cutler? 'I want to finish!
Maybe I have no right to criticise Bill? Do I? Not when
you think about it. After all, all those girls he went with
probably behaved the same way that I behaved when
you were with Alison. They probably threw themselves
at him in the same way that I threw myself at you—'

'I'm not going to let you carry on with such misplaced condemnation,' he told her calmly, shaking his dark head to silence her. 'And I seriously doubt whether you would have let me make love to you.'

'That isn't what you said the other day!' She blushed as she remembered his cutting taunt. The deliberately crude way he had phrased it, insulting her and exciting her at the same time. Panties round her ankles...

Aleck sighed as he saw her cheeks colour. 'I know it isn't. But the other day I was angry, confused.' And too hot with desire to think straight. Like now. 'Besides, I wasn't even married to Alison at the time. Stop beating yourself up about what happened all those years ago, Clemmie. It's all in the past now.'

But the past had long tentacles which reached into the future. They were touching her now. And dangerously.

Clemmie stood up, her legs as wobbly as if she'd spent the evening at sea. 'Time I was going, I think.'

Aleck rose to his feet unenthusiastically, wanting her to stay but anticipating what kind of reaction he would get if he asked her to. 'I guess it is.' She walked right by him then, to get to the sitting room door, and impulsively he reached out for her, pulling her into his arms, staring down at her upturned face, at the freckles which spattered her cute little nose.

'Sure I can't persuade you to stay?' he murmured.

Clemmie made a half-hearted effort to struggle free. 'You said that last time—and I thought then that it was the corniest line I'd ever heard!'

'I know. So, can I?' he persisted, tightening his arms around her waist, just itching to capture her mouth with his.

'You can try!' she challenged. 'But I must warn—'

She got no further. Aleck did what he had been wanting to do ever since she had arrived here to-night, with those snaky hips in the lean black jeans and the soft sweater hugging her luscious breasts. He bent his head and took her lips by storm.

It was like being roller-coastered back through time, only better. Much better. Clemmie was older— and hopefully a little wiser. Aleck had been the first man she had ever kissed, but there had been others since, and every one—Bill included—faded into insignificance when compared to *this*.

For Aleck kissed like no other man. Made her feel like a different kind of woman. She melted against him, swaying as he tangled her hair between his fingers, sighing his pleasure deep into her mouth. As he pressed his body hard against hers, she could feel a tension building in him which matched her own. A special kind of tension which could only be released in the way that nature had intended.

And the children were just along the passage…

Gasping, Clemmie pulled away from him, wondering if her eyes were as black with passion as his, wondering what it was with this man which made her want to give in so easily.

'Oh,' he groaned, on a low note of disappointment. Her breathing slowed. She could feel the heat between her legs, the warm rush of desire where she ached so sweetly, and she could have wept. One kiss and he could have her in such a compliant state? Would he do the same with anyone? 'Maybe you should have asked Maggie to stick around,' she lashed out.

His eyes narrowed. 'And just what is *that* supposed to mean?'

'Just that I know she was your lover—she told me.'

He didn't react. 'And?' He gave a hollow laugh. 'Surely you aren't outraged or shocked at *that*, are you, Clemmie? We were two consenting adults, without any ties at the time, just like you and I are now. It isn't a crime to want to make love, you know.'

He made it sound like an exercise session in the gym, Clemmie thought indignantly! Where was all the tenderness in *that*? 'Well, maybe you should have chosen Maggie tonight—she might have proved more responsive to your attentions.'

His face darkened. 'That's a pretty cheap remark.'

'Well, it was pretty cheap behaviour, wasn't it?' she breathed, her breasts tingling fiercely beneath the black sweater. 'The kind we always seem to indulge in whenever we're together!'

They were facing each other like boxers squaring up for a fight when they heard a muffled yelp from outside the open door, and Aleck frowned. 'Who's that?' he called out.

There was silence for a moment, and then the sound of a sob being stifled, and Aleck and Clemmie both rushed to the door in alarm.

Outside, rubbing her eyes with her fist, stood Stella, her shoulders shaking with sobs.

Aleck was crouched by her feet in an instant. 'Darling, what is it?'

'It's L-Louella,' she cried. 'She—punched me and kicked me! She was horrible to me, Daddy—and I don't like her!'

CHAPTER FIVE

JUSTINE and Louella came flying down the corridor to glare at Stella, and for a moment accusations and counter-accusations were hurled across the room.

'*She* started it!' yelled Louella.

'No, *she* did!' shouted Stella. 'You hit me first!'

The angry words Clemmie had exchanged with Aleck evaporated. She had rarely seen her younger daughter look quite so hurt or so furious. She tried to take some of the fire out of the situation. 'Shh, Louella,' she whispered. 'What on earth is the *matter*?'

'I hate her!'

'Louella!'

'It's not just Louella's fault, Mummy,' said Justine stolidly.

'What happened?' asked Clemmie steadily.

The three girls all clamped their mouths together and stared at nothing in particular.

Clemmie threw Aleck a resigned glance, and he gave her a 'search me' kind of look in return. He was standing with his arm around Stella, his face serious, but he had not started dishing out any blame and for that Clemmie was grateful. She strongly suspected that tempers were too frayed to get any sense out the girls tonight.

It seemed that Aleck thought the same way. 'Why don't we sleep on it?' he suggested quietly. 'Go upstairs and get ready for bed, Stella, and I'll be up in a minute.'

Stella's mouth trembled, her blue-green eyes filling with angry tears as she turned and ran up the stairs.

'I'd better get my two home as well,' Clemmie said, and gave them both a squeeze. 'It'll all look completely different in the morning—you'll see!' But the looks on their faces remained mutinous.

'I'll fetch your coats,' said Aleck heavily, and he went to the cupboard to find them, feeling more raw than he'd felt in a long time. What the hell was going on with the kids? And what were all these mixed messages which Clemmie was sending out to him? She had wanted him to kiss her—he *knew* she had. She'd kissed him back, stirred his blood, left him wanting more. And *she* had wanted more, too. Yet all of sudden she had started rebuking him, as if he had overstayed his welcome.

He handed Justine and Louella their coats and they put them on in stony silence. Then he held Clemmie's open for her, a question in his eyes.

She hesitated. It had been a long while since a man had helped her on with her coat, and she was feeling emotional enough to overreact—the kiss and then the ensuing drama had seen to that. But she didn't want to add to the atmosphere by grabbing it out of his hands and insisting on putting it on herself. So she slid her arms in, feeling stupidly cosseted and protected as he shrugged it on over her shoulders.

Aleck found himself touching the worn cuff with the tip of his finger, finding its old shininess oddly moving. 'You need a new winter coat,' he said slowly.

Clemmie grimaced. 'I need a lot of new things—so does the house and so do the girls. And I'm afraid that a new coat is right at the bottom of the list! Come on, Justine, Louella—say goodnight to Mr Cutler, would you?'

She was half afraid that they would stomp out in a huff, but years of having good manners drummed into them had obviously paid off.

'Goodnight, Mr Cutler,' said Justine politely.

'Goodnight,' piped up Louella, in a small voice.

'See you!' said Aleck cheerfully, but more with hope than conviction.

The girls went out onto the porch, but Aleck signalled to her with his eyes and Clemmie held back a little.

'Disaster averted,' she said in a low voice.

He frowned. 'What do you suppose that was all about?'

'I'll find out,' she promised, and hesitated. She had turned him on, and then turned away and acted as if he was behaving outrageously. And there was no excuse for that kind of behaviour. When she spoke her voice was so quiet that Aleck had to strain his ears to hear. 'Back then, I didn't mean to be—you know—the kind of woman who—'

But he shook his head, her faltering little speech making him feel like some kind of marauding brute. 'You carry on doing exactly what you feel like doing, Clemmie,' he told her huskily. 'There's no book of rules to say how we should behave with one another—and if there was, I think I would have torn it up by now!'

Amazingly, Clemmie laughed, even with two woebegone daughters looking on as though she had no right to.

'We'll sort it out,' he promised her. 'Whatever this thing is—we'll sort it out.'

She nodded, believing him, tempted to reach up and touch his face with her hand, but she didn't dare. For the girls' sake. For her sake. 'Goodnight, Aleck.'

The girls didn't say a word on the way home, and when Clemmie had let them in to the house she sent them straight upstairs. 'Go and put your pyjamas on, will you, Justine? Lou? I'll heat some milk and bring it up—so scoot!'

By the time they were tucked up in their beds in the warm, pink glow of their Mickey Mouse nightlight, Clemmie thought how impossibly innocent they both looked. She put the two mugs of milk down on the locker and sat on the end of Louella's bed.

'So,' she began, 'want to tell me about it tonight? Or we can talk about it tomorrow morning, if you're too tired?'

They exchanged worried glances and then Justine spoke.

'Stella said you'd been kissing her daddy!'

Clemmie felt colour steal up the side of her neck. She swallowed. 'And?'

'Were you, Mummy?' asked Louella.

Clemmie swallowed. She had vowed never to lie to her daughters, but right now she wished she hadn't made herself such a foolish promise. 'Yes, I was,' she agreed calmly.

'Do you love him, then, Mummy?' asked Justine, quite seriously.

Clemmie thought about this. How much more uncomplicated it would be if she could look her daughters in the eye and tell them truthfully that Aleck Cutler meant nothing to her. 'I...like him,' she admitted carefully, though she might have added that she had no idea *why* she liked him so much. 'And I'm attracted to him. I can't deny that. But love is different. Love takes time. And trust.'

'Did you love Daddy?' asked Louella plaintively, and Clemmie could have wept at the naivety of her question.

She struggled to contain her emotions, and to honour their father as best she could. 'Of course I loved him, darling, but I was very, very young at the time much too young to know what love really meant. And to marry young and go and live in a different country—well, that places a lot of strain on a marriage.'

'Is that why you split up?'

Clemmie drew in a deep breath, knowing that she couldn't protect them for ever from the cruelty of the truth. She had decided a long time ago that keeping the truth from them was the only way of keeping their father's image relatively untarnished. For what child could cope with the fact that their father was an unrepentant womaniser? One day she might tell them more, but not now. 'In a way,' she prevaricated. 'I guess you could say that we weren't getting along, and we just couldn't live together any more.'

'But why doesn't Daddy come to see us any more?'

'Because his home is a long way away, darling. You know that.'

'But he didn't come very much when we were living in the next State, did he, Mummy?'

Clemmie bit her lip. It was one of the things which had finally given her the courage to leave the States—the fact that Bill might as well have been residing on another continent for all they saw of him. 'Well, Daddy's got a new baby now, and a new girlfriend…and they make demands on his time…which is perfectly natural. And I expect he's saving up to come here to visit you. H-he told me that he was.'

Anxious to change the subject, she turned to Justine. 'So is that what all the row was about? The fact that Stella saw her daddy kissing me?'

Justine looked down.

'Justine?'

Justine twiddled with her plait.

'She said that even if he *did* kiss you it didn't mean anything. She said you could never take her mummy's place, because her mummy was beautiful and Mr Cutler loved her more than anything in the world.'

Maggie's words came floating back, adding fuel to what Justine had just said. 'No girl can compete with a dead, beautiful wife.' And Clemmie felt ashamed at the sharp pang of jealousy which ripped through her belly.

'I'm sure he did,' Clemmie said steadily. 'And she *was* very beautiful. I used to see her at school. She had turquoise eyes and pale hair and looked exactly like a princess. And Stella is right, you know—no one could ever take her place. What is more—I don't want to.' She picked up the mugs of cooling milk and handed one to Justine and the other to Louella. 'Now, drink this and sleep on it,' she advised. 'It'll all look better in the morning.'

'I'm sorry, Mummy,' said Louella in a small voice.

'Do you think Stella will still want to be friends?' asked Justine plaintively.

'I expect so. But we'll have to wait and see,' said Clemmie as she bent down to kiss them. 'Won't we?'

The morning brought rain, lashing loudly against her window pane like an animal banging to get inside. Clemmie woke up shivering. She had worn a baggy tee-shirt and a pair of thick socks to bed, but she could see that she was going to have to invest in some warm pyjamas. The house was *freezing*—and she certainly couldn't afford to have the heating on all the time.

She glanced at the clock on her bedside table. Getting on for ten o'clock—now that *was* a lie-in! She would go downstairs and make a pot of tea.

She popped her head round the girls' door, but

they were sound asleep—sprawled out beneath their duvets with all the abandon of the young, oblivious to the world. Late night and too much emotion, she thought wryly, and went downstairs.

The pale, rain-soaked light of morning meant that it was bright enough to see by, and Clemmie didn't bother to switch the light on as she sat on the kitchen table, swinging her legs and waiting for the kettle to boil. Then she heard a faint tapping at the window, and she looked up to see a rain-soaked figure there.

Aleck!

She wished she could admit that she was surprised to see him, but she wasn't. Or that she was dreading seeing him, except she wasn't.

Swallowing down the anticipation and excitement which had caused some kind of tingling restriction in her throat, she padded barefoot to the back door and opened it, and a sudden gust of wind brought raindrops and leaves whirling into the kitchen.

Clemmie's eyes were huge. 'What are you doing here?'

'Getting wet!' came his terse reply.

'Then you'd better come in.' Tugging the tee-shirt right down to mid-thigh, so that it camouflaged her bottom, and wishing that she had bothered to put a brush through her sleep-tousled hair, Clemmie stood back to let him pass.

'Where's Stella?' she asked, trying to sound as normal as possible. As though it was nothing out of the ordinary for a man to be standing in her kitchen while she was still in her nightclothes.

'I dropped her off at the stables—she goes riding on Saturday mornings. It was a bit of a struggle getting her out of bed this morning, but I figured that fresh air and exercise might be just what she needed.'

'Yes.'

His gaze flicked around the kitchen and settled on the open door leading to the hallway. 'And your girls?'

'Fast asleep. Or rather they were, when I checked a minute ago.' The kettle began to steam. 'Would you like some tea?' she asked, a trace awkwardly.

'Love some.' He removed his dripping waterproof jacket and hung it over the back of one of the chairs. He sat down without being invited to, stretching his long legs out in front of him, and made a pretence of looking around the kitchen with interest, when really his eyes kept being drawn to Clemmie and the sexy sight she made in her tee-shirt and bedsocks.

Clemmie tried to tip boiling water from the kettle without her hands shaking, tried to act as though she made tea for long-legged men with dark, brooding faces every day of the week. She wished she'd put a dressing gown on. Or jeans. Maybe she should excuse herself and do just that. But if she went upstairs to change now, then not only might she wake the girls, but wouldn't it also draw attention to her semi-clothed state? And the fact that she was self-conscious about it?

She put the cosy on the teapot, asking, 'Would you like any toast? Or cereal?' Then could have kicked herself for sounding so eager to please. As though she couldn't wait to start waiting on a man!

He shook his head, a faint smile touching his lips. 'Just tea, thanks.'

She poured them both a mug, watching while he immediately cradled his for warmth between his large hands. She sat down at the table opposite him with her knees tucked in, keen to keep her bare legs hidden. It hadn't exactly escaped her notice that he had been watching her. And it wasn't that she *minded*—it was just so…so…*distracting*. 'Did you talk to Stella?' she asked.

He watched the steam rise from his mug—anything to keep his mind away from the infinitely more absorbing glimpse of her thighs. 'Yeah.'

Clemmie looked at him expectantly. 'And?'

He stared at her oval face, with the freckles standing out in relief, like stars against the paleness of her skin. Her big eyes were velvety-dark and startled—like a fawn's—and her hair was mussed and messy, as if she hadn't bothered brushing it. She looked, he decided, as he picked up the mug again and sipped some tea—nearly burning his mouth in the process—all rumpled from bed and as sexy as hell.

'And she's jealous,' he said bluntly. 'Simple as that.'

'But there's nothing to be jealous of!' protested Clemmie.

'Isn't there?' His eyes mocked her.

Clemmie studied her hands. Her ringless fingers, the neat, unvarnished nails. 'What did she say?'

Aleck shrugged. 'That she didn't want another mummy.'

Clemmie stared at him. 'One kiss doesn't put me up for the role of stepmother, does it?'

'Maybe in a child's eyes it does.'

'But this must have happened before, Aleck. Doesn't she know that you had an—affair—with Maggie?'

His eyes narrowed. 'How do you have the knack of making something which is perfectly natural sound in some way sordid?'

'You're guilty of the same,' she reminded him quietly. 'You made my slightly drunken antics as a schoolgirl sound like I was a nymphomaniac! But does she? Know about Maggie, I mean?'

'I don't think so.' He shrugged. It wasn't something he particularly wanted to talk about—his short-lived affair with the pretty schoolteacher. Certainly not to Clemmie. But she was just sitting there, looking at him expectantly, with her lips pursed together and that inquisitive look on her face. What could he do other than tell her? If he didn't, it would look as though he had something to hide. And there was nothing.

'We kept the affair very quiet,' he growled reluctantly. 'We thought that best, since she worked at the school. It lasted less than six weeks and ended amicably.'

'Did it?'

'Yes. We've stayed friends.' He met her questioning gaze unflinchingly. 'Which is why she was at my party.'

In Clemmie's experience, an 'amicable' break-up

usually meant that one person was pretending like crazy not to mind! 'Really? So Maggie was happy with the outcome?'

Aleck sighed. 'You can be a very persistent woman, Clemmie Powers,' he observed wryly. Not the sort of woman you could fob off with a vague reply. 'Okay,' he admitted. 'Maggie may have thought she was in love with me—'

'Well, if Maggie *thought* she was in love, then presumably she knew her own mind,' Clemmie corrected acidly. 'She's an intelligent woman, after all. Maybe she *was* in love with you, Aleck, have you thought of that?'

'Well, maybe she was, but it wasn't reciprocated—and for God's sake, don't look at me like that, Clemmie! I can't help it if all I felt for Maggie was a deep affection.'

'And sexual attraction, presumably,' she pointed out. 'You aren't forgetting that, are you, Aleck?'

'No, but I wasn't actually going to spell it out in words of one syllable,' he said, in a voice which was tempted to snarl.

'So Stella knows nothing of the relationship?'

He shook his head. 'A child of seven, which is what Stella was at the time, is a lot less curious about human behaviour than a ten-year-old. She knew we were friends, and that's probably as far as it went in her eyes. Now she's older she's more switched on. Kids today tend to know more than we did at their age. And…' He wondered how honest he dared be.

She met his eyes. 'And?'

'And she probably can't bear the thought of us being a couple.'

'Which I suppose you're using as a euphemism for having sex?'

His sigh was midway between admiration and exasperation. 'Do you always say exactly what's in your head, Clemmie?'

Only to you, she was tempted to say. Only to you. Except that it wouldn't be the whole truth. She was only outspoken about topics she had no reason to fear. And so far she had successfully managed to avoid talking about what was uppermost in her mind. Not the woman he'd had a brief, uncommitted fling with. Not Maggie.

Alison. The woman he had loved, whose child he had fathered. The dead, beautiful wife that no one, including herself, could ever compete with.

'I'm too old for games,' Clemmie said instead. 'I had enough of them in my marriage to last me for life.'

His mouth tensed as he thought about his own marriage. 'Yes,' he agreed roughly.

'And who said anything about us being a couple?'

'It seems I just did.'

'Is that why you're here now?' she whispered to him, as if someone was listening.

'I don't *know*,' he whispered back. 'Maybe. Probably. Why did you come up to see me the other day, Clemmie? Turn up at my party when you clearly didn't feel you should? Is it because something powerful draws you to me as much as I am drawn to you? What *is* it between us, Clemmie?'

The schoolgirl Clemmie would have cited love as the reason for their confused feelings, but the older Clemmie was a lot more cynical about relationships. She tried to order her words so that Aleck wouldn't think she was building happy-ever-after fantasies about him. 'I told you before that it was lust.'

'So you did.'

His mouth turned down at the corners. For a moment, Clemmie thought disbelievingly, he'd looked almost *disappointed*.

'But I was wrong.'

His eyes narrowed. 'Oh?'

'I think it's a combination of things. You were right—our youthful attraction was thwarted. Unfulfilled. We never got those feelings out of our systems.'

'Sounds like there's only one sensible solution, then,' he murmured, in a voice of velvet, as rich as Turkish delight.

Clemmie's skin turned to ice, her stomach to mush at the way he was looking at her, the blue-green eyes travelling slowly up her legs, looking as though he would like to…like to… Clemmie swallowed.

He was the sexiest man she had ever met, and that was the truth. And it had been a long, long time since she had tumbled into bed joyfully with anyone. There had only ever been Bill, and towards the end sex had been nothing but a mechanical chore. Then, when she'd had proof that there *were* other women, that her fears weren't just the product of an over-active imagination—well, then she had sought the sanctuary of the single bed in the spare room.

But now she felt the sweet, unaccustomed ache of desire piercing her, and appreciated how easy it would be to open her arms to him and be caught in his, be welcomed there. But at what price?

'I want you,' he said deliberately.

'I know you do.'

'And you want me, too.' It was a statement, not a question.

'I know that, too.'

'Well, then?'

'Well, then, what, Aleck?' Her voice reflected her disbelief that he could be so naive. 'I'm a mother, remember? I'm a role model for my daughters! I'm not into red-hot short-term affairs—it would confuse the life out of them! Me too, if you must know. And I can't just leap into bed with you because we both happen to feel the urge! I can't compartmentalise sex like that.'

'But I'm not asking you to.'

Clemmie frowned. 'Then what exactly *are* you asking?'

'That we take things one step at a time.'

She screwed up her eyes in bemusement. 'Oh?'

He swallowed down the last of his tea and thumped the empty mug onto the table. 'Stella doesn't want to fall out with Justine and Louella; she likes them—'

'And they like her!'

'I like you,' he said softly.

She read the question in his eyes. 'Snap!'

He smiled, biting down the urge he felt to pull her into his arms and kiss her, because now was not the right time. 'Well, then, why don't we all try being friends?'

'Do you think we can?'

'I think we could accomplish absolutely anything,' he told her teasingly. 'Unless you think that I'd be unable to keep myself from laying a finger on that delicious body of yours.'

'I'm not *that* conceited!' she told him primly.

Well, you should be, he thought hungrily, but didn't say so. 'So. Friends?'

'Just friends?'

'For the moment,' he agreed, and picked up his empty mug to drain it unnecessarily, so that she wouldn't see the glint in his eyes. 'How about we start with the five of us having Sunday lunch tomorrow?'

'Do you think Stella will want to?'

'I'm sure of it.'

'Shall I…?' She hesitated, not wanting to come over as Little Ms Domestic.

'Mmm?' He loved the way her mouth softened into that cute little pucker when she was uncertain.

'Cook? The lunch, I mean.'

Aleck imagined a warm kitchen full of good smells. Imagined watching Clemmie move around in it, all relaxed and easy. 'Oh, yes, please,' he said softly.

CHAPTER SIX

LUNCH the following day was a success, judging by the plates scraped clean and the second helpings of apple crumble and custard which were demolished. Clemmie beamed at the children like a mother hen, then glanced up to find Aleck watching her so intently that she could scarcely meet his eye and immediately began stacking dishes as though her life depended on it.

Aleck's eyes were thoughtful. 'So now we walk it off?' he suggested, as he finished his coffee.

'Oh, Dad—*no!*'

Justine pulled a comical face. 'Mom, do we *have* to?'

Clemmie risked another look at Aleck and found that she wanted to walk beside him, outside, with the wind on her face and the freedom to talk without the girls listening. Four walls could hem you in sometimes. 'We most certainly do!'

They went up through the woods just beyond his house, where most of the leaves now lay in great drifts beneath the trees.

He told her about the school which had just been built—a school he had designed—in the nearby cathedral city of Salisbury. 'Best job of my life,' he sighed.

Clemmie scrunched a leaf underneath her boot. She noticed the way his face lit up whenever he talked about his work. 'You sound so fulfilled by your job, Aleck.'

He smiled. 'I am. It's like a dream come true. You start out with an idea, you put it down on paper, and the end result is a beautiful, functional building. And buildings make such a difference to people's lives!' He looked at her closely. 'How about you, Clemmie?' His voice was soft. 'Do you like working in the general store?'

She shrugged. 'It's okay. I'd be lying if I said it was the job of a lifetime. It's certainly not demanding—but then it isn't stressful, either. And my priority is the children—and jobs which fit around them are hard to find. It's the eternal problem facing working mums. And besides—' she wrinkled her nose at him as she smiled '—I enjoy chatting to the customers.'

Lucky customers, he thought as he watched a dark strand of hair catch her lips and stay there, wishing he could brush it aside and place his mouth there instead. 'Stella says you make the most fantastic cakes.'

Clemmie grinned. 'Does she? That's nice! Why don't you send her over on Saturday afternoons after riding, if she'd like to, and she can help bake?'

* * *

Saturday afternoon cake-making became a regular thing, and Aleck would join them afterwards to eat up what had been made. There had been no repeat of the arguments between the girls, and the baking sessions gave Clemmie the chance to get to know Stella better. She was a sweet child—confident, but occasionally diffident. Like the first time Clemmie had piled the cake mixture into the tins and pushed the bowl across the table towards her.

'Want to lick it clean?' she'd smiled.

Stella bit her lip. 'Am I allowed?'

Clemmie was taken aback. 'Of course you're allowed!' she said gently. 'Why wouldn't you be?'

Stella shrugged. 'Mummy never let me. She said it was messy.'

Clemmie nodded, and busied herself with putting the tins in the oven. It was not her place to criticise. 'Well, everyone's different,' she conceded. 'I expect that there's things I won't let my girls do that you're allowed to.'

'Like *what*, Mom?' asked Justine, who had been listening.

Clemmie searched for inspiration. 'Like horse-riding!'

'You mean you'll let us go horse-riding?' queried Justine doubtfully.

'We'll discuss it in the warm weather,' said Clemmie firmly, and then her face lit up like a Christmas tree as she looked outside and saw Aleck on the doorstep. 'Here's your father, Stella!'

He was carrying a big bunch of mauve Michaelmas daisies in his hand.

'Oh, you shouldn't have done,' she protested, burying her nose in their musky scent when he gave them to her.

His voice was casual. 'Maybe there's something else you'd prefer to flowers?'

Their eyes met in a long, silent message of longing, and Clemmie hid her blush in the blooms. He knew damn well there was! She wanted him so badly she couldn't sleep nights, and yet some instinct kept telling her that this thing between them was much too precious to rush.

He had said 'friends,' and 'friends' was clearly what he had in mind. And it was an education for Clemmie. She had never been friends with a man before. Not like this. Had never experienced this warm feeling of camaraderie with a member of the opposite sex. Bill's friends had been men; women were for sex and housework. His attitude had made her feel like an object, not a person.

But with Aleck, Clemmie began to relax. To unfurl. Like a cat stretched out before the blaze of a fire, she started to bask in the warmth of his affection. For the first time in her life she felt like part of the human race, instead of an outsider. She had been the latchkey kid, then the displaced stepdaughter, the young foreign bride, and finally the divorcee. Yet now she felt poised on the brink of something new and good.

Yes, she was still the divorced mother of two, but she no longer felt so isolated. And Aleck's friendship gave her an undoubted feeling of protection. In a small town where people tended to judge before they knew you, being close to a man like Aleck helped Clemmie regain the confidence which Bill had steadily chipped away at over the years.

But the downside of this patronage was envy.

Maggie Cummings was now cool and distant whenever she and Clemmie met. And she seemed to take great pleasure in coming into the shop and asking for the most bizarre items. Lavatory brushes and bottles of air-freshener! Clemmie thought that she was being mischievous, but she didn't bother telling Aleck. The last thing she wanted to appear was weak, or spiteful. Particularly as she had—to some extent— what Maggie so obviously wanted.

Aleck.

Except…and she could have laughed if there had been any real humour in it…she didn't have Aleck at all. Not in the real sense, the biblical sense. She had him in the big-brother sense, and yet thirsted for him secretly, in the wasteland of her lonely bed at night. She had told him proudly that she wasn't into short-term affairs and she wished she'd had the sense to know when to shut up! Now she felt she would have him on any terms at all—and if three very impressionable little girls hadn't been involved, then she might have done just that.

And Justine had been very quiet of late. Clemmie had caught her hanging around waiting for the postman. Waiting for a letter from her father which never came. Clemmie sighed. She had written to Bill twice, pleading with him not to forget Christmas, but he hadn't even had the courtesy to reply. Soon, she realised with a sinking heart, she would have to tele-phone him.

One Monday lunchtime, in the last week of November, Clemmie trudged home up the hill from the shop in the driving rain. She let herself in, peeling off her raincoat and realising that the rain had soaked right through to her underclothes. She was just debating whether to run a bath when there was a knock on the door. She opened it slightly and stuck her nose round the crack, and there stood Aleck.

There was a moment's pause, a moment's hesitation. She didn't need to ask why he was here. She wasn't into playing games, not with Aleck, and she could read his intentions as clearly in his eyes as if he had written them on a placard and held it up in front of her.

'Come in,' she said.

He closed the door behind him. In the rain-darkened hall he seemed taller, more dominant and more vital than any man had a right to be. Clemmie sighed. He stared very hard at her, then reached out a fingertip to catch a raindrop which hung like a tear on her cheek.

'You're wet,' he observed huskily.

Clemmie felt the potent throb of desire as it hummed like a presence in the air around them. 'Then dry me,' she whispered shakily.

'Oh, *Clemmie*.' His voice shuddered softly as he took her by the hand and led her straight upstairs, as if he didn't trust himself to touch or kiss her properly until they had found the haven of her bedroom.

There was a big pink fluffy towel drying on the radiator, and he plucked it off and rubbed gently at

her hair, so that the sodden strands began to puff out
with static. His face was almost grave as he began to
unbutton the little camel cardigan she wore, until it
flapped open and the lushness of her breasts were revealed, straining uncomfortably against the shiny
coffee-coloured brassière.

'Oh, *God*,' he breathed, and sucked in an almost
agonised sense of longing. '*God*, Clemmie…'

The chill on her skin was forgotten. Her body felt
alive and on fire, the look in his eyes promising her
so much   promising her everything. He looked, she
thought, with a dizzying sensation of recognition, almost as though this was his first time. The sense of
wonder in his eyes was not feigned. The tremble in
his fingertips no sham.

As he began to unbuckle the belt of her jeans, she
lifted her own hands to undo the thick cambric shirt
he wore, sliding each button through the hole until
she found the hair-roughened chest, the flat, hard
planes of his abdomen.

As he eased the denims over her hips she fleetingly wished that her underwear matched. She bent
her head and covered one deep pink nipple with her
mouth, and he gave a groan of pleasure.

'That's not fair!' he gasped. 'I haven't even
touched you yet.'

Not *touched* her? Didn't he realise that she was on
fire where his palms were sliding her black bikini
pants down over her hips? And he might as well have
been caressing her breasts, the way they were peak-
ing and craving for his mouth.

The slow undressing became more frantic.

'I think we'd better get you out of these wet clothes as quickly as possible, don't you?' he murmured.

'Y-yes,' she managed, on a shuddering sigh, as she felt his nails scrape tantalisingly at the apex of her thighs.

By the time they were both naked the towel was dropped redundantly to the floor, since her skin had already dried in the heat his hands had produced.

He pulled back the duvet—a brand-new duvet, she thought fiercely. She had thrown all her marital bedding away on the very day her decree had become absolute. It was suddenly very important that Bill had no place here. This was Aleck's place—and his alone.

I love him, she thought, with the slightly stunned surprise of someone who had just recognised a simple truth.

I love him so much.

He drew her down beside him, the feather-filled duvet resting like a cloud on top of their seeking bodies. He tried to take things slowly, to explore every single centimetre of her as he had dreamed of doing, night after night, ever since she had come back into his life with all the light and beauty of a Christmas angel.

But it was no good. This time he just needed to claim her, impale her. Make her his. Make her…

Lifting his dazed head from her breast, where he had been licking voluptuously at her nipple, Aleck managed to formulate a half-coherent question.

'You're not on the pill?'

She shook her head.

'Damn!' He draped his arm over the side of the bed and scrabbled around for his jeans until he had located the packet of sheaths in the back pocket.

Clemmie was caught between blush and giggle. 'Seems like you were planning this,' she observed. 'Want me to put it on for you?'

But Aleck shook his head violently. One touch of those slender white fingers *there*, and he suspected that he would possess all the control and finesse of a teenage boy. 'Next time,' he promised, as he slid it down. 'Or maybe the time after that.'

'How many have you brought with you?' she teased.

'Not enough!' he growled, and turned her onto her back.

He rose over her, proud and hard as a stallion, looking with pride and lust at her flushed cheeks and sparkling eyes. 'God, Clemmie,' he groaned. 'You are something else.'

With a stroke he possessed her, filled her, shot her with a fire which burned in her heart, and she found herself shuddering and clenching around him with a speed and an intensity which made her cry out.

He saw the tears which spilled like rain down her cheeks just as he closed his eyes, and he moaned out his own disbelieving pleasure in a cry which sounded loud in the silence of her bedroom.

And then, though they both fought against it like children, they fell sound asleep, the experience too shattering for either to lie awake and sane after it.

* * *

Clemmie woke to the sound of raindrops drumming against the window and the feel of a man's arms wrapped tightly round her, the warmth of his breath on her neck. She felt no shame, no regret, just an impression of something being overwhelmingly *right*. She savoured the sensations for a quiet moment—not moving, not opening her eyes—but something must have made him aware that she was no longer asleep, for he said softly, 'Hello.'

Clemmie let her eyelids flutter open, and she was caught and dazzled by the lancing blue-green light from his eyes.

'Hi.'

He moved slightly away from her, positioned himself so that her whole face was exposed to his searching gaze, as if seeking there the answer to an unspoken question. He nodded, as if satisfied. 'So,' he observed, his voice slumberous. 'No regrets.'

Clemmie raised her arms and wriggled luxuriously. 'Am I so terribly transparent, then?'

He shook his dark head, all mussed now, where she had run her frantic fingers through it. 'You just looked...' He shrugged his naked shoulders. 'Happy. That's all.'

All? 'Don't knock it, buster,' she chided, and kissed the tip of his nose. 'Happiness is a rare commodity.'

'And are you? Happy?'

'Mmm!' She closed her eyes dreamily. 'Totally.'

He shook his head. 'No. Not totally.'

Her eyes flew open again. Was this his way of telling her not to read too much into a very pleasant session of afternoon delight?

Aleck read the insecurity there and could have cheerfully pulverised the man who had planted it so firmly in this woman's heart. And that man, of course, was one half of the problem... 'Total happiness would be me *not* sneaking down here like a thief on a winter's afternoon—'

She clapped her palm dramatically above her left breast. 'Why—you've stolen my virtue, sir!' she declared through a giggle.

He put his hand over hers and moved it down to cup the breast in tandem. 'Happiness,' he contradicted thickly as he saw her eyes dilate with pleasure, 'would be the freedom to make love wherever it took our fancy.'

'You want to do it in the car?' she questioned innocently.

He felt the blood rush exquisitely, to harden him. He slicked his finger down between her thighs to find her ripe and ready for him, and he watched her mouth suck in an *oh* of shocked pleasure as he slipped right into her without warning.

'I want to do it here. Right *now*. Like *this*...' He was helpless as he thrust deep inside her, as powerless as he'd ever felt in his life and yet filled with power, too. With this woman he became a mass of beautiful, puzzling contradictions.

It was as though her response was completely outside her control. In astonishment, Clemmie felt her climax building with rapid speed into explosive need, her body shattering into exquisite spasms around him. 'I'm coming,' she cried helplessly into his mouth, as he tipped her over the edge of some astonishing universe.

'Oh, *hell*!' he swore, and Clemmie's dazed eyes snapped open. She was startled by the look of fierce intensity on his face when he suddenly withdrew before climaxing.

It took a moment or two for them to gather breath to speak, and Clemmie wantonly trailed her fingers over him.

'You forgot the condom?' she guessed.

'I forgot my own name!'

She pretended to frown. 'Do I know your name?'

He started to laugh, and then remembered that life was never as simple as you wanted it to be. 'So what now? Is this a secret affair?'

Clemmie heard the troubled note in his voice. 'Do we have a choice?'

He thought about his young daughter, who looked so like his late wife. Would she be able to handle the idea of her father being this intimate with another woman? Was it going to be too much? Too soon? 'Isn't it living a lie not to tell them?'

Clemmie turned her head. Outside the window, the bare branches of the cherry tree rocked and shuddered in the grey lash of the rain. 'I don't know,' she said eventually. 'Maybe we should see how it goes for a while. Maybe it's too soon for any of the girls to accept a replacement in their lives.'

She didn't say what she was most afraid of—that

'replacement' was too permanent a word. What if the affair fizzled out after a few months—even weeks— once the novelty had worn off? Surely it would be better for everyone if their daughters were unaware of the depth of involvement between her and Aleck?

She turned back to face him and stroked her finger slowly down the sculpted curve of his cheekbone, wanting to tell him that she loved him. That she had always loved him. That she would never stop loving him. But she didn't want to scare him off! Heavens, the thought even terrified *her*!

The logical side of him—the paternal part—knew that her words made utter sense, while the emotional side of him—the lover part—wanted to tell the world and damn the consequences. But children altered you. Made you stop thinking about what you *wanted* to do. Instead made you think about what you *ought* to do. 'Maybe you're right,' he sighed reluctantly, and pulled her closer to him. 'But if you change your mind—or you think the time is right to tell them...'

'Then we'll discuss it.' She nodded, stupidly wishing he'd insisted. Thinking, too, that Aleck was the kind of man she could discuss *anything* with. Until she realised that there was one subject they had never discussed at all.

Alison.

Something unspoken hovered in the air around them. Their eyes met. Aleck read the question there, his heart softening as he acknowledged her tact. She hadn't asked him a damned thing. Not before bed. Not even *after* it! Clemmie Powers was some woman.

'Clemmie—'

'Mmm?'

'About Alison—'

She heard the tension in his voice, saw the strain which made ravines out of the laughter lines around his mouth, and shook her head. 'You don't have to tell me anything, Aleck,' she told him huskily.

'I know that. But I want to, sweetheart.'

And suddenly Clemmie was certain of only one thing. That this was their moment, hers and his, here and now. And nothing—*nothing* could take this away from them. Not guilt, nor recriminations. This was theirs, and theirs alone.

All along she had been getting mixed messages about Aleck's relationship with his wife. Alison the beautiful. Alison the cold. A woman no other could compete with. Yet Clemmie had noticed that Aleck was strangely reluctant to talk about his late wife.

So was all as it seemed? Or was it like most of life— neither black nor white but variations of grey? And did she really need to know the nature of Aleck and Alison's marriage at this ecstatic stage in *their* relationship? Couldn't the past taint the present that way?

No. She didn't.

Not today. Maybe not even tomorrow.

Clemmie shook her head. 'No, you don't want to tell me, Aleck,' she contradicted softly. 'Not really. In fact, there's only one thing you want right now.'

His mouth quirked into a smile as he saw the look in her eyes. 'And that is?'

She raised her open lips to his. 'This.'

CHAPTER SEVEN

NOVEMBER slid frostily into December, and the children began to get manic and excited. But for once in her life Clemmie was oblivious to the enticement of the Christmas countdown. She was too full of love for Aleck to think about anything else.

She tried very hard to concentrate on the normal yuletide routine of making puddings and cakes, but she was heavy-handed with the treacle, and for the first time ever her Christmas cake had the consistency of a rubber tyre.

Justine stared in wonder as she surveyed the blackened mess still smouldering in the tin. 'Mom, are you okay?'

Clemmie spun round, her eyes dreamy. 'Of course I'm okay, Justine. Why shouldn't I be?'

'You look *thinner*,' observed Justine critically. 'And you keep forgetting things lately.'

'And singin' all the time,' piped up Louella.

'Nothing wrong with singing,' said Clemmie robustly, wondering how on earth she would survive the Christmas holidays without her blissful afternoons in bed with Aleck, and then immediately feeling disloyal to her daughters.

The telephone started ringing and Clemmie absently licked at a wooden spoon before putting it back down on the counter.

'I'll get it!' said Justine and ran into the hall to answer it. She was back minutes later. 'That was Stella,' she announced, her face full of barely suppressed excitement. 'She says can we go up to her house to play?'

Clemmie's heart thumped like a drum. 'I'll walk you up there if you like,' she offered casually.

'Her dad wants to speak to you.'

'Well, why didn't you *tell* me?' exclaimed Clemmie, and then remonstrated with herself as she went out to pick up the phone. Oh, for heaven's sake! She was acting like a nineteen-year-old instead of a twenty-nine-year-old!

She picked up the phone, her stupid voice coming out more breathlessly than she had intended. 'Aleck?'

'Hello, gorgeous.'

Which, she assumed, meant that Stella was not within earshot. Clemmie tried to ignore the butterflies she felt far too old to be feeling. 'The girls said something about coming up to play?'

'That's right. Why don't you follow them up later and I'll cook us all supper?'

Clemmie sighed. 'That sounds perfect.'

His voice was wry. 'Not quite. Perfect would be if you didn't have to go home.'

'What, *never*?' she teased.

'Why not?' he growled.

Clemmie heard footsteps behind her. 'What time shall I come?'

There was a long, telling pause. 'Whatever time you like, honey—I'll be happy to oblige!' he murmured, and rang off.

'Mummy, why have you gone all red?' demanded Louella.

'Because it's hot,' lied Clemmie frantically.

She sent the girls off after lunch, and forced herself through her household chores. She found herself looking unenthusiastically around the sitting room, knowing that she ought to paint it, and that she really ought to try to get it completed before Christmas.

What colour? Lemon, perhaps. Or turquoise. Didn't they say that turquoise was a very restful colour?

Clemmie sighed. The trouble was that she couldn't seem to work up any great eagerness about decorating. Come to think of it, she couldn't seem to work up any great eagerness about *anything*. Her mind seemed stuck in a groove, like a record on a turntable, and the groove began and ended with Aleck Cutler.

She washed the kitchen floor and went out into the garden to clip at some foliage to put in a vase. She needed to work on the garden, too. She had hastily planted a few daffodil and tulip bulbs before the frosts set in, and at least the lawn wouldn't need cutting until the spring, but the bushes were all straggly and in need of pruning, and the beds could do with tidying up.

She glanced at her watch. It was only three o'clock. She couldn't turn up *yet*. Aleck might be working and it would look as if she couldn't keep away from him.

But did she care?

Not really. She suspected that Aleck knew just how much she wanted him. Her body language certainly wasn't subtle whenever he was within hugging distance!

She ran a bath, recklessly squirting her best bubbles into the running tap, and was rewarded with aquamarine water and the heady scent of tuberose. Then she lay submerged up to her neck, while the water cooled and the light faded from the afternoon sky.

It was quiet in the house without the girls. Too quiet. Leaving her too much time to wonder what lay ahead for them all in the New Year. Would this illicit romance continue indefinitely? she wondered. Or would they be brave enough to bring it out into the open?

She just couldn't imagine how they would tell the girls, somehow. Plus, if the truth were known, she had to admit that it was exciting to have Aleck come to the house most afternoons and make mad, passionate love to her. Aleck—her secret lover. It made her feel young and wild and free. And very, very desirable.

Clemmie wasted time until five o'clock, despising her inability to settle to a book or a newspaper, then she locked up the house and set off for Aleck's.

The sky was moonless, the December afternoon as black as pitch. All around her she heard the rustles and hoots of the countryside, but she felt no fear as she strode up the empty lane towards the Cutler house. When she reached the end of the drive, Clemmie paused for a moment and just stared.

From here, Aleck's house looked like an old-fashioned Christmas card—all lit up and bright and welcoming. She imagined a glossy holly wreath on the door, and a big, dressed Christmas tree in that cavernous hall, standing next to the knight-in-armour. Imagined baking batch after batch of mince pies to bring out to hordes of hungry carol singers.

And she had obviously been watching far too many corny old films!

Smiling, she rang the bell, but the door was opened by Aleck almost immediately, and it was as much as she could do not to throw herself into his arms and hug him tightly.

Aleck saw the eagerness on her face and resolved to take action. Hell, he wanted to kiss her. He didn't want her trailing back home to her lonely bed tonight, after he had cooked her supper. He wanted her *here*, in *his* bed. 'We're going to have to tell them,' he said softly.

'Who?'

'The children.'

'What—*tonight*?' Clemmie screwed her face up in alarm.

His expression was wry. 'Well, when would you suggest we do it? Christmas morning?'

'I suppose if you put it like *that*...' she said slowly. 'Where are the girls?'

'Here!' called Stella, and Clemmie and Aleck

turned around to see the three of them trooping out of the study.

'Hello, darlings!' beamed Clemmie. 'Been good?'

Her daughters quickly looked at Stella, as if seeking guidance.

For what? Clemmie wondered.

'We've made tea,' announced Stella. 'And biscuits. In the study. Would you like to come this way?'

'Of course,' smiled Aleck, and winked at Clemmie.

The girls had obviously been working hard to create an impression. A tray of tea stood on the hearth in front of the fire, next to two plates of home-made biscuits.

'Mmm!' said Clemmie automatically. 'Looks *wonderful*! Smells wonderful, too. So what's all this in aid of?'

'We want to ask—' began Louella.

Justine scowled. 'Shut up, will you, Lou!'

'Perhaps you'd like to sit down?' suggested Stella quickly.

Clemmie smiled into Aleck's eyes. Sweet of them!

There was a lull while the girls busied themselves pouring milk and tea, spooning sugar into cups and piling plates with lemon and spice biscuits; it wasn't until they were all settled, and the girls had demolished most of the cookies, that they put their cups down and looked with big eyes at the adults.

'I'm the spokesperson!' announced Stella solemnly. 'And the other two agree with everything I'm going to say. Don't you?'

Justine and Louella nodded their heads in accord.

Clemmie frowned, wondering what on earth was coming next, as Stella fixed her father with a fierce and determined stare.

'We'd just like to know when you and Clemmie are getting married, Dad. That's all.'

Clemmie slopped tea into her saucer while Aleck stared back at his daughter in bemusement.

'That's all, you say?' he commented drily. 'Then heaven help me the day you come to me with a serious problem! And is there a reason for this sudden question, Stella?'

There was a pause. 'Miss Cummings said that she sees you coming out of Clemmie's house every afternoon,' said Stella slowly.

Clemmie met the black expression in Aleck's eyes, and for a moment she almost felt sorry for Maggie Cummings.

'She said *what*?' he questioned, in a voice which was dangerously soft.

'She just started giggling and asked was there something going on that she didn't know about—'

'Only her eyes looked really *angry*,' put in Justine.

'And anyway, we'd kind of guessed that something was going between you two, hadn't we?'

'Definitely,' nodded Justine.

'Def-nitly,' echoed Louella.

'We just don't think you should have secrets from us children, that's all,' added Stella primly.

Aleck felt staggered. Dazed. Bemused. 'Er—do we have to discuss this right now?'

'Yes, we do!' answered Stella firmly. 'Why don't

you just come out and admit it, Dad, and say you love Clemmie?'

Aleck's eyes narrowed with interest. This was a previously unrevealed side to his daughter he was seeing now! 'Maybe because I haven't actually got around to telling *her* that yet?' he murmured.

Clemmie stared fixedly at a spot on the carpet with all the intensity of a person who had spotted a stray diamond twinkling there.

'Well, why *not*?' demanded Stella.

Aleck looked at each of the four females clustered around the fire in turn. Stella and Justine were looking as if they had just taken a degree in determination, while Louella was trying very hard to mimic the expression on both their faces. Only Clemmie looked ruffled, staring down at the carpet, her shiny red-brown hair falling all over her face so that he couldn't see it. He wanted to go over and take her in his arms, love her and kiss all her doubts away. But there were more people involved than just the two of them. He had to take this step by step.

'I'm waiting for the right time,' he said slowly, and wondered if he was ever going to find it.

'Is it to do with Mummy?' Stella asked suddenly.

His eyes were suddenly watchful. 'What makes you say that?'

'Because you keep all Mummy's photos!' Stella accused. 'Loads and loads of them! And you've left the room how she did it—even though you hated it at the time! But you didn't love her, not really! And she didn't love you, either! You were always arguing—you know you were! So why are you always pretending to me, Daddy?'

'And you keep *saying* that Dad will come and see us!' babbled Justine, as if the words couldn't wait to come bubbling out. 'Only he never does, and we both know he never will! He never even writes to us, does he, Mummy?'

Clemmie lifted her head slowly to meet Aleck's eyes.

And suddenly Aleck knew that the only solution to this problem was complete and utter honesty. It might be painful. Probably would be. Some people might even say that it would be inappropriate to give these children an insight into what he and Clemmie were really thinking about their ex-partners. But anything less would be an insult to them all.

'I *did* love your mother, Stella,' he said, very carefully. 'How could I not love her when she gave birth to you?' He looked into his daughter's blue-green eyes, which were like a mirror reflection of his own, and saw the faith and love there which gave him the courage to continue. 'But what you say is true; we *did* argue. We argued a lot. We just weren't very good at living together. And when…' He swallowed down the lump in his throat at the sight of Stella's face turned so trustingly towards his. 'When your mummy died, sweetheart— I felt so bad about that. I wished we could have been happier together. For your sake, more than anything.'

'But you didn't get divorced, did you?' said Stella quickly. 'You stayed together.'

'Yes,' he agreed quietly.

'Because of me?'

'Yes.' Quieter still.

'Thank you, Daddy,' said Stella simply, and Aleck knew then that he had done the best he could. He felt overwhelmed with gratitude as she jumped up to hurl her arms around his neck and hug him.

Clemmie realised that Justine and Louella were now looking at *her* expectantly, and it certainly didn't seem the right thing to do to march them all off to another room to speak 'privately'. Not when Aleck had behaved so openly and so honestly in front of *them*. She cleared her throat as she struggled to choose the right words.

'I don't *know* whether Daddy will come over to see you both, and that's the truth. He has a new girlfriend and a new baby, and he might not have the time or the money to come all the way to England.' Or the inclination, she could have added, but didn't. 'If you like, you could each write him a letter—not the sort of "Hi, Daddy, how are you?" kind of letter that you usually write, more the sort of letter where you tell him exactly how you feel. Tell him you're worried, that if much more time passes by you're afraid he will forget you altogether. Because that's the truth, isn't it, darling?'

'Yes, Mom,' answered Justine softly, her eyes bright, because even at her tender age, she instinctively recognised how much it had cost her mother to say those words. Her mother's life would be easier by far, she realised, if Bill Maxwell just disappeared out of their lives for good. And yet Clemmie was doing everything she could for that not to hap-

pen because of *them* —her and Louella. 'Oh, thank
you, Mom,' she said softly, and kissed her, and then
Louella came over and put her arms around her, too,
and it was as much as Clemmie could do not to start
blubbing.

Aleck could feel all the heightened emotion in
the room which was in danger of swamping them.
Time to lighten up. And besides, he had things he
needed to say to Clemmie. Alone.

'I think I'm going to get a drink for Clemmie and
me. Anything for you girls?'

Silent messages flashed between Stella, Justine
and Louella, and they shook their heads.

'No, thanks, Dad—not at the moment. We're
going off to play!'

'Okay, then.' They skipped out of the room and
Aleck forced himself to go out to the kitchen. He
wanted to leave Clemmie on her own for a moment.
To let her gather her thoughts and make up her mind
what *she* wanted. Because he certainly knew what *he*
wanted.

He found the very best bottle of claret he could—
he was tempted to bring champagne, except that he
couldn't bear to be that predictable. And besides,
Clemmie's pale face had looked more in need of
warmth than cold fizz.

Swinging the glasses between his fingers, he carried the bottle into the study to find Clemmie where
he had left her, sitting by the fire with the flames
picking out the red lights in her hair.

She glanced up as he walked in, then couldn't

look away. She loved him. She loved him so *much*. But hadn't they both made mistakes in the past?

'Hi,' he murmured.

'Hi.'

He wanted to kiss her, because that would make everything right, and yet something told him that it was very important he *didn't* kiss her. Not yet.

Instead he eased the cork from the bottle and put it down on the mantelpiece to breathe. He looked at her. 'Don't you think it's time I told you about my relationship with Alison?'

'Yes,' she said quietly. 'I do.' She sat as silent as the night, her eyes never leaving his face while she waited.

His gaze was steady on her face, but his words seemed heavy. 'As you've probably picked up from what I just said to Stella, it wasn't a happy marriage…'

Quietly, Clemmie rose to her feet and moved close to him, tenderly putting her finger over his lips. 'And don't you think I hadn't started to work that out for myself, my darling?'

His eyes darkened. 'But I never said—'

She shook her head. 'No, you didn't. You never said a disloyal word about Alison, Aleck—and more power to you as a father for doing that. But all the signs were there if you looked for them, which maybe I did. The non-verbal clues, I suppose.'

'Like?'

'Like the fact that you looked tense whenever she was mentioned. Like your reluctance to remove some of her photos—which would be normal after all this time. But I guess your guilt stopped you doing it.'

He sighed. 'Shall I tell it like it really was?'

Clemmie's gaze didn't waver. 'Only if you think I need to know.'

'I do,' he said softly.

'Then tell me.'

There was a long pause before he spoke. 'All my life I'd had everything I ever wanted. I was good at everything I turned my hand to.' He threw her a look of mocking apology. 'If that sounds unbearably arrogant, it isn't meant to. Everything came so easily. *Too* easily. I'd never had to fight for anything or anyone before—'

'But you had to fight for Alison?' Clemmie guessed shrewdly.

He nodded, a faraway look entering his eyes as he tried to remember the boy he had been. Life had been so simple then. Or it had seemed that way. 'She was everything I thought I wanted. So exquisite, with that pale golden hair and those eyes like chips of turquoise…'

Clemmie had expected this to hurt. But not this much. 'Go on,' she said, in a low voice.

'She seemed so aloof and unobtainable…' His voice trailed off, and words spoken by other people about Alison came drifting back to Clemmie's memory.

'*She was a cold fish*'—Maggie's verdict, true, so it might not be the most reliable testament.

'*Mummy never let me*'—that had come from Stella.

'I *had* to have her,' he admitted reluctantly. 'And then, when I *did*—she was so…so…*remote*, I guess.

So distant. Like a beautiful statue. You never knew what was going on in her head, and I suppose that her elusiveness was attractive to someone who wasn't used to it.'

Clemmie felt her cheeks colour with shame as she remembered the way she had virtually flung herself at him in the classroom. 'And elusiveness was the *last* thing you could have accused *me* of.'

He saw her crestfallen face. 'Sweetheart,' he said softly, 'believe me when I tell you that the way you behaved that night completely blew my mind.'

'So that's why you stared at me as though I was something the cat had brought in, was it?'

'Clemmie,' he murmured, 'I was feeling a) guilty and b) frustrated, and so I did the classic macho thing of blaming you. I told myself that you were outrageous, a temptress—and not the sort of girl I wanted to be involved with.'

'And what did Alison say when she found out?'

He sighed. 'That was part of the problem. There's nothing like jealousy to focus the mind. It's the dog-in-a-manger thing—you don't want a person until you think that someone else does. And when Alison discovered that I had been caught in a compromising situation with you, she started coming on to me *very*, *very* strong.'

Clemmie couldn't stop the sarcasm from showing. 'And you, of course, hated every minute of it?'

His gaze was steady. And rueful. 'Sweetheart— what do you want me to say? I was eighteen years old.'

'So what happened next?'

'We went to university. We carried on going out, but as time went on my feelings towards her began to change. And then, in our second year, Alison became pregnant.'

'And was it p-planned?' She saw the hurt and the anger in his eyes.

'What do you think?'

'I th-think I'd like to punch you and kick you and scratch you, except I know I have no right to be jealous,' she told him brokenly, but he pulled her into his arms and held her there, very tightly.

'Shh, sweetheart,' he said into her hair. 'Don't you think I don't feel the same way about Bill, even though *I* have no right to? And you can take it out on me as much as you like,' he promised, on a note of silky anticipation. 'Later.'

'Tell me the rest,' she urged.

He stroked her hair. 'I couldn't leave Alison then, and to be perfectly honest I didn't want to. Not when she was pregnant. I'd been brought up to honour my commitments, but it was more than that. I wanted this baby, Clemmie—she was *my* baby, too, after all. And I didn't lie to Stella when I told her that I loved Alison. She was the mother of my child, so how could I not love her?'

Clemmie heard the tenderness and respect with which he spoke and realised that she admired him far more for honouring Alison's memory than she would have done if he had rubbished her.

His face darkened. 'I could *kill* Maggie Cummings for spreading gossip to a ten-year-old child.'

'Well, don't do that. I have no intention of spending the rest of my life visiting you in jail!'

He smiled. Maybe he *should* have brought that champagne, after all!

Clemmie raised her face to his. 'Aleck?' she whispered.

He thought of all the things she might say. All the things he prayed she would *not* say. 'What is it, sweetheart?'

It was all there in her eyes, and written in the huge smile on her face, but she said it anyway. Just so that there could be no misunderstanding. 'I love you, Aleck Cutler.'

He closed his eyes tightly and thanked God. 'I love you, too, Clemmie Powers,' he whispered huskily. 'And I'm damned if I'm going to wait until Monday afternoon to show you just how much!'

He lowered his mouth towards the sweet temptation of hers and kissed her very thoroughly indeed, and Clemmie was beginning to get that melty, gloopy feeling which meant that if they didn't stop what they were doing very soon…then things were going to get completely out of hand.

'Whoooh!' came a giggled shriek from the doorway. Their daughters stood there, giggling and blushing in equal measures, and when Clemmie looked up into Aleck's face she saw that the two of them were no better!

He cleared his throat. 'What can we do for you, girls?'

'You said you'd cook us supper!'

'And I will,' he smiled.

'But Dad—it's raining really hard outside! And Justine and Louella didn't bring their wellingtons!'

It took Aleck and Clemmie a moment or two to get the message, and when they did Clemmie blushed even more.

'Perhaps they could stay the night, then?' Aleck suggested gravely, before turning to the woman at his side. 'And we could hardly send you back on your own, could we, Clemmie?'

Stella tugged impatiently at her father's sleeve. 'Isn't there anything you want to tell us?'

Aleck knew what they wanted. What he wanted. And what he knew deep inside that Clemmie wanted, too. 'I want to marry Clemmie,' he said. 'And for us all to be one big, happy family—'

'When?' demanded the three girls in unison.

Aleck looked at Clemmie. 'Whenever you like. As soon as possible. Please.'

Clemmie wanted to pinch herself.

She thought of the way she and Aleck had looked at this house from the classroom window all those years ago. The way it had seemed so lit up and welcoming tonight. She thought of the corny films it had reminded her of and she knew that their life would be that good. No. Better!

'As soon as you like. How about later this month?' She smiled into his eyes and nearly melted from the love she saw there.

'Can we be bridesmaids?' Louella's voice was breathless.

'You can.' Her mother smiled. 'And you can wear scarlet velvet and carry white muffs—if you want to, that is!'

'And you can move in here after the wedding—or before it, if you'd like that,' said Aleck as he looked tenderly at the circle of female faces smiling at him. 'Because I'm going to design Clemmie the most state-of-the-art professional kitchen she could wish for to make her cakes in.'

Her eyes shone as they looked at him, and she wondered whether now was the right time to tell him that she hadn't ruled out having more babies. Perhaps it could wait…! 'Everything has worked out perfectly,' she sighed happily, and leaned her head against his shoulder. '*Perfectly!* And just in time for Christmas!'

The Sultan's Seduction

Susan Stephens

Susan Stephens was a professional singer before meeting her husband on the tiny Mediterranean island of Malta. In true Modern™ romance style they met on Monday, became engaged on Friday and were married three months after that. Almost thirty years and three children later, they are still in love. (Susan does not advise her children to return home one day with a similar story, as she may not take the news with the same fortitude as her own mother!)

Susan had written several non-fiction books when fate took a hand. At a charity costume ball there was an after-dinner auction. One of the lots, 'Spend a Day with an Author', had been donated by Mills & Boon® author Penny Jordan. Susan's husband bought this lot and Penny was to become not just a great friend but a wonderful mentor, who encouraged Susan to write romance.

Susan loves her family, her pets, her friends and her writing. She enjoys entertaining, travel and going to the theatre. She reads, cooks and plays the piano to relax and can occasionally be found throwing herself off mountains on a pair of skis or galloping through the countryside. Visit Susan's website: www.susanstephens.net—she loves to hear from her readers all around the world!

Look for Susan Stephens exciting new novel, *Ruthless Boss, Dream Baby*, available in January 2011 from Mills & Boon® Modern™.

CHAPTER ONE

'WHEN you walk through those doors you leave your world behind and enter mine.'

Was that a threat? Lizzie Palmer wondered, drawing herself up as she followed Kemal Volkan's gaze across the vast palace courtyard.

'Who told you where I live?' he demanded as she walked past him through the gilded gates.

Wisely, Lizzie kept her own counsel, but she caught the glint of something in Kemal Volkan's eyes that made the tiny hairs stand up on the back of her neck. In spite of her resolve, she suddenly felt apprehensive. And then he laughed. It was a harsh, masculine sound that bounced off the damp black cobbles between them.

'You've got some cheek,' he said.

Determination? Definitely. Cheek? Perhaps, Lizzie reflected, moving ahead of the man they called *The Sultan*, making for the entrance to his home. But it couldn't be helped.

There were just two things in life that mattered to

Lizzie: her work as a lawyer, and her brother Hugo. And her brother always came first. She only had to remember Kemal Volkan was holding Hugo somewhere in Turkey to know she was right to be forcing her way into his home.

After the static-fuzzed call from her brother, Lizzie had caught the next flight to Istanbul. What she had learned about Kemal Volkan had only increased her level of concern. It seemed he lived like a feudal warlord, surrounded by a wall of silence. She'd had to use all her legal expertise and connections to dig a little deeper into his affairs, and as she had done so, she'd discovered that his acquired name was no exaggeration. *The Sultan* was an immensely powerful man, and accustomed to ruthlessly wielding that power.

When she had turned to the embassy for help, they'd said she was on her own. This was a commercial matter, rather than political or criminal, and the Foreign Office couldn't get involved in the legal process of another country. So she had tracked down a local lawyer who specialised in commercial work, and Sami Gulsan had told her the really bad news: the company Hugo had been working for during his gap year was in trouble.

The passports of company employees were being withheld until parts missing from the machinery Hugo had helped to install arrived on site. Volkan intended to barter the men's freedom for those parts, and heaven knew where he was holding them in the meantime. Even Sami Gulsan couldn't tell her that.

And with the company in financial difficulties, Lizzie knew that the parts would be almost impossible to obtain.

She stole a glance at her adversary, knowing she had to make him see sense. It was almost Christmas; surely he didn't plan to keep the men over the holidays?

'Thank you for seeing me,' she said, in an attempt to build a bridge between them. 'I can assure you I would not have troubled you at home had I not considered this a matter of the utmost urgency.'

He dipped his head briefly without shortening his stride. She couldn't tell if he had softened towards her or not. But he was right about one thing, Lizzie realised as they reached the grand entrance to the palace building—his world was very different from her own. Even the air felt different. It had the peculiar stillness only the extremely rich seemed to gather round them. And there was a faint scent too— sandalwood, she guessed—worn by Kemal Volkan. Normally she reacted violently to any strong perfume, but somehow this was different.

Hearing the gates close behind them, Lizzie knew it was too late to turn back now even had she wanted to, which she didn't. A tip-off from Sami Gulsan had got her this far, and she had no intention of wasting the opportunity.

It might have been better to introduce herself more sedately, but she had not anticipated arriving at the palace in a beat-up old taxi at precisely the same moment as Kemal Volkan in his chauffeur-driven Bentley. On her instruction, the taxi had slewed across the entrance, blocking his way. Volkan had sprung out ahead of his driver and ordered the cab to move on, and she had almost fallen at his feet in her rush to waylay him. She could still feel the imprint of his hand on her arm from when he'd reached out to steady her, waving his bodyguards away…

Jolted out of her thoughts by the sight of men in jewelled, vividly coloured robes opening the splendid entrance doors for them, Lizzie was suddenly acutely aware of where she was—and of the man at her side. She hesitated briefly as he stood back to allow her to precede him, and then, raising her head high, she stepped over the threshold into the palace. She had allowed for Kemal Volkan wearing the mantle of power that came with immense wealth, had even allowed for his looks being different—more exotic, perhaps, than the people she was accustomed to dealing with. But nothing could have prepared her for a meeting with a man who possessed such a forceful aura.

It would take every ounce of her adversarial skill to bring her brother home in time for Christmas, Lizzie realised, mentally preparing herself for the confrontation that lay ahead.

'Welcome to my home, Ms Palmer,' he said, forcing her to turn and look at him.

'Thank you. It is spectacular,' Lizzie said frankly, gazing around. 'I don't think I've ever seen anywhere quite so beautiful.' And he was stunning too, Lizzie conceded, glancing back at her host.

Kemal Volkan was tall, powerfully built, and

rugged, so that in spite of his formal business suit he looked more like a buccaneer returning home from his latest expedition than the billionaire businessman she knew him to be. She could just imagine that by the time most people got over the sight of Kemal Volkan he would have tied them up in knots. But that could not happen to her. She had to ignore the way the blood was rushing through her veins, and stifle her growing sense of apprehension. She would somehow negotiate the release of the men—and she wasn't going to leave until she did.

'Won't you come in, Ms Palmer?' he said, gatecrashing her thoughts.

Glancing up, Lizzie saw that he had paused and turned to her on his way towards some inner door. Hearing her name roll off his lips with just the trace of an accent sucked a response from deep inside her. His deep, husky voice was every bit as disturbing as his striking appearance, she realised, wishing time had allowed for the anonymity of legal letters passing to and fro between them.

'Ms Palmer?'

For the first time he could remember Kemal wished he could free himself from centuries of tradition. He wanted nothing more than to be alone and to relax after his long and particularly demanding business trip, but the code of Turkish hospitality had been hung around his neck at birth. However inconvenient it might be, custom decreed he must grant her a welcome. And he would—before sending her on her way as fast as possible.

She wouldn't even have got this far if she hadn't announced she was Hugo Palmer's sister. And how had that happened? She and her brother were as different as could be. A repressed female on a mission was the very last thing he needed right now...

Repressed? Kemal's eyes narrowed as he turned the word over in his mind. Ms Lizzie Palmer was certainly wound up as tight as a spring, but... His brow furrowed as he inhaled appreciatively. What was that? Lavender? And there was something more...amber, perhaps? Very English—with just a hint of the East. Maybe there was hope for her after all, he conceded, feeling his senses stir.

Lizzie's face burned as she sensed Kemal Volkan's very masculine interest. She avoided his glance, affecting interest in her surroundings instead, and found she was genuinely captivated. The roofed entrance vestibule they were crossing was exquisite. Stretching the whole length of the palace, it was subtly lit, and awash with colour thanks to the moonlight streaming through glass panes as brightly coloured as jewels in the vaulted roof. Semi-precious stones glinted darkly beneath her feet, and there was a fountain playing in a raised central pool. There were even songbirds fluttering through the flower-strewn foliage cloaking the walls.

It was all very beautiful, but so foreign, and so dangerously beguiling. And she was here on business, not a pleasure jaunt. She could only be relieved that she had dressed the part. There was nothing remotely frivolous in her appearance. A plain black overcoat covered an austere Armani suit, and her soft blonde curls were tied back severely. She wore very little make-up, and neat designer spectacles provided the shield she always worked behind.

Before studying law she had longed to become an actress, but the precariousness of life on stage had ruled that out. Hugo's security had always come first. She had embraced the responsibility for him gladly at eighteen, and since then her life had been geared to taking care of him. Over time her dreams of a life on the stage had faded, and now she found an amusing irony in the many similarities between that career path and her current profession: she still wore a gown and a wig—a costume, of sorts—to act as a barrister, and still fine-tuned her performance each day in court.

She understood only too well the importance of the visual message she sent out to men in the course of her work, and was glad of that knowledge now. It gave her the confidence to deal with a man like Kemal Volkan. She needed to treat him like an adversary, rather than waste time lapping up his masculinity like some gullible adolescent.

But the deeper they ventured into the palace, the greater grew Lizzie's sense of foreboding. She looked round anxiously as another set of heavy doors closed behind them. Her own world was growing more distant—just as Kemal Volkan had promised it would.

Finally they came to an elegant square hallway that seemed to belong to a slightly cosier and perhaps even private living space within the vast formal structure of the palace. The floor was white marble, and antique hangings in muted shades of burnt sienna, rose madder and topaz covered the walls. There was a large Turkish rug on the floor: it was undoubtedly priceless, Lizzie thought, pausing alongside Volkan who had drawn to a halt.

The surroundings were breathtaking, but where was Hugo? Where was her nineteen-year-old brother? How could she secure his freedom? The best alternative, Lizzie realised, was to avoid confrontation and appeal to Kemal Volkan's better nature—though she doubted he had one. And if he had hurt one hair on her brother's head…

Lizzie blinked at the look Kemal flared down at her. It was almost as if he had read her mind and issued a lightning response to the challenge. It made her wonder what price he might exact in return for her brother's freedom.

A servant distracted her, coming to kneel by the edge of the fabulous carpet at his master's feet. Loosening the laces on Kemal Volkan's highly polished shoes, he slipped them off, replacing them with a pair of lavishly embroidered Turkish slippers.

Seeing Volkan indulged in this way only fuelled Lizzie's anger. Wherever Hugo was incarcerated, she was quite certain he would not be enjoying luxury such as this. And now the manservant was kneeling beside her, with a second pair of slippers in his hand.

'Don't looked so shocked, Ms Palmer.'

The low drawl seemed to resonate at a frequency that made her whole body thrum in response, Lizzie noticed with resentment. But she could see the sense of protecting the priceless rug. 'I don't need slippers. I'll just slip my shoes off—'

'Indulge me,' Kemal Volkan murmured.

Lizzie's first instinct was to be bloody-minded. She couldn't remember feeling such passion outside the courtroom. Her childhood had left her with an overwhelming urge to control every aspect of her adult life, and up to now she had always succeeded. But the fact was she couldn't be rude to the elderly retainer who was even now trying to ease up her foot. Round one to Kemal Volkan. She would have to yield to his wishes on this occasion.

'Thank you,' she said politely to his manservant.

'*Seni sevdim,*' the old man replied. Slanting a shy smile at Lizzie, he hurried away.

'What did he say?' Lizzie asked.

'Mehmet likes you,' Volkan said dryly. 'The phrase is freely offered here in Turkey—unless of course you do something drastic to prevent it.'

Something drastic? Lizzie thought. She would do something drastic if that was what it took to set her brother free.

'In Turkey, East and West meet seamlessly,' Kemal Volkan continued. 'Hence the slippers. It is a very small concession for me to make to someone who has served my family all his life. Those of us who are fortunate enough to live in Istanbul enjoy the very best of both worlds—'

'I am well aware of the geographical significance of the Bosphorus, Mr Volkan,' Lizzie cut across him, 'but right now my only concern is for my brother.'

She dared to interrupt him? Kemal kept his thoughts behind a mask of indifference as he ushered Lizzie towards his study. 'My time is yours, Ms Palmer,' he murmured politely.

They could only have been sitting down in his study for a few minutes, but Lizzie felt as if she had been talking for ever. Her neck was aching, and all the time Kemal Volkan just sat watching her, without saying a word. In the end, his remorselessly neutral expression pushed her into an uncharacteristic display of passion.

'I won't leave until I know exactly where Hugo is, what's happened to him, and how soon he can return home.'

She waited tensely, fairly sure that her argument was persuasive In her view there was no reason why a satisfactory compromise could not be reached. She was even prepared to act as intermediary between Volkan and the receivers for the bankrupt company, if he thought that would help to expedite the men's return home.

This was turning into a novel encounter, Kemal reflected. He doubted he had ever met a woman so full of determination, and so unswervingly set on defiance. He felt some admiration for her. It took nerve to confront him on his home territory, and she had certainly researched everything thoroughly…a little too thoroughly, he decided, feeling anger start to take the place of his grudging admiration.

She presumed to have an understanding of his complex business dealings in no time flat, and had invaded his privacy to a degree he had never experienced before. But he would not get into a debate with her. She might have found out plenty, but now she was facing a brick wall. And that was how it was going to stay until he decided otherwise. He would tell her absolutely nothing, and wait like a hunter stalking his prey, using silence as a weapon, feigning uninterest, until he was ready to strike.

CHAPTER TWO

DID nothing provoke a response from this man? Lizzie wondered, as they sat across the desk from each other. Her frustration was growing by the minute as she stared at Volkan's watchful face. Did nothing unzip that firm, sensuous mouth?

The more he exercised control, the more she found herself determined to elicit a response from him. The only curb on that determination was the fact that she had to be careful: she couldn't risk antagonising him. She had the sense of a powerful engine idling, waiting for her to make the next move, reveal her hand. But she did have one slight advantage. She was a guest in a very traditional home where custom insisted that Volkan at least listen before he threw her out—an unfair advantage, perhaps, but where her brother's welfare was concerned she had no scruples.

Lizzie averted her gaze from the wide sweep of his shoulders, clad in the finest wool tailoring. The ink-dark suit was almost certainly from Savile Row, and both his grooming and his smooth bronze tan bore the unmistakable stamp of the super-rich. But that didn't exclude him from the human race, she mused angrily. He must have some feelings. Surely he could understand her concern for her brother?

'Ms Palmer?'

As Volkan unexpectedly broke the silence Lizzie's focus became acute. She straightened up expectantly. 'Yes?'

'Shall we have tea?'

Tea? To choke him with, perhaps! Where were the answers to her questions? He still hadn't even told her where her brother was!

Viewing his imperious profile as he turned to call one of the hovering servants forward, Lizzie decided angrily that it wasn't too great a stretch of the imagination to picture him as a sensual, pleasure-loving sultan. It was quite possible one of his forebears had been some self-indulgent pasha. Kemal Volkan was certainly above all normal human feeling. In fact, nothing about him was usual, from the luxuriant black hair he wore a little long, to the dusky shadows cast by his sharply etched cheekbones. And his eyes, she noticed, were the colour of a smoky-grey wolf pelt...

He was staring at her. She quickly looked away, pretending interest in her surroundings. It was hard to remain insensitive to the beauty around her when everything in the room had been designed to please the senses. The wood panelling insulated the study against outside noise, and there was a log fire blazing in the over-sized grate that under other circumstances might have made her feel relaxed enough to grow sleepy. A mellow light was cast by twin table lamps, and aside from the noise of her own heart hammering in her ears there was no sound other than a faint trickle of classical music coming from surround speakers.

It was all quite different from the small modern apartment she shared with Hugo. But then she suspected Kemal Volkan must have inherited many of the beautiful artefacts, whereas she had inherited nothing at the age of eighteen but a bewildered nine-year-old brother, when their hippie parents had taken the ultimate trip late one Christmas Eve.

Lizzie tensed anxiously as she thought about Hugo. She wasn't doing much for him now—and never would if she allowed those childhood memories to get in the way. And she had been so sure they were all banished to the deepest archives in her mind. One day she would deal with them properly. But not now. She couldn't afford any distractions now.

Determinedly, Lizzie closed her mind to the past. She never allowed the past to rule the present. Dwelling on things she couldn't change was a destructive pursuit, and she chose to look forward. Hugo was nineteen now, and had secured a place at a good university where, after his gap year, he would follow in her own footsteps and read law. They had made it through together; that was all that mattered. And no one, especially not an arrogant individual like Kemal Volkan, was ever going to come between them.

'Do you have anything more you would like to say to me?' he said.

Plenty! Lizzie took a moment before resuming, heeding the warnings she had been given about Kemal Volkan, that like the wolf he was a predator—strong and cunning, a hunting beast. But if he thought for one moment that he could frighten her off, or play the 'men rule here' card, he was about to discover how very wrong he was. She was often forced to take on lawyers of the old school, and that experience had given her the mental armoury necessary to do battle with dinosaurs of any nationality—even Turkish entrepreneurs who thought she was a pushover.

Her argument might be couched in the most polite terms, but her hostility was all too evident. Her attitude offended him, and called for a response. He would master her, Kemal decided as Lizzie's soft, insistent voice washed over him. It was a challenge too rich to be ignored, and he would even be doing her a favour. Intellectual jousting was all very well, but there was another, unawakened side to Lizzie Palmer. All her fires were directed at her work, and her sisterly concern for Hugh Palmer. Commendable. But if she did not find something else to spend her passions on Hugo would only shake her off, as all young men must shake off any feminine influence in the home. And work was a poor companion through the night.

He affected close attention as she talked on. She was certainly a formidable opponent where words were concerned, but he had other weapons in his armoury—weapons he would enjoy using on Lizzie Palmer.

It never ceased to amaze him how one sibling could be so different from another. Hugo was so gregarious, so carefree and fun-loving, whilst his sister was none of those things. But apparently Lizzie had brought him up single-handedly, so Hugo was what she had made him. She had done a good job as far as that was concerned, Kemal conceded thoughtfully. Another plus: it had obviously been some time since she last brushed her long blonde hair, and it was escaping in soft tendrils that curled around her face— a face that in spite of the fact that her eyes were spitting fire at him still managed somehow to appeal.

Kemal shifted position impatiently. The world was full of beautiful women, all melting to order like sickly-sweet ice cream. He was tired of them all. His palate was hopelessly jaded, and business was his mistress now. It had been a long day, a difficult trip, a protracted business negotiation. On the drive back from the airport he had dreamed of the many indulgences awaiting him at the palace: a shower, a massage, a Turkish bath, all of which he could enjoy in the luxury of his own home. Or he might have swum a few lengths in the indoor pool first, and then taken his ease later.

Instead, for some reason, he was giving this intense and surprising young woman more of his time than even good manners demanded. So what was it about her that appealed? The answer, of course, was that she was ice and fire—perhaps a perfect combination of the two. He would listen to what she had to say, and then decide what to do with her.

Lizzie's precise movements as she organised the papers in her briefcase distracted Kemal. He was attracted to her. In fact, he wanted her to stay. The physical reaction that followed took him completely by surprise—control was normally his middle name—and it was all he could do to suppress a very masculine smile as he continued to gaze at the extremely uptight, and immensely proper Ms Lizzie Palmer. If she knew the effect she was having on him now, she would run for her life.

Relishing the opportunity to study Lizzie in some detail, Kemal settled back in his chair. Her trim ankles and shapely calves gave some clue as to the rest of the package, though she was pretty well trussed up in her drab business clothes. Still, there were agreeable curves in all the right places, and the way her hair was beginning to wave softly where it had escaped from the tightly drawn ponytail made him want to wind his fingers through the wrist-thick fall and bring those full red lips a little closer.

There was certainly passion contained in that outwardly respectable frame, but all of it was channelled in entirely the wrong direction. And her impertinence intrigued him—she dared to challenge his code of honour, making it clear she thought he had Hugo locked up somewhere. She was without question a most contentious woman, as well as the most contained he had ever encountered. And that made him curious to know if she might succumb to temptation of a more erotic nature. He shifted position again, barely able to contain his pent-up energy. He was restless now, dangerously restless. His hunting instinct was in full spate, Kemal realised, as he gazed at Lizzie through half-shut eyes.

Lizzie's voice caught in her throat as she started to summarise her thoughts on ways of securing Hugo's speedy release. She wondered suddenly if Kemal Volkan was actually listening to her, and tensed, seeing the slight tug at one corner of his mouth. It wouldn't do to encourage the very masculine interest she could see brewing beneath the surface of his harsh exterior. There was too much sensuality in his face for her to risk relaxing in his presence, and far too much confidence radiating from him in hot, compelling waves.

The idea that he might find her attractive came as a complete shock. She had never imagined herself to be overly attractive; she was too pale, too reserved. And she didn't exude the necessary *vibes*, according to her friends. Which was how she liked it. The idea of sex with a man like Kemal Volkan was a terrifying prospect. She had about as much experience as a gnat, whereas he was sure to have a harem stocked with sophisticated temptresses. Better not to think about it, Lizzie decided. She had expected to wrest her brother from the clutches of a jailer, or argue for his release in the safe and sterile confines of a lawyer's office, but this was definitely the worst-case scenario.

'Are you cold?' Kemal said, as she shivered with

apprehension. 'Let me hurry up the tea and send for some food as well.' Without troubling to wait for her reply, he stood up and pulled a velvet cord hanging from the wall.

Freed from Kemal's penetrative gaze, Lizzie battled to regain focus. This was not what she wanted—this ease, this familiarity. She had believed herself ready for anything, but she had not factored a man like Kemal Volkan into her thinking. His phenomenal level of success had led her to assume that he would be a much older man, and she had learned that once they recovered from the initial shock of having to deal with a woman, older men's fatherly instincts usually kicked in, making them easier to handle. There would be no such concessions with this man, Lizzie thought tensely. Her only hope was to get their discussion back on track as fast as possible, and this time nail him to the mast.

'I really would prefer to talk than to eat,' she said when he turned back to her.

'Is there any reason why we can't do both?' Kemal said easily, dipping to stir the blazing logs with a long steel poker.

'Well, no, but—'

'Then we eat,' he said with a shrug.

What harm could eating together do? Lizzie thought. After all, he was as much sinned against as sinner—

What was she thinking of? The circumstances in which he was holding the men made fairness irrelevant. She had come to free Hugo and his colleagues—not to defend their jailer!

'It's really very warm,' Kemal commented as he moved away from the fire. 'Why don't you let me take your coat? You're still cold,' he said with surprise, when Lizzie failed to stop the quiver of awareness that rippled across her shoulders at his touch. 'We will eat soon, and then you will feel much better.'

She doubted that somehow.

As he swung Lizzie's coat across the back of a chair Kemal realised that he liked the way she had felt beneath his hands, and the way she'd responded to his touch. Her skin had felt warm and soft, not cold.

The thought that it might be good to tutor her in all those things that her education had so obviously neglected to teach her was growing. Too often women were like hothouse flowers: too ripe, too blowsy, hardly recognisable one from the other. But Lizzie Palmer was different. She was fresh and un-spoiled—though, like any difficult mount, she would have to be mastered before she could be enjoyed...

She would have to leave soon, Lizzie thought, picking up on Kemal's brooding interest. She had always thought herself a hard-bitten professional, but Kemal Volkan was really beginning to frighten her.

She was distracted by a gentle tap on the door, and when the servants returned with food and drink she realised she was very hungry. Seeing the same elderly servant smiling encouragement at her as he brought over some delicacies for her to sample, Lizzie felt a little reassured. She would stay long enough to eat, and then she would pin Volkan down over Hugo's release. Once that was done she would take the greatest pleasure in putting as much distance between them as possible.

A few nibbles were brought to them, as well as Turkish tea served in tiny vase-like glasses and accompanied by slices of lemon and white sugar cubes.

'Try some,' Kemal insisted. 'The tea is very refreshing.'

Lizzie hesitated. Taking anything from Volkan's hands seemed like a betrayal. His voice might be neutral, but his steel-grey gaze was shrewd and watchful, and she felt guilty indulging her own needs whilst her brother was still being held. But the key to Hugo's release, she reminded herself, was Kemal Volkan. And while she was under his roof she at least had a chance of getting Hugo home in time for Christmas.

'Where have you been staying?' Kemal asked her as they sipped the tea.

'At the Hotel Turkoman,' Lizzie said distractedly. The last thing she wanted was to allow him to steer the conversation away from Hugo and towards her.

'Ah, yes,' he murmured thoughtfully. 'Close to the law courts, and with an excellent view of the Blue Mosque.'

'I'm really not interested in the view, and I don't plan to stay,' Lizzie informed him. Maybe she wouldn't even need a hotel room, she thought tensely. She was quite prepared to take Hugo's place in a far more primitive location than the Hotel Turkoman. 'Look, I don't feel we're getting anywhere. Let me get to the point. Hugo must be released—'

'Released?' Kemal echoed with a hint of impatience. 'What are you talking about?'

'I think you know,' Lizzie countered. 'My brother must be released in time for Christmas,' she repeated impatiently, meeting his steely look head-on.

Did she think he was a barbarian? Kemal wondered as he held Lizzie's gaze. Did she really believe he had the men locked up in a dank cell somewhere?

And was this emotional blackmail now? Her eyes had grown misty at the mention of Christmas. It suggested a change of tactics on her part. All the more reason for him not to be drawn. He would keep his own counsel, just as he had planned to do when they first met.

Kemal leaned forward across the desk that divided them and passed her a card. 'It's very busy in Istanbul at Christmas,' he said. 'There can be confusion. Take my business card. If you have any difficulties at the hotel, just ask them to call me.'

Didn't he get the message? She wasn't going to be around at Christmas if she could help it, Lizzie thought tensely. And neither was Hugo. It was on the tip of her tongue to say that she could manage very well without his help, but when he dropped the card on the desk in front of her for some reason she picked it up.

'Thank you,' she said briefly, slipping it into the front pocket of her briefcase.

'Today is Tuesday,' Kemal murmured thoughtfully. 'You haven't left yourself much time if you want to have your brother home by Christmas Day, on Saturday.'

Was he goading her? Or was this an unexpected moment of concern? Highly unlikely, Lizzie decided. 'Hugo *will* be home in time for Christmas,' she said pointedly.

Her stubbornness should have infuriated him, but instead he was forced to admire her cool. Nothing he could say fazed her at all—except for any mention of Christmas, which for some reason really got under her skin. But that was his curse, Kemal reflected. He noticed everything, and sometimes wished that he didn't.

He turned to murmur an instruction to one of the servants in his own language, asking for some food to be prepared and brought to the sunken lounge for them. Then he turned again to Lizzie. 'I do recommend you confirm and perhaps extend your hotel booking. Every bed is likely to be taken in the city over Christmas.'

'I will be staying in Istanbul until my brother and all the other men are released,' Lizzie assured him. 'And I can see no possible excuse for reasonable and honourable people not to achieve that satisfactory conclusion before Christmas.'

A muscle worked in Kemal's jaw as he curbed the angry words that flew to his lips. She questioned his honour and she constantly rejected his help. She had arrived in Istanbul assuming the worst, taking a tough line with his office, refusing to accept local protocol, refusing to talk to anyone but him—even turning up on his doorstep believing she could bend him to her will! She chose to assume he was a barbarian—so maybe it was time Lizzie Palmer learned that no one bent Kemal Volkan to their will.

'Mr Volkan!' Lizzie exclaimed with concern as he stood up. 'You're not leaving? We haven't finished our discussions—'

'I have finished.' And now she dared to question his intentions! Kemal's gaze blazed down on Lizzie. *Masallah!* But she was beautiful. If only she could have been a little looser, a little more self-indulgent, like her brother. She would certainly have to learn to be a lot more biddable if she stayed around for much longer! 'Ring the hotel, just to make sure you have somewhere to stay tonight,' he instructed, hardly trusting himself to stay in the room with her a moment longer.

'Thank you, but no,' Lizzie said flatly, also standing up.

'Why not?' Kemal said, his eyes narrowing with mistrust as they confronted each other.

'I won't make the call because I don't need to,' Lizzie said confidently.

'You don't need to?' Kemal repeated suspiciously.

'No. If I have a problem at the hotel I will simply find another,' Lizzie said firmly. 'Look, I know this has been hard for you—'

'Hard for me?' Kemal repeated incredulously.

'I do understand the damage caused to your business because of those missing parts,' Lizzie pressed on.

'You understand? You understand nothing!' Kemal said, his voice like a whiplash.

The look in his eyes made Lizzie's spine go cold.

She didn't think she had ever seen anyone so suddenly in a fury, or anyone control it quite so well. She had overstepped the mark. She had attacked his pride once too often. She had refused his offer of help. She had defied him. And for a man like Kemal Volkan such behaviour was incomprehensible

'How dare you come here and lecture me?' he erupted. 'I paid millions up front in good faith, only to be let down very badly by your brother's employer. You see this as a personal problem affecting your brother. I see it as a setback in trading—in trust between our two countries.'

'Don't you think that's a bit extreme?'

'Extreme?' Kemal said icily. 'You talk of your concerns for Christmas, whilst I have to consider the possible long-term consequences for my business and my employees. I have invested a fortune in this project, and *I will not allow it to fail.*'

His final words flew at Lizzie like shot from a gun. She was in no doubt that he meant every one of them. Tension rose between them as he held her stare. This was a far more dangerous situation than anything she had encountered in court. Kemal was a leader of men, unaccustomed to failure, a man to whom nothing was ever denied. And in his eyes she was merely a woman...

Lizzie's mounting anger overtook her caution. The day would never come when a man could intimidate her, and Kemal Volkan would never browbeat her into submission.

'This is not just another case for you to win, Ms

Palmer,' he was informing her as Lizzie drew herself up. 'And I resent the fact that you imply I have acted dishonestly, or illegally, when all I ask is that people honour their obligations. The fact that your brother is one of those people does not alter the situation one bit.'

Now she would demand to be returned to her hotel, Kemal thought, as he waited for Lizzie's response. But for some crazy reason that was the very last thing he wanted. He almost laughed out loud with relief when she levelled an unflinching gaze on his face. He should have known she would have more guts than that.

'In spite of what you think of me,' Lizzie said coldly, 'I can assure you I do understand the problems you've had. I know what honour means to you, and you have every right to feel let down. But I have my own agenda, and you must understand that I will not be swayed by anything you—'

'I *must*?' Kemal interrupted her softly.

'I am determined to stay,' Lizzie told him, 'until I know that Hugo and all the other men will be home in time for Christmas.'

'What do you want me to say, Ms Palmer?'

Lizzie's thoughts were in confusion as silence fell between them. Reason could never prevail when they were poles apart in culture, in thinking—in everything. Her head was throbbing with concern for Hugo, and she was so keenly aware of the influence Volkan wielded she could scarcely think straight at all. And then there was the passion that had so unexpectedly slipped through his guard...

Kemal Volkan was a force on a level she had never encountered before. She had no cards left to play. Her mind raced as she considered the alternatives. She had to make one last big gesture. Something even he could not dismiss. *She should have left everything ready so that Hugo could enjoy Christmas without her, but she had thought of nothing beyond coming to Turkey to negotiate his freedom...*

'Ms Palmer?'

'Consider this proposal—'

'When I know what it is,' he agreed.

Lizzie drew a deep breath. Honour was her code too, and she would stop at nothing to protect her brother. 'Call the authorities,' she said calmly. 'I'm going to take the place of my brother and his colleagues.'

CHAPTER THREE

LIZZIE'S brave speech took Kemal by surprise. Keeping her close a little longer had been plucking at the edges of his mind. He'd been ready to engage in a battle of words and wits—at which he excelled—to keep her there. Instead of which she had elected to stay—and of her own free will. What a battle for his conscience! A beautiful and intelligent woman had just agreed to become his hostage. He should refuse, of course. But, what the hell? For him, Christmas had come early!

'Sit. Sit down again, please, Ms Palmer,' he said, wanting to give them both time to digest this turn of events.

'I still hope to be free in time for Christmas.'

Kemal looked up. His focus had sharpened as she spoke. Could she tune in to his thoughts? And what was this fixation she had with Christmas? Foolish sentiment? Or a poor attempt at working on his emotions? He stared at Lizzie. She seemed so young, almost vulnerable. But that was a trick of the light—or wishful thinking, perhaps. She was at least mid to late twenties, and there was nothing the least bit vulnerable about her. This harping on Christmas was simply a lever to make him release her brother.

'It may not be possible for you to be free for Christmas,' he said coldly. 'We shall have to see.'

He looked again and saw her eyes briefly close against her fate. No doubt she was imagining all the horrors awaiting her. He turned his face with some irritation. Her suspicions insulted him. They made him want to grab hold of the virtuous Ms Lizzie Palmer and shake some sense into her. And that only made him angrier still, Kemal realised. He wouldn't have believed any woman could rouse such passion in him.

But he would never allow such a base emotion to master him. He would retain control of this situation—and of Ms Lizzie Palmer.

'Will you arrange the exchange for me?' she asked, reclaiming his attention.

'That's quite an offer—one woman in exchange for five men?'

'I would have thought it a good bargain,' Lizzie countered.

The challenge on her face made him glad; made the blood race in his veins. He had never met a woman like this before. They locked gazes like two protagonists in the ring, and in that moment she had never appeared more attractive to him. If a man was to have children, wasn't this tigress the mother he would choose for them?

Was he going completely mad? Kemal wondered, launching himself from his seat in front of the desk to pace the room. Tiredness, he realised with relief, swiping a hand across the back of his neck. Only extreme exhaustion could have allowed such a crazy thought to enter his head!

He relaxed briefly, and then tensed again, seeing Lizzie was still staring at him, still doggedly pursuing her crusade to rescue her brother. Would she never give up? He had never met anyone so unshakeably determined to defy him. His feelings were swinging wildly between anger and desire. All he could think of now was that her stamina had better match her determination. But first, he remembered, there was that sheath of steel she was cloaked in to dispose of.

'Do you accept?' Lizzie demanded quietly.

A muscle flexed in Kemal's jaw. Was she daring to put pressure on him? Whatever the consequences, he knew now that he would never rest until he had mastered her. This was no longer an impersonal negotiation for him—if it had ever been. She had made it deeply personal. 'I accept,' he said. 'Now we will eat. We will discuss the detail later.'

His arrogance was outrageous, Lizzie thought angrily as he turned away from her. It was obvious no one had ever challenged his right to impose his will wherever he chose. *Well, prepare yourself, mister, because I won't stand for it!*

For a moment Lizzie indulged herself with wild thoughts of springing out of her seat to beat her fists against the wide expanse of his back. But she remembered how close she was to achieving her aim. Hugo might be free that very night if she could keep her cool just a little bit longer.

Taking his seat across the desk from her again, Kemal leaned back. It was time for the gloves to come off. 'Don't you mind missing out on Christmas?'

As far as Lizzie was concerned, only four words registered: Missing out on Christmas. 'I would hope that as a man of honour and influence you would not take advantage of this situation,' she said shakily. 'I expect you to help me find a solution before then.'

Would the need to mark Christmas never leave her? It was like a great black hole she had brought with her from her childhood, a hole that had to be filled—with festive food, dainty ornaments, fat crackers stuffed with plastic gifts and silly jokes and paper crowns...a tree, and presents—there had to be presents...

'Ms Palmer?'

Lizzie's eyes cleared and focused again as she looked up at Kemal.

'I will do whatever I can to help you,' he said, with an impatient gesture.

Wounding her had brought him no pleasure. And how could he enjoy a woman whose eyes brimmed with tears every time he mentioned Christmas, even if it was just a case of foolish sentiment? Though he still suspected emotional blackmail, there was a haunted look in her eyes that might have been genuine, or might have been some leftover from her acting days. Hadn't Hugo told him his sister had once dreamed of a life on the stage?

Lizzie's jaw firmed visibly. 'If you refuse me, Mr Volkan, I'll make sure you never do business with my country again.'

Was she threatening him? He almost laughed in her face. 'Enough, Ms Palmer,' he snapped, raising one hand to silence her. But the flash of desperation in her eyes made him rein back. He remained still for a moment, until he could see she had become receptive once more, and then added softly, 'There is no reason for us to become enemies. My name is Kemal. You will use it. And I will call you Lizzie.'

Oh, no, she wasn't going to fall for the 'good cop, bad cop' routine, even played by the same man. 'I'd like to make the exchange tonight,' Lizzie said, as if he hadn't spoken.

'You are a very demanding woman.'

'My brother must be home in time for Christmas.'

Kemal held up both hands in a show of surrender to try and slow her down. 'I realise Christmas is important to you, but who's to say you might not enjoy Christmas here in Turkey?'

While I'm locked up, presumably? Lizzie thought, her lips tightening.

'Why not make this Christmas truly memorable?'

Thanks to him, it already was, Lizzie thought, breaking eye contact when she saw the look in Kemal's eyes. She could not risk offending him by admitting that Christmas in Turkey was the last thing she wanted. 'I didn't think you would celebrate the day.'

'Turkey is predominantly a Muslim country, but my mother was Christian.' Lizzie was surprised, Kemal noticed, and he seized the moment to explain. 'Many of the people who work for me celebrate Christmas. I honour every custom wherever I do business.' What was this? Was he trying to win her favour? It had to be a first for him, Kemal reflected dryly.

'I see,' Lizzie said, colour flooding back into her face. 'Then you do understand—'

No, Kemal thought, I do not. But he would find out. Something troubled him—something behind Lizzie's eyes. His glance dropped to her lips. The thought of mastering her had been replaced by another, more pressing need: the need to awaken her, to steal away the shadows in her eyes.

Kemal's senses leapt when he heard Lizzie's sharp intake of breath, but he saw that his interest was making her tense.

'Mr Volkan—'

'Kemal,' he reminded her.

'Kemal.' The name felt strange on Lizzie's lips, and yet it rolled off her tongue like melted chocolate, so that she wanted to say it again, and again.

'You are exhausted,' he observed, in a softer voice than she had ever heard him use before.

Lizzie was instantly on guard. But she was too slow to resist when Kemal leaned across the desk, and she gasped to see that her own small hand was completely swallowed up in his fist. She snatched it away, but not before she had a chance to be aware of his incredible physical strength.

'I would like to leave tonight,' Lizzie said, hoping she sounded calm. *Now! Right now!* Every sensation she had ever known was concentrated in the hand she was nursing in her lap. It was as if Kemal Volkan had scorched her. 'I must see my brother before I am locked up—'

'Locked up? What on earth are you talking about? You will stay here, of course.'

'Here?' Lizzie's gaze darted around the room. She was ready to take Hugo's place in a cell, in a dungeon—anywhere. Staying here at the palace, under the same roof as Kemal, seemed a far worse fate.

'This is a very large residence,' he said, as if reading her mind. 'The palace is every bit as large as the Hotel Turkoman, where you would have been staying. And here you will have your own suite of rooms, complete independence from me. And before you ask, you will not be inconveniencing me in the slightest. In addition you will have the freedom of the palace gardens, the spa, the swimming pool...'

'I can't possibly agree—'

'Why not?' Kemal said impatiently. 'As my guest you will be free to do as you wish. It will not alter the outcome of any discussions between us. You have my word on that.' He sat back, satisfied that she would stay. It was a *fait accompli*.

Still she hesitated. He had not expected indecision. 'It has been a long day,' he said at last. 'You *will* stay here.' He made a decisive gesture.

'As another hostage?' she said tensely.

'No one forced you to take your brother's place,' Kemal pointed out.

'And I still intend to do so,' Lizzie said. 'But I will not stay here with you.' She got up.

Planting his knuckles on the desk, Kemal leaned across. 'You will stay here—because you have no alternative.'

His angry words seemed to vibrate in the air between them, and after a few tense moments Lizzie sat down again. Kemal was right. She could not do anything that might jeopardise her brother's release. *The Sultan* has spoken, she reflected tensely. Kemal Volkan's sobriquet was well earned, but he was not, and never would be, *her* master.

CHAPTER FOUR

'MS PALMER will be staying tonight,' Kemal told Mehmet. 'Make guest quarters ready for her.'

Bowing, the elderly man gave Lizzie a gentle smile. 'This is excellent news,' he said in heavily accented English. 'Welcome to the palace, Ms Palmer.'

Lizzie felt a shiver of apprehension run down her spine. What had she agreed to?

'Perhaps I should put your mind at rest?'

'Yes, perhaps you better had,' Lizzie agreed tensely, levelling a stony gaze on her host.

'The palace is huge. You will sleep in one wing while I will sleep in the other—in *The Sultan's* bedroom.'

Of course! Lizzie thought cynically. Where else would Kemal Volkan deign to lay his head? But she was tired, and she was hungry, and common sense overruled any inclination she had left to defy him.

'Are you reassured?' he demanded sardonically.

Lizzie held his stare. 'Reassured? I am reconciled,

for now,' she said, hoping she wasn't about to make the biggest mistake of her life.

Meeting Lizzie's gaze in those few seconds, Kemal learned many things: she was certainly strong, but however hard she tried to hide it there was sadness behind her eyes. And those eyes, as he had just discovered, were a very attractive shade of aquamarine. But why should he care what the hell he saw behind her eyes? What was so different about her?

He did care, however much he tried to pretend otherwise, and that irritated him. It was doubtless down to curiosity, which was a great driver. The puzzle surrounding Lizzie intrigued him. And, whatever she was trying to hide from him, he would find out.

'I hope I can rely on your complete co-operation tomorrow morning,' Lizzie said as Kemal showed her to the door. 'Whatever the conditions might be where my brother is, I insist on seeing him.'

Kemal maintained a diplomatic silence, knowing Lizzie was in no position to issue commands. She was like a tigress in defence of her cub where her younger brother was concerned, and he could only approve of that. There were certainly qualities to admire in Lizzie Palmer. But Hugo was old enough to make his own decisions. It was time for Lizzie Palmer to let go—in more ways than one.

'First thing tomorrow morning, we will move this matter on,' he promised. He viewed Lizzie's tense features with a very masculine mix of self-interest and desire. The attraction of channelling her fire and honing it in his own direction was keen—and he would only be doing her a service, after all. Someone had to release the pressure building up inside her.

Kemal saw Lizzie's eyes glittering like green ice as she stared back at him. Even when she had every reason to be reassured he could still feel her defiance flying at him. But it only fuelled his appetite. Had her beauty and her bravery derailed his pride? Certainly they made him long for the tussle of words between them to end, and for the combat to begin in earnest.

It would have to be conducted somewhere a lot more comfortable than his study, though, he reflected wryly, and it was still a little soon for the bedroom. She would need maximum reassurance, maximum preparation, maximum foreplay. Any haste on his part would only consign her to a life of repression, of inhibition—and, anyway, it pleased him to make her wait.

'Shall we go somewhere we can relax and talk?' he suggested, when she made to follow Mehmet. 'Now that you are reassured about your brother, the business part of our meeting is concluded.'

'There is no other part to our meeting,' Lizzie pointed out. 'This isn't a social call. I would prefer to be shown to my room.'

'Ah, yes, the dungeon,' Kemal murmured sardonically. 'But may I suggest you take some refreshment before your confinement begins?'

'No, I don't think so,' Lizzie said, heading for the door.

As she reached it, Kemal was forced to lunge forward and snatch her to safety, before it swung open to admit a servant coming to inform him that food was ready to be served in the sunken lounge. Shaking herself free, Lizzie dislodged her spectacles.

'Let me help you—'

'No!'

'I insist.' Taking hold of the delicate gold arms between his lean, tanned fingers, Kemal held them up to the light as if to check for damage. It was just as he had suspected. 'Well, well,' he murmured. 'Why do you hide behind these?'

Lizzie was conscious of the servant still hovering. This was not the moment to make a scene. 'I don't hide behind them,' she said tensely. 'I choose to wear them.' She held out a stiff hand for their return and after a moment Kemal gave them to her.

But she didn't need to wear them, he thought, puzzling over the spectacles as Lizzie put them back on. Both lenses were clear glass. The clues were piling up. She couldn't leave now until he had solved every one of them.

'We will eat in the sunken lounge,' he said, refusing her the chance to object.

'I'm really not hungry,' Lizzie said, reddening with embarrassment when her stomach growled in disagreement.

'Well, I am going to eat,' Kemal informed her. 'You may do as you please.'

She couldn't remain in his study alone, Lizzie realised as the servant silently pivoted on his heels and left them.

Kemal stood back to let her pass, and then led the

way into another sumptuous room. A richly padded seating area was sunk into a floor of snowy white travertine marble, and torches in high brackets on the walls cast a discreet light over the intimate space. The servants had arranged the food on a long, low table set between two plump banks of cushions.

It was a set for seduction, not a business meeting, Lizzie decided, holding back. But it did look incredibly comfortable—and she *was* incredibly hungry.

It was also incredibly decadent, she discovered, struggling to keep her pencil skirt below her knees as she sat down. Kemal had no trouble adapting his powerful frame to the exotic relaxation area. Where he was concerned East and West were one and the same, Lizzie realised as he shrugged off his jacket. Loosening his tie, he tossed that aside too, and a tremor tiptoed down her spine when she suddenly realised that they were quite alone. There wasn't a sound now, other than water splashing rhythmically over tiles somewhere far in the distance.

'Relax,' he said, mind-reading again. Stretching powerful arms along the back of his bank of cushions, he viewed her with amusement. 'Or I promise you will get indigestion when you start to eat. *Borek*?'

Lizzie stared at him. It was hard to believe this was the same man who had ordered the detention of her brother and his co-workers. But then it was a struggle to impose clear thinking of any sort on a mind churning with such unexpected thoughts. She should never have agreed to move into such sultry surroundings, Lizzie realised, checking her skirt. At least in his study there had been the huge expanse of mahogany desk separating them. Here, on silken cushions, their knees were almost touching.

Kemal's gaze was disconcertingly direct as he gestured towards a platter loaded with crisp golden pastries. 'I think you will find *borek* quite delicious...'

His eyes never left hers for a moment, and Lizzie felt a treacherous heat start to invade her veins as he continued to explain the food to her. His low, gravelly voice seemed to be telling her something very different from the ingredients he was listing.

'Or perhaps you would care for a ripe plum?' he suggested finally, in a matter-of-fact tone.

The change in his voice was as good as an alarm bell. It was as if she had been in an erotic trance—a trance into which he had placed her, Lizzie realised, recovering herself fast. 'The food does look delicious,' she admitted coolly, 'but there are other things to talk about. I'm really not interested in taking a culinary safari,' she added in a tone of mild apology, 'but thank you all the same.'

'Then perhaps you won't mind if I do,' Kemal said, refusing to be put off. And, taking his time to select the plumpest fig, he used a small pearl-handled knife to skilfully expose the moist fruit.

Lizzie found she could not look away as he devoured the succulent flesh. His lips, his tongue, the nip of his teeth—the very thorough way in which he went about the task—made the breath catch in her throat.

She shifted position awkwardly on the unusual seating, hoping Kemal's mind-reading skills were taking a break. He had the ability to make her long for pleasure, for self-indulgence, to be the fruit beneath his mouth, the object of his very thorough attention. And there was nothing more dangerous to her cause than that, Lizzie thought, looking at him. Not unless she turned the tables on him…

The idea of seducing *The Sultan*, bending him to her will, played in Lizzie's mind for a moment, until reason won through and she looked away, knowing she had neither the inclination to allow fantasy into her life, nor the talent for putting her wandering thoughts into practice.

'You must excuse me for being so greedy,' Kemal murmured, 'but when the fruit is sweet and full of juice it requires my fullest attention.'

Lizzie's stomach lurched. There was something very dangerous in his eyes. She looked away quickly, feeling her cheeks burn. It was such a human look, rather than the cold and very calculating expression she had come to expect. But even when she looked away the image of Kemal—his lips, his tongue working rhythmically and so very thoroughly on the fruit—took root in her mind and refused to go away.

Kemal watched the transition in Lizzie as she sank a little deeper into the cushions, and he allowed the moment to hang long enough for her full lips to part and her small pink tongue to sneak out to moisten them. Then, reaching for another plump fig, he said, 'Would you like me to prepare this one for you?'

'Thank you—'

'And feed you?'

Lizzie realised some minutes must have passed while she was in a daze. Now he was holding out a plate of prepared fruit. 'That won't be necessary, thank you,' she assured him quickly.

But Kemal brought a piece up to her mouth before she could stop him, and, brushing the warm sweet flesh against the full swell of her bottom lip, he murmured, 'Open wide.'

Lizzie's gaze slid away from the disturbing look in his eyes to the even more worrying strength in his hands. She noticed that he had unbuttoned his cuffs and rolled his shirtsleeves back to reveal powerful forearms shaded with dark hair. There was hard muscle and sinew showing clearly beneath the tanned flesh, and he was so close she could feel his body warmth reaching out to envelop her. Sandalwood invaded her senses and his warm minty breath mingled with her own.

'I'm really not hungry,' she said faintly.

'Of course you are,' Kemal insisted, placing the fruit between her lips. 'And anyway, you don't have to be hungry to enjoy this.'

Well, that was true at least, Lizzie thought, closing her eyes as she drew the fruit slowly into her mouth.

It pleased Kemal to see the faint flush on Lizzie's cheeks, and to hear the raised pitch of her breathing. Her full lips parted again when she had swallowed, as if she was waiting for him to fill them once more. Obliging her, he watched as she tested the next piece of fruit delicately with her tongue. He hardened instantly, and when she drew the firm flesh into her mouth he almost groaned out loud.

Now they were both slaves to erotic thoughts, he mused as his senses soared to a new level. 'This fruit is so ripe,' he murmured, feeding Lizzie another mouthful, 'it is practically begging to be eaten.'

Another sharp intake of breath mingled with his words, and when their fingers brushed, trying to dab at some escaping juice on her lips, their eyes met too.

It was enough for now, Kemal brooded with satisfaction. She was firmly secured upon his erotic hook, and very soon he would reel her in.

'My brother—'

As she spoke she frowned and drew away. She was so sensitive to his thoughts, to his slightest change in mood—he would have to be more careful in future, Kemal realised at Lizzie's soft and unexpected exclamation. She was a far more complex creature than he could ever have imagined, more intriguing than he could ever have wished. He liked it that way.

Lizzie forced herself back into an upright position on the cushions, and, seizing a large linen napkin, wiped every trace of juice from her lips. 'Do you give me your word that Hugo is all right?' she said, fixing a determined expression back on her face. She would not be led astray, or distracted from the only reason she found herself in this position.

'I have given you my word,' Kemal said, straightening up too.

'When can I see him? Tomorrow?'

'Before Christmas.'

Christmas... Christmas... Lizzie swallowed hard,
determined that nothing she was feeling inside would
show. But as she watched Kemal fastidiously clean
each one of his strong, tanned fingers on a square of
linen, she knew, just from the slight emphasis he put
on the word, that he had already begun to understand the power that even the mention of Christmas
allowed him to wield over her. It was as if he could
see where others had been blind, and his intuition
frightened her more than anything else. The ugliness
in her past was not for public view.

The shadow flitted across her face so fleetingly
Kemal might have missed it had he not been watching for precisely that reaction. It confirmed all his
suspicions about Lizzie Palmer, and supplied a
framework into which he could place the pieces of
the jigsaw. When the puzzle was completed he would
know all there was to know about her. Already he
knew that Christmas was the source of some deep-
rooted pain. But there was more.

'Shouldn't you ring your parents to let them know
where you are?'

Up to that point it had been just a game for him.
But instantly Kemal regretted his graceless probe.
From the look on her face he might have hit her.

'They're dead,' she said flatly.

The light that had burned so brightly in her eyes
was completely extinguished, he noticed. 'I'm sorry,'
he said after a while.

'Don't be,' Lizzie said. And the way she compressed her lips warned him not to push her any harder. 'If all the holiday flights are full, how will the men get home?' she asked.

For a moment Kemal was surprised by Lizzie's change of tack, her swift recovery. 'That's my problem,' he said. 'Once everything is resolved to my complete satisfaction we will talk about the men.'

'But I'm here. Why can't they go now? Shouldn't you at least be trying to book their flights?'

Irritation rose inside him. No one pressed him. *Ever.*

Maybe it was time. Maybe it might be more fun this way. Maybe he should try it for a change…

A shiver ran down Lizzie's spine as she tried to gauge Kemal's reaction. His eyes were so changeable—one moment silver-grey, and hard like steel, the next dark and unreadable. The sooner Hugo could get back home, the sooner he could stir up a hornets' nest of lawyers to get her out of this mess. She had to have some sort of goal to work towards. Or did he mean to keep them all as hostages? Had her offer been in vain?

'I must have something to work towards,' she said. 'The least you owe me is a proper answer.'

'I owe you nothing,' Kemal said, his gaze sharpening as he looked at her. 'I accepted your offer, freely made. You will stay here. Your brother and the other men will return home when I say.'

Tension between them was suddenly snapping again, like an electric current along a wire, and there was an edge to Kemal's voice Lizzie hadn't heard before. There was something primal and fierce at work, and it should have warned her off. But instead it only redoubled her determination.

'Sit down. We haven't finished,' she said sharply when he moved to get up.

Kemal froze in position and slowly turned to look at her. For a moment the air hummed with his incredulity. 'Oh, yes, we have,' he told Lizzie in a dangerously soft voice. 'And now I will have someone show you to your room. We will meet again tomorrow, at nine o'clock prompt.'

'Just wait—please—' Lizzie struggled up from the cloying embrace of the soft silk cushions and managed to catch up with Kemal at the door, grabbing his wrist.

Kemal gazed down, noticing how quickly she snatched her hand away from his naked arm. They were an explosive combination. There was nothing about her he would not find out at a time of his own choosing. 'Yes?' he said.

'Where am I to sleep?' Lizzie asked.

'Didn't I tell you?' Kemal said.

'No, you did not,' Lizzie informed him. 'Other than to assure me that it would be in a wing well away from you.'

'And so it shall be,' he assured her.

'So where—where, exactly?' Lizzie pressed.

'Don't concern yourself,' he said. 'I'm quite certain you will be delighted with your suite of rooms.'

'Which is where?' Lizzie asked, glancing around at a number of archways leading to different areas of the palace.

Kemal took a moment, and she didn't like the look on his face one bit.

'In the harem,' he said at last.

'You're asking me to sleep in your harem?' Lizzie demanded, her heart pounding with indignation.

Leaning back against the door, Kemal folded his arms and granted her a long, considering look. 'Don't flatter yourself, Ms Palmer,' he said.

CHAPTER FIVE

DAZED and exhausted, Lizzie woke with a start, disorientated by her nightmare, her surroundings, but most of all by her confused memories of the previous evening's events. Staring blearily at an ornate clock on the marble mantelpiece, she felt as if a bucket of cold water had just been dashed in her face. She was more than an hour late for her nine o'clock meeting with Kemal!

After showering briskly, she dragged on her clothes and raced out of the room. She ran down endless corridors and across acres of marble floor, only slowing when she saw some servants looking at her curiously. Emerging through the archway that led from the sumptuous quarters where she was being housed into the main hall, she stopped dead. Kemal, dressed in full business uniform, was waiting for her outside the door to his study.

He dipped his head in greeting. 'I trust you slept well?'

'Very well, thank you,' Lizzie lied. 'I'm sorry I'm late—'

'I'm also sorry you are late—because you're too late,' Kemal murmured, snatching a look at his wristwatch. 'I have another meeting.'

'Another meeting?' Lizzie echoed. 'But I thought I was seeing my brother this morning.'

'Unfortunately that will not be possible.'

'Not possible!' Firming her mouth, Lizzie blazed a stare up at Kemal. 'So your word means nothing?'

'I do not recall giving you my word that you would see your brother. I merely said we would meet again at nine o'clock. Had you arrived on time—'

'How can I believe anything you say? How do I know you will allow Hugo and the men to go now I am here in their place?' Lizzie demanded angrily, watching with annoyance as Kemal checked his watch a second time.

'You have my word,' he said coolly. 'Had you arrived at nine, as we arranged, I could have given you about fifteen minutes of my time—'

'Fifteen minutes? You could have spared me as long as that?'

This made a change from the cool, prim professional who had turned up on his doorstep the day before, Kemal reflected. He should have known when she lurched out of the taxi-cab that there was a wildcat inside Lizzie Palmer, just waiting to be set free. 'Why, Lizzie,' he said, 'I do believe you're angry.'

'Damn right I'm angry! You rant about honour—now I see how much honour really means to you—'

She broke off abruptly when, seizing her arm, Kemal

brought their faces very close. 'Don't push me too far, Lizzie—unless you're ready to take the consequences.'

'Then explain yourself. If you can—which I doubt.'

Kemal lifted his hands away while Lizzie was still reeling from the close contact.

'Very well,' he agreed. 'I will tell you this much. There has been a complication I could not have foreseen—'

'Hugo's all right?' Lizzie said quickly.

'Your brother is well. I'm afraid the weather is causing problems. All flights to and from Ankara have been cancelled.'

'Ankara?' Lizzie said anxiously. 'Is that where he is?'

A muscle flexed in Kemal's jaw. He didn't have the heart to deny her the truth. 'Yes, Hugo's there—with the other men.'

'But you said I could see him. Is it far?'

'Conditions are forecast to improve tomorrow—'

'Tomorrow?' Lizzie exclaimed. 'But that's Thursday. Christmas Day is on Saturday!'

'I had not forgotten,' Kemal said more gently, hearing the rising note of panic in her voice.

'Hugo will be so worried,' Lizzie murmured distractedly. 'He knew I was coming to Turkey to sort this out—'

'Hugo is a grown man,' Kemal intervened. 'He understands the position.'

'How can he?' Lizzie said. 'When he doesn't even know where I am?'

'He knows.'

'You've been in contact with him?' Lizzie's mouth firmed into an angry line. She could see the truth in Kemal's eyes. 'Why didn't you let me speak to him? No—' She held out her hands as if to ward him off. 'Don't. I don't want to hear it. Just get him out of there. The sooner he leaves the country, the sooner I can follow him.'

'We will share the same relief when that happens,' Kemal assured her. 'And now, if you will excuse me—'

'That's it?'

'Should there be something more?'

'There's a little matter of my liberty, and when you think I'm likely to be free. Let me remind you, I am not on holiday. And I haven't come all the way to Istanbul to be fobbed off with five minutes of your time!'

'Ten,' Kemal murmured, checking his watch. 'And your time's up.'

Lizzie's lips parted with sheer disbelief. 'But what am I supposed to do all day?' she said at last.

'I have no idea,' Kemal said with a shrug.

Lizzie gasped as he took hold of her upper arms and firmly moved her to one side.

'But please don't get in the way of the servants,' he said.

Flinging all the papers she had gathered for their meeting down on a chair in her bedroom, Lizzie tugged her jacket off and tossed it after them. She might have spent the night in his harem, but if Kemal

Volkan thought she was a suitable candidate for assertiveness reversal therapy he was sadly mistaken! And if he thought she was going to sit around all day, doing nothing to secure her freedom, he was wrong about that too.

She still had one card up her sleeve, Lizzie remembered—Sami Gulsan, the local lawyer. And this was the perfect moment to call him. Going to her briefcase, Lizzie retrieved his card and her mobile phone.

Keying in the number, Lizzie was disappointed to be put through to the lawyer's voicemail. But, with time running out if she was to get the men home before Christmas, anything was better than nothing, she reasoned. She explained the position in which she found herself, and the outrageous manner in which her brother and his colleagues were still being held in Turkey against their will, and then for good measure added her suspicions that Kemal could not be trusted to let the men go, even though she had offered to stay in their place.

When she cut the line, Lizzie felt that at least she had done something positive. But until she heard from the lawyer, or Kemal came back and she could talk to him, she was powerless to move things on.

Wondering how she was going to pass the day, Lizzie's glance fastened on a collection of small brass ornaments displayed on a low table. As she picked one up, it was as if the cause for her late arrival at the meeting with Kemal became suddenly obvious. Running her fingertip over the pierced brass surface, Lizzie remembered all too clearly the nightmare that had kept her tossing and turning all night.

There had been many similar ornaments at home when she was little. Of course her parents' drug-warped attempts to recreate the mystical East had been a sham, whereas everything here in Kemal's palace was an expensive original, but the two worlds had become hopelessly entangled as she slept. The incense and the curios from her childhood had been a stage set for a tragedy, and they could never be compared to the beautiful works of art and fragrances with which Kemal Volkan filled his home. But the Eastern ambience, the ever-present scent of sandalwood and spice had trespassed on her dreams, transporting her to a different time. That was why she had suffered one of her worst nightmares for years—and why she had been late for the crucial meeting. She could never allow it to happen again.

Walking slowly around the perimeter of the room, Lizzie made a point of handling and examining everything she believed might have stirred her memories. On close inspection she realised that nothing bore the slightest resemblance to the cheap imitations that had littered the squat where she had been raised.

Satisfied that she had laid the ghosts to rest, her thoughts veered off again in the direction of all the other women who must have waited here for their sultan to return. Had their future been any more secure than her own? Had they been happy to wait in the harem? Or had they felt as she did—trapped and uncertain—birds in a gilded cage? How had they prepared themselves for the moment when the gilded doors opened and they were summoned into the Sultan's presence?

Wandering over to the window, where sunlight filtered in through magnificent stained glass panes, Lizzie opened it and peered out. The courtyard was deserted. She was quite alone. Or was she? She turned back to face the room. How many spyholes existed in these richly decorated walls? How many places where a discreet listener could press an ear? This was the harem—after all, a place of intrigue and voluptuous secrets.

Hugging herself, Lizzie stared properly at the scenes depicted on the wall hangings, and then up at the fabulously painted ceiling arching high above her head. The illustrations on the hangings showed scenes of a gentle and romantic nature, but the paintings on the ceiling were quite different. They were unashamedly erotic. Her pulse began to race as she guessed at their purpose, and the position from which they might best be viewed. And then her mouth firmed angrily at the thought that Kemal must have found it infinitely amusing to house her in the harem.

But a quiver of excitement took hold when she gazed at the silk-draped bed. It had been eighteen months since her last relationship—eighteen long months of celibacy. And she couldn't help wondering how long it might take to view every one of the highly descriptive scenes on the ceiling properly. Dragging her gaze away, she surveyed the plump cushions arranged in shady mirrored alcoves furnished with low tables bearing dishes of fresh fruit. Everything in the harem was designed to delight and seduce the senses. But she would not succumb by so much as a single grape, Lizzie decided, turning away.

Kemal had mentioned a pool, and a spa. Perhaps it was time to make the most of her stay in this gilded cage…

Lizzie made a sound of impatience, remembering she had no casual clothes—they were all at the hotel—then a knock on the door made her start.

It was so timely she should have been pleased, but Lizzie felt a chill run through her as a manservant entered carrying her suitcase. Kemal had clearly given instructions that her belongings were to be removed from the Hotel Turkoman.

'Who told you to bring my things here?' she asked, but the man only bowed low and then left the room as quietly as he had arrived.

'Oh, no— I didn't order anything,' she said, when a maid entered next, with a number of exclusive-looking carrier bags. But she might not have been there at all, Lizzie realised with exasperation, for all the heed the woman paid to her. The maid deposited the bags in a neat line beside the bed, and then walked away from her on silent feet across the cool marble floor.

Lizzie's heart stalled when she saw what she was about to do next. 'No!' she cried out, and raced across the room. But the wicks on the scented candles were already burning strongly. And now the maid was moving on to light a large incense burner.

'No. No! Please—don't!' Lizzie fought to keep her voice steady, but the sweet and pervasive scent was already curling around her nostrils, stealing away every bit of breathable air...

Kemal had always believed it was gut instinct that had brought him success. And it was gut instinct that had made him cancel his meeting and brought him back to the palace. Now he knew why, he realised as he strode across the room. One look at Lizzie was enough to tell him he had been absolutely right to return.

'Leave us,' he commanded the serving woman, his focus never wavering from Lizzie's face. Quickly extinguishing the flame of the incense burner between his thumb and forefinger, he removed it to a window ledge far away from her, beneath an open window. Then, returning to Lizzie, he dragged her into his arms just before she hit the floor.

Lizzie could hardly understand what was happening. She was having trouble breathing. She was confused, bewildered, knew only that for some reason Kemal was holding her up, and that she should push him away. For a moment something new took over, and she felt safe...protected. But that was dangerous. It was a false impression, Lizzie realised, pulling back.

'I don't know what came over me,' she said with a half-laugh, trying to make light of what had happened. But her voice sounded brittle even in her own ears and she could see he wasn't convinced. 'I have always been sensitive to perfume,' she added. 'I have a rather highly developed sense of smell.' She gave another short, dismissive laugh.

'And a highly developed aversion to incense?' Kemal commented lightly.

It gave him no pleasure to see Lizzie hugging herself now, in an instinctive gesture of defence. And a report from one of his servants was still playing on his mind. Mehmet had heard her crying out in the night. Nightmares, he'd thought. That would explain why Lizzie had missed their meeting, and it also explained why he had felt compelled to turn the car around today. Could he possibly be developing a conscience? Kemal wondered dryly. Or had feelings more physical than cerebral brought him racing back to Lizzie's side?

'Would you feel happier in another suite?' he suggested, looking around. 'I have more modern accommodation than this available if you would prefer?'

'This is absolutely fine,' Lizzie assured him, still regretting the fact that she had shown her Achilles' heel to him. 'As prisons go, this is definitely at the better end of the market.'

'Prison?' Kemal murmured, cocking his head as he stared at her.

Meeting Lizzie's gaze, he tried to read her thoughts, but a veil had come down over her extraordinary eyes and it was beyond him. At least she was calm again. He was careful not to show his amusement when she settled the most important part of her armoury back on her nose. Instead, he took the couple of steps necessary to reach her and take them off.

'Why are you still hiding behind these?' he said. 'Why don't I just lose them somewhere?'

Lizzie took them out of his hands again and gave him a look as she put them back on. 'Maybe I like wearing them. What's wrong with that?'

'Or maybe you're frightened of something, or someone, and like hiding behind them,' Kemal suggested softly.

'I am certainly not frightened of you,' Lizzie assured him without breaking her stare. 'You are bigger than me physically, and that is all.'

Kemal's eyes flared with passion. Her defiance amused him, and it aroused him too. No one had ever defied him as she did; they were always too frightened of overstepping the mark, of losing his interest. But Lizzie Palmer was different. She was a woman of fierce contradictions—vulnerable, combative, contained—and passionate? Yes, passionate. He was sure of it. Even though she was staring at him now in that cool and very English way. But one day those fires burning beneath her frosty exterior might just erupt. And he would be there when they did.

Her skin was so fine and pale it was almost translucent, but there was a blush about her cheeks that betrayed a matching interest in him, whether she cared to admit it or not. Just a few minutes ago, when she had been at her lowest ebb, vulnerable, weak and exposed, he could never have touched her, but now...

Lizzie's heart refused to stop racing as she stared up at Kemal. She struggled to ignore the excitement building inside her, and fought hard to dismiss the way her flesh sang where his arms had briefly held her. She could not banish the memory of his drugging warmth, his clean, masculine scent. But at the same time she knew that finding sanctuary and a kind of peace in his embrace would be a huge mistake—fool's gold.

She made a little sound of surprise and refusal deep in her throat when he reached out to take hold of her.

'Yes,' Kemal insisted. And his voice was so soft, so caressing, that just for a moment Lizzie knew he was going to kiss her. 'Are you all right now?' he asked instead, dipping his head to stare straight into her eyes.

'Fine,' Lizzie said, trying not to show how disappointed she was.

'You will find some leisure clothes in those carrier bags. Dress for lunch out. I am going to change, and then we will relax.'

She looked at him.

'Don't pretend surprise,' he said practically. 'You surely don't mean to live in that one black suit for the whole time you are here?'

'I meant to go back to the hotel and change,' she said, tensing again as she remembered the arrival of her luggage.

'You wanted to talk,' Kemal reminded Lizzie. 'So I have cleared my diary for you.'

Lizzie's hand flew to her face as in one deft move he removed her glasses.

'And you won't be needing these,' he said, placing them in the breast pocket of his jacket. 'There will be nothing between us now, Lizzie, but the truth.'

CHAPTER SIX

REMOVING the beautiful designer clothes from the stiff, expensive-looking carrier bags was heaven. Lizzie never indulged herself, and certainly never accepted gifts from someone like Kemal, who was practically a stranger. But these were different— these she would pay for.

Soon the circular fur rug where she was sitting was completely covered in tissue paper and clothes. Everything had been carefully packed, and the rainbow-hued packages neatly sealed with a label from each exclusive store. Her heart was thundering with excitement at each new discovery, and she flushed red as she held up a set of cobweb-fine underwear in delicate flesh tones. She had seen something very similar in England, but it had been so expensive she had just smiled and walked on. But she wasn't about to resist temptation now, and she put them to one side with the other clothes she had chosen to wear that day.

Kemal hadn't meant to stand and watch, but found

it impossible to resist. As Lizzie had suspected, the harem had many secret places from where the occupants might be discreetly observed. He had slept badly the previous night, disturbed by the fact that she was sleeping so close by. He had also felt some guilt, knowing he had exploited her anxieties as well as her loyalty to her brother by accepting the audacious offer she had made to take his place.

This was a unique situation, he had reflected. There were no rules dictating how he should or shouldn't behave. He was far from sure how he wanted it to end with Lizzie—or if he wanted it to end at all yet. Whatever the final outcome between them, instinct had told him he must soften the situation quickly—hence the glamorous clothes he had ordered for her. Her lack of luggage had provided him with the perfect excuse.

But he shouldn't be hanging around here. He had pressing commitments, little time to spare for Lizzie Palmer, however beautiful she might be...but he was interested to see how she would look dressed in something other than formal business attire.

Kemal's eyes hardened as he watched her obvious glee and remembered how easily some women could be bought. He had thought Lizzie Palmer was different. But no matter—he had no thought of creating a permanent space for her in his life, and no inclination to sort out her problems. He pulled back from the fretwork screen as Lizzie stood up. She had an armful of things and was heading for the bathroom. Her modesty touched him. Briefly. She was lodged in the harem for one reason only as far as he was concerned—and modesty wasn't part of his plan.

'I trust everything is to your liking?' he said coolly when Lizzie finally emerged from her suite and crossed the hall towards him.

She looked fabulous. And it was hardly surprising. Her natural beauty needed little adornment, so his instructions to the personal shopper had specified elegant simplicity rather than a selection of blatantly fashionable clothes. The slim-fitting navy trousers, Gucci loafers and tan leather blouson suited her to perfection. The jacket had felt like silk beneath his hands when it had been brought for him to approve. He liked everything to feel good—just like Lizzie, he mused as she walked up to him.

He noticed she was wearing hardly any make-up—something else he approved of—and her thick, glossy blonde hair was secured on top of her head with a couple of the tortoiseshell pins he had ordered with her long hair in mind. One quick movement and the whole shimmering cape would cascade down around her shoulders—but that was for later.

'It's all very nice. Thank you,' she said politely.

Kemal's cynical thoughts were confirmed—even Lizzie Palmer could be bought with a few trifles.

But, breaking into his thoughts, she added, 'Naturally I will pay you back for everything.'

'Of course,' he agreed dryly. 'Whenever you are ready.'

However he tried to harden his heart against Lizzie Palmer, she managed to surprise him, Kemal acknowledged. He didn't know if that was a good thing or not—he only knew that he wanted her in the most pleasurable way.

'A quick lunch, and then we discuss the detail of my departure to take the place of the men?' she was saying optimistically.

She was nervous. He guessed she was untutored—not vulnerable, as he had first supposed—and that made anything possible. He would soon teach her to relax, in a way he hoped she would find dangerously addictive. There was a vacancy on his staff for a short-term mistress, and Lizzie Palmer satisfied his list of requirements perfectly.

'A relaxed, informal lunch,' he corrected her, 'and then we talk.' On his terms, as always, Kemal determined, amused to think that Lizzie might imagine it could be any other way.

Lizzie stared at Kemal. Freedom for Hugo and herself meant she must comply with his every wish. But he was trying to make it easier for her, and this wasn't so hard, she conceded as she linked her arm through his.

Catching sight of them in one of the huge gilt-framed mirrors, she was stunned to see what a striking couple they made. It hardly seemed possible—or even likely. Kemal was so glamorous, in a hard-driven, masculine way, and she had never considered herself particularly attractive. The glamorous clothes certainly helped, but she couldn't help suspecting he had dressed her for a part, and began to wonder exactly what role he expected her to play.

'I've changed my mind,' Lizzie said at the door. 'I'd rather eat here—something quick and simple— and then we can talk while we eat—like we did last night,' she pointed out hopefully. 'Look,' she said, when she saw Kemal's expression harden, 'why don't you arrange for a phone and an Internet connection in my room? Then I can help you to track down the parts for your machinery before I leave—'

'Please leave business matters to me,' he said. 'I need you to help me with something else.'

'Oh?' Lizzie said, surprised. 'What's that?'

'Christmas shopping.'

'Christmas shopping?' She frowned. It seemed so out of context. 'Can't that wait?'

'I'm afraid not,' Kemal said. 'As you are always reminding me, Lizzie, time is running out where Christmas is concerned.'

'But surely you have people to do that for you?'

'This is different,' Kemal said. 'This is something special. I had hoped you might help me.'

Tit for tat? A shopping expedition in exchange for her speedy departure to take Hugo's place? She couldn't refuse, Lizzie realised.

'I have to buy presents for my nieces. And I never know what to buy,' Kemal said impatiently, while she was still deliberating whether or not to agree to his request.

Lizzie studied his face. He certainly looked con- vincing enough. Perhaps this was an opportunity to rebalance their relationship. 'All right,' she agreed. 'But only on condition that the moment we get back you help me with this exchange so Hugo and the other men can go home.'

'That seems fair enough,' he agreed. 'And if it makes it any easier for you, let's say that you are helping me out in return for your bed and board.'

'One night's bed and board,' Lizzie reminded him, only to have Kemal shrug and give her another inscrutable look.

'Surely you don't have a problem with such a simple request?' he said.

'No, of course not,' Lizzie said.

If they only knew it, Kemal's nieces were in for the best Christmas they'd ever had!

'I want you to consider my three nieces very carefully,' Kemal said as they halted first outside an exclusive clothes store.

Everything in the window was displayed beautifully beneath carefully angled lighting, with spotlights picking out the choicest pieces in each range, and Lizzie was dazzled by the array of handbags, costume jewellery, gloves and silk scarves. The colour scheme was a stylish mix of winter white and tan, with highlights of a soft chalky red, and her eyes widened when she recognised a tan jacket that looked very similar to her own. It would take her an age to pay Kemal back for that item alone, she realised with concern.

'My first niece, Anya,' Kemal said, reclaiming her attention, 'does not indulge herself as I believe she should. I've seen her looking in this window, and judging by her face we're sure to find something just right for her here.'

'These had better really be your nieces,' Lizzie said, as a pang of suspicion caught her unawares.

'Why, Ms Palmer,' Kemal retorted mildly, 'what sort of man do you take me for?'

'I wouldn't like to say,' Lizzie admitted truthfully, walking past him into the shop.

Kemal didn't bat an eyelid as the sales assistant, under Lizzie's direction, wrapped up the most expensive handbag, gloves and silk scarf in the shop.

'My second niece—'

'Her name?' Lizzie prompted as they walked further down the fashionable shopping arcade.

'Kerola.'

'Tell me something about her, so I can get a picture of her in my mind,' Lizzie suggested.

'Feminine, and rather studious. She likes to read, and I guess she likes to write long letters to her friends.'

'You guess?'

'She's the type,' he said with a shrug.

Kerola didn't sound like mistress material Lizzie concluded, reassured. And now it was her turn to lead the way into a small, wood-panelled shop she'd spotted, specialising in writing materials. Picking out a beautiful fountain pen in sapphire blue lacquer, she held it up to the light admiringly. There was a gem inset at the top of the cap, and the nib was pure gold. She tested it thoughtfully between her fingers, before trying out a few words on a clean vellum sheet presented to her by the sales assistant.

'Do you like it?' Kemal asked.

'It is perfectly balanced, and quite beautiful,' Lizzie said. And very, very expensive, she thought. Apart from wreaking a very female type of vengeance on her tormentor, she couldn't help but smile when she imagined the look of pleasure on Kerola's face when she opened this package on Christmas morning.

'We'll take it,' Kemal told the shop assistant. Turning to Lizzie, he added, 'Don't you think Kerola would like this five-year diary too? She could confide all her secrets inside and then lock them away.'

Lizzie had to move very close to peer over Kemal's shoulder as he stared into a glass display cabinet, and it was a struggle to concentrate when she was inhaling the by now familiar scent of sandalwood and clean, warm man. She saw that the diary was covered in fuchsia suede, and there was a tiny gold lock complete with miniature key. 'Perfect,' she agreed.

'I was hoping you would think so,' Kemal murmured, turning his face up to look at her.

Their faces were very close now, and as he smiled Lizzie's heart lurched.

'Only one more niece to go,' he announced, straightening up abruptly. 'And then lunch,' he added, offering Lizzie his arm.

Lizzie hesitated a beat, but then linked her arm through his. It was better for everyone if they stayed on friendly terms.

As they walked along her mind strayed back to the sight of him, his arms locked around the sides of the display cabinet in the shop. The wide spread of his shoulders, and the waves of thick, glossy black hair licking over the collar of his casual jacket. There was so much strength contained in his hands it was almost impossible to believe how gentle he could be. But she had seen him peel a fig with the utmost delicacy, and the careful way in which he had handled each of the precious items they had bought reflected a very different side to Kemal's character from the tyrant she had imagined him to be. He was a powerful man, but he was a connoisseur too.

These were very dangerous thoughts, Lizzie reminded herself. 'Don't bother with lunch,' she said suddenly, determined to keep her thoughts under control. 'We still have to find a gift for your third niece, and we have to talk—'

'I'm sure we can find time to do both and have lunch,' Kemal told her calmly.

There was nothing for it, she would just have to curb her impatience, Lizzie realised. 'So, what do you think we should be looking for?'

'Jewellery.'

'Real jewellery?'

'Is there any other kind?'

Seeing the quality of the jewellers in the arcade down which they were strolling, Lizzie became suspicious. This gift was surely for someone other than a niece. But if it was, why should she care? She would be just as objective about selecting this Christmas present as she had been with all the others.

But then Kemal said unexpectedly, 'Do your best. She's been having a really hard time.'

Lizzie looked at him in surprise as they stopped in front of another exclusive store. She would leave her cynical self outside the shop, she vowed, and try her best to choose something special.

Lizzie knew the moment they walked in that this was the hushed and reverent showroom of a serious gem dealer. She felt anxious suddenly. She knew nothing about good jewellery. 'At least tell me your niece's name,' she said while they were being escorted to a discreet booth to view the gems. 'I need help here.'

'You don't need help,' Kemal assured her. 'Just go with your gut instinct.'

'That's quite a responsibility,' Lizzie murmured.

'I'm sure you're up to it,' Kemal countered, turning away from her to speak to the assistant. 'Aquamarine?' he suggested. 'Something special, unique—a necklace, perhaps?'

'Certainly, sir.' Excusing himself, the man hurried away.

'You're very generous,' Lizzie said.

'I can be.'

Lizzie was relieved when the jeweller returned. For a few moments no one spoke. The collection of fabulous gems took her breath away.

'This is our most exclusive range,' the jeweller explained. 'Each item is fashioned by our finest craftsmen, and each piece has its own story to tell.'

'Pick out whatever you like,' Kemal said, turning to Lizzie.

For an instant Lizzie almost envied the young woman who was to receive such a fabulous gift, but then she made herself concentrate on choosing something special, as she had promised to do.

It was like dipping into the most fantastic dressing-up box in the world—there was so much choice—but finally she settled on two pieces upon which she hoped Kemal would make a final decision: a large oval aquamarine ring, set with diamonds, and a fine aquamarine drop hanging from a white gold chain. The drop was particularly pretty, as it hung from a tiny bow studded with brilliant white diamonds.

The jeweller applauded her choice.

'These pieces are from one of my favourite designers,' he said. 'I like the necklace in particular— if you look you can see the drop here represents a tear, and the bow represents the love that prevents that tear from falling.'

'Why, that's beautiful,' Lizzie murmured, entranced by the jeweller's romantic description. Looking in the mirror, she held the necklace up to her neck and sighed.

'It suits you,' Kemal observed dryly. 'I'm quite sure my niece will be very pleased with your choice.'

He was right—it wouldn't do to get too fond of it! Lizzie thought, quickly replacing the beautiful necklace on the velvet tray.

'I'll take it,' Kemal informed the assistant. 'Please have it gift-wrapped and delivered to the palace.'

Bowing, the jeweller escorted them both to the

door. 'It has been a pleasure doing business with you,' he said, including Lizzie in the pleasantry.

'Oh, no—it's nothing to do with me.' Lizzie blushed red.

Her determination to exact a penalty from Kemal had been well and truly scuppered by his incredible generosity, she realised. And now she felt deeply guilty, thinking of the amount of money she had forced him to part with.

'Come along,' Kemal said briskly, apparently unconcerned by the huge sums of money involved, 'or we will be late for lunch.'

Lizzie became so relaxed over lunch she hardly realised she was talking non-stop about her brother.

It had almost taken the edge off his appetite, Kemal thought ruefully, but not quite. 'What would you like to do now?' he said, after calling for the bill.

'Chase those parts you need for your machinery, sort out flights for Hugo and the other men, and get the exchange underway,' Lizzie suggested.

'Quite a shopping list.'

'I'm sorry,' Lizzie said, seeing Kemal's face had darkened. 'But you're right—there is a lot to do, and not much time left.'

Was leaving all she thought about? Kemal wondered. He had thought she was becoming more relaxed—big mistake.

'I would at least like to make a flight reservation for Friday—Christmas Eve—if that's possible,' Lizzie said. 'If I don't make it, so be it.'

'You are not in a position to book your flight yet.'

'Just a reservation,' Lizzie reminded him. 'I can't imagine what I'll do for Christmas if I'm still here.'

He would not allow those wide-set eyes to soften his resolve, Kemal determined, or those tremulous lips to do anything other than his bidding. 'Well, I shall be very busy,' he said crisply. 'Irrespective of Christmas, I have matters that must be attended to. What you choose to do is, of course, entirely your affair.'

'That's if I'm still here…'

Kemal shrugged, and Lizzie could be in no doubt that her options were limited to whatever suited him.

Maybe she could just close her eyes and sleep through the whole thing, Lizzie reflected tensely. She had no intention of weakening now, allowing him to see how badly she needed to be home for Christmas. She had nothing to barter for her freedom. Taking in Kemal's firm, sensuous mouth, with the shading of rough stubble already showing on his jaw, Lizzie knew she had nothing to offer that he could possibly want. Seducing the Sultan and making him give in to her demands might have been easy for some women, but she didn't have a cat in hell's chance—

'The lady's jacket, please,' Kemal demanded, cutting brutally into her thoughts. 'We're leaving now.'

CHAPTER SEVEN

SEATED an arm's length away from Kemal in his sleek black limousine, Lizzie felt as if she had tumbled down Alice's rabbit hole and woken up in someone else's shoes. In a matter of hours it seemed as if her whole life had been transformed. She had been swept up into Kemal's glamorous and very addictive world. His reality was most people's fantasy, and it was dangerously beguiling.

Was this how it felt to be a rich man's mistress? Kemal's mistress? she wondered, and her throat dried as she pictured that bird in the gilded cage, being brought out for the occasional treat—a resource to be dipped into at will. The pun tugged at her lips until she had to smile.

'It's good to see you smile.'

Not if you knew what I was thinking about, Lizzie thought, knowing she would have to be more careful in future. She was going home as soon as she could. She didn't belong here. She didn't belong with Kemal.

But still her pulse speeded up just from stealing a

glance at him. He was staring out of his window, clearly preoccupied with something or someone else, while her thighs were tingling at the thought of possible contact between them—not that that was very likely, unless the limousine picked up speed and swerved around a corner.

She reddened guiltily when Kemal swung around to face her, as if he knew exactly which route her thoughts were taking.

'When we get back, you will join me in the spa.'

'I will?' Lizzie queried, collecting her wits. Half-naked bodies? Cocoon-like warmth? Clouds of hazy steam? No way!

She had to think up with some reason why she couldn't. No, in fact she didn't have to make excuses, Lizzie determined. She would just refuse—

'I bought you swimsuits, didn't I?' Kemal said, in the manner of a man who knew very well that he had. Gym clothes, swimsuits, trainers…the list went on and on. 'Do you have a problem?' Kemal pressed. 'They do fit?' he added dryly.

'Yes,' Lizzie admitted. 'Perfectly.'

OK—truce. She couldn't let Kemal think he could intimidate her to the point where she wouldn't even share a swimming pool with him. What chance would Hugo stand then? And, after pounding the pavements all afternoon, she really did feel like a cooling swim.

'All right,' she said. 'Why not? The spa sounds great.'

What harm could a swim do? She didn't imagine icebergs were his type.

* * *

Kemal's idea of a spa was having the most sumptuous health club imaginable installed at home for his own private use. And when your home was a palace, that allowed for something on rather a splendid scale.

He was waiting for Lizzie at the foot of a wide sweep of marble steps: bare feet, black jogging pants, tight-fitting black vest. *Amazing.* She pretended not to notice.

'We will take a Turkish bath before we enter the pool,' he said, heading off.

'We?' Lizzie demanded coolly, staying exactly where she was. Apart from the fact that she was determined to set the rules here, she needed a moment to deal with the sight of a bronzed male body blatantly made for sin.

'You will see,' Kemal murmured, pausing to look at her, his arm resting on a heavy arched door. 'Well, are you coming?'

Thankful her every erogenous zone was concealed beneath a baggy tracksuit, Lizzie went past him through the arch into a vast, echoing, marble-tiled room.

'The changing rooms are over there,' he said, pointing them out to her. 'And you will need these,' he added, swooping down to pick up what looked like a pair of wooden clogs.

Not exactly what she would have chosen to go with her outfit, but...

'The floor gets slippery with soapsuds,' he warned. 'These *nalin* will keep you safe.'

It would take more than a pair of wooden clogs, Lizzie mused, levelling a cool glance on Kemal's fiercely arrogant face. 'Soapsuds?' she queried evenly.

'Lots of them,' he promised.

She didn't like the look on his face one bit. She felt like a very small mouse that had lost its way in the wolf's den.

'Oh, and by the way,' he added, easing away from the door, 'strip naked, will you?'

'I'll do no such thing,' Lizzie assured him.

'There are plenty of towels in the changing cubicles,' Kemal said, as if she hadn't spoken a word. 'Help yourself to as many as you want.'

He was enjoying her discomfort just a little too much, Lizzie thought as she tilted her chin at a rebellious angle and moved past him towards the changing cabin.

Her heart was pounding nineteen to the dozen when she stepped out again. Every inch of her body was concealed under towels, apart from her head. She had redressed her hair, using the tortoiseshell clips to keep it off her shoulders, and was wearing the wooden clogs as Kemal had advised…but where was he? she wondered, looking around.

'I'm in here.'

She followed the sound of his voice through an archway into another room. Slipping off the clogs, Lizzie looked around. It was a wet room, with a huge hot tub in the centre of the tiled floor. A series of raised platforms ran around the tub like giant steps, and there was a domed ceiling above the water towards which steam was billowing in dense white clouds.

Kemal was already in the tub—and naked, she guessed, certainly from the waist up. If a man could be called beautiful, then he was beautiful. His wet torso gleamed like polished bronze, every muscle perfectly delineated. The wide sweep of his shoulders reminded her of an etching she had seen of naked gladiators, and there was an unconscious grace to his movements as he lazily slicked soapy water across his powerful chest.

'I'm quite happy to join you,' Lizzie said briskly. 'But as a man of honour, I take it you will respect my modesty.'

This *was* novel, Kemal mused, sinking a little lower down into the suds. After a moment of wry consideration he averted his face.

As soon as Kemal turned, Lizzie sprinted up the steps, dropped her towels, climbed in, and sank beneath the bubbles. Quickly lowering the straps of the swimsuit she was prudently wearing, she kept just her face above the foaming water. 'OK,' she announced. 'You can turn around now.'

Kemal's dark slanting stare held just enough humour to make Lizzie feel gauche. Doubtless his more sophisticated female companions would have taken a very different line, perhaps stripping off and parading themselves in front of him. She had neither the confidence nor the inclination. And she was in a unique position—neither companion nor guest; she was merely the bird in his gilded cage.

Hearing Kemal speak in his own language, Lizzie turned to see an older woman who must have come silently into the room. Dressed neatly in a white uniform, she stood discreetly in the shadows, obviously awaiting instruction. Before Lizzie could question Kemal, he relaxed back against the side of the tub, arms widespread, and closed his eyes. The next minute the woman was standing next to Lizzie, and gesturing with a smile that she should climb out.

Lizzie couldn't get out fast enough. Kemal might look harmless enough, with the warm bubbles frothing around him, but his stillness seemed deceptive somehow.

The attendant quickly fashioned a comfortable bed with clean towels on one of the wide lower steps at the base of the hot tub. When she picked up soap and a sponge Lizzie supposed she must lie down, but as she went to position herself the woman gave a cluck of disapproval and a smile, and mimed that she should take off her swimming costume.

Glancing back to the tub, Lizzie realised that Kemal couldn't see, so after a moment's hesitation she did as the woman had suggested.

After the soaping came an abrasive mitt, and finally, when she was glowing like a beacon, the woman walked away to turn on the drench shower, leaving Lizzie gazing at the tantalising stack of fluffy white towels she had left just out of reach.

'Do you intend to lie there all day covered in foam?'

Lizzie tensed as she looked back up at the tub. 'Are you speaking to me?'

'Who else?' Kemal said. 'Well? What are you waiting for?'

Not for you to get your ounce of fun out of me, that's for sure, Lizzie thought as she got to her feet. A naked back view was regrettable, but unavoidable. She held her head high as she stalked across the soap-covered tiles towards the shower.

'*Nalin*,' Kemal reminded her dryly, sweeping her up into his arms moments before she hit the floor.

'Let me go!' Lizzie insisted, struggling to escape.

'Not a chance,' Kemal informed her. 'I guess we'll have to miss the steam bath…'

'Put me down!' Lizzie warned, painfully aware that she was completely naked and in his arms.

'And the massage…' Kemal complained, as if he still hadn't heard her.

'Please!' Lizzie gasped throatily, kicking her legs. Kemal's warm, hard body seemed to be making embarrassing contact with every single part of her.

'Shall I drop you here?' he said.

'No!'

She turned her face away from him, shutting out his mock-innocent expression. Worst of all, he must have registered the tremors scorching through her…and he must know as surely as she did that they had nothing whatever to do with her fall.

'Say please,' Kemal prompted, settling Lizzie more comfortably in his arms, 'and then I might let you go.'

Lizzie's lips compressed as she considered her options. 'Please,' she said at last, grudgingly.

At least he had the good grace to ask if she was all right, she thought mutinously, testing first one foot and then the other on the ground. 'I'm fine,' she said. 'No harm done… Thank you,' she muttered somewhat belatedly, crossing her arms over her chest.

She watched Kemal cock his head to one side, and knew he was trying hard not to smile. The towels were still out of reach. But that didn't stop her making a lunge for them.

'Not so fast!' Kemal said, stopping her. 'Towels are for *after* the shower, not before—didn't you know that?'

Lizzie shook herself free angrily, her skin burning where he had touched her, her temper rising when she saw the laughter in his eyes. Her hands balled into fists, but she dropped them back to her sides again. Wouldn't he love that? A slippery, soapy tussle in the nude? A tussle she couldn't hope to win!

And then she saw that the hunt had sparked fire in his dark gaze, and there was a confident twist to his hard, sensuous mouth. There was no escape route available to her and he knew it. For some crazy reason Lizzie realised she was incredibly aroused. And he knew that too. She made one last desperate attempt to reach for a towel.

But Kemal caught hold of both of her arms and brought her round in front of him. 'Now what are you going to do?' he demanded huskily.

'I would hope you are a gentleman,' Lizzie challenged, staring him straight in the eyes.

'Would you really?' Kemal murmured, as if he didn't believe a word of it. He gave a short, virile laugh, and then there was silence.

Lizzie's breathing sounded loud in her ears. She was intensely conscious of Kemal's naked body, only inches from her own, and then he reached up, freeing the tortoiseshell clips from her hair so that it tumbled around her shoulders like a shimmering golden cape.

'Beautiful,' he murmured, sifting it through his fingers.

As Lizzie opened her mouth to protest he kissed her hard on the lips.

The shock made her sway towards him, and before she could pull away he tightened his grip. And then she stayed because she wanted to—because she had to. The kiss was long and perfect, the sensation streaming through her intense. He could kiss away her heart, kiss away her soul—but what to do about it? How to hold back? How to distance herself from him? She had no answers, only wordless sounds that spoke of need and pleasure until finally, responding to her wishes, Kemal deepened the kiss.

At last he broke away, leaving her breathless. 'Shower,' he suggested.

'Good,' Lizzie blurted half with relief, thinking it a sign that the kiss was out of his system.

'Excellent,' Kemal murmured. 'Because now I want to wash every part of you, taste every inch of you.'

A small cry leapt from Lizzie's throat as her veins were infused with sensation. It was as if every nerve-ending was naked and exposed, awaiting Kemal's attention. And then, cupping the back of her head in one hand and using the other to drag her close, he kissed her again.

Kemal tested the stream of water and made sure that it was warm before allowing Lizzie to stand beneath it. Then he joined her, throwing his head back so that the whole of his beautiful body was exposed for her enjoyment.

And now she did look, her gaze lingering on every perfect inch of him: the long powerful column of his neck, the hard chest tanned to the shade of nutmeg, the shading of black hair that narrowed to a vee as it tracked down below his waist. She quickly looked up again and slicked back her hair self-consciously, and as she did so she became aware of the effect her innocent action was having on Kemal: her breasts were fully exposed for his perusal, the pert nipples taut and outthrust, damp pink peaks, provoking him, tempting him—

She jumped when he hit the switch that turned off the shower.

'I'm taking you to bed.'

'Just like that? No, *Please may I?* Or, *How do you feel about it?*'

'I know how you feel about it,' he assured her.

His confidence was compelling, the look in his eyes irresistible. Sensation was already pooling in sharp insistent pulses between her legs by the time Kemal wrapped her in towels and swung her into his arms.

'This is *The Sultan's* palace, and you are my captive,' he teased her provocatively.

'Will you tie me down with ribbons of silk and tantalise me with feathers?' Lizzie demanded, responding in kind to his wicked mood.

'You have been indulging in far too many fantasies,' Kemal observed as he shouldered open the door. 'I have something far more fulfilling in mind for both of us.'

She didn't doubt him for a minute. But, as for fantasies, she had never indulged in them before coming to Turkey. Happily, it seemed all that was about to change.

CHAPTER EIGHT

KEMAL took Lizzie in the opposite direction from her own rooms. He stopped outside some fabulously carved doors in a grand hallway, where everything was the same exotic mix of exuberant ornamentation and vibrant colour. But the moment they walked through the doors they might have been in another world.

Kemal's private kingdom was a triumph of ice-cool minimalism. The chocolate-brown leather chairs and sofas would be from Italy, Lizzie guessed, and the rest of the furniture looked as if it might have come from Scandinavia. Huge rugs in neutral shades provided pools of contrast on a stark white marble floor, and on the pure white walls just two large, colourful modern paintings were expertly displayed.

The totally unexpected decor, and the realisation that it must reflect Kemal's inner self, fascinated Lizzie. Like him, this apartment was powerful and controlled, with a touch of the audacious—the perfect mix in any man.

Laying her down on the bed, Kemal stretched his

length against her so that Lizzie felt at once extremely dainty by comparison. She started to tremble when he lightly ran the fingertips of one hand very slowly down from her slightly parted lips to the apex of her thighs, and then she gasped, wanting more…wanting much, much more.

'Not yet,' he whispered reluctantly, kissing her lips with frustrating restraint.

But his mouth was a channel from which pleasure poured, and her limbs were running with molten honey. Lizzie groaned with impatience as she shamelessly angled herself towards him.

The cool and oh, so contained Ms Lizzie Palmer was a volcano waiting to erupt, Kemal realised. That vacancy on his staff for a mistress had just been filled.

And now he would take the greatest pleasure in spinning everything out, taking even longer than he had planned over her seduction. She was beautiful, and ripe like the figs they had both enjoyed. She needed release and he would give it to her—but her defiance must be curbed. Everything would happen at a time of his own choosing. He would tease and tantalise until she was in a realm beyond reason. He was a master of the art, and she would be a most responsive pupil.

He watched in fascination as Lizzie cupped her breasts, to taunt him with the sight of her extended nipples. It was as if she was seeking his approval— and he did approve, Kemal allowed with a groan of contentment. Dipping his head to suckle, he felt her arch towards him, and, reaching down, he cupped her buttocks with his hand, spreading his fingers and using his thumb to caress her—just enough. It pleased him to hear her cry out—a short, sharp cry of need. But he would never accede to her will in such matters, and instead pinned her beneath him, holding her still while he pleasured her at his own pace.

'You're very greedy,' he observed softly with satisfaction. 'But greedy must wait.'

He smiled again, hearing her small cry of disappointment. And, looking down, he saw that her nipples were pink and taut, stretching out to him as if begging for his attention. With a growl of triumph he rasped the rough stubble of his chin across the tender peaks, and revelled in the sound of her whimpers of desire.

Kemal recognised that he was just as hungry as Lizzie, but he was eager to find out just how high he could push her capacity for pleasure. And that quest, he realised with surprise, was even more important to him right now than his own pleasure.

Reaching down, he eased her thighs apart and gently parted her swollen lips with one skilled and searching finger.

'Oh, Kemal, please—'

'Not yet,' he murmured, pretending regret. He held her firm as she bucked beneath him. 'You must stay very still,' he instructed softly, whispering against her lips.

'I will—I promise…anything,' Lizzie cried hoarsely. 'But don't make me wait too long.'

'You will wait as long as I think is necessary,' Kemal said quietly. 'You must learn to pace yourself.'

'Will you teach me?' Lizzie challenged, trying to stop herself moving beneath him.

'I said still,' he reminded her. 'Or I won't touch you at all. In fact,' he said, moving away, 'I don't think I will touch you more tonight—'

'What?' Lizzie lashed out at him furiously. 'Where do you think you're going? Don't you dare!' she warned, when he threatened to get off the bed.

Kemal whirled around. In that moment Lizzie saw the warrior he might have been centuries before, his face so harsh and fierce…but his eyes, she noticed as they held her glance, were still warm, still full of passion, and glinting now with a very potent mix of humour and desire.

'You drive me to the limits,' he confessed huskily.

'And my penalty is?' Lizzie demanded, holding his gaze.

'You will touch yourself,' he instructed her steadily. 'I think that would please me.'

'What?' Lizzie's eyes widened with surprise.

'You seem to think that we Turks have a monopoly on erotic practices; I don't want to disappoint you.'

'Brute!' Lizzie exclaimed, knowing he was teasing her. 'Monster!'

'Anything but, I can assure you,' Kemal said steadily. Seizing one of her hands, he slowly dragged it to his mouth, and, keeping his gaze locked on Lizzie's face, took each finger into his mouth and began to suckle her fingertips in turn until they turned pink.

Lizzie felt faint with pleasure and surprise when he brought her own hand down between her legs. It was so unexpected…forbidden, and so very, very good. Closing her eyes, she groaned as Kemal guided her. It was intensely erotic—the most erotic moment of her life.

She exceeded all his expectations, Kemal realised, relishing every nuance in Lizzie's expression as she climbed to a plateau so high even he hardly knew how she sustained her hold upon it without tumbling off. She had been so very cool, ice-cool, and now he watched as her face flushed pink with arousal. Only he could have guessed what lay beneath the frigid façade.

'Stop, stop… No, I mustn't—' she protested huskily, trying not to lose control; it seemed so very wrong.

'Why? Why mustn't you?' Kemal demanded softly, giving her all his attention again. And then he decided to tantalise her a little more, by holding her arm above her head and kissing her breasts, before finally transferring his kisses to bring her the release she craved.

She cried and moaned in his arms for ages afterwards, while he held her close, stroking her until at last she was calm. 'Didn't I tell you it would be good for you?' he murmured wryly when finally Lizzie grew quiet. And when she said nothing Kemal pulled back to look at her, and saw she was asleep.

'Lizzie…Lizzie…'

The voice came from far away, down a long, dark tunnel of sleep.

It wasn't an angry voice, or muffled, like her parents when they were locked in their den. No, Lizzie realised with surprise, it was Mrs McConnell from next door.

'Lizzie, dear, what are you doing?'

The little girl looked up, worried because she knew she was doing something wrong, but still eager to share her plans. Mrs McConnell was always kind to her, always smelled so good. 'I'm sorry, Mrs McConnell, but we don't have holly on our side of the fence. And yours has got such lovely bright red berries.'

'Look at your hands.' Mary McConnell made a sound of concern as she bent low to take hold of two grubby fists in her own workworn hands. 'You're all scratched and bleeding, Lizzie. No need to ask whether your mother has any antiseptic, I suppose?'

'She has magic mushrooms. Maybe those—'

'Heaven protect you, child!' Mary McConnell exclaimed with alarm.

And then later, when they were in the food-scented haven of Mrs McConnell's kitchen, she asked, 'And what were you going to do with my holly, Lizzie?'

'I wanted it for Christmas,' Lizzie explained, forcing in a last bite of mince pie even before she had swallowed the first. 'I saw your decorations and so I knew it must be time—'

'No need to hurry, Lizzie,' Mrs McConnell said, in that soft voice of hers, which made Lizzie painfully aware of how hungry she was, and how hard she must try not to seem so. 'I'll send you home with a batch of mince pies, and then you can share them with your brother and your parents—when they wake up,' she added under her breath.

She wasn't supposed to have heard that, Lizzie realised, watching Mrs McConnell bite her lip to stop the flow of words. Now she had swallowed down the last delicious crumb, Lizzie's attention was drawn back to the kitchen table, loaded with freshly baked pies. 'Couldn't I stay here with you for Christmas, Mrs McConnell?' she asked, already anticipating the refusal that was sure to come. 'The baby too… I could bring Hugo with me. Mum would never notice—'

'No, dear,' Mrs McConnell said softly. 'I'm afraid that's just not possible.'

'*Please!*'

Of course she hadn't begged, Lizzie recalled, tossing restlessly in the half-world between sleeping and wakefulness. She had just slipped down from the kitchen stool, placed her hand in Mrs McConnell's and, with the box of mince pies tucked safely beneath her arm, walked dutifully back with her kindly neighbour to her own house. But she had so wanted to stay with Mrs McConnell. She would have loved nothing better than to stay and help her put up the last of the decorations, finish the tree…

Lizzie groaned as she snapped her face away from the reflection of her younger self's pale, resigned face in the hall mirror at Mrs McConnell's home. It was like seeing someone else altogether—a stranger—someone she wanted to reach out to and help, but couldn't. She started thrashing about in angry frustration on the bed.

'Wake up, Lizzie…wake up.'

The low voice grew more insistent. A man's voice—one the child didn't recognise. But the woman Lizzie did.

'You've had a bad dream, Lizzie,' Kemal said, bringing her into his arms. 'But it's all over now. You're safe here with me,' he said, murmuring against her hair. 'You'll be all right now.'

Would she? Lizzie wondered, dashing the tears from her eyes. Would she ever be all right?

CHAPTER NINE

BACK in her own fabulous suite of rooms at the palace, Lizzie sat on the bed with her head in her hands. Had she lost every semblance of self-respect and control? No wonder the nightmares had returned. She had allowed herself to be seduced by a cold-blooded man who meant nothing but harm to her family. And Hugo *was* her family—her only family; Hugo, her brother—had she forgotten him?

And she hadn't even been properly seduced. A contemptuous sob escaped Lizzie's lips at she remembered her behaviour. She was a freak, a bumbling, unsophisticated idiot where sex was concerned. And she had let Kemal humiliate her. How could she have allowed it to happen?

Kemal Volkan. She need search for no other answer. A wave of panic rose in Lizzie's chest as she thought about him. Just the image of his face in her mind sent shock waves racing through her. Kemal had stirred fires she had never guessed might be inside her. But they were destructive fires. She came.

He saw. He conquered. Some stand she'd made! And when she'd finally woken up this morning, after suffering one of her worst nightmares for years, he'd already left her. Too much trouble for too little return, she suspected.

Lizzie buried her head in her hands, wondering what she might have called out during her nightmare. She knew that by revealing the demons she lived with to Kemal she had made herself look like a victim—something she had always refused to be.

Kemal Volkan was one of nature's predators, and she had rolled over for him in every way that a woman could roll over for a man. What an outstanding victory! She would have to be sure to try those tactics in court some day. She had certainly learned some bitter lessons in Istanbul, Lizzie reflected. And Hugo still wasn't home. But she would get him home for Christmas, whatever it took. Firming her lips, she went to find her phone.

For once the lawyer she had found in Istanbul, Sami Gulsan, answered immediately. He advised Lizzie to sit tight, stay calm and do nothing other than leave her phone on until she heard from him again. The situation had been dealt with, he said reassuringly. But Lizzie refused to be reassured. It was about time someone knew exactly what kind of man Kemal Volkan was.

She was forced to cut the conversation short when she heard the door open.

'Kemal!' Springing up, Lizzie backed away instinctively. There was a look on his face that frightened her.

'Don't end your call on my account,' he said.

Putting the phone down on the table beside her, Lizzie stood tensely—waiting.

Kemal stopped a few feet away from her and Lizzie saw that he had a sheet of paper tightly clutched in his hand; so tight, in fact, his knuckles had turned white.

'What's that?' Lizzie said.

'Honour,' Kemal told her. 'A shining example of your idea of honour.'

Lizzie flinched as he flung the paper at her feet. Swooping down, she picked it up and read quickly, backing away at the same time to put some urgently needed space between them. It was a hand-delivered document written in English from Lizzie's lawyer, Sami Gulsan, questioning Kemal about her illegal imprisonment. Gulsan demanded her immediate release, and added that a claim for damages would shortly follow.

'There is nothing in this letter that I am ashamed of,' Lizzie said, looking up. 'Far from impugning my honour, it shows yours in a poor light, don't you think?'

'Did you really imagine you could make money out of this situation?' Kemal demanded contemptuously, when she had finished.

'Money?' Lizzie exclaimed. 'What are you talking about?'

'If it wasn't the money, then what—what made you stoop to this?' Kemal said icily.

'It has nothing to do with money,' Lizzie said.

'I'm perfectly within my rights to consult a lawyer if I choose—'

'Your rights!' Kemal turned away, as if he couldn't bear to look at her a moment longer.

'I consulted a lawyer regarding my position,' Lizzie said, addressing his back. 'So what? Are you telling me you wouldn't have done the same?'

'I might have chosen my lawyer with a little more care,' Kemal replied, turning back to face her again. 'I might have exercised diplomacy, for instance.'

'What do you mean?'

'Just this,' he bit out. 'You went behind my back and consulted with a lawyer who represents my strongest competitor.'

'But how could I know?'

'That's the point,' he said icily. 'You don't know anything, but you continue to meddle in things you know nothing about. What do you think Gulsan will do with this information? He's no friend of mine. Another thing you don't know is that as one of the major creditors I was given first option to buy the company Hugo works for. Now Gulsan has pushed my competitors into submitting a counter-bid.'

'But I couldn't possibly have known that—'

'Fortunately,' Kemal continued, ignoring her, 'they were too late. My deal was too far down the line. But, had it not been, you could have spoiled it for me.'

Lizzie looked at Kemal, shaking her head slightly in bewilderment.

'Yes,' he said with satisfaction. 'In spite of your best efforts, I agreed terms some time earlier.'

'Agreed terms?' Lizzie repeated in a dry voice. She wanted to stop up her ears. She wanted to stop him speaking. But he went on relentlessly.

'I agreed terms to buy the company Hugo was working for out of receivership the morning after you arrived.'

'You…did…what?' Lizzie stared at him open-mouthed. Ice streamed through her veins and into her heart as she realised everything this information meant to her.

'That meeting I had to postpone when I came back to the palace to see you?' Kemal reminded her brusquely. 'Luckily I was able to hold it by conference phone. And just as well I did. But I had no idea until I received this letter from Gulsan that it was you who had betrayed me.'

Lizzie stared at him in disbelief, barely hearing his last words. 'Why didn't you tell me you had bought the company?' she asked hoarsely.

'I am not in the habit of discussing my business decisions with anyone. I make them; I execute them. It's that simple.'

Lizzie felt each of his statements as a physical blow. She couldn't believe anyone could be so callous. She had to be sure. 'You knew all along that the situation was resolved,' she said, 'and yet you allowed me to make a fool of myself. You used a situation you knew didn't exist any longer to force me to stay—'

'Force?' Kemal cut across her harshly. 'You were in no hurry to leave, as I remember.'

'You used me,' Lizzie accused him bitterly, 'and you abused my trust. What kind of person are you?' Her mind was in turmoil as Kemal went on listing her supposed offences. Finally, Lizzie could stand no more of it. 'How dare you accuse me of ruining your plans? If you had told me the truth in the first place this would never have happened!'

'I am not in the habit of discussing my plans. My business is my affair.'

'And me?' Lizzie demanded tensely. 'What about me, Kemal? What about us?'

'Us?' he said, stiffening.

'Oh, I see,' Lizzie said bitterly, determined at all costs to maintain her composure. 'There is no *us*. There is only Kemal Volkan, *The Sultan*: the man who uses everyone for his own ends. You manipulated me, Kemal. You led me to think that you were as much a victim in all of this as my brother, when all the time you were controlling the situation. You seduced me—'

Kemal's contemptuous laugh, short and harsh, cut her off. 'You were eager to be seduced.'

Lizzie cheeks flared red and she grimaced with disbelief. 'Where is Hugo?' she demanded furiously. 'What have you done with him, Kemal? Tell me where he is,' she warned, 'or never mind calling a lawyer, I'm calling the police.'

'Oh, no, you're not,' he said, catching hold of her wrist as she went for her phone.

'Get off me!'

He ignored her.

'You disgust me!' Lizzie raged, trying to shake him off.

'That's not what you said last night,' Kemal reminded her roughly.

'You're contemptible! You made love to me, knowing how things were. I demand to see my brother.'

'And so you shall,' Kemal assured her in a low, fierce voice.

Lizzie whipped her face to one side so that she would not have to stare any longer into his wolf-grey eyes. 'Will I share Hugo's cell?' she challenged him derisively.

At once she felt Kemal tense, felt it in every tissue by which they were connected.

It was as if every inch of him was balled up, ready to spring to the defence of his honour, Kemal realised. There was not a single insult left for her to throw at him.

His grip on Lizzie's arm tightened as he brought her closer still, but rather than keeping her face averted as he expected, she snapped around to blaze a look of defiance straight into his eyes. She was more than a match for any man. For him?

Kemal wasn't sure if that thought pleased him or not, he was still too busy deflecting her insults.

'Hugo isn't in a cell,' he said. 'He has never been in a cell—he was in a camp out in the wilds, where my new factory is being set up, yes. But now, as you never allow me to forget, it's almost Christmas, so he's due to land with his workmates at Heathrow round about—now.' As he released her to check his watch, Lizzie lurched back and away from him.

'You bastard!'

Kemal stared at her in shock.

'You knew all along that my brother was in no danger!'

'Danger! What kind of man do you take me for?'

'The worst—the very worst,' Lizzie assured him.

'Then why are you still here?'

Lizzie stared at him, speechless with disbelief. 'Because you kept me here.'

'I have never tried to stop you leaving,' Kemal said. 'Do you want to go so badly?'

'Damn right!' Lizzie agreed. 'And I want transport out of here—'

'No problem!' Kemal cut across her with an angry gesture. 'My private jet is standing on the tarmac in Istanbul. Why don't you use that?'

As the executive jet soared high above Istanbul, Lizzie felt her emotions might overwhelm her. It was a battle to keep the expression on her face neutral for the sake of the flight attendants.

Her time in Turkey had been an absolute disaster. Instead of returning home with her mission successfully accomplished, she was returning home as the villain of the piece. And her brief affair with Kemal Volkan had left a wound so deep she knew it would never heal.

Kemal was right about one thing, Lizzie conceded wryly. She would never forget this Christmas. *And what about Christmas Day?* She still felt numb. Maybe it would be better to sleep through it—let this one be the Christmas she never had.

'Hugo? Can you hear me?' Kemal demanded. 'Isn't it about time you got yourself a decent mobile phone?'

'Kemal! Is that you? How can I help you?'

'This isn't about business. It's personal,' Kemal said tersely.

'Personal?'

Kemal heard the wariness in Hugo's voice in that one word, but he had to press on. 'It's not about you,' he said. 'It's your sister.'

'Lizzie?'

Hugo's anxiety proved how much he loved his sister, Kemal realised. 'Yes, Lizzie,' he said.

'What do you want to know?'

'She's been here with me in Istanbul…'

'I should have known she would jump on the next flight,' Hugo said. 'I should never have called her. The line was so bad—'

'It's too late to worry about that now,' Kemal said, cutting across him. 'I couldn't get hold of you at the camp, otherwise we could have talked sooner—I could have reassured you. If the weather hadn't been so bad, and communications so poor, I would have let you know that she was here. But she's OK, Hugo. She's on her way back to England right now in my jet. Will you be there?'

'Yeah—sure. But I'm not at the flat.'

'I gathered that,' Kemal said, hearing a girl in the background. 'Can you go somewhere private to talk?'

'It's important, I assume?'

Kemal heard the subtle change in his voice. 'Yes, it's important,' he said.

'Give me a minute.'

Kemal pulled the receiver away from his ear and waited until Hugo came back on the line. 'I'm afraid I have to talk to you about your past,' he said. 'And I need answers, Hugo.'

'OK,' Hugo said, but Kemal sensed his reluctance.

'I'd like to start with your childhood,' he said.

'Not much to tell,' Hugo said evasively. 'What do you want to know?'

How to get the most out of him? Why should Hugo put the family skeletons on show for him? Kemal wondered, his mind racing. 'Tell me about Christmas,' he said, choosing the direct approach.

'Any bar will do,' the younger man said flippantly.

'Hugo, this is serious,' Kemal said quietly. 'Why does Christmas mean so much to Lizzie?'

'Does it?'

'Don't stonewall me, Hugo,' Kemal warned. 'Why does she wear those damned glasses? Why does she have nightmares? Why does she call out in her sleep? What happened to her, Hugo?'

'I'm sorry, Kemal, I don't want to talk about it.'

Kemal forced himself to wait. He had to give him space. 'Did you often see Lizzie upset when you were younger?' he said at last. 'Did she ever tell you why she was crying?' There was a long silence, and every moment he expected Hugo to cut the line. But he didn't.

'No one cries when it's really bad, do they?' Hugo said at last. 'They just hold it all in.'

Kemal sat back, and then he said carefully, 'Can you tell me about it, Hugo?'

'Lizzie didn't tell you?'

'No,' Kemal admitted.

'Then I can't. Sorry,' Hugo said gruffly.

Kemal let the silence hang. The line rang with silent tears and he had no wish to trample on Hugo's memories. 'I need this information, Hugo' he said at last, 'for Lizzie's sake. She can't go on like this. You must know that.'

For a few seconds that seemed a lot longer there was nothing. And then: 'Lizzie found our parents dead,' Hugo said, talking in a fast monotone. 'There was incense everywhere in the house. It nearly choked her—nearly choked me. I was only nine. I was hiding in my bedroom with the window open. When I heard Lizzie scream I ran out. She was downstairs, looking through the glass door that led into the kitchen— She'd been bringing stuff in for Christmas decorations: holly, red berries. She did it every year—it was sort of a tradition—'

'Stop there,' Kemal interjected softly. 'Go slowly, Hugo. I need to understand.'

'They OD'd,' Hugo told him. 'Lizzie was standing outside the glass door, looking in at Mum and Dad slumped dead on the floor.'

'And she's worn glasses since then?'

'How did you know that?'

'It's not important,' Kemal said. 'She doesn't wear them any more.'

'Does that help?' Hugo said, clearly uncomfortable that he had betrayed some long held secret.

'It helps a lot,' Kemal assured him. 'And now I want you to forget about business for a while, Hugo. I need you to do something else for me.'

The flat seemed smaller than Lizzie had remembered, and it was cold   very cold. She tried to get hold of Hugo on the phone the moment she got in, but he was staying round at a friend's. A girlfriend's, Lizzie guessed, judging by the muffled giggles in the background.

'Thank God you're safe!' she exclaimed with relief.

'Safe?' Hugo demanded. 'The only danger here is a couple of girls from uni, and I seem to be coping!'

'Er, thank you, Hugo. That's far too much information,' Lizzie said, dragging her coat a little closer. 'Don't you ever put the heat on at the flat?'

'When I'm there.'

'OK, so tomorrow's Christmas Eve. Will I see you?'

'I have to go on somewhere from here,' Hugo said. 'What about if I come round to the flat tomorrow morning?'

'I promised to go into Chambers in the morning,' Lizzie said, thinking out loud, 'and then I expect there will be drinks, Christmas lunch—that sort of thing—'

'I could come round really early in the morning?' Hugo offered.

Lizzie smiled, knowing that was quite some sacrifice. 'Thanks, Hugo. I'd appreciate it. I want to talk to you about Istanbul.'

'No problem. Look, I'm a bit tied up right now...'

I bet you are, Lizzie thought. Kemal was right again—her kid brother was all grown up.

Pacing around the small flat, Lizzie tried hard not to think about Kemal. His chauffeur had taken her to the airport. There had been no sign of anyone else from the palace. Kemal had made his feelings towards her crystal-clear before they parted, so why should she have expected things to be different?

But for some reason a stubborn kernel of hope kept on refusing to give up—even though she knew it could never have worked out between them. They were like twin tornados, cancelling each other out. They were both in the wrong, both too passionate, too intense to give an inch. It was time to get on with the rest of her life, Lizzie told herself, and file *The Sultan* away, along with her other memories.

Flicking open the well-used diary on her desk, Lizzie saw that, just as she had told Hugo, Christmas Eve was going to be hectic. There would be barely enough time to dash round the shops to try and gather up some last-minute seasonal goodies. She looked around the cold, modern flat. She would have to make time. It was all so drab. Wandering across to the window, she pushed the curtain aside and looked out. Under the street lamp she could see the holly bush flourishing beneath her window. It was covered in red berries.

* * *

Lizzie woke early on Christmas Eve morning. Bouncing out of bed, she hurried about the flat, barefoot in her pyjamas. Munching toast, and slurping coffee out of her oversized mug, she backed into the tiny sitting room to check over the simple Christmas arrangements she had fashioned late the previous night.

But her gaze flew instinctively to the telephone. Her heart gave a lonely thud. There was no winking light. No message. Stuffing the last piece of toast in her mouth, she crossed over to her desk and logged on to her computer to check her e mails. Nothing. There was nothing—no voicemail, no text, no recorded message—nothing.

'So, that's it,' she informed the empty room.

Unless…

All she had to lose was her pride, Lizzie thought, remembering the business card Kemal had insisted she keep. She still had his private number…

For a moment Lizzie was surprised to hear a woman's voice. Then she realised that of course Kemal would have a PA. She wished she hadn't made the call. Kemal might have said to call him if she needed help—but the only help she needed was in getting over him! Giving a false name to the woman, Lizzie said she worked for one of the Financials, and then casually dropped into the conversation the name of the company Hugo had been working for.

It was now part of the Volkan group, the woman

said economically, before asking if there was anything else she could help Lizzie with.

'No. No, nothing else, thank you,' Lizzie said, cutting the line.

Hugo's visit lasted about five minutes. He was clearly in a hurry to get somewhere else, Lizzie realised when he joined her for some coffee. Any detailed chat about Istanbul would have to wait—not enough time now, he explained. But enough time to request a new mobile phone for Christmas, Lizzie thought with a wry smile. Typical brother!

And then later in the day she just couldn't say no to her colleagues when they insisted she join them for Christmas lunch. They all arrived together at the luxury hotel in a fleet of taxis, but, quite suddenly, she was on her own. How could seven people simply melt away? Lizzie wondered, looking with bemusement around the brilliantly lit entrance foyer.

She tensed as the elevator doors slid open. But in spite of the frisson that tracked down her spine it was just a young mother, laughing as she struggled to manage two excited children and the pile of presents in her arms. Lizzie looked away quickly, but then, drawn to the sound of happy laughter again, she turned back and smiled at the family.

It was then Kemal saw her.

After speaking to Hugo he had to come and find her. He couldn't allow them to part on a wave of acrimony and recriminations. His business was under control—always had been, in spite of Lizzie Palmer's best endeavours. But his personal life was not under control, Kemal realised as his heart lurched at the sight of Lizzie.

She was even more beautiful than he remembered. But now she was relaxed and smiling, and he had failed there. He had never succeeded in bringing Lizzie that type of uncomplicated happiness, because they had spent all their time fighting—almost all their time, he amended with a faint smile. But they only fought because no one had ever stood up to him as she did, and he had come to admire her for that. That was why he had come to London. He could not draw a line beneath their relationship yet.

CHAPTER TEN

'KEMAL!'

Lizzie froze when she spotted him. In spite of everything that had happened, when he walked towards her she thought she might faint.

'Lizzie.'

He stopped a few feet away, giving her that half-smile that always knocked her off balance. And even after despatching her from Turkey with all speed, his voice was low, even intimate, as if they were lovers.

'Kemal,' Lizzie said coolly, regrouping fast. He was so self-possessed, so confident of his reception. The same very masculine humour shaped his gaze. She held out her hand to him politely. 'You're the last person I expected to see.'

Did she seriously expect him to shake her hand? Kemal thought, ignoring it as he moved to kiss her on both cheeks, continental-style. Her face was ice-cold, he noticed, but she still trembled at his touch.

'I'm glad to see you,' he said with matching formality. 'I know how busy you must be so close to Christmas—'

'How did you know I would be here?' Lizzie said. 'This isn't a coincidence, is it, Kemal?'

'I followed you,' he said casually. 'And your colleagues were most helpful.'

'My colleagues told you—'

'They're not at fault,' he cut in. 'I wanted to find you. But, look, if I'm keeping you…'

For a moment she was so shocked she couldn't speak, and she saw Kemal's gaze turn cool.

'I mustn't keep you from your friends,' he said, moving as if to go.

'No. Wait.' Self-consciously Lizzie drew her hand back from touching him. 'We could have a drink first, maybe?'

'Won't your friends be waiting for you in the restaurant?'

'Perhaps, but…'

'But?' he demanded quizzically.

'For old times' sake?' Lizzie suggested, finding she was unable to meet his gaze.

'Have we known each other that long?' he said, affecting a weary tone, but as she looked up she saw the spark of humour in his eyes.

'It feels like it sometimes,' Lizzie admitted, smiling a little 'Aren't you going to eat lunch somewhere?'

'Perhaps. I hadn't thought about it, to be honest.'

'Why don't you join us?' Lizzie suggested on impulse. It would be a safe environment inside the restaurant, with her colleagues around to chaperone them. There was no reason for her to part from Kemal on bad terms.

'I don't want to intrude,' he said. 'And afterwards there'll be things you want to do. You'll be too busy—'

'Oh, no—that's fine,' Lizzie heard herself say. 'There's loads of time.'

She looked up at him. She didn't want him to go. Not yet.

She didn't want him to leave. It was a shock, and a pleasant one, Kemal discovered. He took every woman on earth for granted, but not Lizzie—never Lizzie.

'OK, so I give in,' he said softly.

Lizzie flushed red. The tone of his voice was everything she had ever hoped for—more than she could possibly have expected. She loved everything about him, she realised as Kemal linked her arm through his: the power radiating from him, his amazing build, his intoxicating scent, the thick black hair that always escaped so wilfully from his careful grooming. She even loved the piercing gaze that could strip her to the core in an instant. But most of all she loved the harsh mouth that had kissed her so very thoroughly, and that even now was tugging up in a smile.

She was quite sure that every one of her X-rated thoughts was printed in large type across her forehead. But this was nothing more than two people parting as friends, she reminded herself. It was the civilised way to behave.

'Oh, that's a shame,' Kemal murmured, looking round the dining room. 'Your friends seem to have gone. They must have decided to move on.'

'But where—'

'Does it matter? We can eat here—unless, of course, you want to try and find them?' Kemal offered, unlinking her arm and standing back.

'No,' Lizzie said quickly, 'that's fine. I'm quite hungry now, aren't you?'

'Very,' Kemal agreed, smiling into her eyes.

Was the secluded table at Kemal's request? Or was the *maitre d'* particularly sensitive to his client's requirements? Lizzie wondered, as she handed over her coat. She was becoming neurotic, she decided. Glancing in the mirror, she wished there'd been time to change. Dressed all in black for work, she looked as pale as a wraith. Whereas Kemal dressed in black—Italian tailoring, she guessed—seemed more vibrant than ever. Black looked fabulous against his tan.

As he held the chair for her Lizzie felt Kemal's forcefield pulsing behind her. And when he settled himself across the table and she glimpsed the hard, bronzed torso beneath his open-necked shirt she could taste his warmth on her tongue again, feel the silky texture of his hard, muscled frame beneath her hands.

Drawing a deep breath, Lizzie closed her eyes, revelling in the warm, musky man scent, laced with sandalwood. Suddenly aware that he was staring at her, she accepted the menu from a waiter with relief, and quickly buried her head in it. But she had chosen to wear the fragile silk and lace underwear

Kemal had bought for her in Istanbul beneath the severely cut suit. And she felt as if he knew. If ever there had been an occasion for wearing blue serge gym knickers, this was it!

'Don't I owe you some money?' she said quickly, to distract herself, looking up.

'For what?' Kemal asked, leaning back comfortably in his chair.

'For the clothes you bought for me while I was in Istanbul.'

'It was nothing—just some underwear, wasn't it?'

He *did* know! And in case he was in any doubt, her cheeks were on fire.

'Won't you accept it as a gift?'

'I don't accept gifts from anyone.'

'That's a pity.'

'You'll send me the bill?' she pressed.

'I hear the food is very good here, and the waiter is waiting for our order,' Kemal pointed out. 'Won't you choose something?'

'Don't change the subject,' Lizzie warned. 'You have to give in.'

'Do I?' he murmured. 'Perhaps later.' And then he turned to concentrate on his own menu.

Lizzie was so flustered she asked for the first thing that came into her head. And very soon after that the hors d'oeuvres arrived.

'Just tell me how much I owe you,' Lizzie said again.

'I'll let you know when I've worked it out,' Kemal said. 'But now we eat.' He dipped an asparagus spear into thick, buttery sauce. 'This has come all the way from Peru, just for our enjoyment,' he pointed out, offering one to Lizzie. 'It would be churlish of us to let it go to waste.'

Lizzie drew the succulent stalk slowly into her mouth, trying not to look at Kemal. But her face was burning beneath his steady gaze.

'Would you like to taste the wine, sir? Sir…?'

'No. Thank you,' Kemal said politely, wiping his lips on a large linen napkin. 'I'm afraid we have been called away—some urgent business.'

'I quite understand, sir.'

Lizzie sincerely hoped he didn't. But then she was on her feet, her hand in Kemal's. 'My coat!' she exclaimed, when they were almost at the door.

'Someone will return it,' Kemal said, pulling her behind him.

Lizzie pressed back against her own side of the elevator. Kemal was leaning against his. They didn't speak. They didn't need to. The space in between them was a forcefield crackling with energy and intention. Maybe she was mistaken, Lizzie thought wildly. Maybe she was going crazy—maybe her imagination was running away with her. Yes, that must be it, she decided. Kemal was so calm—too calm.

'We're here,' he said at last, standing aside to let Lizzie pass him when the lift doors opened.

The same silent retainers she had seen in Turkey opened double doors for them, and Lizzie walked past them into a sitting room the size of a small ballroom. The cream carpet was so thick it felt like a mattress, and the air was filled with the subtle scent of roses.

'Do you like them?' Kemal asked conversationally, as he waited for the servants to leave.

'I love roses,' Lizzie admitted, touching one of the velvet petals with her fingertip. 'Especially cream roses. They are so delicate.'

'I had them flown in especially for you.'

'For me?' Lizzie said incredulously, looking up. 'Why?'

'You don't know?'

'Should I?' Lizzie said, turning to him.

'You are without question the most surprising woman I have ever met.'

'Good surprise or bad surprise?'

'That depends on the moment,' he said. 'Fortunately, I like a challenge.'

As the door closed on the last of the servants Kemal dragged her to him. Pushing her jacket off her shoulders, he turned impatiently to the tiny pearl buttons on her blouse.

Placing her palms firmly against the wall of his chest, Lizzie pushed weakly at him. 'Kemal…'

The word was little more than a sigh, but he stopped it with a kiss. 'We've talked enough,' he said at last, releasing her to watch her reaction as he moved to trace the swell of her breasts very lightly with his fingertips.

Lizzie's lips parted to drag in air as Kemal used the firm pads of his thumbs to chafe impatiently against her fine lawn blouse. She didn't want subtlety, or foreplay. They had explored that particularly frustrating activity to the limits.

Soon they were tearing the clothes off each other and flinging them aside, dropping them and kicking them away. And Kemal was lifting her, entering her even as he lowered her down onto the nearest surface—which, fortunately for Lizzie, was a heavy sofa that held her securely as Kemal moved above her, thrusting deep.

They were greedy for each other. Ravenous. They had waited too long, and Lizzie was every bit as demanding and as forceful as Kemal. Her hands grabbed for him, her fingers mercilessly pushed and pressed, forced him on while she cried out repeatedly, wondering if she could ever get enough of him filling her, stretching her, pounding her. There was only one thought in her mind now—one goal, one driving, overwhelming need. And finally, crying out to him in triumph, she brought him with her in a series of shudderingly intense, pleasure-filled waves.

They made love in every room in the plush apartment—every room and every corner—until finally they made it to the bed. There was no conversation, no need for speech; they could communicate very well without it. And the longer they were together the more perfectly they understood each other.

'Tomorrow is Christmas Day,' Kemal reminded Lizzie, when she was drifting off to sleep at last in his arms. 'Do you have any last-minute preparations to make?'

Remembering Hugo's request for a new mobile phone, Lizzie was instantly alert. Glancing at her wristwatch, she exclaimed, 'Oh, my goodness!' And then she swung out of bed. 'I'm so sorry—I feel terrible about this—but I have to make the shops before they close. I promised Hugo—'

'I understand,' said Kemal, lazily stretching out his length on the bed. 'You'd better get going if you want to catch the shops.'

'Will I see you again?' Lizzie asked, pausing with her hand on the bathroom door.

'I'd say there's a very good chance,' Kemal promised, slanting her a grin. 'But hurry up, Lizzie, or you will be too late.'

CHAPTER ELEVEN

'HUGO? Yes, I'm here. Of course I'm at the flat. You're speaking to me, aren't you?' Lizzie said, breaking off to suck hard on the thumb she had just pricked with the last of the holly. 'You are still coming here for Christmas lunch tomorrow? Bring friends, if you want.'

There had been no call from Kemal since she had returned home from the shops, and Lizzie was beginning to wonder if there ever would be. He had surely made his own plans for Christmas Day by now. She didn't want to think about it, because each time she did the words 'used and abused' sprang to the forefront of her mind.

'You don't have to come, if you have other things to do,' she said, remembering that Hugo had a new girlfriend.

'Don't be an ass, Lizzie. Look, sis, I have to go—people are waiting for me.'

'OK, have a good time—but just be careful,' Lizzie said, smiling down the phone. She stared thoughtfully at the receiver after the line was cut. This was a new phase in her life. Hugo didn't need her as he'd used to. That was good. It was what she wanted for him.

And she was not going to spend Christmas feeling sorry for herself. She had a brilliant career, a fantastic brother, and was still throbbing from the attentions of her billionaire ex-lover—not bad for someone raised in a squat.

From then on Lizzie concentrated on the bare flat, making it look the best she could, with candles and a home-made holly wreath on the front door. She had kept plenty of baubles over the years, and she hung those on a small fake tree. There was no way she could get a real one up two flights of stairs, which was a pity, but it couldn't be helped. When she was finished, she went to her small refrigerator and took out a bottle of champagne. But champagne was for sharing…

She was just about to put it away again when Hugo burst in through the front door like a tornado.

'Where did you come from?' Lizzie exclaimed delightedly, hugging him.

'We have to go now. *Now!* Right this minute,' Hugo said, breaking away from her.

'Where are you talking about? Hang on—where are you taking me?' Lizzie asked, as he started dragging her towards the door.

'Don't ask so many questions.'

'I have to,' Lizzie pointed out. 'Do I change into a tracksuit? Are you taking me down the pub for a drink? Or is this an outing to one of your crazy parties? Just tell me if it is, so I can put something washable on—'

'We don't do that sort of thing now,' Hugo informed her, adopting a pious expression. 'I'm all grown up,' he added ironically. 'Or hadn't you noticed yet?'

'I've noticed,' Lizzie said dryly. 'So. What do I wear?'

'Something pretty,' Hugo said, giving it a moment's thought. 'Something really special.'

'All right,' Lizzie said. 'I'll see what I can do. Give me half an hour?'

'Five minutes.'

'Fifteen,' Lizzie bartered, flashing him a smile; Hugo's enthusiasm was infectious.

The Carlton Towers?' Lizzie grimaced when she heard Hugo instructing their taxi driver. 'Do we have to?'

'You can't change your mind now; it's already booked,' Hugo informed her grandly.

'You shouldn't have,' Lizzie said, squeezing his arm. 'A meal there costs a fortune. And look at you— you can't go like that. You've got glitter dust on your jacket. How did that happen?'

'It's nothing,' Hugo said, quickly brushing it off. 'There's glitter dust everywhere at this time of year.'

'I'll come with you to the Carlton Towers if you promise me we'll go halves,' Lizzie said, looking at her brother.

'You should have a treat for a change,' Hugo insisted. 'You've done so much for me. I only wish—'

'Hugo,' Lizzie broke in. She had never seen her brother in sentimental mode before. 'This Christmas is going to be really special,' she promised softly. 'Just knowing you're safe makes it special for me.'

'It had better be special,' he muttered tensely.

They were both locked in their own thoughts as the taxi wove in and out of traffic on the busy streets. When it finally drew to a halt outside the brightly lit hotel Lizzie got cold feet, and hung back as Hugo leapt out.

'Come on,' he insisted, poking his head back into the taxi. 'We can't leave the doorman holding the door for ever.'

Lizzie shook her head. 'You don't understand,' she said. 'Kemal's staying here. I know you and I never got the chance to talk properly about Istanbul—but honestly, Hugo, he's the last person I want to see—'

'That's good to hear.'

'Kemal?' Suddenly Hugo was nowhere to be seen, and Kemal was standing in his place.

'Shall we move inside out of the cold?' he suggested, extending his hand to help her out.

'This is crazy,' Lizzie murmured with shock, sitting back in her seat.

'Crazy is one way of describing it,' Kemal conceded. Leaning into the taxi, he drew her out onto the pavement beside him.

'I'm with my brother…' she said faintly, already wondering if that was strictly true.

'You're with me now,' Kemal said.

* * *

'Basimin ustunde yereniz var.'

It was the same old gentleman who had welcomed her to *The Sultan's* palace, Lizzie remembered, smiling with pleasure when she saw him again. 'What did he say?' she asked Kemal as they walked past him into the presidential suite.

'You're sure you want a literal translation?'

'I'm prepared to risk it,' Lizzie said, laughing with happiness.

'OK,' Kemal agreed, trying not to smile. 'He said, you can even sit on my head if you want to! It means you pass the test; he really likes you. In fact, he will do pretty much anything for you.' As I will, he wanted to add, but it was too soon for that.

His old friend Mehmet had done him better service than he knew, Kemal thought, seeing Lizzie so happy. 'Have you eaten yet?' he asked, pausing at the door to the main room.

'I think Hugo has arranged dinner for me here at the hotel,' she said uncertainly.

'And so he has,' Kemal assured her softly. 'Happy Christmas, Lizzie.'

As the door swung open Lizzie gasped. The sumptuous room was lit by hundreds of candles, and there was a Yule log blazing in the modern open fireplace. There were even Christmas stockings hanging above it, bulging with gifts, Lizzie noticed, her eyes widening with amazement.

'And look at this,' Kemal said, drawing her attention to another part of the room.

As Lizzie turned she saw the Christmas tree.

Stretching almost to the ceiling, it had the faintest tang of pine. 'It's real!' she exclaimed, moving straight towards it.

Hung with dozens of baubles in red and gold, and strung with glittering bands of tinsel, it was the best tree she had ever seen in all her life. 'You did all this for me?' she murmured incredulously, running her fingertips lightly over the supple spines.

He could not remember the last time he had felt so much emotion, Kemal realised. He wanted to do this every day for her—make it Christmas every day for Lizzie, for the rest of her life.

'And look!' Lizzie said, hands clasped with excitement as she moved away to examine something else. 'There's a sleigh, and Father Christmas with all the reindeer, and presents—' Whirling her hands around, she laughed delightedly. 'I just can't believe it.'

Her voice was breaking now, but her expression…her expression…

Kemal crossed the room in a couple of strides and brought her into his arms.

'You've got glitter dust on your jumper,' Lizzie accused softly, looking up into Kemal's eyes. 'Just like Hugo—' She stopped as understanding dawned.

'I wonder how that could be?' Kemal murmured dryly, staring down into her eyes as if he could never get enough of looking at her. 'Why don't you go back to that sleigh and see if Santa has brought anything for you?' he said at last.

'For me?'

'Go on,' Kemal chivvied her, pushing Lizzie in the direction of the sleigh full of presents he had arranged on a side table.

'Do you mean this?' Lizzie said, hugging a box wrapped in silver paper.

'Why don't you take a look and find out?' he said, walking over to her.

Lizzie's eyes widened as Kemal took the velvet case from her hand and removed the aquamarine and diamond pendant she had chosen for his 'niece'.

'For me? It's far too much,' she breathed.

'No, it isn't,' Kemal assured her as he fastened it around her neck. 'And it goes perfectly with your lovely dress.'

The dress he had bought for her in Istanbul, Lizzie realised, smoothing down the soft chiffon folds. When Hugo had said to choose something special it had been the first thing she thought of when she opened her wardrobe. Had Kemal planned this all along?

'I'm not sure what to believe any more,' she said out loud.

'Do you like it?' Kemal said, turning her round to face him.

'I love it,' Lizzie breathed against his lips.

'Then that's all that matters. But there is one condition.'

'What's that?'

'You have to stay with me. Always.'

She wanted to, Lizzie thought, fingering the fabulous jewel on her neck. She wanted nothing more in all the world than to be with Kemal. But she was too independent to make a very good mistress, and there were too many ghosts in her past…

'I know, Lizzie,' Kemal murmured, tipping up her chin. 'I know all about the past.'

'You know?' Lizzie repeated softly, seeing understanding in his eyes.

'Hugo told me—don't be angry with him,' Kemal said quickly, holding her a little way in front of him. 'I asked the questions. I made him answer.' With a sigh he brought her close when she started to pull away. 'It's over,' he whispered fiercely. 'The nightmares are over, Lizzie.'

Kemal's heart ached for her when she looked up at him. There was so much hope in her eyes. 'I promise you, they're over,' he said steadily.

When he released her, Lizzie looked around at everything Kemal had done for her…the candles, the Yule log blazing, every type of delicious food she could think of laid out on the table, champagne chilling in an ice bucket. And there were crackers, and chocolates, and candied fruit for nibbling…

'So, you and Hugo…'

'Hugo played a critical role in my plan,' Kemal assured her, giving credit where it was due. 'Without Hugo I could never have got all this done in time— What?' he asked, seeing the expression on Lizzie's face.

'But where *is* Hugo?' Lizzie exclaimed anxiously. 'How will he spend Christmas if I'm here with you?'

Kemal's lips tugged up in a wry smile.

'I know what you're thinking,' Lizzie said, putting her hand on his chest as if that could stop his thoughts. 'You think he's far too old for me to be worrying about him.'

'I think you'll always worry about each other,' Kemal said. 'You are brother and sister, after all. But you can stop worrying now,' he said, dipping his head so he could look directly into Lizzie's eyes. 'I've invited Hugo and his new girlfriend to join us for lunch tomorrow—if that suits you?' But he could already see that it did. Lizzie's face was radiant.

'You've thought of everything,' she said.

'I hope so,' Kemal agreed. 'What about looking on the tree for something now?'

'Another present?' Lizzie exclaimed. 'I can't—'

'Why not?' Kemal demanded softly.

'Because your gift is back at the flat.' She had intended to send it to him—a small silver fruit knife to remind them both of the famous figs.

'There will be time for you to get that later— when you return to the flat to pack up your things,' Kemal pointed out.

'Pack up my things?'

'I'm sure there will be some things you want when you come to live with me.'

'You're very confident.'

'Isn't that what you like about me?' Kemal said softly.

'But I can't be your mistress,' Lizzie said, as Kemal started backing her towards a convenient sofa.

'I realised some time ago that having Lizzie Palmer as my short-term mistress would never work,' he admitted wryly, holding her still.

'What do you mean?' Lizzie said, feeling all her new-found happiness draining away.

'I have a much longer arrangement in mind.'

'What are you saying, Kemal?'

'I'm saying that I love you, Lizzie,' he murmured, dropping kisses on her lips, her eyelids and her brow. 'More deeply and more intensely than I would ever have believed possible. We are equal partners, you and I. You're so courageous, so tender, and I want to be the one to cherish you, to make you happy every day of your life. My life is nothing without you, Lizzie. I am nothing without you.'

Reaching up, Lizzie touched Kemal's lips with her fingertips. 'And I love you too,' she said softly. 'More than life itself.' And it was true, she realised. Whatever the consequences might be for her future.

By the time the backs of Lizzie's legs touched the sofa Kemal had freed the zip on her dress, and the catch on her bra, and was already pushing her tiny lace thong down over her hips.

'You are incredible,' she breathed, reaching for his belt.

'I certainly hope you think so,' Kemal agreed, dark humour flashing in his eyes.

And he was, Lizzie realised, closing her eyes as he sank deep inside her. She was hungry for him, starving, as if they had never been together in this way. And as if he was infected by her sense of urgency, Kemal went purposefully about his task—no teasing, no delays.

'More,' Lizzie cried out greedily, moments after he had tipped her over into fulfilment. 'I need more,' she exclaimed, wriggling out from under him. 'There,' she cried with satisfaction, straddling him and throwing her head back in ecstasy as he bucked beneath her to bring her satisfaction. 'I can never get enough of you,' she confessed, collapsing on him at last, only to feel that Kemal was still ready to give her more.

'I'm pleased to hear it,' he said. 'I've a pretty healthy appetite myself.'

And with that he swung her beneath him and took her again, firmly. 'But now we take it a little more slowly,' he said, controlling the pace.

'Anything you say,' Lizzie agreed, breathless from an overload of sensation.

Kemal paused momentarily to look at her. 'Is this the key to mastering you?' he demanded, slanting her a look.

'Could be,' Lizzie agreed wickedly, urging him on.

'Presents?' Kemal murmured later, when they were dozing together, exhausted.

'I've had my present,' Lizzie managed, too drugged by all their lovemaking to even form the words properly.

'More presents,' Kemal said, easing her off him. 'Remember the tree? Here,' he said, 'wrap yourself in this.' He tossed a silk throw from the sofa over to her.

'This is all very mysterious,' Lizzie said, as Kemal led her across to the Christmas tree.

'Is it?' Kemal asked, reaching for a small package.

'Shouldn't you get dressed first?' Lizzie murmured, hardly able to keep her hands off him.

'Not much point in my getting dressed, is there?' he pointed out. 'But I would like you to have this before we return to bed.'

'What is it?'

'Open it and see.'

Lizzie turned the small box over in her hand, and, flashing a glance at Kemal, responded to his nod of encouragement. Tearing off the paper, she opened the case and gasped. The aquamarine and diamond ring matching the teardrop pendant she was wearing flashed spectacularly from a nest of deep blue velvet.

'Would you like to put it on?' Kemal said.

'Are you serious?'

Taking it from her, Kemal placed it on the third finger of her left hand. 'I'm extremely serious,' he said, staring deep into Lizzie's eyes. 'In fact, I've never been more serious in my life. I want to marry you, Lizzie Palmer. There's no one else on earth I want to be my wife and bear my children. Will you marry me?' he asked. There was an edge of tension in his voice as he waited for her answer. 'Will you agree to become my wife?'

'If you will be my husband,' Lizzie challenged softly, holding her face up for his kiss.

'Let battle commence,' Kemal murmured wryly. 'Or in this case, let it continue for ever.'

And then he kissed her.

The Millionaire's
Christmas Wish

Lucy Gordon

Lucy Gordon cut her writing teeth on magazine journalism, interviewing many of the world's most interesting men, including Warren Beatty, Charlton Heston and Sir Roger Moore. She also camped out with lions in Africa, and had many other unusual experiences which have often provided the background for her books. Several years ago, while staying Venice, she met a Venetian who proposed in two days. They have been married ever since. Naturally this has affected her writing, where romantic Italian men tend to feature strongly.

Two of her books have won the Romance Writers of America RITA® award. You can visit her website at www.lucy-gordon.com

Look for Lucy Gordon's new novels, *A Winter Proposal* and *His Diamond Bride*, available in January 2011 from Mills & Boon® Cherish™.

PROLOGUE

IT WAS the most glorious Christmas tree in the world: eight feet high, brilliant with baubles, tinsel and flickering lights, with a dazzling star shining from the top.

Around the base brightly coloured parcels, decorated with shiny bows, crowded together, spilling lavishly over the floor.

The whole thing presented a picture of generous abundance. It was a family tree, meant to stand in a home, surrounded by happy children eagerly tearing the wrapping from the parcels, revealing longed for gifts.

Instead, it stood in the corner of Alex Mead's huge office. The presents were fake. Any child removing the pretty wrapping paper would have found only empty boxes.

But no child would do so. The whole confection had been designed and carried out by Alex's secretary, Katherine, and as far as he was concerned she had wasted her time.

She entered now with some letters in one hand and

a newspaper in the other, and he noticed that she couldn't resist glancing proudly at the tree as she passed.

'Sentimentalist,' he said, giving her the brilliant grin that won him goodwill at every first meeting. Often the goodwill was short-lived. It didn't take long for rivals and associates to discover the predator who lived beneath the charm.

'Well, it looks nice,' she said defensively. 'Honestly, Alex, don't you have any Christmas spirit?'

'Sure I do. Look at your bonus.'

'I have and it was a lovely surprise.'

'You earned it, Kath. You did almost as much as I did to build this firm up.'

He was a generous man where money was concerned. Not only her bonus but that of several other vital employees had been more than expected. Alex knew how to keep good staff working difficult hours.

'Some of them want to come in and thank you,' she said now.

'Tell them there's no need. Say you said it for them, and I said all the right things—Happy Christmas, have a nice time—you'll know how to make it sound good.'

'Why do you have to try to sound like Scrooge?'

'Because I *am* Scrooge,' he said cheerfully.

'Liar,' she said, with the privilege of long friendship. 'Scrooge would never have let his employees go a day early, the way you're doing. Most firms keep everyone there until noon, Christmas Eve.'

'Yes, and what's the result? Nobody does any work on Christmas Eve morning. Half of them are hung over and they're all watching the clock. It's a waste of everyone's time.'

She laid the newspaper, open at the financial page, on his desk. 'Did you see this?'

It was the best Christmas gift an entrepreneur could have had. There was a page of laudatory text about Mead Consolidated and its meteoric rise, its impact on the market, its brilliant prospects.

Backing this up was an eye-catching photograph of Alex, his grin at its most engaging, telling the world that here was a man of charisma and confidence who could steer his way skilfully through waters infested by sharks. You would have to look very closely to see that he was one of them.

The picture was cut off halfway down his chest, so it didn't show the long-limbed body that was just a little underweight. He was thin because he forgot to eat, relying on nervous energy for nourishment, just as he relied on nervous force to make an impact.

It was Alex's proud boast that he had no nerves. The truth, as Kath knew, was that he lived on them. It was one of the reasons why he looked older than his thirty-seven years, why his smile was so swift and unpredictable, and why his temper was beginning to be the same.

When she'd come to work for him his dark eyes had sparkled with ambition and confidence and his complexion had had a healthy glow. The glow was gone now, and there were too often shadows under his eyes. But he was still a handsome man, only partly through his looks. The rest was a mysterious talisman, an inner light for which there were no words.

She had been on business trips with him and seen the female heads turn, the eyes sparkle with interest. To his credit he had never collected, although whether that was out of love for his wife or because he couldn't spare the time from business, Kath had never quite decided.

'"Here's the one to watch,"' she read from the newspaper. '"By this time next year Mead Consolidated will threaten to dominate the market." Well, you might try to look pleased. It's so brilliant you might have written it yourself.'

He laughed. 'How do you know I didn't?'

'Now you mention it, you probably did. You're conceited enough for anything.'

'So conceited that if *I'd* written it I wouldn't have stopped at "threatened" to dominate. That's not good enough for me. I have to be at the top, and I'm going to get there.'

'Alex, you only started eleven years ago, practically working from a garden shed. Give yourself time.'

'I don't need time. I need Craddock's contract, the biggest that's ever come my way.'

'Well, you've got it.'

'Not until he's signed it. Dammit, why did he have to get this tomfool idea about going to the Caribbean?'

George Craddock, the man whose signature he was determined to get by hook or by crook, had been all set to sign when he'd been struck by the notion of a gathering on the tiny Caribbean island that he owned. He'd called Alex about it that very afternoon.

'And a big contract signing party to end it,' Alex groaned now. 'It's a pointless exercise because the deal's already set up.'

'So why the party?' Kath asked.

'Because he's old, foolish and lonely and has nobody to spend Christmas with him. So I have to forget my plans and catch a plane tonight.'

'Weren't you supposed to be seeing your family over Christmas?'

'Part of it. I was going to arrive tomorrow and stay until the next day. Now I'll have to call Corinne and explain that I've been called away. I just hope I can make her understand.'

Tact prevented Kath from saying, *Sure, she understands so well that she's divorcing you.*

'You should have told Craddock to get stuffed,' she told him robustly now.

'No way! You know how hard I've fought for this contract, and I'm not going to see it slip through my fingers now.'

Seeing disapproval on her face he said, defensively, 'Kath, there'll be other Christmases.'

'I'm not so sure. Children grow up so fast, and suddenly there aren't other Christmases.'

'Now you're being sentimental,' he said gruffly.

That silenced her. 'Sentimental' was Alex's strongest term of disapproval.

'I'm sorry,' he said. 'I'm not in the best of moods. Go home, Kath. Have a nice Christmas.'

'And be in early on the first day,' she said in a reciting tone.

'I never need to tell you that.'

When she'd gone he sat down tiredly and stared at the phone. What he had to do could not be put off any longer. If you had to break a promise it was best to do it quickly and cleanly.

He hoped there wouldn't be any trouble with Corinne. She was used to the demands of his job, and the fact that it often took him away from his family. The only time she'd ever fought him about it was at Christmas.

And it would have to be Christmas now, wouldn't it? he thought, exasperated. Just when he'd wanted to put a good face on things and show that he wasn't a neglectful father, as she'd accused him!

He'd planned to join her and the children tomorrow, just for one day, because that was all he could spare. But he would have arrived, overflowing with presents, and they would have been impressed whether they liked it or not. They would have *had* to be. He would have seen to that.

So the sooner he called, the better. Dial the number, say, I'm afraid there's been a change of plan—

He reached for the phone.

CHAPTER ONE

'MUM, it's the best Christmas tree we've ever had. A tree fit for Santa.'

Bobby was nine, old enough to have his own ideas about Santa, kind enough not to disillusion his adults.

'It's beautiful, isn't it, darling?' Corinne agreed, regarding her son tenderly.

The tree was five feet high and covered in tinsel and baubles which had been fixed in place by eager, inexpert hands. Perhaps the star on top was a little wonky, but nobody cared about that.

'Do you think Dad will like it?' Bobby wanted to know.

'I'm sure he will.'

'You will tell him I did it, won't you? Well, Mitzi helped a bit, but she's only a little kid so she couldn't do much.'

'She's six years old,' Jimmy said, from where he was standing behind Corinne. 'It's not that long since you were six.'

'It was ages ago,' Bobby said indignantly.

Jimmy grinned. He was a cheerful young man with a round face that smiled easily, the kind of man who seemed to have been designed by nature for the express purpose of being an uncle.

He was in the army, on two weeks' leave, and had gladly accepted Corinne's invitation to spend Christmas. They were only third cousins, but, with no other family, they had always clung to their kinship.

'You thought you were a big man at six,' he reminded Bobby.

'I was,' the child said at once. 'And I'm an even bigger one now. Put 'em up.'

He lifted his fists, boxer-style, and Jimmy obligingly responded with the same stance. For a moment they danced around each other, Jimmy leaning down to get within the child's range.

Suddenly he yelled, 'Help! He got me, he got me,' and collapsed on the floor, clutching his nose.

At once Bobby, the tender-hearted, dropped down beside him.

'I didn't really hurt you, did I, Uncle Jimmy?' he asked anxiously.

Jimmy wobbled his nose and spoke in a heavy nasal whine. 'I dink you spoiled by dose.'

Bobby giggled.

In falling, Jimmy had dislodged some of the presents and the two of them began to pile them up again. Corinne helped, trying not to be too conscious of the parcel with the tag that read, *To Daddy, with love from Bobby.*

'Daddy will like it, won't he, Mummy? I got it specially with my pocket money.'

'Then he'll love it, whatever it is,' she assured him. 'Aren't you going to tell me?'

Bobby shook his head very seriously. 'It's a secret between me and Daddy. You don't mind, do you?'

'No, darling, I don't mind.'

She watched how carefully he replaced the box under the tree, and her heart ached for him. Both children loved their father so much, and had been let down by him so often. And the more he failed them, the more anxiously they loved him.

But he would make up for it this time, she thought desperately. Please, don't let anything go wrong. Make him be here.

When Bobby had gone away, Jimmy murmured, 'That has to be the sweetest-tempered kid in the world.'

'Yes, and it scares me. He's wide open to be badly hurt by Alex.'

'But that won't happen, will it? Alex gave his word that he'd arrive on Christmas Eve.'

Corinne made a face. 'Yes, but a promise to us was always conditional on business.'

'But not at Christmas?' Jimmy said, shocked.

'Especially at Christmas, because that was when he could steal a march on all those wimps who spent it with their families.'

'But he promised to spend this Christmas with you and the kids.'

'No, what he promised was to arrive on Christmas Eve and leave on Christmas Day.'

'So little time? Then surely you don't have to worry about him cancelling that?'

'I wish I could believe it. Do you know? I'm not sure the children even realise that our marriage is over. They hardly see less of him now than they did then. Apart from the fact that we've moved house, not much has changed.

'I don't mind for myself, but if he disappoints Bobby and Mitzi again I'll never forgive him.'

'And you've put up with that all these years?'

'Yes,' she said, almost in a tone of surprise. 'Until the day came when I wouldn't put up with it any more. And now we're separated, soon to be divorced.'

Put like that it sounded so simple, and that was how she wanted to leave it. This wasn't the time to speak of the pain, misery and disillusionment she'd endured as she had finally given up the fight to save her marriage.

It had been twelve years, starting in unbelievable happiness. And perhaps unbelievable was the right word, because she had believed the impossible.

At eighteen you convinced yourself of whatever suited you. You thought you could marry a tough, ambitious man and not suffer for it. You told yourself that love would soften him, that he would put you first, not every time, but often enough to count.

When that didn't work you told yourself that the babies would make a difference. He was so proud of his children. Surely at least he would put *them* first?

'He can't have missed everything, surely?' Jimmy asked now.

'No, he was there for some birthdays, even some Christmases. But I always knew that if the phone rang he'd be off somewhere.'

Jimmy looked into her face, trying to see past the wry resignation to whatever she really felt. He doubted that she would let him catch a glimpse. She'd perfected that cheerful, unrevealing mask by now. That was what marriage to Alex Mead had done for her.

To Jimmy's loving eyes there was little change from the dazzling bride of twelve years ago, gloriously blonde and blue-eyed in white satin and lace, unwittingly tormenting him with the opportunity he'd missed. But opportunities sometimes came again to a man who was patient.

'By the way,' he said, 'is there somewhere I can hide my costume so that the kids don't find it?'

He was playing Santa at Hawksmere Hospital that evening, roped in by Corinne, a member of the 'Friends of Hawksmere Hospital.'

'It means going round the wards, ho-ho-ho-ing,' she'd said. 'And then you settle down in the grotto for the children who can walk out of the ward, or who happen to be in the hospital visiting someone.'

And Jimmy, good-natured as always, had agreed, just to please her.

'You can put it in the boot of my car,' she said now. 'I'll be leaving at five to take Bobby and Mitzi to a kids' party. When I've dropped them off I'll come back for you at six, and deliver you to the hospital by seven.'

'Yes, *sir*!' He saluted.

'Idiot!' She laughed.

'I'm paying you a compliment. You've got this organisation thing down to a fine art,' he said admiringly.

It was true; she was good at arrangements. Years of last-minute changes of plan, because Alex had been called away, had made her an expert.

'At eight o'clock,' she resumed, 'I collect the kids and take them to the hospital, where they'll find Santa already in place. They'll never dream it's you.'

'What about coming home?'

'Easy. When Bobby and Mitzi have finished I'll take them to the "Friends" office on some errand that I'll suddenly remember, while you get changed. When we leave the office we bump into you. We'll say you've been visiting a friend.'

'By the way, Alex won't mind my staying here, will he?'

'It doesn't matter if he does,' she said firmly. 'Our marriage is over in all but name, and he has no say. Besides, you and I are related.'

Which wasn't quite fair because she knew how Jimmy had always felt about her. But that was something she wasn't ready to confront just yet.

'It could be such a happy time,' she said, 'if only that phone doesn't ring. But I'll bet you anything you like that in the next few minutes Alex will call and say, "Corinne, there's been a change of plan." And I'll be expected to be "reasonable" and not "make a fuss".'

Her voice rose sharply on the last words, making

her bite it back with an alarmed look at the door in case Bobby or Mitzi could hear.

'Hey, steady.' Jimmy gently took hold of her shoulders. 'That's all over, remember?'

'It's not really over.' She sighed. 'Not while Alex and I share children who can be hurt by him.'

'In the end they'll see him for what he is.'

'But that's just it. I don't want them to see him for what he is. I want them to go on believing in him as the most wonderful, glorious father there ever was, because that's what they need.'

'Just don't let *yourself* be hurt by him.'

'No, that can't happen any more.'

'I wish I believed that.'

'Believe it. I'm completely immune. Whatever was between Alex and me was over a long time ago.' She gave him a bright smile. 'Honestly.'

'*Mummy!*' came a shriek from the garden. '*Uncle Jimmy! Come and look. It's going to be a white Christmas.*'

It wasn't merely snowing; it was coming down in drifts, huge, thick snowflakes that settled and piled up. Jimmy immediately bounded out into the garden to join the children in a game. Corinne stood in the window, watching them jumping about and laughing. Dusk was falling and the only light came from the house. Through the driving snow she could only just make out the fast moving figures. They could have been anyone.

They could have been the newly-weds, blissful in their first Christmas, hurrying together through the snow to the shabby little flat that had been their first home.

And the happiest, she recalled now.

The next one had still been happy, but they had already been in their first proper house, with Alex promising her 'a palace by next year'. She hadn't wanted a palace. All she had asked was for her joy to last, but the first cracks were already appearing.

Even so, she hadn't realised yet that she had a rival, a beloved mistress called Mead Consolidated. And, as years had passed, the rival had grown all-consuming. How wearily used she had grown to the phone calls, and Alex's voice saying, 'There's been a change of plan.'

But not this year, she thought desperately. I don't mind for myself, but don't let him disappoint the children.

The phone rang.

For a moment she couldn't move. Then, in a burst of anger, she snatched up the phone, and snapped, 'Alex, is that you?'

'Yes, it's me. Look, Corinne, there's been a change of plan—'

On the last lap of the journey the snow began to come down even harder. Alex cursed and set his windscreen wipers to go fast.

It had been an awkward sort of day, with people forcing him to change course at the last moment, which he disliked. First Craddock and his mad Caribbean party, then, just as he was reaching out to call Corinne, the phone had rung.

It had been Craddock's secretary to say that her boss had been rushed to hospital with suspected appendicitis. The whole trip was off. The signing would have to be done later.

The upside was that he could call Corinne and say he would be there a day earlier.

'Alex, that's wonderful. The children will be thrilled.'

'OK, I'll be there tonight, but I'm not sure when. The traffic's difficult.'

'We're going out, but I'll leave the key in a little box in the porch. Maybe you'll be there when we get back.'

'Fine. I'll see you.'

The snow was coming down harder, and his car began to slide over the road. He slowed, but then more snow seemed to collect on his windscreen.

Why had she insisted on moving out to the very edge of London instead of staying in the mansion he'd bought her? It was a beautiful house, full of everything a wife could possibly want, but she had fled it without a backward glance.

And where had she chosen instead? A dump. A cottage. He knew he was exaggerating because it was a five-bedroom detached house, far better than where they'd lived when they were first married, but nothing compared to what he'd given her later.

It still hurt when he thought of the home he'd provided for her. The price had been extortionate, but he'd paid it willingly, thinking how thrilled Corinne would be.

It had had everything, including a paddock for

the pony he intended to buy as soon as Bobby had learned to ride. Those riding lessons had been a kind of eldorado in his mind. How he would have loved them in his own childhood! And how different the reality had been!

But, for Bobby, everything would be perfect.

As always, he felt something melt inside him when he thought of his children, Mitzi, wide-eyed and appealingly cheeky. Bobby, quiet, self-assured even at nine, rapidly growing up to be a companion to his father.

And then Corinne had blown the whole dream apart. He'd come home one day to find the beautiful house empty and his family gone.

When he'd seen her again she'd talked about divorce, which he didn't understand. There was nobody else for either of them, so who needed divorce? He'd refused even to consider it.

He had thought his firmness would make her see sense and come home, but she had quietly refused to budge. She would wait out the divorce, if necessary.

She didn't actually say that the important thing was to be away from him, but the implication hung in the air.

He was nearing his destination now. He had never been there before, and darkness and snow made it hard to find the way. It was this road—no, the next!

Relieved, he swung the car into the turning and immediately saw a man crossing in front of him, moving slowly.

What happened next was too fast to follow, although later his mind replayed it in slow motion. The man saw him and began to run, and at the exact same moment he slammed on the brakes. The sudden sharp movement made the car skid over the ice that lay on the road beneath the snow.

It was the merest bad luck that the car went in the same direction as the man. Whether he, too, slithered on the ice or the car actually touched him nobody could ever be sure. But the next moment he was lying on the ground, groaning.

Alex brought the car to a cautious halt and got out. By now a woman had appeared from a house and hurried over to the victim. She was wrapped up in a thick jacket whose hood concealed everything about her head.

'Jimmy? Oh, God, Jimmy, what happened?'

'That idiot was going too fast. Hell, my shoulder!'

He winced and, clutching his neck, gasped with pain.

'Corinne, can you give me your arm?'

'Corinne?'

Alex drew back the side of the hood to her indignation.

'Hey, what are you—? Alex! Did you do this?'

'He slipped on the ice.'

'Which I wouldn't have done,' Jimmy said, 'if you hadn't been going too fast to stop.'

'I was barely doing—'

'Shut up both of you,' she said fiercely. 'This isn't the time.'

'Right. I'll call an ambulance.'

'No need,' Jimmy groaned. 'We were on our way to the hospital anyway. Corinne, let's just go. I'm sure it's only a sprain and they can patch me up before I do my stuff.'

He climbed slowly to his feet, holding on to Corinne and refusing all offers of help from Alex. But when Corinne touched his arm he yelled with pain.

'Be sensible,' said Alex, tight-lipped. 'If you don't want an ambulance I'll take you. Wait here!'

He strode off to where he'd parked. Jimmy, clinging to Corinne, gasped, 'Corinne, please, anybody's car but Alex's.'

'Fine. Mine's just here.'

In a moment she'd opened the door and eased him into the passenger seat. She was starting the engine when Alex drew up beside her.

'I said I'd take him,' he yelled.

'You don't know the way. Wait for us in the house, Alex.'

She pulled away without waiting for his answer. Muttering angrily, Alex swung around to follow her. He'd just about recognised Jimmy from their wedding. As Corinne's sole relative he had given her away, but his languishing looks had suggested that he would rather have been the groom.

Soon the main entrance of Hawksmere Hospital came into view. He followed Corinne and drew up behind her as she was opening the passenger door. From the way Jimmy moved he was more badly hurt than had appeared at first. Alex marched ahead into the hospital and up to the reception desk, emerging a few moments later with an orderly and a wheelchair.

'He's right, Jimmy,' Corinne said. 'Let them take you in.'

Jimmy muttered something that Alex didn't catch, which made Corinne exclaim, 'To blazes with Santa Claus! It's you that matters.'

They made a little procession into the hospital, the orderly wheeling Jimmy, Corinne beside them, and Alex bringing up the rear.

Once inside, Jimmy was whisked away to an examination cubicle. Now, Alex thought, he would get the chance to talk to Corinne, but she insisted on going too. There was nothing for him to do but sit down and wait, which he found the hardest thing in the world to do.

Relief came ten minutes later with the whirlwind arrival of an elderly lady of military aspect and forthright manner.

'Where is he? I was told he'd arrived and we're waiting for him.'

'Who?' asked Alex.

'Santa Claus. Jimmy. Corinne promised he'd do it, but where is he?'

'In a cubicle, having his shoulder examined,' Alex said. 'He met with an accident.'

'Oh, dear! I do hope it isn't serious. That would be most inconvenient.'

'I dare say he'd find it inconvenient as well,' Alex said sardonically.

She whirled on him like an avenging fury.

'It's easy for you to sit there and mock, but you don't have a crowd of children who are expecting Santa to arrive with his sack and give out presents, and you've got to tell them that he isn't coming.'

Alex was saved from having to answer this by the arrival of Corinne.

'Mrs Bradon, I'm so sorry,' she said at once. 'Jimmy's got a broken collar-bone and a cracked rib. I'm afraid he can't be Santa.'

'But can't he be Santa with a broken collar-bone?' Mrs Bradon asked wildly. 'The children won't mind.'

'It's being set now. He's in a lot of pain,' Corinne explained.

'Well, they can give him something for that.'

'They *are* giving him something, and it's going to send him to sleep.'

'*Oh, really! That's very tiresome!*'

Alex's lips twitched. He couldn't help it. Mrs Bradon's single-mindedness would have been admirable in a boardroom, but here it was out of place.

'There must be a way around the problem,' he said.

'Like what?' Corinne confronted him, eyes flashing. 'This is your fault. You ran Jimmy down, driving like a maniac.'

'I was doing ten miles an hour, if that. He slipped on the ice. He always was a slowcoach.'

'Well, he can't be Santa, whatever the reason, and it was your car.'

The sheer injustice of this took his breath away.

'What does it matter whose car it was if I didn't hit him?'

'Jimmy says you did.'

'And I say I didn't.'

'Will you two stop making a fuss about things that don't matter?' Mrs Bradon said crossly. 'We have a crisis on our hands.'

'Surely not,' Alex said, exasperated. 'How hard can it be to play Santa? A bit of swagger, a ho-ho-ho or two—anyone can do it.'

'Fine!' said Corinne. 'You do it!'

'I didn't mean—'

'What a wonderful idea!' Mrs Bradon cut across him. 'You're about the same height so the costume will fit you. You have got it?' This was to Corinne.

'Yes, it's in the car. And you're right, the size is fine.'

'I'm sure you don't need me,' Alex said defensively. 'This is a hospital. There must be a dozen men around—'

'There are a hundred,' said Mrs Bradon firmly. 'But they are doctors, nurses, ward orderlies. Which one of them do you suggest should be taken off his duties to save you from having to do *your* duty?'

'It's hardly my—'

'You deprived us of our Santa Claus,' said Mrs Bradon implacably. 'It's your job to take his place!'

'Look, ladies—'

Alex met Corinne's eyes, seeking her support. But she was looking at him angrily.

'After all,' she echoed him, 'how hard can it be? A bit of swagger and a ho-ho-ho or two.'

'All right, all right,' he snapped.

'Splendid!' Mrs Bradon hooted triumphantly.

'You'd better get to work right away. Corinne will show you what to do. Hurry up!'

She bustled away.

'You're finding this very funny, aren't you?' Alex growled.

'It has its moments. When was the last time someone spoke to you like that without you flattening them in return?'

'I can't remember,' he admitted.

'I'll get the costume and you can get to work.'

'Corinne, wait.' He detained her with a hand on her arm. 'Must I really do this? Surely—'

'Aha! Backing out!' She began to cluck like a hen.

'I am not chicken,' he said furiously.

'Sez who?' she jeered. 'You're just afraid you're not up to it. That's the first time I've heard you admit that there is something you can't do better than the next man.'

'I didn't mean that.'

'No, you meant that it's beneath you.'

'I just think that there has to be another way.'

'Of course there is. All you have to do is find a replacement who can do this in exactly ten minutes' time.'

He ground his teeth.

'All right. Get the costume and let's get this over with.'

'I'd rather you came out to the car with me. I don't want to let you out of my sight.'

'Dammit, Corinne!' Alex said furiously. 'Why must you overreact to everything? I've said I'll do it, and I'll do it. After all, how hard can it be?'

She fetched the costume and took him into a small kitchen where Jimmy had planned to change. As Alex dressed she explained his duties.

'You have to go around both the children's wards with your sack, giving out presents.'

'How will I know who to give what?'

'Leave that to me. I'll be there. I'll tell you who everyone is and hand you the right present. After that you go and sit by the big tree in the hall and you'll get some children who are in here visiting people. Then I'll have to leave you for a few minutes to collect Bobby and Mitzi.'

'Did you tell them I called? That I was coming a day early?'

'No, I thought I'd let it come as a nice surprise when you turned up.'

'You mean you thought I'd let you down?' he asked wryly.

'Well, if I did I was wrong,' she conceded. 'Maybe I've done you an injustice. When I heard your voice I thought you were going to cry off again. But you didn't, and that's wonderful. It'll be the best Christmas ever.'

Remembering how close he'd come to cancelling, he had the grace to feel awkward and was glad that fiddling with his beard gave him an excuse not to look at her.

'Here,' she said, laughing. 'Let me fix that.'

'There's an awful lot of stuff to put on,' Alex said. 'I thought it would just be a white thing with hooks over the ears.'

'Well, there are hooks, but there's also glue so that it fits your mouth and stays in place. Jimmy believes in doing things properly. He got this from a theatrical costumier, and he chose the best.'

'Jimmy?'

'Jimmy is spending Christmas with us—or he was before he was knocked down by some maniac driver.'

'I did not knock him down,' Alex said through gritted teeth. 'He fell.'

'Whatever. He chose the costume, and it's a good one.'

Alex had to admit that it was the best. The beard was soft and silky, gleaming white, with a huge moustache that flowed down into the beard itself. When it was fixed in place it covered his mouth almost completely.

But there was something else.

'A wig?' he protested.

'Of course. How can you be convincing with a white beard and brown hair?'

'Won't my hair be covered by a hood?'

'Even with a hood they'd notice. Children notice everything these days. They see wonderful special effects on films and television, and when they get close up to reality they expect it to be just as convincing.'

He grumbled some more, but when the wig was on he had to admit that it looked impressive. Long, thick and flowing, it streamed down over his shoulders, mingling with the beard, which was also long and flowing.

He looked nothing like himself, and that was some consolation, he reflected. At least nobody would be able to identify him.

He was beginning to get into the part now, driven by the instinct that governed his life—to be the best at whatever he undertook.

If you weren't the best there was no point in doing it. Right?

In some respects he had the physique, being over six foot. But there was one flaw.

'I'm too thin,' he objected. 'This suit was made for someone a lot bigger.'

'There's some padding,' Corinne said, diving back into the bag.

With the padding in place he had a satisfactory paunch.

'Will I do?' he demanded.

'Your cheeks need to be rosier.'

'Get off! What are you doing?'

'Just a little red to make you convincing.'

'I won't even ask what you've just put on my face.' He groaned. 'I don't want to know.'

'You look great. Completely convincing. Now, let's have a ho-ho-ho!'

'Ho-ho-ho!' he intoned.

'No, you need to be more full and rounded. Try it again, and make it boom this time.'

'*Ho-ho-ho!*'

To her surprise, he made a good job of it.

'Well done,' she said. 'That was really convincing.'

'You thought I couldn't be?'

'Jimmy never manages it that way. He tries but it comes out sounding reedy.'

'What about my eyebrows?' Alex asked. 'Are they white enough?'

He was right. His dark brown eyebrows now looked odd against the gleaming white hair and whiskers.

'There aren't any false eyebrows,' she said, inspecting the bag. 'You'll have to go as you are.'

'No way. We'll do this properly. This is a kitchen, right? Won't there be some flour?'

'The kitchen's just for making tea,' Corinne objected, opening cupboard doors.

But, against all odds, she found a small bag of flour with some left inside.

'Fancy you thinking of that,' she said, rubbing it into his eyebrows until the natural colour faded.

'When I was a kid I wanted to be an actor,' he said.

'You never told me that before.'

'I was never trapped under half a ton of gum and whiskers before.'

She stood back and regarded him.

'You look great,' she said. 'Here's your sack of toys, all labelled. Are you ready?'

'Let's go!'

CHAPTER TWO

ELEPHANT WARD had been designed and decorated for children. Streams of cheerful-looking cartoon elephants walked around the walls and played games with their trunks.

Alex stood in the doorway and boomed, '*Ho-ho-ho!*' to an accompaniment of shrieks from the rows of beds. When it quietened, Corinne murmured, 'First bed on the right, Tommy Arkright, broken pelvis. Fascinated by ghosts.'

Whoever had planned this had done it well, Alex realised as soon as he began talking to Tommy. The name, the ailment and the interest were all accurate, and when Tommy unwrapped his gift, which turned out to be a book of ghost stories, it was a triumphant moment.

It was the same with the next child, and the next. From being self-conscious, Alex began to relax, and even to enjoy himself. In part this was due to the knowledge that he was unrecognisable. Not that people here would have known him anyway, but the total anonymity still made him feel easier.

He was in a good temper when he came to the end of the ward and turned in the doorway for a final wave and a cry of, 'Goodbye, everyone.'

'*Goodbye, Santa!*' came the answering roar.

'I'll say this for that Bradon woman,' he growled as they headed down the corridor towards Butterfly Ward. 'She prepared the ground properly.'

'What do you mean?'

'Every detail was right. Good preparation is the secret.'

'I agree. But why do you give the credit to her?'

'Didn't she organise all this?'

'No, *I* did, you rotten so-and-so,' she said indignantly. 'I personally went round every child, asking questions, trying not to be too obvious about it.'

'You?' His surprise was unflattering but she told herself she was past being bothered by him now.

'Yes, me,' she said lightly. 'Feather-brained Corinne who can just about manage a shopping list, remember? I prepared the ground, gathered intelligence, surveyed the prospects—er—' She clutched her forehead, trying to think of other businesslike expressions.

'Appraised the situation?' He helped her out. 'You did a great job.'

'So did you.'

'Much to your amazement,' he said with a grin that she could just detect behind the beard.

'You see over there—' she said, not answering directly '—the Christmas tree in the corner?'

'Yes.'

'When you've finished on Butterfly Ward that's where you go and sit. I'm off to collect Bobby and Mitzi, and I'll be back as soon as possible.'

'Are you going to tell them it's me?'

'No, I think it will be nicer not to. Let's see if they guess.'

'Of course they'll guess. I'm their father.'

She did not reply.

On Butterfly Ward it was the same as before, except that now he was full of confidence and performed his part with a touch of swagger that went down well.

Corinne stayed long enough to see him settle in before leaning down to murmur, 'I'm off now. Back soon.'

It was only a few minutes' drive to the house where the party was being held. Bobby and Mitzi piled into the car, wearing party hats, clutching gifts and giggling.

'No need to ask if you had a good time,' Corinne said.

'And now we're going to see Father Christmas,' Mitzi yelled gleefully.

Bobby touched Corinne's arm and spoke quietly. 'Is Daddy still coming?'

'Yes, darling, he's still coming.'

'He didn't cancel while we were at the party?'

'No, he didn't.'

He searched her face.

'Are you *sure*?'

Until then Corinne had been feeling in charity with Alex, but at the sight of Bobby's painful anxiety she discovered that she could hate him again. No man had the right to do that to a child, to destroy his sense of security in his parents, so that every moment of happiness had to be checked and rechecked to discover the catch.

'Darling, I give you my word. Daddy has not cancelled and he isn't going to.'

He settled into the car, apparently satisfied.

'By the way—' she said as she drove to the hospital '—Uncle Jimmy had an accident. He fell over on the icy road and broke his collar-bone.'

They were loud in their cries of dismay.

'Will Uncle Jimmy be in hospital for Christmas?' Bobby asked.

'I don't know. They're putting him in plaster now. When I've delivered you to Santa I'll go up to see him.'

At the hospital she took them straight to where Alex should be sitting by the tree, only half expecting him to be there.

But of course he was there! Alex had run his pride up this flagpole and it was really no surprise that he was doing well. He had one child on his knee and another standing beside him, while their mother looked on, smiling. There were three others waiting.

Corinne inched forward carefully, keeping her eyes on Bobby and Mitzi, waiting for the moment of recognition.

It didn't come.

Of course it was the beard and hair, she realised.

The disguise was magnificent. It would be different when they were closer.

At that moment Alex looked up. His eyes went first to Corinne, then to the children, then back to Corinne, while his eyebrows signalled a question. Almost imperceptibly she shook her head.

She took them to the end of the little queue, said something to them and walked away.

Alex was glad that he'd bothered to dress up properly when he heard one child mutter, just audibly, 'He looks like a real Santa, Mummy.'

At last his own two children stood before him, Mitzi keeping back a little. It was weeks since he'd seen her, and he'd forgotten how fast children grew. Her hair, which had been short, was now long enough to wear in bunches which stood out from her head, giving her the appearance of a cheeky elf. He couldn't help grinning at the picture she presented.

But right now she was solemn and seemed unwilling to come forward.

'Go on,' Bobby urged her.

But she shook her head.

'She's a bit shy,' Bobby confided to Santa.

'But I'm—' He checked himself, and amended the words to, 'But I'm Santa Claus. Nobody is shy of me.'

He waited for one of them to say, Daddy! But neither of them did.

Of course, he thought. They were pretending not to know, enjoying the joke.

He leaned down to Mitzi. 'Aren't you going to tell

me what you want for Christmas?' Big mistake. Mitzi was surveying him, wide-eyed with astonishment.

'But I already told you. I put it in my letter. Didn't you get it?'

'Of course I did,' he improvised hastily.

Over her head his frantic eyes met Bobby's. The boy mouthed 'Marianne doll set.'

Since he'd never heard of this, Alex had to signal bafflement with his eyebrows. Bobby mouthed it again, more emphatically, and this time Alex understood. 'Ah, now I remember. You want a Marianne doll set,' he echoed, and saw his daughter's eyes light up.

'The one in the riding habit,' his son mouthed at him.

'The one in the riding habit,' Alex repeated.

Mitzi's beaming smile told him he'd got it right.

'But is that all?' he asked. 'Isn't there anything else you've thought of since?'

Mitzi hesitated until her brother nudged her gently and whispered, 'Go on.'

Emboldened, the little girl reached up to say, 'And can I have a necklace?'

'Of course you can,' Alex said.

Suddenly the little girl hugged him. He tensed, thinking of the beard that might be dislodged. But it held, and he became aware of her arms, holding him without restraint.

She had hugged him before, but not like that. Now he knew what he had always sensed in her embraces. It had been caution. And it wasn't there now.

Before he had time to take in the implications, she

had released him and moved aside, making room for her brother, who came in close.

But before addressing Santa he wagged a finger at his sister.

'Don't wander off,' he told her severely.

She stuck out her tongue.

'Does she give you much trouble?' Alex asked with a grin.

'She's OK most of the time,' Bobby said seriously. 'But sometimes she won't do as I say 'cos I'm not very much older than her.'

It was a three-year difference, but a sudden inspiration made Alex say, 'About five years?'

Bobby looked pleased. 'Not quite as much as that,' he admitted. 'But almost. And it's a great responsibility being the man of the family.'

'The man of—? Don't you have a father?'

Bobby made a face. 'Sort of.'

Alex felt an uneasy stillness settle over him.

'What do you mean, sort of?'

'Well, I don't really know him very well,' Bobby said. 'He's not around much.'

'I expect he's busy,' Alex said.

'Oh, yes, he's always very busy. Too busy for us. He and Mummy aren't together any more.'

'Do you know why that is?' Alex asked carefully.

Bobby gave a shrug.

'They were always rowing, and Mummy cried a lot.'

A strange feeling went through Alex. Corinne had never let him see her cry. Not for a long time.

'Did she tell you why she cried?' he asked.

Bobby shook his head.

'She doesn't know I've seen her and I have to pretend not to, because she doesn't like anyone to know.'

'So you don't know why?'

Bobby shook his head.

'Perhaps she misses your dad?' Alex ventured.

'I don't think so. He's nasty to her.'

'How?' Alex asked, a touch more sharply than he'd meant to.

'I don't know, but when they talk on the phone she cries after she's hung up. But he doesn't *mean* to be nasty,' Bobby added quickly. 'He just doesn't know how people feel about things.'

Alex hesitated for a while before saying, 'So maybe it's better that they're not together?'

'Oh, no,' Bobby said, shaking his head vigorously. 'He's coming home for Christmas and it's going to be brilliant—that is—if he really comes.'

'Has he said he will?'

'Yes, but—' Bobby's shrug was more eloquent than a thousand words.

Alex could not speak. There were too many thoughts swirling around in his head, and they were all of the kind he found hard to cope with. The best he could manage was to put his arm around Bobby's shoulders and squeeze.

'You think he'll back out?' he asked at last.

'I keep telling myself he'll be there,' Bobby said. 'It isn't for long. Just Christmas Eve until Christmas Day. He could spare us that, couldn't he?'

'I should think he could spare you more than that,'

Alex managed to say in a voice that he hoped didn't shake too much.

'Could you fix it?' Bobby asked.

'You want me to arrange for him to stick around for longer than that?'

'Oh, no,' Bobby disclaimed quickly, as though saying that nobody should ask for the impossible. 'Just make sure he's there for when he said he'd be.'

'All right. It's a promise.'

Bobby searched his face anxiously. 'You really mean it?'

'You think I can't do it?'

Bobby shook his head, his eyes fixed on Santa with a look in them that was almost fierce.

'You can do anything,' he said, 'if you really want to.'

The air seemed to be singing in Alex's ears. He wondered if he'd imagined the emphasis in the last words.

'Then I promise,' he said.

'Honestly? Dad will be here until Christmas Day, and he won't leave early?'

Alex was swept by a mood of recklessness. 'I can do better than that,' he said. 'He'll arrive early, and he'll stay longer than Christmas Day.'

He waited for the effusion of joy. It did not come. If anything, the fierce scrutiny on the child's face intensified.

'Really and truly?' he asked. 'Cut your throat and hope to die?'

'Of course. When I give my word, I keep it.'

'That's what *he* says,' insisted Bobby. And suddenly it was a child's voice again, forlorn and almost on the edge of tears.

Alex put his hands on both Bobby's shoulders.

'He will be there tonight,' he said. 'You have my solemn promise. Word of a Santa!'

Bobby nodded, as though satisfied.

'Now,' Alex said, 'tell me what you want for Christmas.'

'But I just did,' Bobby said.

'That's it? Nothing else?'

'That's the thing that matters. And you said I could have it. You promised.'

'Yes, I did. So you just go on home and see what happens.'

Bobby smiled, and for the first time it was the happy, natural smile of a child. It made Alex feel as though he had been punched in the stomach.

'All right, you two?' It was Corinne, appearing suddenly. 'Move along. Father Christmas still has customers.'

Another three children had joined the little queue, and Bobby and Mitzi moved off to join their mother.

'How's Uncle Jimmy?' Bobby asked. 'Can he come home?'

'We might get him home tomorrow. We'll have to wait and see. Come on, let's be off home. Goodbye, Santa.'

'Goodbye, Santa,' they chorused.

Alex raised a hand in a gesture of farewell and turned back to his next 'customer' with reluctance.

He wasn't sure how he got through the next few

minutes. His mind followed Corinne and the children out of the hospital and into her car, watching them talking, wondering what they were saying.

At last it was over and he was free to go. To his relief, Mrs Bradon joined him in the kitchen just as he finished changing. He would not have thought it possible that he could have been glad to see her.

'What about the costume?' he asked.

'Just take it with you. Corinne will know what to do with it.'

He packed up the costume into its bag and tossed it into the back of his car. On the journey, he wondered how much Corinne would have told the children after they left.

When he reached the house he intended to go straight in. Instead, he found himself sitting in the silent car, trying to psyche himself into taking the next step.

It should be his great moment. He would burst through the front door, keeping Santa's promise and enjoying the look on his children's faces.

Without warning, his courage failed. He didn't know why. His son had spoken like a child who loved his father and looked forward to seeing him. Yet he had said, 'It isn't for long, just Christmas Eve until Christmas Day. He could spare us that, couldn't he?'

Something about those words haunted Alex painfully.

He could spare us that, couldn't he?

Was that how Bobby saw his father? Doling out his time in small, begrudged amounts?

He did not want to go inside the house.

Cowardice. The weakness he had always despised most.

With sudden decision, he got out of the car. In the porch he hunted for the key that Corinne had left out for him, hearing sounds inside the house. There was her voice.

'Bobby, what are you doing in the hall?'

'Nothing, Mummy.'

'Come and have an iced bun.' That was Mitzi, a little more distant, sounding as if her mouth was full.

'In a minute,' Bobby replied. His voice still came from the hall.

Then Corinne's voice.

'Darling, why are you watching the front door?'

Suddenly, as though a spotlight had come on inside him, he saw his son's face, staring at the front door with painful intensity, not daring to believe.

He didn't know where that light had come from, except that it had something to do with his talk with Bobby. It lit all the world from a new angle, showing what had always been there, but which he'd never noticed.

He turned the key.

'*Daddy!*'

The ear-splitting shriek came from Mitzi. Corinne was standing by the kitchen door, watching his arrival with pleasure. Only Bobby did not react. He stood completely still, his face a mask of total and utter disbelief.

Alex wanted to cry out, But I promised you. You

knew I was coming. Instead, he concentrated on hugging his daughter, who was almost strangling him with the exuberance of her embrace.

'Hello, darling,' he said.

'Daddy, Daddy,' she carolled.

'Hey, don't choke me,' he said, laughing. 'How's my girl?'

She gave him a smacking kiss, which he returned. Then it was time to face his son.

Bobby was strangely pale. 'Hello, Daddy,' he said.

'Hello, son.'

To his dismay, Bobby held out his hand politely, almost as though meeting a stranger. Or a ghost.

'Hello, Daddy.'

Then he broke suddenly, as belief came rushing through, and flung himself against his father, burying his face against him.

Alex's arms closed protectively about his son as he felt the storm of emotion go through the child. He didn't know what to do except stay as he was, trying to understand but feeling helpless.

Looking up, he found Corinne's eyes on him. Her expression was gentle but he had the feeling that she was conveying a warning.

Bobby drew back to look at his father. His face bore the marks of tears, which he rubbed aside hastily. Alex brushed some of them away with his own fingertips.

'It's all right, son,' he said quietly. 'I'm home.'

Bobby sniffed. 'Hello, Daddy.'

'Hey, is that any way to greet your old man? Crying? Shall I go away again?'

It was a feeble joke and a badly misjudged one. Bobby clung to him, his eyes full of sudden dread, and Alex drew in his breath. He was floundering badly.

'You're not getting rid of me that easily,' he backtracked, saying anything that came into his head. 'I'm here now and I'm staying. You've got me for Christmas, whether you like it or not.'

Mitzi began hopping about, yelling, 'Yippee, Yippee!' Bobby, the thoughtful one, smiled.

'Come on, kids,' said Corinne. 'Let Daddy come in and get his breath back.'

Alex straightened up and kissed her cheek. Corinne did the same, smiling to present a show of cordiality for the children.

'You said you weren't coming until tomorrow,' Mitzi reminded him.

'Well, I got away early and thought it would be nice to see a bit more of you.' He tweaked her hair. 'You don't mind, do you?'

She shook her head ecstatically and pointed to the centre of her mouth. 'I lost a tooth,' she informed him proudly.

He studied the gap with great interest. 'That's very impressive. When did that happen?'

'Last week,' she said.

'I'm sorry I missed that.'

'I saved it for you,' she reassured him.

'Then I'll look forward to seeing it,' he said gamely.

Mitzi promptly pulled it out of her pocket. Alex heard Corinne give a soft choke of laughter.

'How about selling it to me?' he said. 'I'll bid you a pound.'

Mitzi made a face.

'One pound fifty?'

She finally got him up to two pounds and the deal was struck. Mitzi pocketed her profit and went off to explain to Bobby how to do business.

'A chip off the old block,' Corinne said when Alex joined her in the kitchen.

'Better,' he agreed. 'At her age I'd have settled for fifty pence.'

'Ah, but don't forget inflation,' she said, teasing. 'I'll say this for you—you coped very well with that tooth. I thought it was going to faze you.'

'Nothing fazes me,' he insisted. Then he looked at the tooth in his hand. 'What am I supposed to do with this?'

'Treasure it.' She laughed. 'You just paid a high price for it. I expect you're ready for something to eat.'

'I don't know when I last ate,' he admitted.

'I do,' she said, giving him a friendly smile. 'Breakfast was a cup of black coffee. You meant to catch up at lunchtime, but you were caught between meetings so you made do with a sandwich.'

'Am I that predictable?'

'Yes.'

'I had a roll in the car on my way here.'

'Oh, well, then. You don't need the steak I got for you.'

Suddenly he was ravenous. 'Just try me.'

She poured him some tea, very strong and heavily sugared, as he liked it, and he wandered into the next room. Like the rest of the house, it was decorated with paper chains and tinsel.

It was an old house, full of a kind of shambling charm. The original fireplace was still there, although only a vase of artificial flowers adorned it now, and, out of sight, the chimney was blocked to keep out draughts.

Beside it stood the tree. It was smaller and less impressive than the one in his office, and the fairy on the top looked wonky, as though she were clinging on for dear life. But the parcels around the base were all addressed to people and, when picked up, rattled reassuringly.

Alex stood looking at it and suddenly the inner light shone again, showing him that this was a real tree, with real presents, for real people.

He looked at some of the labels. There were gifts from Corinne to the children and from them to her, gifts from Jimmy to all of them, and from them to him. It occurred to him how often Jimmy's name appeared.

'Time for bed, kids,' Corinne called. 'There's lots to do tomorrow.'

'I want Daddy to put me to bed,' Mitzi said at once.

'All right,' Alex said. To Bobby he added, 'What do you want?'

'I put myself to bed,' the child said gruffly. 'But you can look in, if you want.'

'Fine.'

His daughter bounded all over him and rode on his back down the hall to her bedroom, which turned out to be a shrine to horses. Horse pictures adorned the walls; horses leapt all over her duvet cover. Her slippers were shaped like horses and picture books about horses filled her shelves.

Alex spoke without thinking. 'Now I understand.'

He meant the Marianne doll in the riding habit that she had mentioned to Santa earlier. With his little girl's eyes on him he remembered, too late, that he was supposed to know nothing.

'Now I understand what you've been doing recently,' he improvised. 'We'll have lots to talk about tomorrow. Goodnight, pet.'

He kissed her and departed hastily before he could make any more slips.

Bobby's bedroom was curiously unrevealing. There were no pictures on the wall, or books, beyond a few school books. Alex flicked through one of these.

'Good marks,' he observed. 'You're working hard, then?'

Bobby nodded.

'That's good. Good.' He was floundering. 'Are you all right, son? All right here, I mean?'

'Yes, it's nice.'

'Don't you miss your old home?'

Bobby hunted for the right words. 'Places don't really matter.'

'No. People matter. Right?'

'Right.'

'Well, I'm here now.'

'Yes.'

Alex searched his face. 'You are glad, aren't you?'

'Yes, of course I am.'

He would have doubted it if it hadn't been for their memory of the earlier conversation. How could all that have gone?

Because now he knows it's me.

'Tomorrow's a big day,' he said cheerfully.

'Yes.'

It was becoming a disaster. He had resolved to act on what he'd learned from Bobby that evening, and use it to make this visit a triumph. That was the secret of success—good intelligence and knowing how to use it. But all his gains were slipping away.

'Daddy—'

'What is it?' His voice betrayed his eagerness.

'Tomorrow, will you ask Mitzi about the school play? She was ever so good in it.'

The school play? The school play? His mind frantically tried to grapple with this. When had it been? Why hadn't he known?

'It was a pantomime—' Bobby said, reading his face without trouble '—and Mitzi was an elf. She had two lines.'

'Er—?'

'It was last week. You were abroad.'

'Of course—yes—otherwise I'd have—'

'Yeah, sure. You will remember to ask her, won't you?'

'Of course I will. Goodnight, son.'

Corinne said her goodnights after him. As they passed in the corridor she said, 'I've put you in that room at the end. Your things are in there.'

He looked in before going downstairs. It was a small, neat room with a narrow bed.

Alex thought about the other rooms. Presumably Corinne had the big room on the corner of the house, but where, he wondered, had she put Jimmy?

CHAPTER THREE

HE CAME down the stairs so quietly that Corinne didn't hear him, and he had a moment to stand watching her as she worked in the kitchen.

The steak smelled good, and suddenly he was transported back to the early days of their marriage, when steak had been a luxury. But somehow she had managed to wring the price out of the meagre housekeeping money they had.

They had been partners—laughing at poverty, competing with each other in loving generosity, squabbling to give each other the last titbit. But that was long ago.

The years had barely touched her, he thought. The slim, graceful figure that had once enchanted him was the same, two children later.

She had been gorgeous at eighteen—beautiful, sexy, witty, knowing her own power over young men and enjoying it. They had all competed for her, but Alex had made sure that he was the one who won her.

Her face had changed little, except that it was

thinner, and the ready laughter no longer sprang to her eyes. They were still large, beautiful eyes but there was a sad caution there now.

'It's ready,' she called, seeing him.

Like every meal she had ever cooked him it was excellent—the wine perfectly chosen, the salad exactly as it should be.

Their last meeting had been three months ago, and it had ended in a fierce quarrel. Since then there had been communication between lawyers, and the odd phone call that had left each of them resolved that it should be the last. Her invitation for Christmas had been delivered through a letter addressed to his office.

'Thank you for letting me come,' he said quietly.

'I didn't think you would. I was amazed that you actually turned up early. What happened? Did something more important fall through?'

He winced.

'I'm sorry,' she said at once. 'I didn't mean it like that.'

'There's nothing more important than being with my family,' he said emphatically.

'It means the world to the children.'

'What about you, Corinne?'

'Never mind about me. This is their time.'

'But I do mind about you. It's ours too, isn't it?'

'Well, it's a chance for us to be civilized with each other. We haven't done much of that lately.'

'And that's all?'

'Yes, that's all. I'm not your wife any more—'

'The hell you aren't!' he said with the swift anger that sometimes overtook him these days. 'We're not divorced yet, and maybe we never will be.'

She regarded him with a quizzical air that was new to him. 'You have to win every negotiation, don't you? But you won't win this one, Alex. So why don't we just leave it there? I don't want to spoil this holiday.'

'Is there someone else?'

The question jerked out of him abruptly, without finesse, tact or subtlety.

She sat silent.

'Tell me,' he insisted.

'No, there's nobody else. I don't want anyone else. That's not why I left you.'

'Just to get away from me, huh?'

'If you care to put it that way—yes. But why must we put it that way or any way? It's Christmas, Alex. Let it go.'

'All right,' he said hastily.

As she set coffee before him she said, 'How about you?'

'I beg your pardon?'

'Do *you* have someone else?'

'Do you care?' he growled.

'If you can ask, so can I,' she said lightly.

'Except that you broke up this marriage. That hardly gives you a stake in the answer.'

She shrugged. 'You're right. Do you want a drop of brandy in that?'

'Thanks.'

As she was pouring the brandy he said, 'The answer's no.'

She didn't answer directly, but she took his cup and carried it and her own into the next room, where the tree glowed.

'Sit down and relax,' she said. 'You look dead on your feet.'

He leaned back in an armchair, closing his eyes, desperately tired in a way that had nothing to do with work. Mercifully he felt the strain begin to drain away, leaving him as close to being relaxed as he ever came.

'How did it go after I left the hospital?' Corinne asked. 'Did the children recognise you?'

'No,' he said slowly. 'At least, they didn't show it if they did.'

'Mitzi would have shown it,' Corinne said at once. 'She's got no subtlety, that little one. Her riding instructor says she has no nerves, but lots of nerve.'

'Riding instructor?' Alex queried. 'She's learning to ride too?'

Corinne shook her head. 'Just her. Bobby gave it up.'

'Don't tell me he was afraid?' Alex said sharply.

'No, not afraid. Bored. It just didn't interest him, and there are other things he wants to do. But Mitzi is crazy about horses, so she does it instead.'

He was silent, swallowing his disappointment. Corinne eyed him sympathetically.

'Come out of the nineteenth century,' she chided.

'What do you mean by that?'

'In those days you could have told Bobby what he had to be interested in, but not now. He doesn't have to ride a horse just because you wanted to and couldn't.'

Alex's father had mucked out stables for a race-horse trainer. Alex had grown up surrounded by beautiful animals, none of which he had been allowed to touch.

'And it has to be your son who carries on your dream, doesn't it?' Corinne pursued. 'Somehow a daughter isn't the same. Pure nineteenth century.'

'That's nonsense,' he growled.

'No, it isn't. It's the way your mind works. But you ought to go and see Mitzi ride, see how good she is.'

'All right, I will.'

'You'd be proud of Mitzi. She's a real natural. In fact, I think you ought to learn yourself.'

'Me? Take riding lessons?'

'Why not? You used to tell me how it was your dream when you were a boy. What's the point of making all that money if you don't spend some of it making your dreams come true?'

It flashed across his mind that he was too busy earning it to enjoy spending it, but all he said was, 'Sure, and let my six-year-old daughter make rings round me!'

'Well, she's bound to at first, because she's had some practice and you're just a beginner,' Corinne said, 'but I'm sure she'd make allowances for you.'

He gave a reluctant grin at her teasing. Suddenly he remembered, 'She says she wants a Marianne doll set, the one in the riding suit. What's she talking about?'

'"Marianne" is the latest craze. It's a doll that comes with its own lifestyle—ballgown, ballet tutu, riding habit.'

'Where do I get one?'

To his bewilderment Corinne rocked with laughter.

'You don't think I left it to the last minute, do you? It's Christmas Eve tomorrow. People have been trampling each other to death in toy shops for the last two months. Don't worry, I've got one tucked safely away. You can give it to her, if you like.'

'Do you think I haven't bought her a present?'

'No, I think you've probably got her something very expensive. But what she wants is that doll, and if you give it to her you'll be her hero.'

'Thanks,' he said gruffly. 'I'd like that. And she also wants a necklace.'

'I've got that too,' she assured him.

'Like I said earlier, you're really well organised. I could do with a few like you in the firm.'

'Funny, Jimmy says the same.' Corinne laughed. 'Only he says they need me in the army. It makes me wonder how the country has muddled along without me for so long.'

Alex scowled. He didn't want to talk, or even think, about Jimmy.

'Anyway, Mitzi's easy to understand,' Corinne went on. 'Bobby is more complicated, and it's much harder to know what he's thinking. Did he recognise you?'

'I don't know,' Alex said slowly. 'I honestly don't know. He didn't say anything, but—Corinne he was just a few inches away from me. Surely he *must* have recognised his own father?'

'It was a very complete disguise,' she reminded him. 'The wig and the hair and the padding. And he wasn't expecting you to arrive today.'

The words, And he hasn't seen you for weeks, hung in the air.

'Did he tell you what he wanted?' Corinne asked. 'I think I've got that covered too, but I'd be glad of any "insider tips" you picked up.'

Oh sure, he thought, *my son said he wanted me home for Christmas, like it was an impossible fantasy. He reckons he has a 'sort of' father, and he's bracing himself for when I let him down.*

'Hey, there!' Corinne was waving. 'Anybody home?'

'Sorry!' he said, forcing himself to smile. 'No, I didn't get any inside information. You'll have to tell me. What's his big interest?'

'Drawing, painting—anything to do with art.'

'Doesn't he like soccer or any sports?'

'He watches them on television, but his interests are the quiet ones.'

'Corinne, are you sure? He's never said anything about drawing to me.'

'Of course not. He knows you wouldn't like it. But he's passionate about drawing and painting since he discovered that he has a talent for it. He's just getting deep into water-colours now, and if you gave him something connected with that he'd be thrilled. But I'll bet you've bought him a pair of riding boots.'

'Among other things,' Alex growled. 'I suppose you don't want me to give them to him?'

'That's up to you.'

'Sure!' he snapped. 'Like I'm going to dig my own grave by giving him something he doesn't want, thus proving I'm the useless father that you claim! You'd like that, wouldn't you?'

Once in a blue moon Corinne lost her temper. She did so now—big time!

'Don't be *stupid*, Alex! I know it's hard, but try not to be laughably, moronically stupid. If that's what I wanted I wouldn't be warning you now, would I?'

'No,' he said hastily. 'Sorry. I didn't—I just fly off the handle sometimes. I don't mean to. I shouldn't have said it.'

'It doesn't matter. It's the children who matter. Just try to see Bobby as he is, and not as "Alex Mead's son." How I've come to hate "Alex Mead's son"!'

'What the devil do you mean by that?'

'He's a character who's hung around our home ever since Bobby was born. He has plenty of "boy's interests." He likes the "manly" sports and anything that involves getting dirty. He's got no time for art or music or thinking, and he's the opposite to Bobby.

'That boy has spent his life so far pretending to care for things that bore him rigid because that was the only way to get your attention. He knew ages ago that he didn't fit the picture of your ideal son. In fact, the only person I know who does fit it is Mitzi.'

He was silent, too shocked to speak.

At last she got up and brought him another brandy.

'Thanks. I need it.'

When he'd revived his courage a little he managed to ask, 'If I'm so hateful why does he bother to pretend?'

'Because he *adores* you,' Corinne said. 'He worships you. He'd go through fire and water for you. Haven't you got that through your thick skull yet?'

She broke off and gave a sigh of frustration. 'We're quarrelling again.'

'Yeah, well—' He shrugged, sharing her frustration.

He was saved from needing to say any more by the sound of his cellphone coming from the hall. He answered it with relief.

It was Mark Dunsford, his assistant, as zealous about business as he was himself. Mark was jealous of Kath, who had been with Alex longer and had his total trust. He tried to compensate by giving himself to the job, body and soul, twenty-four hours a day, and making sure that his employer knew it.

'I just wondered if you had any final instructions for me,' he said now.

'No way. It's Christmas. Get off home to your family.'

'I don't have a family.'

'Well, get off home, anyway. Or wherever you get off to.'

'Wherever I am, I'll be keeping an eye on things. I thought that you would be, too.'

'Mark, lighten up. It's Christmas. There's nothing to keep an eye on.'

'All right, but perhaps you'd better give me a contact number where you are. I know I can call the cell-phone, but another number is always useful.'

He hesitated. Nothing was likely to happen, but it was as well to be prepared.

'OK. The phone number of this house is—'

He stopped. Corinne had wandered out into the hall and was looking at him, her head on one side.

'No,' he said. 'This is a private number. I can't give it out and I'd rather you didn't contact me at all. In an emergency, use the cellphone, but it had better be life or death or there'll be trouble. I'll call you when I'm ready.'

'But—'

'Goodbye, Mark.'

He hung up and looked at Corinne with a touch of defiance.

'Thank you,' she said warmly.

He put out his hand and she took it between both of hers. 'I'm glad you came,' she said. 'It's going to be a great Christmas.'

Her eyes were as warm as her voice and he tight-ened his hand. But the next moment she stepped back, smiling and saying, 'It's time for bed. I'll see you in the morning. Goodnight.'

Next morning the snow lay thick on the ground as they had Christmas Eve breakfast.

'Are we going to see Uncle Jimmy?' Mitzi asked.

'No need,' Corinne said. 'I've already called the hospital and he can come home. I'm going to fetch him later. You three can go shopping.'

The children cheered, but a few minutes later Alex took her aside.

'It's a bit soon for him to be leaving hospital, isn't it?'

'Hospitals don't encourage people to stay over Christmas, and it's only a collar-bone. I can look after him here. Jimmy's been kind to me.'

She saw him scowl and said firmly, 'Alex, I am not leaving him to spend Christmas in hospital. Besides, you'll be the gainer.'

'How?'

'I'll be spending a lot of time with Jimmy, leaving you with the children. So, you make the most of it.'

For a man who wanted to be with his children it was a good bargain. But 'I'll be spending a lot of time with Jimmy' had a melancholy sound.

Alex became aware that Bobby was signalling to him, and remembered.

'So, tell me how the school play went,' he said, tweaking Mitzi's hair. 'I want to know all about it.'

She produced her photo album so fast that it was clear she'd had it ready, and they began turning the pages together. There she was in a green hat and green costume with bells, giving the world her wide, gap-toothed grin.

Alex gave her an answering grin, but it was too late to smile back at her. It was only a week ago but that mischievous imp was already gone for ever.

Along with many other things.

After that he made a good job of it, showing an enthusiasm that Mitzi, the unsubtle, accepted at face value. When she'd gone away happy he met Bobby's eyes, silently asking the child if he'd done all right. And his nine-year-old son nodded in approval.

They split into two parties. Corinne headed for the hospital, while Mitzi and Bobby piled into Alex's car and directed him to the shopping precinct.

It was quieter than Alex had expected, with most shoppers having finished the day before. On the lower floor an amateur brass band played carols, with spectators joining in. Bobby and Mitzi enthusiastically sang 'While Shepherds Watched their Flocks' while Alex, suddenly inspired, sang 'While Shepherds Washed their Socks,' at the top of his voice, until compelled to desist by the glares of a large woman shaking a collecting box.

Under her reproving gaze he put a very large donation into the box and scurried away, his children clinging to his hands and rocking with laughter.

'Oh, Daddy, you are funny.' Mitzi giggled.

'I used to sing that at school,' he remembered. 'It got me into trouble then, too.'

Strolling around later, Mitzi noticed something that made her gasp with joy.

'Daddy, look! Santa Claus!'

The precinct's Santa was just embarking on his last stint, complete with grotto and tree. Mitzi looked up at her father eagerly, but Bobby touched her arm and shook his head.

'We already saw Santa,' he urged. 'Yesterday.'

'We saw him last week too,' she pointed out, 'and the week before.'

Alex watched to see if his son would be stuck for an answer. But he wasn't.

'They were just pretend Santas,' he said. 'The one we saw last night was the *real* Santa.'

'How do you know?' she demanded rebelliously.

'I just do.'

'How?'

'I *do*.'

Mitzi subsided, apparently satisfied with this brand of logic. Bobby looked up at his father and received a wink, which he returned.

'Why don't we go in there?' Alex said, pointing quickly at a store that sold books, CDs and various related items.

As soon as they were inside he struck lucky, coming across a display of 'Marianne' picture books, with one prominently displayed featuring Marianne as a rider.

'Has she got that?' Alex muttered to Bobby.

'No.'

'Here.' He shoved some notes into Bobby's hands. 'You get it while I distract her.'

The teamwork went like clockwork. In a short time Bobby was back with a parcel wrapped in anonymous brown paper.

'What's that?' Mitzi demanded.

'What?' Bobby looked innocently around.

'That!'

'I don't see anything. Do you, Dad?'

'Not a thing.'

Making a covert purchase for Bobby was harder,

because he couldn't use Mitzi as an agent. But he struck lucky, noticing a series of video cassettes titled 'Water-colour Technique'. Managing to catch the assistant's eye, he mouthed, 'How much?' pointing at Bobby to explain the reason for silence.

She indicated the price and Alex produced his card. The videos vanished and reappeared safely wrapped.

Luckily, Bobby had started bickering with Mitzi and noticed nothing.

'How about something to eat?' Alex asked. All this undercover work was exhausting.

They found a café and Alex studied the menu, but the other two knew what they wanted.

'Cocoa and cream buns,' Mitzi said blissfully.

'Yes, please,' Bobby chimed in at once.

'But what about your lunch?' Alex objected. 'If I take you home already full your mother will kill me.'

'It's real cream,' Bobby pointed out.

'Lots and lots of it,' Mitzi said ecstatically.

'Does Mummy allow you to eat cream buns before lunch?'

They considered.

'No,' Bobby said regretfully.

'No,' Mitzi agreed.

'Well, then!'

Bobby regarded him innocently. 'But Mummy isn't here.'

Alex made the mistake of engaging him in debate.

'But aren't you equally bound by her rules even when she's absent?'

'No,' Bobby explained. 'Because it's Christmas, so she might have changed her mind, just this once. We don't know, do we?'

'I suppose we don't,' Alex said, eyeing his son with new respect. 'Mind you, I've got my phone. We could call and ask her.'

'That wouldn't be fair,' Bobby said quickly. 'Mummy's very busy, doing last-minute things. We shouldn't interrupt her.'

'Ah!' Alex gave this idea his full attention. 'You think we could simply assume her agreement—out of consideration for her?'

'Yes,' Bobby said firmly.

They shook hands.

'When you want a job,' Alex told him, 'come to your old man. The thought of you arguing on the other side scares me stiff. You've got every trick.'

'I learned them from my dad.'

'Oh, no, you don't!' Alex said at once. 'I'm not taking the blame for your devious mind.'

Bobby grinned.

They each had three cream buns and two cups of cocoa, and Alex thought he'd never tasted anything so delicious. Then they went home to confess to Corinne. But she wasn't fazed.

'Fine. It'll save me cooking a big lunch. Uncle Jimmy's here, kids.'

Overjoyed, they dashed into the next room where Jimmy, swathed in plaster, was reclining on the sofa. Alex followed and was in time to see them climbing up beside him, moving carefully, not to hurt him.

Mitzi was on his uninjured side and put her arms about him. 'Poor Uncle Jimmy,' she said. 'Is it very bad?'

'Not really,' he said cheerfully.

'What did you do?'

'Fell in the road,' he said at once. 'Silly me.'

Alex regarded him with mixed feelings. It was decent of Jimmy not to have blamed him. On the other hand he couldn't like him, especially as Mitzi was greeting him with real affection. Bobby was less effusive, but he was on Jimmy's injured side.

'Tea up!' Corinne called, entering with a cup.

She handed it gently to Jimmy, who smiled, receiving it, while Mitzi solicitously plumped up his cushions.

A shiver went through Alex. It was absurd, of course, but for a moment they had looked like a family.

The stockings and socks were in place, hanging from the mantelpiece. Jimmy, clowning, had produced one full of holes, which had reduced the children to fits of laughter.

'Right now, you two,' Corinne said. 'Bed.'

'Mummy, we haven't left things for Santa,' Mitzi urged. 'In case he gets hungry and thirsty.'

'What do you want to leave, pet?'

'Jam tarts and milk,' Mitzi said at once.

'Ginger biscuits,' Bobby said. 'And some beer.'

'You can't leave beer,' Mitzi said, scandalised.

'Why not? He'd hardly be drunk in charge of a reindeer after just one beer!' Bobby said.

'But it won't be just one,' Mitzi pointed out. "Cos

he'll have been to lots of other people first, and drunk what they left, and—'

'Well, they won't all have left beer,' Bobby argued.

'Will.'

'Won't.'

'Will.'

'Won't.'

'Will.'

'Won't.'

Corinne tore her hair. 'Break it up, you two. Peace on earth, goodwill to all men.'

'And all women?' Jimmy suggested.

'Especially all the women,' Corinne clowned. 'They're so busy cooking for everyone.'

'I'd do it for you if I had more than one arm.'

'Yeah, sure you would,' she jeered.

'You're a hard woman.'

They grinned at each other. Alex tried to tell himself that they were like brother and sister, but there was something about the cheerful ease of their relationship, the way they shared the same sense of humour, that troubled him.

'Anyway, I vote for jam tarts and milk,' Jimmy insisted.

'I vote for ginger biscuits and beer,' Alex said at once. 'I think Santa gets left a lot of milk, and beer will come as a nice change for him.'

In the end they compromised, which meant that Bobby left out a can of beer and some biscuits, while Mitzi stubbornly left out a carton of milk, jam tarts, and two glasses.

'Why two?' Bobby demanded.

'So that he doesn't have to drink milk and beer out of the same glass,' she riposted.

'He won't drink the milk at all.'

'He will.'

'He won't.'

'Will.'

'Won't.'

'*That's enough!*' Corinne roared. 'Get to bed, both of you.'

They vanished.

'I think I'll go up too,' Jimmy said.

'You look all in,' Corinne agreed. 'Have you had your pills?'

She fussed over him until he'd taken his medication and at last, to Alex's relief, Jimmy took himself off to bed.

'That's it!' Corinne brushed the hair back from her brow. 'I'm bushed.'

'It's been a great day,' Alex said.

'Yes, it has. You've been terrific.'

'Have I?'

'The kids are so happy. Haven't you seen?'

But it wasn't quite what he wanted to hear.

'What about you?' he insisted.

'It's not about me. It's about you and them. Alex, I've never seen them so much at ease with you. And Bobby—surely you've noticed how he—?'

He kissed her.

He did it so fast that she had no time to resist. Surprise had always brought him results in business, and for a moment he thought it was working here. Corinne didn't try to push him away, but neither did she embrace him back. Instead, she remained so still that it finally got through to him.

'Corinne—'

'Alex, please don't. It's been so lovely. Don't spoil it.'

'Is it spoiling it to say that you're still my wife and I still love you?'

'Don't talk like that,' she begged.

'Corinne, what is it? I thought that when we'd been apart for a while—'

'I'd "see sense"? That's how you think of it, isn't it? You think I had to be crazy to leave you, and that I'll realise I made a mistake.'

'Are you going to say you didn't?'

'Yes, I am saying that. I wanted a home, husband and children, and all I got was the children. They're lovely kids, but I wanted a husband as well.'

'And you couldn't love me?'

'You weren't there. You haven't been there for years.'

His eyes kindled. 'Tell me about this man you want to love. He wouldn't be called Jimmy by any chance?'

'Don't be ridiculous.'

'Is it? I can see that he's a lot of things I'm not— things you might want.'

'Yes, he is. He's kind and dependable, and I always know where I am with him, but—'

Corinne checked herself, on the verge of saying, But he's not you.

It had been a risk, asking Alex to stay for Christmas, but she'd told herself that she must take it for the children's sake. Now she knew it had been a mistake. Her love was not sufficiently buried, or perhaps not sufficiently dead. It threatened her too often and too piercingly.

Alex watched her, willing her to say something that would ease his heart.

'But?' he urged. 'But you haven't forgotten "us." Have you?'

'No,' she admitted unwillingly. 'I can't forget that. I'm not sorry we married. We were very happy back then, and I'll never regret it.'

'If we had the time over again—you'd still marry me?'

'Oh, yes. Even knowing how it would end, I'd still do it.'

'It hasn't ended yet. We don't know how it's going to end.'

'Alex—'

He took hold of her shoulders, very gently. 'It's too soon to say,' he told her. 'Don't let's rush to part, Corinne.'

She gave a wry smile. 'I thought we *had* parted. I should have remembered that no position is ever final until you've agreed to it.'

'Tell me that you don't love me any more,' he said insistently.

'And you're an ace negotiator, always knowing the other side's weak spot.'

'Then you do love me.'

'I don't know.' She sighed. 'I'm trying not to.' She added reluctantly, 'But it's hard.'

He drew her against him, not kissing her this time but wrapping his arms about her body and holding her close while he rested his cheek on her head.

After a while he felt her arms slowly go around him, and they stayed there peacefully together for a long time.

CHAPTER FOUR

WHEN his tiny illuminated clock showed midnight, Bobby slid out of bed and went quietly into the hall. The house was completely silent and almost dark, except for a faint glow he could see downstairs.

Moving noiselessly, he crept down the stairs and into the room where the tree glowed. On the threshold he stopped and an expression of relief crossed his face.

'I knew you'd be here,' he whispered.

The red-clad figure by the tree turned and smiled at him through his huge white beard.

'Come in,' he said.

Bobby moved closer. In dim light, and on his feet, Santa looked bigger than ever.

'Did you have trouble with the chimney?' he asked. 'I was afraid it might not be big enough.'

Santa looked down at his wide girth. 'You mean with there being so much of me?'

'I wasn't being rude.'

Santa laughed, not a *ho-ho-ho,* but a kindly, understanding sound.

'It's not as bad as some places I've tried,' he said.

'What about when there's no fireplace?' Bobby asked. 'How do you get in then?'

Santa tapped the side of his nose and winked. 'Trade secret,' he said.

He sat down in the armchair, put down the can of beer he was holding and signalled for Bobby to sit. Bobby plonked himself down on the floor.

'You know how I got so fat?' Santa asked.

Bobby shook his head.

'In their kindness, people leave more out for me than I can possibly eat.' He indicated the hearth. 'How about you have the milk and we'll split the tarts and biscuits? I've had most of the beer and it was great. Whoever left that was a genius.'

'It was my idea,' Bobby said eagerly. 'Mitzi insisted on putting out a glass for you as well. I said you wouldn't be bothered, but you know what girls are.'

'Actually, Mitzi was right,' Santa confided, holding up a glass with beer in it. 'Drinking from the can is awkward when you've got a beard.'

He poured milk from the carton into the other glass and the two of them sat sipping and sharing tarts.

'So what happened?' he asked. 'Did your dad show up?'

'Yes, just like you said. A day early. How did you know?'

Santa hesitated. 'Inside information.'

'Do you know everything?'

'No,' Santa replied at once.

'So you can't tell me how long he's going to stay?'

'I already did, when we talked yesterday. Longer than tomorrow.'

'But after that?'

'What do you really want him to do?' Santa asked thoughtfully

'Stay as long as possible.'

Santa looked at him keenly. 'Are you hoping I'll wave a magic wand?'

But his thoughtful son shook his head. 'No,' he said. 'He has to want to, or there's no point.'

'That's right,' Santa agreed. 'You can't make people choose what you'd like them to.'

'You mean he doesn't really want to stay with us?'

'Oh, yes, he does. You're his family, and he loves you all more than anything else on earth, even if he doesn't always show it very cleverly. But he got confused and other things got in the way. Now he's trying to find the way back to the place where he took the wrong turning, but it isn't easy. The road seems different when you're looking backwards. But you could help him.'

'How?'

'I can't tell you that. You have to sense it for yourself. But you will. Don't worry.'

Santa indicated the tree.

'Have you got your presents sorted out?'

'Yes. I got a scarf for Mum and a picture book for Mitzi.'

'And your dad?'

'Well—I got him a pair of cufflinks.'

'It sounds like a good choice, so what's the problem?' Bobby's voice had hinted that all was not well.

'I got him something else too, but I'm not sure if I should give it to him.'

'If it's from you, he'll love it,' Santa said without hesitation. 'You can rely on that.'

'Can I show it to you?'

'That would be really nice.'

'It's upstairs.' Bobby went to the door, then hesitated. 'You won't go away?'

'Cross my heart and hope to die.'

Bobby vanished and reappeared a moment later with a large, flat object that he put into Santa's hands, switching on a side lamp so that he could see.

It was a picture of a family sitting under the trees by water, evidently having a picnic. There was a man in a red shirt, a woman in a green and white dress, a small boy of about five and a toddler in a pink dress. It had been painted in water-colours by an inexperienced but talented hand.

'Did you paint this?' Santa asked in a strange voice.

Bobby nodded. His eyes were on Santa's face.

'I think you should definitely give it to him,' Santa said at last.

'You think he'll understand?'

'You put a lot of work into it, and he'll think it's wonderful that you took so much trouble to please him.'

'But will he *understand*?' Bobby asked with a touch of desperation.

'Yes,' Santa said decisively. 'He will.'

'Everything?'

Santa put his hand on the child's shoulder. 'He'll

understand everything that you want him to understand,' he said. 'I promise you.'

A smile of pure, blinding relief broke over Bobby's face.

'You'd better go and wrap it now,' Santa said. 'I have a lot of other houses to visit.'

'Goodnight.'

'Goodnight.'

At the door Bobby paused and looked back. 'I didn't used to believe in you. But I do now.'

He vanished quickly.

The brilliant sunlight flashed and glinted off the water and bathed the river-bank with warmth. The man and the woman picnicking under the trees leaned back in the welcome shade and smiled at each other with secret knowledge.

'That was good,' he said. 'The best I ever tasted. Happy birthday, darling.'

She didn't answer in words, but she blew him a kiss. Her arms were curled around the two-year-old girl sleeping in her arms, but her eyes, full of love, were on the man.

'It's not much of a birthday for you, though,' he mused, 'having to do the catering for a picnic.'

'You helped.'

'Did I? Oh, you mean when I dropped the butter?'

They laughed together.

'Wouldn't you rather have had a big night out?' he asked. 'Fancy restaurant, champagne, everything of the best?'

She looked down at the little girl sleeping in her arms. 'You've already given me the best,' she said.

He nodded. 'Yes, this is as good as it gets.'

Suddenly she chuckled.

'What?' he demanded, looking around. 'What?'

'It's that bright red shirt you're wearing. It's so un-you. You're usually so sober-suited.'

'On the contrary, this is the real me. The suit is a uniform, although sometimes it gets to feel like a second skin.'

'So the truth is that you're a bit of a devil?' she teased.

He winked. 'You know more about that than anyone.'

He shifted position to get closer to her, but then something that came into view made him leap to his feet.

'*Bobby*, not so near the water. Come back here.'

He dashed over and scooped up the five-year-old child, who chuckled with delight as his father carried him back to the picnic.

'Whadaya mean by giving your old man a heart attack, eh?' he demanded as he sat down beside his wife. 'What's the big idea?'

As he joked he buried his face against the child, who screamed with laughter.

'Don't scare him,' the woman protested.

'He's not scared of me. He's my boy. Aren't you?'

'Yes,' said the little boy firmly, putting his arms around his father's neck.

The man turned his head to smile at the woman.

'Do you have any idea how much I love you?' he whispered.

She gave a soft laugh. 'Not a clue. You'll have to tell me.'

He leaned sideways to kiss her, and she leaned towards him. It was awkward because they were each holding a child, but they managed somehow between love and laughter. And the little boy in his father's arms went contentedly to sleep.

Alex awoke with a start and found that he was already sitting up. The dream had been so clear, like being taken back four years to relive the moment.

He'd seen it all again—the trees, the water, the sun. More than that, he'd felt again the blissful contentment of that day.

This is as good as it gets.

That had been his feeling. When had he known it since?

He'd thought of it as something between himself and Corinne. Who would have imagined the little boy was imprinting it all on his mind, to carry there for years until his hands had the skill to reproduce it, like a silent reproach to the adults who had let the happiness slip through their fingers?

He discovered that he was shaking and pulled himself together. He'd been lucky. He'd remembered in time.

Bobby looked in. 'C'mon Daddy. We're opening presents!'

He pretended to lie down again. 'Already? I was hoping for a lie-in.'

'*Daddy!*'

He grinned and allowed himself to be hauled downstairs in pyjamas and dressing-gown. 'Sorry about this,' he told Corinne. 'I wasn't given any choice.'

'You and me both,' she said, laughing. She'd managed to dress, but only in hastily flung on jeans and sweater, before getting to work in the kitchen.

'Mummy, can we open the presents now?' Mitzi cried.

'Just a moment, pet. Let Uncle Jimmy come downstairs.'

When Jimmy had come cautiously down and settled on the sofa it was time to start. The children first, tearing off gaily coloured paper with excited screams.

Alex held his breath as Bobby opened the watercolour videos and then became totally still, so that Alex feared the whole thing had misfired. But then Bobby looked at him with eyes so full of incredulous joy and relief that Alex's own eyes blurred suddenly.

With Mitzi he scored a double hit, giving her not only the Marianne book but a pair of riding boots. They were too large, but Alex immediately clutched his head, swore he couldn't understand how the mistake had happened, and offered to change them as soon as the holiday was over, and Mitzi was happy.

'Brilliant,' Corinne murmured appreciatively when she had him alone for a moment.

'Even those of us who are moronically stupid have our clever moments,' he riposted.

'Oh, don't be smug.'

His gift to her was a small bottle of expensive perfume, one he'd bought for her in the past. He had thought it a safe present, but suddenly it seemed intimate enough to draw down her disapproval. But she only thanked him with an impersonal smile and said nothing more. He found himself strangely relieved, almost as though he'd been afraid.

Her gift to him had been as impersonal as her smile— a scarf of very fine cashmere, beautiful but meaningless. It told him nothing beyond the fact that she wanted the children to see them being friendly.

The present-giving was nearly over and there were only a few small items left around the base of the tree.

Alex found himself studying them in hope, but none seemed exactly right. The severity of his disappointment shocked him. He was grown up, for Pete's sake! Grown-ups didn't get upset because the right gift wasn't under the tree.

Yet for a moment he was a child again, fighting back the tears because Mum had bought the wrong book and shrugged the mistake aside with, 'Oh, well, it's the same thing, really, isn't it?' And he couldn't explain that it wasn't the same thing at all because she had more important things to worry about than his feelings.

Then he saw his son gradually easing something out from behind an armchair, and relief swept him.

'This is yours,' Bobby said, holding out the brightly wrapped parcel.

'Thank you, son.'

Alex unwrapped it slowly, revealing the picture inside—a water-colour of the happy family sitting by the river. As he gazed at it he became aware of his son watching him, full of tension, waiting for what he would say.

'It's beautiful, son. Did you do it?'

'Yes, I painted it myself.'

'But how do you recall that day? You were only five years old.'

'You remember, Daddy?' Bobby asked breathlessly.

'Sure I do. It was Mummy's birthday, and we went out for a picnic. You wandered too near the water and I had to run and grab you. That was a great day, wasn't it?'

Bobby nodded. Corinne's eyes were on Alex.

'Do you remember?' Alex asked her.

'Oh, yes, it was lovely.'

'You've even got the details right,' Alex said, returning to the picture. 'Right down to that red shirt.'

'Mummy still has it,' Bobby said.

'Really? Well, that's lucky.'

Corinne was suddenly doing something else. Alex couldn't even be sure she'd heard the words, although they seemed to sing in his own ears.

Mummy still has it.

It changed everything. Suddenly he was no longer fighting darkness.

He put a hand on Bobby's shoulder. 'Thank you,' he said quietly.

The rest of the day was standard-issue Christmas—

turkey, plum pudding, crackers filled with silly jokes and funny hats, Christmas cake, more crackers. Alex faded contentedly into the background, doing nothing that might spoil the atmosphere.

There was the odd awkward moment. From somewhere Jimmy produced a sprig of mistletoe and wandered into the kitchen where Corinne was cooking. Alex heard a giggle, then a silence that tested his control to the utmost. But he forced himself to stay where he was.

And nothing could really spoil the one blazingly beautiful gift that had been given to him unexpectedly.

Corinne had kept the red shirt. He could live on that for a while.

Alex insisted on helping with the washing-up.

'You can't ask the kids and spoil Christmas for them,' he explained. 'And poor Jimmy isn't up to it.'

'Poor Jimmy!' she exclaimed indignantly. 'You're a smug hypocrite, you know that?'

He grinned. 'It's what I'm good at.'

She gave a reluctant laugh and accepted his help.

'I'll wash,' he said. 'I don't know where to put things. Pinny?'

'The only one I have,' she said defiantly, 'has flowers on it.'

'I'll be brave.'

He looked so ridiculous in the flowered apron, with a garish paper hat still on his head, that Corinne's heart melted. He did a good job too, washing and rinsing properly, and it reminded her of how domesticated he was. He'd always done his share in the old days.

'What made you pick this house?' he asked. 'You could have had something better.'

'You mean more expensive? I don't think it comes any better than this. It has a big garden, is full of atmosphere, and the kids love it because it's a house where they can be untidy.'

Bobby appeared in the doorway.

'What is it, darling?' Corinne asked.

'Nothing.'

'Did you want something?'

The boy shook his head. His eyes were fixed on Alex.

Suddenly the little kitchen clock gave three clear chimes, and Alex understood.

Three o'clock. The time when he had originally meant to leave. Bobby was watching him intently.

'It's all right,' he said. 'I'm not going anywhere.'

It was a pleasure to see the smile that came over Bobby's face, but in the very same moment Alex's cellphone rang in the hall. Without a word, Bobby went and fetched it, handing it to his father, his face a careful blank.

The screen was showing Mark Dunsford's number, and for a moment Alex hesitated, tempted to shut it off without answering. But he didn't.

'Mark,' he said in his most discouraging voice.

'Simply checking to see if you need me,' came his assistant's tinny voice.

'For pity's sake, it's Christmas Day!'

'I just thought you'd like to know that I'm on the ball.'

Alex ground his teeth. 'Go and eat some Christmas cake, Mark, and don't call me back unless it's a real crisis.'

He hung up. Bobby's eyes were shining, but all he said was, 'Are you coming back soon, Dad? We haven't used up all the crackers.'

'I'll be there in a moment, son. Put this back for me, will you?'

He handed him the cellphone and Bobby disappeared.

'I'm glad you got rid of that man,' Corinne said. 'I don't like him.'

'Have you met Mark? Oh, yes, he came to the house once.'

'Horrible man.'

'I suppose he reminds you of me,' Alex said wryly.

'Not really. You were always full of fire and enthusiasm. It lit you up inside, and it was exciting. I remember once you got out of bed at one in the morning to work out some brilliant idea. Your eyes were shining and your voice had an edge, as though you'd seen a vision. I never knew what you were going to do next. But Mark Dunsford is a robot. He never had an original thought in his life, and he's trying to make his name by standing on your shoulders. You should watch out for him.'

The same thought had occasionally occurred to him. Now he marvelled at the shrewdness that had shown Corinne so much in one brief meeting.

'That must be the first time you've said anything good about me and the business,' he observed.

'I grew to hate it because it always came first—before me, before the kids.'

'You never understood how driven I felt.'

'You're wrong. I saw you being driven all the time. At first, like I say, it was exciting, but later I saw what it did to you. I used to dream that there'd come a time when you could ease up, but of course there never did, and it went on and on, getting worse and worse.'

He gave a mirthless grunt of laughter.

'Funny! I thought of it as getting better and better, because I could provide for you properly. A nice house, holidays—'

'Half of which we ended up taking alone,' she reminded him. 'Where's the fun in that?'

'But can't you—?'

She stopped him hurriedly. 'Alex, it's all right. It's finished. It doesn't matter any more. Let's leave it.'

The washing-up was done. Alex looked up at the sprig of mistletoe that Jimmy had fixed overhead.

'Do I get a Christmas kiss?' he asked, speaking lightly to take the sting out of the refusal he expected.

'Of course,' she said.

Moving quickly, she reached up and kissed him on the cheek. He had a brief sensation of her sweetness, the faint tang of the perfume he'd bought her, the warmth of her breath against his face. Then she was gone before he could catch her.

At the end of the day the last cracker had been

cracked, the last silly joke read out, the last paper hat reduced to a crumpled wreck. Jimmy opted for an early night. Mitzi, already asleep, was carried to bed, and Bobby went without protest.

'I'm going up now,' Corinne said to Alex, who was drying a cup in the kitchen.

'I'll stay down for a little,' he said. 'There's a late film I want to see.'

'Goodnight, then.'

'Goodnight.'

He kissed her cheek and she put her arms gently around his neck, resting her head on his shoulder. He held her close, swaying back and forth a little in a gentle rhythm.

'It's been a lovely day,' she whispered.

'Yes,' he said. 'Thank you for everything, Corinne. Thank you for making it possible, and not driving me away.'

'I could never want to do that,' she said, raising her head and looking into his face.

It was once more the face she loved, not distorted by anger or masked against her as it had been in the worst days of their failing marriage. For a moment she saw again the vulnerability that had always been there beneath the arrogance, and which had touched her heart.

It touched her now and she turned away quickly.

'What is it?' he asked.

'Nothing.'

He brushed his fingertips across her eyelashes and found them wet.

'Sometimes I feel like doing that,' he said. A tremor went through him. 'I miss you so much.'

'I miss you too. The love doesn't just switch off.'

'Even though you're trying to make it?' he asked.

'I'm working on it. I don't pretend it's easy.'

He kissed the top of her head.

'Goodnight,' he whispered.

She went upstairs and he was left alone.

Midnight. The clock in the kitchen chimed. The room was in darkness except for the tree lights that still glowed and flickered.

Santa smiled at the figure in the doorway. 'Have you come to say goodbye?'

'I wasn't sure if you'd be here,' Bobby said. 'You're supposed to have gone back to the North Pole by now.'

'That's one of the advantages of being the boss. You can change the rules to suit yourself. I thought I'd pop back to see how it was going.'

'It's been brilliant.' Bobby sighed happily. 'He's still here. He liked the picture and everything. He even remembered what it was.'

'Did you think he wouldn't? Yes, well, I suppose you couldn't be blamed for thinking that.' Santa's voice was gentle as he added, 'Let's face it, he's not much of a father.'

'Yes, he is,' Bobby said instantly. 'He's the best.'

'Doesn't spend as much time with you as he should, though, does he?'

'He's very busy. He has lots of other things to

think of. But he always comes back to us, because he loves us best in all the world.'

For a moment Santa seemed lost for words. At last he said, 'I know he does.'

'Did he tell you?'

'I just know. He loves his family so much that it hurts, but he's not good at saying things.'

'And we love him best in all the world too,' Bobby said firmly. 'I do, and Mitzi does, and Mum does.'

'Well, I don't know—'

'She does. I know she does.'

There was a silence before Santa said, 'Never mind that. Tell me about Mitzi. Did she have a good day?'

'Oh, yes. Dad gave her that Marianne doll with the riding habit—the one she asked you about the other day. You must have told him.'

Santa grinned. 'Let's just say that I can give him a nudge in the right direction. That's not always easy, because he's a stubborn fellow who doesn't listen as often as he ought.' Seeing Bobby about to flare up, he added quickly, 'Now, be fair; you know that's true.'

'Sometimes,' Bobby conceded.

'Always,' Santa insisted.

'Now and then.'

'All right, I'll settle for now and then. You're quite a negotiator.'

Bobby giggled. 'That's what Daddy says. He says he wants me working for him when I grow up.'

'I thought you wanted to be an artist?'

'Couldn't I be both?'

'You could. But it's better to be what you really want. Your way might be better.'

'Will you be back again, after tonight?'

'I don't know,' Santa said. 'Christmas is passing.'

'But it's not gone yet. Tomorrow's still sort of Christmas. Dad won't leave tomorrow, will he?'

'No, he won't. And if you have him, you don't need me.'

'It's different. I can talk to you.'

'And not to him?'

'Not about everything. He minds too much, you see, and I don't want to hurt him.'

Santa spoke gruffly. 'How do you know he minds so much?'

'Because he tries so hard to pretend that he doesn't,' Bobby said simply.

Santa turned away. 'Goodnight,' he said huskily. 'Go to bed now. Wait for what tomorrow may bring.'

Bobby moved towards the door. As he reached the hall he paused a moment, wondering if he really had heard a noise. But all was dark and quiet. After a moment he sped upstairs.

Alone by the tree, Santa did not move but stood with his head bent, as though trying to bear up under a heavy load.

'Are you all right?'

He turned quickly. Corinne was standing there.

'Of course I am.' He added feebly, 'Ho-ho-ho!'

'You seemed a bit tired.'

He shrugged. 'It's a great responsibility being Father Christmas. It's scary.'

'It must be.' She hesitated. 'I'm glad you came back. He needed to talk to you again.'

Abruptly Santa asked, 'Did you know he was protecting his father?'

'Yes. He always talks about him protectively. Nothing is ever Daddy's fault. If he ever lost that faith it would hurt him more than he could bear.'

'Actually not discussing things in case his father can't cope? This is a nine-year-old child.'

'Nobody really knows what Bobby is thinking,' Corinne said. 'Except maybe you. He tells you things he can't tell anyone else.'

'Not even you?'

'He's protecting me too. Santa Claus can help because he's not involved. And my husband—'

'Your husband's a thick-head, and don't let him tell you any different.'

'He's not that bad.'

'Yes, he is. Take my word.'

Corinne smiled. 'Well, he may have a thick head but he has a thin skin. Only he doesn't know it.'

Santa made a sound like a snort.

'It sounds to me as though you're protecting him too. I'll bet he doesn't know that, either.'

'I don't think it's ever occurred to him.'

'You invited him here for Christmas for his sake as much as the children's, didn't you?'

'You're very astute.'

'Well, maybe a little more than I was,' Santa said gruffly.

'He's lost so much already,' Corinne said. 'I don't

want him to lose any more, otherwise it'll soon be too late.'

Santa stared into the fireplace. 'I think he knows that. Tell me something. Do you know why Bobby chose that picnic to paint?'

'I think it was the last completely happy time we had together. Alex's business was building up fast, but we were still a family. When the picnic was over we went home and put the children to bed. And then we made love—' her voice softened '—and it was the most beautiful thing that had ever happened. He told me over and over how much he loved me and how our love would fill his heart and his life until his very last moment.'

'Is that why you kept the shirt?'

'Yes,' she said softly. 'That's why I kept it.'

'Perhaps you should have thrown it out of your life, along with him.'

'I haven't thrown him out of my life. I never could. It was really the other way around. The day after that picnic he got a call that changed everything. Suddenly it was "big time," and he was never really ours after that. That's why I was surprised he recognised the moment. I should think it feels like another life to him by now.'

'Maybe it does,' Santa said wistfully. 'Another sweeter life that he lost somewhere along the way.' He gave a brief laugh. 'He's not a very clever fellow, is he?'

'Cleverer than I thought,' she murmured.

'I think you should go now,' he said abruptly.

'Can't I stay? I could get you a beer and—'

'Go,' he said with soft vehemence. 'It's better, believe me.'

'Yes,' she said with a sigh. 'I suppose it is.'

When she'd gone Santa stood looking at the doorway, as though hoping she would return. When she didn't, he switched out the tree lights and sat for a long time in the darkness.

CHAPTER FIVE

ALEX could still remember the first Christmas of his marriage, when he and Corinne had gone out early on December the twenty-sixth, and dived into the sales. She had an eye for a bargain, and they had triumphantly carried back home several pieces of household equipment at rock-bottom prices.

As they'd prospered they hadn't needed the sales and Alex, who had been able to buy her anything she wanted, had been bemused by her continued enthusiasm. So it hardly came as a surprise that she was set on attending this year.

He came downstairs to find several newspapers spread out on the kitchen table with four eagerly debating heads leaning over them.

'Washing machine!' Jimmy was making a list.

'Shoes,' Corinne added. 'And a lawnmower—'

They went on compiling the list and Alex, who had learned wisdom, stayed in the background.

At last Mitzi looked up and noticed him, giving him a hug and offering to make him some tea—an offer her mother hastily overruled.

'I'll do it, darling.'

'Morning, Jimmy,' Alex said affably. 'How are you feeling today? You're not looking so good. I expect yesterday took it out of you.'

'It did a bit,' Jimmy admitted. 'But, heck, I wouldn't miss it for anything. I can be ill later.'

'Uncle Jimmy's a soldier,' Bobby said in explanation of this reckless heroism.

'And a good soldier doesn't give in,' Alex agreed, straight-faced. 'But you're looking a bit seedy now. Are you taking your medication?'

'Well, I skipped a bit,' Jimmy conceded. 'You can't drink if you're taking the pills, and it is Christmas—'

'Of course,' Alex agreed. 'But now it's time you took proper care of yourself.'

Corinne turned around, her jaw dropping with indignation at what she could clearly see him up to. But she was pulled up short by the sight of Jimmy's face. He really was pale and strained.

'Oh, Jimmy, you are an idiot.' She sighed affectionately. 'You should have said—or I should have noticed. Stay in bed today.'

'No way. There's masses of sport on television. But I wouldn't mind staying in and watching it with my feet up. You won't mind if I don't come out with you?'

'We'll bear up,' Alex assured him.

He sauntered innocently out into the hall, looking back to catch Bobby's eye and send him a signal. Bobby glanced at Mitzi and Alex nodded.

Message received and understood.

After a moment the two children followed him out.

'Listen, kids,' Alex said hurriedly. 'You're fond of your Uncle Jimmy, aren't you?'

'Yes,' said Mitzi.

Bobby nodded, alert, ready to tune in to his father's signal.

'Well, you wouldn't want to leave him all on his own at Christmas, would you?' Alex asked. 'It wouldn't be a very kind thing to do. Why don't you both stay here with him?'

'What's it worth?' Bobby asked.

'What—? You're my son.'

'And I'm up to every trick. You said so.'

'But, like any skill, it should be used wisely,' Alex said. 'There's a time for using it and a time for not using it.'

'This is a time for using it,' Bobby said firmly.

Alex eyed him with respect mixed with caution.

'I want to come to the shops,' Mitzi said. 'Mummy said she'd get me a doll's house.'

'It's in Bellam's Toys,' Bobby explained. 'There's a big range, and number four is going cheap now because they've just brought out number five. So Mum promised her number four.'

His eyes met Alex's. 'Of course, Mitzi would really prefer number five.'

'Mummy said it would cost too much.' Mitzi sighed.

'But we're holding all the cards,' her brother told her.

'You are, aren't you?' Alex said in appreciation of these tactics. 'Number five it is, on condition you stay at home.'

Mitzi scampered off to tell Jimmy, whose head was aching, that he was going to have the pleasure of her company and they could talk and talk and talk.

'What about you?' Alex asked his son. 'What's your price?'

'Nothing,' Bobby told him.

'But you just said—'

'I always meant to stay at home anyway.'

Alex looked at him with sheer admiration, although he felt compelled to point out, 'But, like you said, you have all the cards. I'd have paid. You missed a trick there, son.'

Bobby shook his head. 'No, I didn't,' he said earnestly. 'Don't you see? I didn't really.'

Alex's amused irony faded and he took Bobby's hand. 'Yes, I do see,' he said seriously.

'Good luck, Dad.'

He knew everything, of course, Alex thought.

'I'll do my best,' he promised his son.

The road to the shopping centre lay through open country. The snow had stopped falling and now lay settled thickly on the ground, the perfect picture of a white Christmas.

They went in Corinne's car, which was larger than Alex's sleek vehicle, made to accommodate children and big enough for the mountain of things she was planning to buy.

'I haven't seen this before,' he observed as they climbed in.

'I got it a month ago.'

Third-hand, from the look of it, he thought. He was wise enough, now, not to say he could have bought her something better, but it flashed through his mind that this was one more thing she'd done without him.

How many other things, now and in the future?

Corinne had on a thick sheepskin jacket and jeans which showed off her long, slim legs, and seemed in high spirits this morning.

'You were rotten to poor old Jimmy,' she chided Alex.

'I advised him to rest and take care of himself, and he was only too glad to accept. He really is feeling poorly, so how can you blame me?'

'Very clever! You know, if there was one thing about you that got up my nose more than any other it was your way of making your most self-interested actions seem perfectly virtuous.'

'But what possible ulterior motive could I have for wanting Jimmy to stay at home?' he asked innocently. 'You're not suggesting that I was scheming to be alone with you?'

A sideways glance showed her that he was grinning.

'If I wasn't driving I'd thump you,' she said, falling in with his humorous mood. It was hard to be anything but cheerful in the brilliant white scenery around them.

She reckoned that must be the reason for her new sensation of well-being this morning. It was strange how she had awoken full of contentment, almost happiness, and the feeling had lasted so that now she felt oddly light-hearted, like a teenager again.

The shabby old car saw them safely through the treacherous conditions and into the shopping centre car park. They went from store to store, bagging the washing machine first and then working their way down the list.

'Doll's house!' Alex said, seeing Bellam's. 'Quick, before they sell out of number five.'

'Number four,' Corinne objected. 'That's what I promised her.'

'That's a little out of date,' Alex said cautiously.

'What have you been up to?'

'Who? Me?' Under her suspicious gaze he confessed, 'Mitzi and I discussed it and came to a joint decision that number five was a better choice.'

'You mean you bribed her?'

'Bribed is a harsh word.'

'But true.'

'Let's hurry,' he said diplomatically.

Just inside the shop they found a counter with a sale of tiny Christmas trinkets that nobody had bought. To Corinne's surprise Alex lingered there a surprisingly long time, but she didn't see whether he bought anything because an assistant asked her if he could be of help and she hurried to claim the doll's house.

Alex secured the last number five available and bore it out of the shop in triumph, refusing the shop's suggestion of delivery. 'Next Monday?' Alex echoed, aghast. 'If I don't take it home now I won't live that long.'

The box was so big that it blocked his view, and

Corinne had to guide him into the elevator, then out and to the car.

'A bit to the left—bit more—stop.'

'Corinne, I can't see a thing,' came a muffled voice from behind the box.

'It's all right, trust me. Take two steps forward. Oh, dear!'

'What does "Oh, dear!" mean?' came a plaintive cry.

'There are some steps just ahead. Go slowly. That's it. Put your foot down very carefully.'

'I didn't need telling that!'

'Now another one—and another—just one more. Now you're on land again. Walk forward.'

'Will you please stop laughing?'

'Who's laughing?' she chuckled, opening the back of the car so that he could edge the box through and finally release it.

'I need something to eat after that,' he said.

They found a café and tucked into fish and chips.

'That'll teach me to make rash promises,' he said, grinning. "She never warned me it was almost as big as a real house."

'Alex,' she said abruptly, 'how long can you stay?'

'That's up to you.'

'As long as you like. I have to return to work on Monday, but there's no reason for you to go.'

'Work?'

'Yes, I've got a job.'

'Don't I give you enough to live on? You should have said—'

'You give me far more than I need. That's why I can afford to work part-time. I get the kids off to school first, then I go in to work. In the afternoon my neighbour collects them and they stay with her until I come home. Don't pull a face. They like going there. She's got a dog they can play with.'

'Where do you work?'

'A lawyer's office. It's really interesting. Eventually I thought I could train and get some qualifications.'

'Be a lawyer, you mean?'

'Yes. Not just yet. In five or six years, when the children are more independent. For the moment I just do part-time secretarial work to get the feel of it. I took a computer course and my boss says I'm the best in the office.'

'How long will your training take?'

'About four years to pass all the exams. I reckon I'll be qualified about ten years from now.'

He was silent for so long that Corinne thought he was about to fight her on this, and braced herself to stand up to him. She didn't want to fight, but nor was she going to yield.

But all he said was, 'You must be brilliant if you did that computer course so quickly.'

'I started doing it six months ago. I used the computer you bought for Bobby.'

'Six months? While we were together?'

'Uh-huh!'

It was painful, like discovering that she'd had a secret life—which, in a way, he supposed she had.

'And you made sure you didn't tell me?'

'No, Alex, I didn't "make sure" of not telling you. I'd gladly have told you if you'd shown any interest, or even been there. But you were such an absentee that I could have got away with murder. I could have had a dozen lovers and you'd never have suspected.'

'Very funny.'

'Don't glare at me. Many men who live for their work secretly know that their wives are getting up to every kind of mischief behind their backs. But my furtive trysts were with a computer. My "clandestine mail" came from a correspondence course, and you never surprised my guilty secret because it never occurred to you that I was interesting enough to have one.

'Well, I had, and I passed with very high marks. My boss is very glad to have me around. They've just had a load of state-of-the-art machines delivered and I'm the only one who knows what to do with them. I can't tell you how—' She stopped suddenly.

'How proud that made you?' he suggested.

'No, how sad it made me. There was nobody to tell.'

He nodded. 'And you need someone to tell your triumphs to or they don't amount to much. I always told things to you. Nobody else's opinion ever mattered as much as yours.'

'I'd have loved to tell you, but I knew it would look very trivial to the boss of Mead Consolidated.'

After a moment he asked, 'Does Jimmy know?'

'Only since he came here last week.'

'And I suppose he's rooting for you?'

'Yes, he thinks it's great.'

Alex was silent. He was afraid to ask any more about Jimmy. Instead he said, 'You've got the rest of your life pretty well mapped out, haven't you?'

'It's good to have a goal.'

'Yes, I see that. Ten years—heck! I don't know anyone who plans that far ahead.'

'I must. I'm thirty already. I have to make the most of my time.'

'Where do I come into your plans?'

'You're still the children's father.'

'I'm still your husband, and I want to go on being your husband.'

'Alex, nothing's going to change. You are as you are. What's the point of saying all this? I tried to explain when we broke up, and you weren't listening then, either.'

Alex sighed. 'Yes, I was. I know it didn't seem like it, but I heard. You were saying you were better off without me.'

Dumbly she shook her head. It was less a denial than an attempt to fend off confusion.

'I never said that,' she said at last. 'And I never, never will. Not with all the things I remember.'

'What do you remember?' he asked gruffly.

'You, as you were when I met you,' she said wistfully. 'You were wonderful—the most wonderful, generous, loving man in the world.'

Her words hurt him unbearably. 'I'm still the same—' he pointed to himself '—in here.'

'I wouldn't know,' she said sadly. 'It's a long time since I've known what was happening in there.'

'Nothing's changed. Not towards you. Tell me it's the same with you. Or can't you say it?' His voice was ragged.

'Yes.' She sighed. 'I can say it. But we're not youngsters now, and it's not enough.'

'Are you happy?' he asked abruptly.

'I don't know,' she said slowly. 'I'm not sure it really matters.'

He realised that she had altered in some indefinable way. There was a calm about her now, as though she had settled something that had long been troubling her.

'Alex,' she said suddenly, 'will you tell me something honestly?'

'Fire away.'

'But I mean honestly. No polite lies. No gilding the lily. The unvarnished truth.'

'All right.'

'Why did you arrive here early and stay late?'

He hesitated, knowing that he was going to confirm her worst suspicions. Yet she'd asked for honesty and he could give her no less.

'Something fell through,' he said reluctantly. 'Craddock set up a party in the Caribbean, to settle the contract. Then he got ill.'

She faced him. 'And if he hadn't got ill?'

It was the question that he'd dreaded, but he said, 'Then I wouldn't have come at all.'

She didn't seem to react, only nodded slightly, as though something had been confirmed.

It made him burst out, 'But I did come, and I

found myself talking to my son, who didn't know it was me. And I found out a lot of things I didn't know before. Maybe it's my fault that I didn't, but I know them now. It makes everything different.'

'Between you and the children. Not between you and me.'

'But it can if we let it. Corinne, come home. I want to try again. Don't you want that too, in your heart?'

'I can't come back to that soulless place, Alex. I hated it. My home is here.'

'Then I'll come here.'

'Here? You mean move into where I'm living now?'

'It doesn't matter as long as we're together. If we stay here you'll still have your job and—'

'Wait, Alex, please. I know you when you've set your heart on something. You go bull-headed for it without thinking it through. How long would it be before things went wrong again? I know you've understood things these last few days, but that isn't the complete answer you seem to think.'

'But if we still love each other—'

'I do still love you, but—'

'But you think I'm beyond redemption,' he said wryly.

'You don't need redemption. I think you might need a different kind of wife—one who can enjoy the entertaining you want, and wear glamorous clothes, and be a credit to you.'

'To blazes with that!' he said impatiently. 'None of that stuff matters. I want you, and the children. My

God!' He was growing angry. 'You've not only mapped out your own life but mine too. I'm headed for a trophy wife, am I? You'd better tell me her name now, because I'm sure you've picked her out.'

'Calm down!'

'I'm damned if I will! What do you suggest—a luscious little blonde with a cleavage, or a busty brunette who'll marry me for my gold card? Do you think I want anyone like that after being married to *you,* or is that all you think I'm worth?'

'I'm sorry,' she said in anguish. 'I didn't mean to hurt you.'

He didn't say any more. But he took her hand and laid it against his cheek, closing his eyes.

'Alex—'

'Hush,' he said. 'Don't say anything.'

She nodded and lifted her other hand to touch his face gently.

'There won't be anyone,' he said in a voice that was both fierce and quiet. 'It's just you. Nobody else. Sometimes I wish that wasn't true. Hang it, Corinne, I'd like to be able to forget you and pass on to something new as easily as you've done. But I can't. If that's inconvenient, I'm sorry, but I always was an awkward cuss, and I haven't changed in that way either.'

She wanted to tell him that it was all an illusion. She hadn't passed on to something new because he still haunted her and always would. But those would be dangerous words to say to him.

Suddenly he seemed to pull himself together.

'Come on,' he said. 'It's time we got back to work. There's a lot still on that list.'

He rose abruptly, leaving her no choice but to do the same. The subject was closed, she thought. He had simply put it behind him.

It was two hours before they had completed the list and were able to start the journey home. By that time the temperature had fallen sharply and Corinne drove in silence, concentrating on the road, which had become treacherous.

When they left the town and reached the country stretch they slowed.

'It looks like it snowed here in the last half-hour,' he said, 'and there hasn't been much traffic, so it's probably icy—'

The words were barely out of his mouth when the car began to make choking noises.

'What's that?' Alex asked.

'Nothing,' she said quickly. 'It's done it before. It doesn't mean anything. It'll go back to normal in a moment.'

But instead of going back to normal the vehicle choked some more, slowed, and then quietly died in the middle of the road.

'Oh, heck!' she said wretchedly. 'Is anything coming?'

'No, but let's get this to the side before anything does.'

Together they set their shoulders to the rear and pushed the car until it glided on to the grass verge, where it settled, out of danger but totally useless.

Alex pulled his cellphone out of his pocket and called the rescue service. As he'd expected, he was at the end of a long line.

'An hour, minimum,' he groaned as he hung up.

'We have to stay here for an hour?' she asked, horrified.

'Not necessarily here. If we take a walk through those trees I think there are some buildings on the other side. There might be a pub where we could get a sandwich.'

'Can I borrow your phone?'

She called home and was answered by Bobby.

'Everything's fine, Mum. Mitzi's looking through her books and Uncle Jimmy's watching telly.'

'Can I talk to him?'

Jimmy assured her that all was well and there would be no trouble about her being late. Corinne hung up, satisfied.

'Let's see where the trees lead,' she said to Alex.

He took her hand and kept hold of it as they wandered beneath the great oaks. The sun was beginning to set, sending golden beams slanting through the branches and on to the snowy ground, and for a while they walked in silence.

It was magic, Corinne thought; the kind best enjoyed in silence. But when she looked at Alex she saw that he was walking with his head down, scowling with tension. His misery reached her almost tangibly, defeating her resolve to keep her distance.

'Alex—' She stopped and turned him to face her, and at once it seemed natural to put her arms about him and pull his head on her shoulders. Hang good resolutions, she thought. He was in pain, and she could no more refuse to comfort him than refuse to breathe.

'Corinne, I'm afraid,' he whispered.

'Afraid of what, my dearest?'

'Everything. Going back to that empty house, that empty life, knowing it's all I'm fit for now. I'm losing everything I care about, and I don't know how to stop it.'

Her heart ached for him. She longed to say, Come home. Everything is all right again, and see the happiness return to his face.

But she knew she mustn't say it. Everything was still not right. Perhaps it would never be right. She shared his sense of helplessness. It was too soon to think that a reconciliation could be easy, or even possible. Until she could see the way ahead she could say nothing to comfort him.

This visit wasn't working out as she'd expected. She had sent the invitation to the brusque, hard-faced man he had been at the end. But the man who'd arrived had been closer to the old Alex, reminding her of the unexpected touch of defencelessness that he'd always tried so hard to disguise, and had succeeded with everyone but her.

She'd vowed to keep her heart to herself in future, but he'd exerted his dangerous spell on it again, filling her with confusion.

'Don't be afraid,' she said. 'You're the man who's never afraid, remember?'

'That's all a con,' he admitted. 'Underneath, my knees were always knocking. Except with you. They never really stopped. Hold on to me.'

She did so, feeling him clinging to her in return, holding her as tightly as a drowning man might clutch a lifeline.

'I love you so much,' he said huskily.

'I love you,' she told him truthfully.

Let's try again.

The words trembled on her tongue, but somehow they couldn't be spoken, although she could sense the longing to hear them in every tremor of his body. Instead she raised her face to him and felt his lips cover hers.

He had kissed her before, on Christmas Eve, but that had been different. That kiss had lacked the driving intensity of this one. Last time he'd been overconfident and it had made her freeze. Now he kissed her like a man who feared he might never be able to do so again, with a dread and desperation that made it impossible for her to hold out against him.

His lips still had the skill to excite her, carrying the reminder of a thousand other times when a kiss had been the prelude to lying naked in his arms and being taken to another world that they made themselves out of love and desire. The memories crowded in on her now, making her ache with longing for what she had renounced.

She was kissing him back. She didn't mean to, but she couldn't help herself, for she too thought this might be the last time, and there was so much that she wanted to remember.

Alex, the generous lover, seeking her delight before his own, as subtle in his lovemaking as he was unsubtle in his daily life—the man who could be hurt by a word or a look, and who would move heaven and earth to hide it. He had been hers, she had let him go, and soon she would send him away for good.

'Corinne—Corinne—'

Just that. Just her name, spoken in a voice of racking anguish. It tormented her, but she would stay firm somehow.

'Don't cry,' he whispered.

She hadn't known that she was crying, but she knew why she couldn't help it. She was saying a final goodbye to the only man she could love, and though it broke his heart, and her own, she was resolved on doing it.

'*Excuse me!*'

It took a long moment for them to return to reality enough to realise that a man was trying to attract their attention.

'*Are you the gentleman who sent for a tow?*'

'Yes,' Alex said raggedly. 'I am.'

'I know we said an hour, but I managed to get here a bit early,' the man called. 'Right, let's get to work. Can I have the keys?'

Alex was pale and his hands shook, but he had regained command of himself. He stood aside as Corinne handed over the keys to the car, then they all walked back through the trees in the setting sun.

CHAPTER SIX

ALEX supposed it was natural for reaction to set in as Christmas passed. That was the only reason he could think of for the weight that suddenly seemed to descend on Bobby. He had always been a thoughtful child, but now he was more silent than usual, as though burdened by some extra care.

'Do you know what ails him?' Alex muttered to Corinne, joining her in the kitchen on the morning of the twenty-seventh.

'No, all I know is that it happened suddenly, some time yesterday evening. But if I ask him about it he swears nothing's wrong. It's best to leave him alone, then maybe he'll tell us.'

Alex nodded and tried to do as she said, but it was hard to realise that the newly established trust between himself and his son was melting away, and be unable to understand. It was also painful to see the forced brightness that Bobby sometimes remembered to assume.

To divert him, he started a snowball fight in the

garden, with Mitzi joining in and Jimmy cheering from the sidelines. When they had got each other wet they dashed back into the house, dried off hastily and continued the fight with cushions.

To Alex's pleasure, Bobby became caught up in what he was doing and laid about him vigorously with a big soft cushion, yodelling with glee.

Totally absorbed in the tussle, Alex failed to hear the front doorbell, or observe Corinne go to answer it. It was taking all his attention to deal with Bobby, who wielded the big cushion expertly until suddenly it collided with Alex's shoulder and split. A cloud of little feathers flew up to the ceiling and settled back over Alex, who had fallen on to the sofa in a paroxysm of laughter.

He was madly blowing feathers away when a figure he recognised walked into the room.

'Mark!' he exclaimed.

Mark Dunsford regarded his employer with something close to disapproval in his eyes.

'I've been trying to get hold of you since yesterday,' he said. 'It's very urgent.'

Out of the corner of his eye he saw Corinne grow very still. Little Mitzi did the same. But the stillest of all was Bobby.

'It can't be that urgent,' he said. 'You could have called me.'

'I tried. Your cellphone is switched off.'

'No way,' Alex said at once. 'I never switch it off.'

'I assure you, it's switched off now.'

Frowning, Alex rose and went out into the hall

where his coat hung, plunged his hand into the pocket and pulled out the phone. It was off.

'But how did—?'

Alex checked himself. The air was singing about his ears, and suddenly he knew that what he said next was going to be critical.

'Well—' he said at last '—so I switched it off and forgot. Is that so strange at Christmas?'

'What is strange is that it seems to have been switched off after I made a call,' Mark observed.

'That's impossible. You must be mistaken.'

'It definitely rang several times, long enough for my identity to be displayed on the screen. Then it was turned off. I was curious, as you've never done such a thing before.'

Alex shrugged. 'There's a first time for everything. I must have been overcome by the Christmas spirit.'

'But to do it now, when such an important deal is hanging in the balance!' Mark sounded aghast at the thought that his idol might have feet of clay. 'That's simply not like you.'

The next moment he had another shock. Alex's voice was cool as he asked, 'What was so urgent that it couldn't wait?'

'I called you to let you know of the change of plan. It seems that Craddock's illness was a false alarm—just indigestion—so the Caribbean is on again. The flight leaves this afternoon. You've just about got time.'

'Time for what?' Alex asked blankly.

'Time to catch the plane. I went to the office first, and collected your passport and ticket. Luckily your address book was there and I was able to discover where your wife was living.'

'But how did you know I'd be here?' Alex asked quietly. 'I didn't tell you.'

'It was a reasonable supposition, and luckily correct, otherwise I wouldn't have known where to find you at all.'

'I see. Well, I would rather you hadn't done that. Please remember for the future.'

'But to put yourself completely out of touch when—well, I've found you now. You'll have to hurry.'

Alex rubbed his eyes. 'I'm sorry, I'm afraid I'm not quite with you. I'm not going anywhere, Mark.'

'You don't understand. The contract—'

'I understand all right. Old man Craddock thinks he can snap his fingers and everyone will jump.'

'He knows we need that contract—'

'No, we don't need it,' Alex interrupted him firmly. 'We want it, but we don't need it. He won't find another firm that'll do the job as well for such a reasonable price, and he knows it. *He* needs *us,* and I'm not cutting short the best Christmas of my life just to dance to his tune.'

'But—'

'Mark, do you know why he wanted to gather us all round him on the other side of the world? Because he's a lonely old man with no family. He has no children and both his wives left him. I'm sorry for him, but I'm damned if I'm going to end up like him.'

Mark was aghast at this heresy.

'But somebody ought to be there, representing the firm. If you won't go, then let me.'

Alex shrugged. 'OK, you can do it if you like. I'm sure you've got your passport, because I always used to carry mine, and you strike me as frighteningly like myself as I was in those days.'

'Frighteningly?'

'Terrifyingly. Appallingly. You've got that look in your eyes. It's like talking to a ghost of myself.'

Mark looked indignant.

'I'm not ashamed of following your lead. And if, as you say, I can go—'

'You can if you want to, but if you've got any sense you won't. I know you have no family, but isn't there a girlfriend you ought to be with?'

'I do have a girlfriend, and I've spent some time with her this Christmas—'

'*Some* time? God help you!'

'But she understands that I need to seize every opportunity—'

'Spare me the speech.' Alex was talking to Mark, but he was aware of Corinne, watching him, holding her breath. 'I wrote that speech myself, long ago. Now I'm tearing it up. Catch the plane if you want to, Mark, tell Craddock I've got a bug or something, and you're fully empowered to sign for me. Otherwise tell him I'll be back in the office next Monday, ready to do business. It's up to you, but try to be wiser than I was.'

Mark was stiff with outrage.

'Then, with your permission, I'll go to the Caribbean and watch over your interests there.' His tone implied that somebody needed to mind the shop until his employer recovered his senses.

'Fine, I'll see you when you get back and knock some sense into you then.' Alex grinned. 'We'll have cocoa and cream cakes in my office.'

At this, Mark's hair practically stood on end. 'Cocoa and—?'

'Never tried it? You haven't lived. You'd better be off if you're going to catch that plane.'

When Mark had left nobody spoke for a while. For the first time Alex realised that he was still covered with feathers. No wonder Mark had thought he was crazy.

He caught Corinne's eye and realised that she'd had the same thought. She was smiling at him, but not just in amusement. There was a warmth and tenderness in her eyes that he had not seen there for a long time.

She came forward, hands outstretched to him.

'You really did that?' she asked eagerly. 'You really switched the phone off and blocked his call?'

For a moment the temptation to say yes was overwhelming, but with her candid eyes on him he had to say, 'No, I didn't do that. I don't know how it happened. I'm glad of it, but it's a mystery to me.'

'It was me.'

For a moment they had forgotten Bobby standing there, silently watching everything. Now they saw his face, white and determined.

'It was me,' he said again.

'What do you mean, son?' Alex went and sat on the sofa, taking Bobby's hands in his.

'I was in the hall last night, and I heard your cell-phone ringing,' Bobby said. 'I took it out of your coat pocket. I was going to take it to you, but—then I didn't.'

'Why not?' Alex asked gently.

'Because I knew it was that man,' Bobby said desperately. 'It was displayed on the screen, the same as last time he called. I knew he'd want to take you away, and I didn't want you to go, so I switched it off and put it back in your pocket, and I never told you.'

'Oh, darling,' Corinne said quickly, fearful of Alex's anger at this interference and wanting to protect the child from it. 'I know why you did it, but you really shouldn't have—'

She broke off. Alex's hand was suddenly raised to silence her. He was looking intently at his son and there was no anger in his face.

'Were you going to tell me about it?' he asked gently.

'Yes, but only when it was too late,' Bobby blurted out with such fierce resolve that Alex's lips twitched. 'I knew you'd be angry but I didn't want you to go. It's been brilliant this Christmas—the best ever. You've really *been* here, *really* been here, not just pretending like other times, but talking and—and *listening,* and being interested, and I didn't want it to end. I wanted you to stay and stay for ever, but he'd have made you go away and—and—'

'Hey, steady on, calm down,' Alex said softly,

brushing back a lock of tousled hair from his son's forehead. 'You wanted me that much?'

Bobby nodded vigorously.

'Well—' Alex had to stop for a moment to control his voice, which was beginning to shake. 'I can't be angry at you for wanting me, can I?'

'I'm sorry, Daddy.'

'Sorry for what?'

'Your trip—and your contract.'

'I didn't want the trip, and I haven't missed the contract. Or, if I have, I'm well rid of it if that was the only way I could have it.'

Bobby looked at him uncertainly. 'Really?'

'Let me tell you something, son. What you did was completely unnecessary. If I'd spoken to Mark last night I'd have said the same as you heard me say today.'

Bobby didn't reply. He was gazing at his father, as though longing to believe what he'd just heard, if only—

Alex spoke again, in a rallying tone. 'You don't think I'd want to go away from all of you, do you?'

Bobby shook his head.

'Well, then!' Alex smiled at his son. 'I tell you what, it proves what a great team we make. You did exactly what I'd do, just as though you'd read my mind.'

Those words brought forth Bobby's own beaming grin, full of joy and relief. The next moment he was in his father's arms.

With Bobby encircled by one arm and Mitzi by the other, he looked up at Corinne. She was not smiling, as he'd hoped, but looking at him with a kind of satisfaction, as though he'd just confirmed something that she'd known in her heart all the time.

'This is our last meeting,' Santa said. 'I don't usually stick around this long, but I did this time, just for you.' He leaned down to look at the boy. 'Do you think you'll manage?'

'Oh, yes,' Bobby said simply. 'It's all right now. But you will come back next year, won't you?' he added anxiously.

'Yes, I'll be back. In the meantime, keep this to remember me by.'

He handed Bobby a small object that he took from his pocket—a medallion made of wood, with the head of Santa Claus in relief. It was a trivial thing, such as anyone might have bought cheap in the sales now that the season was over. But to Bobby it was a precious talisman.

'For you,' said Santa. 'Until we meet again.'

'Goodbye,' Bobby whispered. 'Until we meet again.'

When he'd gone Santa stayed there a while, wondering. He'd almost given up when another figure appeared in the doorway.

'You're a wise man,' she said. 'Tell me what I should do.'

'It depends whether you're thinking of him or yourself,' Santa told her. 'For your own sake you should send him on his way and marry Jimmy.'

'That's your advice?'

'It's what's best for you.'

'Would it be best for him?'

Santa shook his head. 'It would finish him. He couldn't cope. He told you about going home to an empty place, but he didn't say how bad it is without you—how he makes excuses to work extra late so that he doesn't have to go back and face the emptiness, or how he jumps whenever the phone rings in case it's you, and curses when it isn't.

'I know he's a difficult man, but he understands things now that he didn't understand before. Doesn't he deserve a chance to show you? I'm not saying it'll be easy. He's still going to get it wrong a lot of the time, maybe most of the time. But he loves you and he needs you, and without you he's going to turn into a mean, miserable old man. Are you simply going to abandon him to that fate?'

'But you just told me that I ought to marry Jimmy.'

'He's steady and reliable, and he'll give you no trouble.' Santa couldn't resist adding, with a marked lack of Christmas spirit, 'He'll also bore the socks off you.'

'That's true. And maybe I feel I could cope with a little trouble.'

He looked at her uncertainly, as though not sure that he'd heard correctly.

'So—what are you going to tell him?' he asked cautiously.

'Nothing.' She gave Santa the smile of a conspirator. 'You're such a great ambassador. Why don't you tell him?'

'Tell him what?'

'Whatever you think he most wants to hear.'

She kissed him on the cheek. Then she was gone.

Jimmy was up early the next morning, packing his suitcase with one inexpert hand.

'Will you be all right for the journey?' Corinne asked, coming to help him. 'You surely don't have to go yet?'

'Yes, I do,' he said sadly. 'I'm a soldier, remember? I know when I'm beaten.'

She didn't ask what that meant.

Alex drove him to the station, and they parted on reasonably cordial terms, considering. Alex was feeling cordial to the whole world this morning, although there was still a touch of anxiety in his manner when he returned and went to find Corinne. He found her upstairs in her bedroom, pushing clothes aside in the wardrobe.

'It's still a bit cramped,' she said. 'But your things can overflow into the guest room now Jimmy's gone.'

'Are you sure?' he asked quietly. 'There's still time to send me away.'

She smiled. 'Is there? Would you go if I told you to?'

'Nope.' He took her into his arms. 'This is home now.'

'You don't mind moving in here?'

'I wouldn't have it any other way. This is the home where we became a family, and where we'll stay a family.'

'Suddenly you're very wise,' she said.

'I've been taking advice from a mysterious friend.

He's a very old man who knows a lot because people tell him things. He says the problems won't simply vanish, but if the love is there we should never
give up on it.'

'And the love *is* there,' she said.

'Yes. Always.' He took her face between his
hands. 'I love you, Corinne, with everything in me.
Promise me that you'll remember that when I act like
a jerk.'

'Are you likely to do that?'

He nodded wryly. 'Oh, yes.'

'Me, too.'

'We've just taken the first step,' he said seriously.
'I don't know where the other steps will lead, but if
you're with me I'll follow the path in any direction.'

'It may lead to some strange places,' she reminded him.

'Just keep tight hold of my hand.'

He drew her close and kissed her. If their last kiss
had been one of farewell, this was one of greeting,
neither quite knowing who the other was any more,
but glad to be introduced.

They didn't see the door open and two heads look
in, then withdraw silently.

'Told you,' Bobby said triumphantly. 'I *said* Dad
would come back for good.'

'You were just guessing,' Mitzi accused.

'I wasn't.'

'Was.'

'Wasn't.'

'Was.'

'I knew he was coming back. I had—' Bobby looked around significantly '—inside information.'

'Go on! Who?'

'Santa Claus.'

Mitzi looked at him with six-year-old sisterly scorn. 'You're batty, you are!' she announced. 'There is no Santa Claus.'

'There is.'

'Isn't.'

'Is.'

'Isn't.

'Is. What's more, I talked to him.'

'Batty!' she said again. 'Batty, batty, batty!'

She ran off down the stairs, yodelling the word happily.

Bobby was not upset by this reaction. At six, Mitzi still had a lot to learn about life, and people, and Santa.

'Santa Claus,' he said. 'Santa Claus—Father Christmas.'

He took the little wooden medallion from his pocket and turned it over in his fingers, still murmuring softly. 'Father Christmas, Father Christmas—'

He smiled to himself with secret contentment.

'*Father.*'

EPILOGUE

One year later

'YOU see, I kept my word,' Santa said.

Bobby nodded, slipping into the room and regarding his friend with shining eyes.

A year had made him two inches taller, and the shape of his face was a little different. His eyes were, perhaps, a little too wise for his age, but that was his nature. The tension and sadness were gone.

'I knew you'd come because you said you would,' he said.

Santa looked around him at the room. 'I hardly recognise this place.'

Bobby nodded. 'We've been redecorating. Dad tried to do this room himself, only he's rotten at it, and Mum said he should chuck the paintbrush away and she'd get a firm in to do it, and anyway they had better things to do, now that I'm going to have a baby brother or sister.'

He turned to look at a small figure who had appeared in the doorway.

'Come in. I told you he'd be here.'

Mitzi came further into the room, eyeing Santa with a touch of suspicion, then coming close and poking him in the stomach.

'Ow!' he remembered to say.

'You see, I'm not batty,' Bobby told her.

'Yes, you are,' she said firmly.

'Aren't!'

'Are!'

'Aren't!'

'Are!'

'That's enough, the pair of you,' Corinne said, coming in. 'Go to bed, now. Santa still has a full night's work to do.'

He leaned down to them. 'That's right. I'll say goodbye now. I won't be back tomorrow, like I was last time.'

'And next year?' Bobby asked.

'We'll see.' Santa added thoughtfully, 'Most boys of your age don't believe in Santa Claus.'

Bobby regarded him with a faint quizzical smile. 'I believe in *you,*' he said.

Mitzi nodded. Then she put her arms around his huge girth as far as they would go, which wasn't far. Santa leaned down and she vanished into his white hair.

'Goodnight, both of you,' he said huskily.

When the children were gone Corinne looked at Santa's belly, then at her own, which was about the same size.

'I wouldn't have much luck cuddling you, either,'

she said, chuckling. 'Cross fingers that we'll make it through Christmas.'

'Well, if not, that husband of yours is here.' Beneath his beard Santa paled slightly. 'He may not be much use, but he's here.'

'Don't you say a word against my husband. The clinic said he was doing the breathing exercises very well. Better than me.'

He grinned, but then the grin faded. 'Are you going to be all right?' he asked seriously.

She smiled. '*We're* going to be all right. All of us.'

'Sure?'

'I'm like Bobby. I believe in *you*. Happy Christmas, Santa. Now and always.'

A Wild West Christmas

Linda Turner

Linda Turner began reading romances in school and began writing them one night when she had nothing else to read. She's been writing ever since. Single and living in Texas, she travels every chance she gets, scouting locales for her books.

PROLOGUE

Ten Years Ago

IT WAS THE hottest part of the day, when the shadows were short and there wasn't so much as a whisper of a breeze to stir the dust off Priscilla Rawlings's boots. When she'd first come to the Double R to spend the summer with her cousins at their ranch, she was sure she'd never be able to survive the hot New Mexican sun that baked the earth until it was granite-hard and bleached the very color from the sky. It hadn't, however, taken her long to appreciate the heat…and the men who worked out in it day after day.

But it was one man in particular who made her smile. One man in particular who stole her breath and weakened her knees. Wyatt. Wyatt Chandler. Five years her senior, he, too, was a cousin to the Rawlings—but on their mother's side, which made him no relation to her—and was, like her, spending the summer at the Double R. She'd taken one look at him and fallen like a ton of bricks.

He hadn't wanted anything to do with her, of course. Not at first, anyway. She was only seventeen and off-limits to a man who had his future all mapped out for him. He'd graduated from college in May and would head for L.A. at the end of August and a job he already had lined up with one of the largest architectural firms in California. He'd taken one look at her and labeled her a little girl looking for someone to sharpen her flirting skills on. He'd sworn to her face that it wasn't going to be him. He'd called her "baby" and "jailbait" and everything else he could think of to discourage her, but all the while his eyes had held a hunger that had called to her like something on the wind. In the end, he hadn't been able to resist her anymore than she had him.

What had followed was, without a doubt, the most wonderful summer of her life. Under the very noses of their watchful—and very protective—cousins, they'd laughed and played and fallen in love without anyone being the wiser. But nothing lasted forever, and their time together was almost over. August was only two weeks away and soon Wyatt would be leaving for L.A. and his future.

And she meant to go with him.

The decision had come to her while she was swimming at the creek with her cousin Kat an hour ago, and suddenly nothing had been as important as finding Wyatt and telling him. She'd left a stunned Kat at the creek and rushed back to the house, taking time only to change before searching the ranch for him. In her haste, she'd overlooked one of their favorite meeting places—the barn—until Alice, the family housekeeper, had told her he was waiting for her there with an old college friend who had dropped in unexpectedly while she was at the creek.

Hesitating at the shadowy entrance to the barn, she knew she probably shouldn't intrude. Whoever his friend was, he obviously had something important to say to him or he wouldn't have driven halfway across the country to see him. She could wait until tonight to speak with Wyatt, she decided reluctantly. She'd just step inside, meet the man, and make arrangements to talk to Wyatt later.

A smile of welcome already stretching across her face, Priscilla stepped into the darkened interior of the barn and waited for her eyes to adjust to the change in light. Blinking, she caught sight of Wyatt standing by the horse stalls and started forward, but she'd only taken three steps when she stopped short, shock strangling the gasp that rose in her throat. A woman, she thought dully. Wyatt's visitor wasn't a man as she'd so foolishly assumed, but a long-legged blonde in a short skirt and a halter top. And they weren't talking…they were kissing.

CHAPTER ONE

"WELL, I DID IT," Priscilla said grimly as soon as her cousin answered the phone. "I broke things off with Tom this afternoon."

"Oh, no," Kat gasped. "Not on Thanksgiving Day, Cilla!"

"I know—my timing stinks. But he insisted on going over the wedding music, and something in me just snapped."

"How did he react? Was he devastated?"

"Furious is more like it," she retorted dryly. "He fired me…after he told me that his mother warned him months ago that I would leave him high and dry at the altar. That old lady never did like me."

Kat chuckled. "And now you've gone and proved her right. Talk about having a happy Thanksgiving. You just made hers."

As miserable as she felt, Cilla had to laugh. "I've finally done something she approves of." Her smile fading, she said quietly into the phone, "Tom's a good man. I hated hurting him, but I know this was the right decision. He has all the qualities I thought I wanted in the man I married, but something was always missing between us. I'm fond of him, but that's not enough."

"Of course it's not!" her cousin replied with satisfying indignation. "Hold out for the fireworks. I did, and it was worth the wait. So what are you going to do now?"

With a will of their own, Cilla's eyes drifted to the princess-style wedding dress hanging on the door to her bedroom. God, how had she ever gotten herself into this mess? "Take back an unused wedding dress, then see about getting another job, I guess. Though God knows where I'm going to find one this time of year. Most places don't hire until after the holidays."

"Speaking of the holidays, what are you doing about them? Are you going to go home or what?"

"And listen to Mom go on about what a mistake I'm making in letting a dependable man like Tom go? I don't think so."

"Then why don't you come to the ranch and stay for awhile? Don't wait for Christmas—come now. You said yourself no one hires in December, so there's no reason for you to stay in Denver. You can stay at the main house and go riding whenever you like and just veg out. And no one will even mention Tom's name—I swear it."

Cilla hesitated, tempted. She hadn't been back to the Double R for an extended stay since she was a teenager, but she could still remember the sound of the wind in the grass and the peace of the wide open spaces that stretched in all directions for as far as the eye could see. Right now that sounded like heaven, but it was the holidays and she didn't want to ruin it for anyone.

"Oh, I don't know, Kat. I'd be lousy company—"

"Then we'll cheer you up. It's settled, Cilla. You're coming within the week. I'll call Gable and Josey and let the rest of the gang know. Okay?"

What could she say? Kat could be as stubborn as a rock when the mood struck her, and when she spoke in that don't-mess-with-me tone, she wouldn't take no for an answer. "Okay," she laughed. "I'll see you soon."

At the ranch headquarters, Gable picked up the phone on the second ring and grinned at the sound of his cousin's voice. "Hey, man, what's going on? How was your turkey day?"

"Let me give you a hint," Wyatt said. "Does 'the holiday from hell' tell you anything?"

"Uh-oh." Gable chuckled. "Sounds like you've got a problem. What's her name?"

"Eleanor." He fairly spit the name out in distaste. "And it's not what you think."

"Yeah, yeah, that's what all you diehard bachelors say."

"No, I mean it. She's not a girlfriend. Hell, I don't even really know her. She saw me at a building site in Beverly Hills and decided I was just the man she'd been looking for all her life."

"So what's wrong with that? Maybe it was love at first sight."

Wyatt snorted. "Make that *Fatal Attraction* at first sight. I tell you, Gable, she's a nut case. And a spoiled brat whose daddy has more money than God. I took one look at her and knew she was trouble, but when I tried to be nice and explain that I wasn't interested in a relationship right now, she got nasty. She had her daddy make some calls and almost got me fired from a government project."

"Are you kidding me? Dammit, Wyatt, she sounds dangerous. Have you talked to the police?"

"Yeah, for all the good it did me—they didn't do jack squat. Her old man's best buddies with the police commissioner. Now she's started showing up wherever I go. If I stay home, she calls day and night to make sure I haven't got another woman with me. I've already had the number changed twice, and she's found out what it was both times. She's driving me crazy."

"You need to get out of Dodge, man. I mean it. I know you're tied up with work—"

"Actually, I'm finishing up a project by the middle of the week and don't have another one starting till after New Year's, and it's in Oakland. How would you feel about having a visitor for a month or so? I know it's a lot to ask—"

"Stuff it, Chandler," Gable growled. "You're family, remember? Stay as long as you like. We've got plenty of room."

"Thanks, man. I owe you. I'll see you in a couple of days."

Her mother hadn't exactly been thrilled with her decision not to spend Christmas with her, but as Cilla drove through the simple, unadorned gates of the Double R late Wednesday afternoon, she felt as if a huge weight had been lifted from her shoulders. The ranch had always been a refuge for her, a place to go to get away from the world, and that was something she really needed right now. Here, there would be no pressure to make a decision about what she was going to do with the rest of her life, no questions about what went wrong in a relationship that had seemed so right for her. She could, for a while at least, take this time for herself and forget a wedding that was never going to be.

As she left the highway behind and drove deeper into the ranch, civilization was left far behind. There were only miles and miles of grass-covered grazing land and the shadowy, rocky ridge of mountains that marked the western boundary of the ranch. Rolling her window down so she could hear the whisper of the cold wind across the open plain, Cilla smiled for what felt like the first time in days. She felt like she was coming home.

Then the huge Victorian house that had been the ranch headquarters for more than a century came into view, the lighted windows a welcoming beacon in the gathering twilight, and suddenly she couldn't get there fast enough. Pressing down on the accelerator, she raced toward it, dragging a rooster tail of dust behind her.

There was a sports car parked in the circular drive in front of the house, the kind that cost the earth and ate up the road with intimidating ease, but Cilla hardly had time to lift a brow at the sight of it before a very pregnant Kat and the rest of her cousins were pouring out of the house to greet her, all talking at once.

"Cilla! You look wonderful!"

"How was the drive? We heard it was sleeting up north. D'you have any problems?"

"You must be tired. What time did you leave this morning?"

They were all there, Gable and his wife, Josey, Cooper and Susannah, Flynn and Tate, and Kat's husband Luke. And the children, of course. There seemed to be more every time she came, and for the first few moments, it was a madhouse as everyone hugged her, then passed her onto the next Rawlings. Then Alice, hovering around them all like a mother hen, waved them toward the porch as she tossed out orders like a drill sergeant. "Don't keep the poor girl outside in the cold. Can't you see she's freezing to death? And Kat, you need to put your feet up—you haven't rested today like you're supposed to. Gable, get Cilla's suitcases. Cooper, help her with that bag of presents. Land sakes, it looks like she's been to the North Pole."

Laughing, Cilla hugged the housekeeper affectionately. "Alice, you never change. Are you going to make me a Mexican chocolate cake while I'm here?"

"It's already on the kitchen table," she admitted with a grin. "And let me tell you, you're lucky it's still in one piece. These cousins of yours would have already had it half-eaten if I hadn't take the broom to a few of them."

"We were only trying to do you a favor," Flynn told Alice innocently as they all started up the porch steps. "We just wanted to test it to make sure it was done before you served it to company."

"Yeah," Cooper added. "We know how you pride yourself on your baking. We didn't want you to be embarrassed."

When the older woman only snorted at that, they all laughed and swept Cilla along with them to the front door. Kat, however, wasn't laughing when she pulled Cilla to the side just before she could step inside. "Cilla, there's something you should know—"

Surprised by the worried glint in her cousin's blue eyes, Cilla frowned. "What is it? The baby? Is there a problem? Alice said something about you resting—"

"No, no, I'm fine," she said, distracted. "I should have called you back after I found out you both called the same night, but I thought it might be better if I stayed out of it. Now I'm not so sure, and it's too late—"

"Too late?" she repeated with a confused laugh. "Too late for what? Kat, you're rambling. Just spit it out—"

But Kat didn't have to. An abrupt, apprehensive silence from the rest of the group caught Cilla's attention, and she looked up…only to stop dead in her tracks at the sight of the man standing just inside the front door in the entrance hall.

Wyatt.

The smile that curled her mouth froze, then vanished completely. No! she cried silently. It had been ten years since she'd seen him last, ten years since he'd broken her heart. Determined not to lay eyes on him ever again, she'd timed her visits to the ranch when she knew he wouldn't be there. But she hadn't even thought to ask this time because the last she'd heard, he was tied up with some big government project in L.A. What was he doing here?

She wanted to turn and run. Now! But she'd be damned if she'd give Wyatt Chandler the satisfaction of seeing her run for cover like a scared rabbit. With her heart thumping crazily in her breast, she stood her ground and lifted her chin, reminding herself that he no longer had the power to hurt her. But it didn't feel that way when her gaze met his.

He'd changed. She'd have given anything not to have noticed or cared, but much to her dismay, her eyes were already searching his face, noting the differences between the man she'd loved and the one who stood before her. There was no boyishness to his lean, angular face now, no softness in the sharp green eyes that boldly met hers. His wavy black hair was still as dark as midnight, but the sun had carved lines at the corners of his eyes and weathered his skin. He'd matured, filled out, hardened.

And he was still the best-looking thing she'd ever seen in cowboy boots and jeans.

The thought hit her like a stray bullet in the dark, catching her off guard. Horrified, she stiffened, but it was too late. He'd always been able to read her like a book and that, apparently, hadn't changed. His green eyes suddenly glinting with amusement, he grinned at her. "Well, if it isn't Prissy all grown up," he drawled. "Long time no see, cousin."

They weren't cousins and he knew it, but like a trout rising to a fly, she took the bait so beautifully, he almost laughed aloud. "The name is Cilla, *cousin*," she snapped, glaring at him. "And just for the record, absence doesn't make the heart grow fonder. What are you doing here?"

"The same as you," he chuckled. "Spending Christmas here."

"What? You can't be!"

He laughed, not the least offended by her outburst. "'Fraid so. Knocked me for a loop when I heard you were coming, too. Did you bring me a present?"

Not amused, she gave him a withering look. "What do you think?"

What he thought was that she still hated his guts, and he couldn't say he blamed her. He hadn't forgotten what had happened between them that summer ten years ago, any more than she had. She had been just a kid, barely old enough to drive, and still finding herself. He shouldn't have given her a second look, but she was cute and so outrageous, he hadn't been able to resist her. He'd told himself he wouldn't lose his head or do something stupid—just flirt with her and kiss her a couple of times. But one taste and she'd gone straight to his head. The next thing he knew, he was making love to her. When he finally came back to his senses, she was looking up at him with wedding bells in her eyes. It had scared the hell out of him.

Looking back now, he readily admitted that he'd handled the situation badly. But he hadn't been much more than a kid himself and he'd panicked when she started talking happily-ever-after, and all he could see was her father coming after him with a shotgun. So he'd done the only thing he could to convince her they weren't made for each other. He'd called a friend from college and arranged for Cilla to find the two of them in a hot clinch.

He wasn't proud of what he'd done, but his back had been against the wall. And even though she'd never believe it now, he'd done it for her own good. She'd gone home that very day and had managed to avoid him ever since. Until today.

Shaking his head over the quirks of fate, he couldn't help wondering if it had all been for nothing. Here they both were, back at the ranch and snipping at each other like two kids again. Only this time she wasn't seventeen.

And that could be a problem, he thought with a frown as the others quickly stepped in then to fill the awkward silence. All these years, whenever her memory had slipped up on him unaware, he'd pictured her frozen in time with freckles dusting her cheeks, her long, auburn hair caught up in a pony-tail, cutoffs hugging her slim hips and a faded T-shirt molding her slight breasts. But that girl was long gone and in her place was a Priscilla Rawlings he could have passed on the street and not known.

Sophisticated. Over the course of the last ten years, he'd never once pictured her as sophisticated, but the woman who stepped around him like he was a bug to be avoided had somehow acquired polish and grace. Where was the little hoyden he remembered so fondly? The wild Indian who used to ride hell-bent for leather across the ranch, her laughter trailing behind her in her dust? There was no sign of her in this Cilla, who was a city girl through and through. Dressed in black wool slacks and a sapphire-blue angora sweater, with her hair cascading to her shoulders in soft curls that glinted with fire, she was a stranger.

Dear God, when had she become so beautiful? And why hadn't anyone told him? The family had kept him apprised of every boyfriend she'd had since her senior year in high school, dammit, but no one had thought to tell him that she could stop traffic with a smile. If he'd known, he could have least prepared himself for the sight of her, he told himself, then snorted at his own wishful thinking. Yeah, right. Who was he trying to kid? With her oval face, high cheekbones and flawless skin, not to mention a mouth that looked more kissable than ever, the lady was drop-dead gorgeous. And nothing anyone could have said could have prepared him for that. Somehow, over the course of the next month, he was going to have to deal with that. He had a sinking feeling it wasn't going to be easy.

Her stomach knotted with nerves, Cilla escaped upstairs to her room to unpack and tried to convince herself she could do this. Just because she was staying in the same house with the man didn't mean she had to be anything more than polite to him. After all, it wasn't as if they'd even see each other that much. Wyatt had never been the type to hang around the house in the past, and the ranch was a big place. If she was lucky, she wouldn't have to deal with him except at mealtimes, and then the others would be around.

"All you have to do is smile and make small talk so the rest of the family won't be uncomfortable," she told her reflected image in the mirror as she put the last of her things away and checked her appearance. "It'll be a piece of cake."

It sounded easy enough, but the second she stepped out into the hall, the door to the guest room directly across from hers opened and she once again found herself face-to-face with Wyatt. For a second, he looked as surprised as she felt, then that slow, maddening grin of his propped up one corner of his mouth. "We've got to stop meeting like this, sweetheart," he taunted softly. "The cousins will start to talk."

Heat blooming in her cheeks, Cilla just barely resisted the urge to hit him. "I agree," she retorted. "So why don't you do us both a favor and go back to where you came from?"

"Why should I do that?" he chuckled. "I was here first."

"Dammit, Wyatt, this isn't a game! I'm serious. You're not any happier to see me than I am you. If you were a gentleman, you'd leave."

For all of two seconds, he actually considered her suggestion. She was right—neither of them was thrilled to see the other and that would make for an awkward holiday for the rest of the family. But his gut knotted just at the thought of going back to L.A. right now. He could handle Cilla and her hostility. Eleanor and her insane fanaticism was something else entirely. If he never saw the woman again, it would be too soon.

"Sorry, darlin'," he drawled, "but you should know better than most that I'm no gentleman. But you don't have to stay just because I am. I'm sure the family would understand if you decided the house wasn't big enough for the two of us. You could always go to your mother's in Florida."

"And let everyone think you scared me off?" she snapped, arching a delicate brow at him. "Not on your life, Wyatt Chandler. If you can suffer my company, I can stomach yours."

Satisfied, he only grinned. "Have it your way, honey. Whatever makes you happy."

She gave him a withering look, not the least impressed. "Please…spare me. If you really wanted to make me happy, you'd do the decent thing and at least go stay with Flynn or Cooper for awhile."

"Why? So you won't have to worry about running into me every time you turn around? What's the matter?" he teased. "Afraid you'll fall for me again?"

"Fat chance," she retorted with a laugh, truly

amused. "I'm over you, cowboy. So if you're sticking around in hopes of rekindling an old flame, you're wasting your time. It ain't going to happen."

CHAPTER TWO

WHEN the entire Rawlings clan got together for a meal, they had to put two tables together and use every chair in the house. Even then, they sat shoulder to shoulder, crowded in like a herd of calves at a feeding trough. You could hardly move without bumping the person next to you, and at times, the different conversations going on around the combined tables were so loud that you couldn't hear yourself think. Cilla loved it.

The family hadn't been nearly as large when she was a teenager. No one had been married then and there'd just been Gable, Cooper, Flynn and Kat. And Alice, of course, who had fussed over them like a mother hen and helped Gable keep them all in line and the family together after their parents died. To Cilla, who had never had any brothers or sisters of her own, every visit with her Rawlings cousins had seemed like something out of "The Brady Bunch." And meal times had been the best of all. The Double R had always been known for its hospitality, so there'd always been a place at the table for anyone who cared to drop by. The more the merrier.

Glancing around at the laughing faces of her cousins, Cilla was glad to see that that hadn't changed. There were seven children now—good Lord, when had that happened?—who ranged in age from Flynn and Tate's sixteen year old Haily all the way down to Cooper and Susannah's Holly, who would be two on Christmas Eve. As close as brothers and sister, they were a lively group and kept everyone laughing with their antics. Especially Holly. An unabashed flirt, she grinned across the table at Wyatt and giggled as he rolled his eyes at her playfully.

Watching him under lowered lashes, Cilla couldn't help but notice he was still a flirt, still a ladies' man, and it didn't matter if the lady was two or eighty—he could still charm the pants off her. All of their cousins were happily married and settled in life, but Wyatt showed little interest in marriage or having a family. Oh, he was great with the kids, just like a favorite uncle. But when the holidays were over, he'd go back to L.A. and a life that didn't require commitment or responsibility.

And that irritated her no end. He was still footloose and fancy-free, and she was, she told herself, lucky she'd gotten over him long ago.

Seated at the far end of the table from him, she tried to ignore him but Holly and the other kids' laughter made that impossible. Fighting the urge to smile, she watched him blow the toddler a kiss, and just that quickly, his eyes were on *her*. Her heart skipped a beat, then thundered frantically in her ears. Damn him, she fumed, glaring at him. How did he do this to her? She'd deliberately taken a seat as far away from his as possible, but his wicked, dancing, *knowing* eyes pinned her in her chair and just reached out and physically stroked her, stealing her breath.

So you're over me, are you? he seemed to taunt silently. *Well, we'll just see about that.*

He was staring and he didn't care who noticed. She wanted to kill him.

Seated across from her, Kat gently tapped her tea glass with her fork. "Hey, everybody, I need the floor for a second," she said over the low roar of the different conversations making their way around the table. "I have an announcement to make."

"Oh, God, here it comes," Flynn groaned teasingly. "She's come up with another name for the baby. What is it this time, brat? Michelangelo Valentine or Abraham Lincoln Valentine? They've both got a ring to them."

"Cute, Flynn. Real cute," she retorted, grinning as the others laughed. "Actually, I was thinking about Michelangelo *and* Lincoln. That sounds better than Fred and Barney, don't you think?"

Puzzled, he frowned. "You're going to give the kid two names?"

Her eyes twinkling, she reached for her husband, Lucas, who sat next to her, and smiled as his strong fingers closed around hers. "No, we're going to give the *kids* names of their own."

For a moment, there was nothing but stunned silence. Then her words really registered, and in the next instant pandemonium broke out as all the adults seemed to surge to their feet at once.

"Twins?" Cilla whispered, thrilled. "You're having twins?"

Tate and Josey, the two doctors in the family, immediately started throwing questions at her. "Are you okay? Are you still seeing Thompson in Silver City? What does he say about you working with those longhorns of yours?"

"Should you even be working?" Gable asked, frowning. "Josey spent the last four months in bed before the boys were born. Are you sure you're following the doctor's orders?"

"Yes, for once in my life I'm following orders," Kat laughed as she was swept from her brothers to her sisters-in-law to her cousins for a round of hugs and kisses. "Lucas is making sure of it. And yes, I'm seeing Thompson, and no, I'm not working anymore, not since last week. Give me a chance to catch my breath and I'll tell you everything."

Wyatt, the last to congratulate Lucas and hug his cousin, drew back suddenly to grin down at her. "You're going to make a hell of a mother, brat. But two? Lord, if they're anything like you, they're going to lead you a ragged chase. Think you're going to be able to keep up with them?"

Her blue eyes twinkling, she only grinned. "What do you think?"

Alice, beaming like a proud grandmother, swept in then with champagne and the cake she'd been guarding all afternoon. Just that easily, dinner became a party, and long after the cake and the champagne were history, they sat around the table talking and laughing and discussing everything from the most outlandish names everyone could think of to where the new babies would go to college when the time came.

"College is the least of our worries," Kat laughed. "Right now, I'm just worried about where we're going to put them if we get a mixed set instead of two of a kind. The cabin's only got one spare room."

"Well, that's easily solved," Wyatt said. "I'll draw you up some plans while I'm here, if you like."

"But you're on vacation. We couldn't let you do that."

"I don't know why not if I want to do it," he said reasonably. "Consider it my present to the new arrivals."

Kat hesitated, looking to Lucas for help, who said dryly, "That's a pretty expensive present, Wyatt. Most people give a stuffed teddy bear. You sure you want to do this?"

"I wouldn't have offered if I wasn't sure. Anyway, I can't sit around here all month and just twiddle my thumbs. I'll go nuts."

Lucas glanced back at Kat, a silent message passing between them before he finally shrugged and grinned. "Well, if you're sure you want to do it, I guess we'd be crazy to turn you down. Thanks, Wyatt. We appreciate it."

"Things are pretty slow around here right now," Gable said thoughtfully. "If we all pitched in, we

could have that room up and finished in no time once
the plans are drawn up."

That started a discussion on who could do what
and when they could start and soon Wyatt was drawing a sketch of the cabin on his paper napkin while
Kat described her dream nursery. Watching them
from the far end of the table, Cilla found herself staring at what could have been. *She* could have been the
one who was pregnant and it could have been a nursery for his own child that Wyatt was designing.

Not in a million years, Cilla Rawlings, a voice
growled in her ear. *Don't even think it.*

But it was too late. Old dreams and forbidden needs
flashed in front of her eyes, teasing her, taunting her
with yearnings that she had locked away in a secret
part of her heart eons ago. A baby. Wyatt's baby. At
seventeen, she'd imagined and fantasized and dreamed
of the day in the far distant future when she would hold
a tiny infant in her arms, an infant that would have a
fascinating combination of her and Wyatt's features,
a precious baby that would be the embodiment of their
love for each other. But that dream had shriveled up
and died—she'd thought forever—when she found
him in the arms of another woman.

God, what was she doing?

Pale, suddenly in desperate need of some time
to herself, she pushed her chair back and immediately drew the attention of every adult at the table.
Including Wyatt's. Avoiding his sharp gaze, she
pushed to her feet with a smile that wasn't quite as
easy as she would have liked. "Sorry to be a kill-

joy, but I'm really bushed, guys. It's been a long day, and if I don't go to bed, I'm going to crash right here."

"You do look a little pale," Josey said with a frown. "Are you feeling all right?"

"The flu's been going around," Tate added, studying her in concern. "Josey and I have been tripping over patients all week. Have you had any kind of a fever?"

"No, Dr. Tate. I'm fine. Really," she insisted with a smile as she rose to her feet. "It's nothing that a little sleep won't fix. I started at five this morning and I finally ran out of gas. So don't break up the party on my account. I'll see you all in the morning."

Promising to catch up on all the family gossip in the days and weeks to come, she hurried upstairs to her room, sure she would be out like a light the second her head hit the pillow. But long after she'd showered and crawled into bed in her favorite flannel gown, her thoughts were still jumping around like popcorn in a hot skillet.

Downstairs, she heard the sleepy good-night calls of the children and their parents as Flynn and Cooper and their families left for their own nearby homes, which were also part of the Double R. Kat and Lucas followed soon after that, and then the house started to quiet down as Josey and Gable got their own brood ready for bed. One by one, Cilla heard them all come upstairs, the whisper of their feet on the hall runner, the quiet thump of doors shutting up and down the hall. Finally there was nothing but the silence of the night, and still she lay flat on her back and stared up at the ceiling, sleep a thousand miles away.

Across the hall, she caught the muted sounds of Wyatt getting ready for bed—the running of the water in the bathroom, the sound of boots dropping, first one, then the other, to the floor—and suddenly she'd had enough. She couldn't do it. She couldn't lie there and listen to those intimate sounds without imagining him undressing, stretching out on the bed with a tired sigh, thumping his pillow into a comfortable shape...not without dreaming about him and that was something she hadn't done in years. She didn't intend to start now.

Her heart thumping crazily in her breast, she bolted up and reached for her robe. Seconds later, she carefully eased open her bedroom door and cautiously peered out into the hall. There was a nightlight on at the top of the stairs, providing the only illumination. As quiet as a mouse, she hurried downstairs in her bare feet to the den and switched on the TV. She needed a movie, something old and draggy and preferably in black and white that would bore her to death inside of five minutes. Maybe then she'd be able to go to sleep.

But what she got was *It's a Wonderful Life*. And it was just starting.

She groaned. Of all the miserable, rotten luck. It was her favorite holiday movie, the only one she made a point to watch religiously at least once every year. Frowning at the stark black-and-white images of Jimmy Stewart and Donna Reed, she reminded herself that she needed to get some serious sleep if she was going to hold her own with Wyatt tomorrow. But she was a real sucker when it came to the holidays and traditions. And *It's a Wonderful Life* was definitely a tradition. Unable to resist, she sank down onto the couch, her chenille robe flaring out around her, and tucked her bare feet up under her folded legs. Clutching one of the throw pillows to her breast, she hugged it to her, her eyes glued to the screen.

That was the way Wyatt found her twenty minutes later.

On his way to the kitchen for another piece of Alice's Mexican chocolate cake, he heard the muted sounds of the TV coming from the den and stepped into the doorway to see who was still up. At the sight of Cilla huddled on the couch with tears streaming down her cheeks, a slow, crooked smile tugged at the corners of his mouth. She always had been a pushover for a sappy movie.

He should have left her alone. She was enjoying the movie and her tears and wouldn't appreciate his showing up in the middle of either. But he wasn't going to go away; he couldn't. Not when there were tears sliding down her cheeks and they were the only two people awake in the house. Alice's chocolate cake forgotten, he walked silently into the den and dropped down onto the couch beside her. Without a word, he reached into his pocket, pulled out a handkerchief, and held it out to her.

Startled, she stared at the folded cotton handkerchief as if it was a snake that was going to strike any second. "Go ahead, take it," he said, laughing softly as he reached for her hand and closed her fingers around the cloth. "It's not going to bite you."

She took it…warily. "What are you doing down here? I thought you'd gone to bed."

His smile flashed in the darkness, wicked and teasing. "I was just about to ask you the same thing. What's the matter? Can't sleep for dreaming of me?"

"Fat chance, Chandler," she snorted. "I know this may come as something of a shock to you, but my every thought doesn't begin and end with you."

Grinning, he pressed a hand to his heart like a man who had just taken a mortal blow. "No kidding? And here I had the distinct impression that just being around me made you nervous. Guess I was wrong."

"You're darn right you were wrong," she retorted. "I couldn't care less what you do. Now, if you'll excuse me, I'm going up to bed."

"Oh, no, you don't. The movie's not over yet." His eyes dancing, he settled his arm about her shoulders and leaned back, all his attention innocently focused on the movie.

Cilla wasn't fooled for a second. Wyatt Chandler didn't have an innocent bone in his body. And the day he actually wanted to watch a sentimental movie like *It's a Wonderful Life* was the day he'd been out in the sun too long.

But God, his arm felt wonderful around her! It had been so long. She'd thought she'd forgotten what it felt like to be held by him, to lean against him and draw his scent in with every breath and know that nothing in the world could hurt her when he was this close.

Except him.

And it took nothing more than the throb of a hurt that even now, ten years later, hadn't quite healed to make her reach hurriedly for the arm around her shoulders and shrug out of it. "You haven't changed, Wyatt Chandler. You'll use any line, any situation, to get a woman in your arms. Let go! I'm going to bed."

He made no move to stop her, but his taunt followed her across the den. "Go ahead. Cut and run like a scared little girl. And here I thought you were all grown up."

Later, she told herself she should have ignored him and gone on upstairs. At the very least, she should have held on to her temper and given herself time to think before she answered him. But his needling words struck a nerve, and before she had time to ask herself why she cared what he thought, she was whirling and bearing down on him with fire in her eyes.

"Don't pull that garbage on me, Chandler. I know what you're doing and it's not going to work. I *am* all grown up, and in case you haven't noticed, I'm not running scared from you or anyone else. I'm tired. T-i-r-e-d. Got it?"

Not the least impressed, he only grinned up at her crookedly as he sprawled against the couch with his arms spread wide against the back. "A likely story," he drawled. "You've been avoiding me ever since you got here. Admit it, cousin, you've still got a thing for me—"

"A thing for you! God, I don't know why I even bother to try to hold a rational conversation with you. You always were the most insufferable, conceited—"

"And it's got you all shook up," he finished, chuckling, as insults fell from her tongue. "Why else would you be spitting at me like a scalded cat? You're scared."

She gave him a scornful look that would have felled a lesser man. He didn't even blink. Annoyed, frustrated, she wanted to shake him until his teeth rattled…and, just once, shake up that irritatingly smug self-confidence of his. Glaring at him, she said, "I couldn't care less what you do or where you go and I can prove it."

His mouth twitching, he arched a dark brow at her. "Oh, really? And how do you plan to do that?"

"Like this," she retorted, and sank down beside him on the couch. A heartbeat later, she grabbed him by the ears and kissed him.

CHAPTER THREE

SOMEWHERE in the back of her head, she told herself she could do this. She could lay a kiss on him that would curl his hair and leave him panting, then walk away without a second glance. After all, it was no more than he deserved. He might think he was God's gift to women, but not where she was concerned. By the time she got through with him, he wouldn't know what hit him. And she wouldn't feel a thing.

At least, that was the way it should have happened. But nothing, she discovered too late, was that easy with Wyatt. The second her mouth settled on his, she felt things she hadn't allowed herself to even think about for a very long time. Things like need, the kind that came from her very soul. And a hunger that was immediate and fierce, as familiar as the sound of his name on her tongue. Stunned, she should have pulled back right then and there, but she couldn't think, couldn't move, couldn't tear herself away from the wonder that was and always had been Wyatt. His arms came around her, snatching her close, wrapping around her like he'd never let her go, and between one heartbeat and the next, she felt like she'd come home. Finally.

Dizzy, her heart doing somersaults in her breast, she swallowed a whimper as the truth slipped into her heart like a switchblade between the ribs. *This* was what had been missing in her relationship with Tom. This instant heat, this fire in the belly that threatened to burn you from the inside out, this passion that swept over you like a crashing breaker and dragged you down into full blown raging desire before you even thought to note the danger. A passion that she'd never come close to finding with Tom, not even when she'd thought she loved him with all her heart.

She'd known something was missing, something that she'd been yearning for, searching for, something she'd never felt for any man...except Wyatt. Something that, in spite of everything, was still there and stronger than ever.

Have you lost your mind, Cilla Rawlings? a caustic voice demanded in her head. *This isn't Prince Charming you've got in a lip-lock, you know. He's the worst kind of rat, and he'll break your heart again if you give him a chance. Last time you were a kid—you didn't know what you were doing. But you're not seventeen anymore. What's your excuse this time?*

The painful words forced their way through the cloud of need that shrouded her brain, tugging at her until they got her attention and brought her up short. Horrified, she stiffened. Dear God, what was she doing? She was supposed to be teaching the man a lesson, not melting in his arms and kissing him like there was no tomorrow!

She jerked back abruptly, her breathing ragged and the thunder of her heartbeat loud in her ears. She'd eat dirt before she'd let him see what he could do to her with just a kiss. Calling on all her self-control, she looked him right in the eye and gave him a cool smile that was guaranteed to set his teeth on edge. If her blood was still hot, her pulse racing, no one but she knew that. "Not bad, Chandler. Your technique's improved with age."

His eyes narrowed slightly, but he only grinned. "So has yours. But if that little demonstration was supposed to show me how indifferent you are, I think I missed the point. Maybe we should try it again."

"Oh, no you don't!" Her laugh shakier than she would have liked, she quickly shied out of reach. "Nice try, but if you think I'm going to stand here and trade kisses with you, all those years of working in the sun must have fried your brain. I'm not interested."

"Oh, really? That's not what your body was telling me just a few seconds ago."

"Oh, I didn't say I didn't enjoy it," she said with an airiness that was nothing but pure bravado. "I enjoy hot fudge sundaes, too, but that doesn't mean I want a steady diet of them. Some things just aren't good for me, and you're one of them. So you see," she continued with an easy smile, "I'm over you, cousin. Totally and completely. I can enjoy the company—and occasional kiss—of a man who's not good for me, but I no longer fall head over heels like a teenager with a bad case of hero worship. So you don't have to worry about me making a fool of myself over you again. It's not going to happen."

Watching him closely, she saw his usually laughing eyes darken with irritation and grinned cheekily. "Now that we've got that cleared up, I think I'll go to bed. It's been a long day. 'Night, Wyatt. See you in the morning."

Turning on her heel, she walked away from him with unhurried grace. She could feel his eyes drilling into her back, but he didn't move, didn't say a word, for which she was profoundly grateful. Because if he'd just have called her name, he could have tempted her to change her mind. But he didn't, and she didn't spare him a glance. She didn't dare.

With the sound of her footsteps loud in the quiet of the night, it seemed to take her forever to cross the length of the den. Then she finally reached the door and quietly stepped into the hall. It wasn't until she was around the corner that she realized how shaky her knees were. Alone, out of his sight, she ran for the stairs and the privacy of her room.

Long after she disappeared from view, Wyatt stared after her like a man who had just been flattened by a stampeding herd of longhorns that had come out of nowhere. For the life of him, he couldn't say what the hell had just happened. One second he was teasing her, lighting that fire in her eyes that always delighted him, and the next, she was kissing him with a determination that set every nerve ending he had humming.

He should have pushed her away. If nothing else, he damn sure shouldn't have kissed her back. She was trouble—she always had been. The second he realized they'd both been invited to the ranch, he should have gotten the hell out of there. But by then, she'd been walking through the front door with that glint in her eye that warned him not to come anywhere near her, and something deep inside him had balked at the idea of conveniently disappearing just so *she* could be more comfortable. He had just as much right as she did to be there.

Damn his stubborn pride, he thought irritably. If he hadn't stayed, he would have put her out of his head the minute he drove away, but there was no way in hell that was going to happen now. Not after that kiss.

She'd just caught him by surprise, he tried to tell himself. That was the only explanation for his response. After all, he wasn't a monk. When a beautiful woman laid one on him, he was damn well going to enjoy it.

As far as excuses went, it sounded good. But his common sense wasn't buying it. It wasn't just any beautiful woman he'd kissed. It was Cilla. And there was enough electricity in that kiss to light up the whole West Coast.

Over her? he thought grimly. Like hell!

Damn! Now what was he going to do? She wasn't the only one who'd thought the past was dead and buried. Oh, he'd never really forgotten her—even at seventeen, Cilla hadn't been the type of woman a man walked away from unscathed. She'd stuck like a burr to his memory, pricking his consciousness at the most inopportune times and refusing to let any other woman push her from his head.

But it'd been ten years, dammit! And you couldn't look back. Time had a tendency to blur the memories, to enhance them, to make them better than they were. A long-ago summer was always longer, hotter, the music better, the romance sweeter than anything in the here and now. Which was ridiculous, he tried to tell himself, because it couldn't have been that good. Nothing ever was.

So where did he go from here? Regardless of the need that was still churning in his gut from that damn kiss, he wasn't looking for a relationship with Cilla or anyone else. It wasn't that he didn't ever plan to settle down—he did when the right woman came along, but so far, he'd run into nothing but one roadblock after another. If they weren't too young—as Cilla had been when they'd first met—they were too old or too afraid of getting hurt or too career-minded.

And then there was the problem he'd left behind in California. Eleanor. Just thinking about her made his gut clench. He'd searched his memory a dozen times, trying to pinpoint some innocent word, some unsuspecting action, that had led her to believe not only that he was available, but that he was interested in her. But there was nothing, not even a smile. He didn't deny that he had a reputation for flirting, but he didn't encourage anyone that he wasn't first attracted to. And Eleanor had left him stone-cold. There'd been something about her that he hadn't liked from the second his eyes had met hers, and he'd been as curt as he could without being rude. She hadn't taken the hint. If anything, she'd somehow seen his coolness as a challenge and had given him misery ever since.

Compared to Eleanor, Cilla didn't come close to being a problem. She wasn't, thankfully, jailbait anymore. She'd grown up, filled out, and learned to control that impulsive streak that had once nearly gotten them both into serious trouble. And she despised him—he'd made sure of it by setting up that kiss with Sharon all those years ago. The sparks might still sizzle between them, but he'd destroyed her youthful illusions and flung her love back in her face, and no woman forgot or forgave that. And that just might be both their salvations.

Still, when he locked up and went upstairs, he couldn't stop his gaze from drifting to Cilla's closed door. All too easily, he could picture her getting ready for bed, slowly stripping out of her sweater and slacks, revealing inch by inch that beautiful body that had only gotten better with the passage of time. Was she still shy about that mole on her hip? And still so sensitive—

Suddenly realizing where his thoughts had wandered, he swore under his breath and wondered whose brainy idea it had been to put them at this end of the hall together. It wasn't as if these were the only two available rooms. The house was as big as a small hotel. They could have easily been given rooms at opposite ends of the house. So why hadn't they?

If he were a suspicious man, he'd swear someone was playing matchmaker, but that was downright ridiculous. The entire family knew that Cilla couldn't stand the sight of him—she'd been avoiding him for years, for God's sake! She'd even, according to Gable, planned her visits to the ranch at times she knew he wasn't going to be there. No one in their right mind could possibly think there was anything between them but hostility.

Unless they'd happened to witness the kiss they'd just shared downstairs. Whatever he'd felt for the lady at that moment, it hadn't been hostility. Swearing, he turned away from her room and went into his own, determined to put Cilla and that damn kiss out of his head.

The lady, however, didn't make it easy for him. He'd barely drifted off to sleep when she wandered into his dreams as if she owned them, teasing and touching and kissing him until he was hot and hard and reaching for her, only to come up with nothing but sheet. He'd dreamed of her before, of course, but that was in the past, and the Cilla who had tormented him then was little more than a girl who was just discovering her powers as a woman. She'd tied him in knots with her innocent seduction, and he hadn't resisted her as he should have, but in the end, he'd found a way to walk away from her because it was for her own good. This Cilla was something else entirely. Older, wiser, more sure of herself, she was a grown woman who knew exactly what she wanted and how to get it. And that was what made him more than a little bit nervous. How was a man supposed to handle a woman like that without getting burned?

Disturbed by the thought, he rolled over on his stomach and punched his pillow into a more comfortable shape, determined to put the lady out of his head once and for all and get some sleep. They were going to spend the next month together under the watchful eye of the family, and he had no intention of dreaming of her or any other woman every night. He had better things to do with his time...like come up with the plans for the addition to Kat and Lucas's cabin.

Over the course of the next six hours, he designed additions to half a dozen cabins and even came up with plans for an office complex in L.A. But it didn't help. Nothing did. Every time he drifted into sleep, Cilla was there, waiting for him with a smile that was as distracting as hell. He woke reaching for her, cursing her, cursing himself. If she'd really been there beside him in bed, he didn't know if he would have kissed her or shook her until her teeth rattled. He just knew that in all the years since that long-ago summer, he'd never once met a woman who could fascinate and irritate him at one and the same time the way Cilla could.

Giving up all pretense of trying to sleep, he was up before dawn and standing under the shower by the time the first rooster crowed. The hot water didn't do a thing for his dull head, though, so as soon as he was shaved and dressed, he headed downstairs to the kitchen. Coffee. He needed lots of coffee.

The house was quiet as a tomb—with the slower pace of winter, it would be another hour before the rest of the family started to stir—but he was no stranger around his cousins' kitchen. For as long as he could remember, Alice had insisted that everyone help get the meal on the table and clean up afterward, and he hadn't been spared that chore when he was a kid just because he was visiting. Retrieving the ground coffee from the pantry, he put on a pot and sat down at the old oak kitchen table to wait for it to brew.

Thirty minutes later, he was on his second cup and enjoying the sight of the first streaks of morning sunlight creeping over the ranch when Gable appeared in the doorway wearing nothing but his jeans and a frown. "I thought I smelled coffee," he said in a voice gravelly with sleep. "What are you doing up so early, man? You're on vacation!"

"Someone forgot to tell my brain," he said, sipping at his steaming cup. "Sorry I woke you."

"Hey, don't worry about it. I needed to get up, anyway. Josey's got the early shift at the clinic this morning, and she needs a ride. Her water pump went out yesterday, and I've got to run into town to get her another one. Any more of that coffee?"

"A whole pot," Wyatt said with a grin. "I figured it would take that much to jump-start my motor this morning. Help yourself. I hope you like it strong."

Strong didn't even begin to describe the brew Gable poured into the mug he'd grabbed from the cabinet. Black as tar, it could have, in a pinch, served as battery acid. Filling his mug to the rim, Gable took a cautious sip and sighed in satisfaction, a slow grin stretching across his rugged face as the potent liquid hit his stomach. "This stuff damn near ought to be outlawed," he growled. "Where'd you learn to make coffee like this?"

"Visit any construction site anywhere in the world, and this is pretty much what you're going to get," Wyatt replied, his green eyes glinting with amusement. "I've been told it puts hair on your chest."

"Then remind me not to let Josey have any," he chuckled as he settled into the chair across the table from him and took another cautious sip. "Damn, that's good. So tell me," he said casually, studying him with eyes that missed little, "what kept you awake last night? Cilla or the woman in California?"

Caught in the act of swallowing, Wyatt choked. "Cilla? What's she got to do with anything?"

"I don't know," his cousin replied. "You tell me. It's been—what? Ten years since you've seen each other? And you didn't exactly part on the best of terms. I guess it was no surprise that she wasn't thrilled to see you."

"That's putting it mildly," Wyatt snorted. "If looks could kill, I'd have dropped dead on the spot."

"Probably," Gable agreed, grinning. "But she's sure grown into a fine-looking woman, hasn't she? She was engaged, you know."

Wyatt took the news like a man who had just been shot. Stunned, he blurted out, "Engaged! To who? When? How come I wasn't told about this?"

"I guess because no one thought you'd be interested one way or the other. After all, it's not as if you two have kept up with each other over the years. Anyway, nothing came of it. She broke things off last week."

"Why?"

Gable shrugged. "I don't know. I guess she decided she didn't love him. She told Kat all about it, how the guy was her boss and fired her when she gave him his ring back. That's why she's here. She's trying to decide where to go from here. I think she's sort of had it with Denver."

Still reeling from the news that she'd actually been on the verge of getting married, Wyatt hardly heard him. All these years, he'd known she wasn't standing still in time. She'd gone on with her life just as he had. He'd pictured her growing up, graduating from high school and college, getting a job, a place of her own, even a boyfriend or two. But he'd never pictured her loving another man. And he found, to his disgust, that he didn't like the images that sprang to mind. He didn't like them at all.

"Have you got a problem with her being engaged?"

Lost in his thoughts, it was a minute before Gable's words even registered. When they did, he retorted sharply, "Why the hell would I care if she was engaged or not engaged? She's nothing to me."

"Good, I'm glad to hear it," Gable said easily. "I wouldn't want to see her get hurt again. Or you. So your problem must be the woman in California. Right? I know if I had someone like that showing up every time I turned around, I wouldn't be able to sleep nights, either."

It was a logical conclusion, but still Wyatt hesitated, considering. In the end, however, there was nothing left to consider, not if he was going to get any sleep at all the next month. "Right," he said, taking another bracing swig of coffee. What else could he say?

CHAPTER FOUR

"DADDY, can we get the Christmas tree today? Ple e-a-ase? You said we'd do it this weekend."

"I want to drive. Can I drive the wagon, Daddy? Brian got to do it last year."

"Did not! Mandy did. She always gets to do things like that cause she's the oldest."

Gable, grinning at his kids as they argued good-naturedly about who did what and when, lifted an inquiring brow at Josey, who was seated across the breakfast table from him. "Well, Mom, what'da you say? It's your day off. Do you want to spend it getting the tree and putting it up or did you have something else planned?"

Her dark green eyes twinkling, Josey pretended to consider. "Well, I was going to go through everybody's sock drawers today and sort them out—"

"Aw, Mom, you can do that any time!" Joey grumbled.

"And Cilla and Wyatt really want to go with us to get a tree," Mandy pointed out. "They've been here nearly a week already and haven't got to do anything fun."

In the middle of spreading jam on one of Alice's homemade biscuits, Cilla glanced up in surprise. "Oh, but I have," she told the eight-year-old. "I've slept late every morning and visited your mom and Tate at the clinic, and caught up on all the gossip with Kat. Tomorrow, I'm having dinner with Cooper and Susannah, and later this week, I'm going shopping with your mom. I'm having a great time." And in the process, she'd successfully stayed out of Wyatt's way. Life couldn't be better.

"Yeah, she's hardly been here at all," Wyatt said dryly, the glint in his eyes warning her he knew exactly what she'd been doing. "And neither have I. I've been working on the plans for the addition to Kat's cabin and ordering all the supplies, but that doesn't mean I haven't been having a good time. And we don't need to be entertained, anyway. We're family."

"Does that mean you don't want to go with us to get the tree?" Brian asked, hurt.

"Oh, no!"

"Hey, sport, you know better than that. I love picking out Christmas trees."

Cilla almost choked on her coffee at that one—the Wyatt she'd known in the past had been cynical and mocking about anything that had to do with tradition and sentiment and holidays—but before she could remind him of that, Gable was rising to his feet with a grin. "Well, then, it looks like we're all taking a trip to the canyon to get a tree. Who's going to help me hitch up the wagon?"

"I will!"

"Me first!"

"I'm the oldest!"

Grabbing their father's hands, the kids were off like a shot, laughing and shouting in excitement as they dragged him off to the barn while Josey yelled after them not to forget their coats. His green eyes twinkling, Wyatt glanced down the table at Cilla and arched a brow at her. "Does this mean we're going to have the pleasure of your company today, Prissy?"

The nickname was old and hated and no one knew that better than him. Put on the spot, Cilla gritted her teeth and gave him a smile that should have lowered his body temperature ten degrees. She was trapped, and if she hadn't known better, she would have sworn he'd somehow finagled the whole thing. "It looks that way, Earp," she said sweetly, returning tit for tat when it came to hated nicknames. "We can sing Christmas carols and everything. It'll be fun, don't you think?"

"Oh, yeah," he drawled, his grin broadening. "I intend to make sure of it."

Cilla didn't like the sound of that—or the wicked mischief dancing in his eyes—but what could he possibly do in front of Gable and Josey and the kids? Oh, he would tease her, but she could handle that. It was the touching—and the kissing, God help her— that stole her breath and turned her into putty in his hands. She didn't, however, intend to be an easy mark. She'd just keep her distance and everything would go fine. And it wasn't as if she'd have to spend the entire day with him. How long could it take to pick out a tree?

It was a cold morning, but clear, with a playful wind that grabbed at hats and hair and chilled any exposed skin. Thankful that she'd brought her mittens and stocking cap, Cilla started to pull them on as she stepped outside with Josey a few minutes later, only to stumble to a halt as her gaze fell on the old wagon pulled up before the front steps. She'd assumed that the wagon Gable had gone with the kids to hitch up was some kind of modern ranch trailer that was pulled behind the family Jeep to carry the Christmas tree back to the house. But the wagon parked in the drive was definitely the old-fashioned wooden kind, complete with a pile of hay in the back and a team of horses hitched to the front. Gable was already lifting the kids up to the long bench seat they would share with him so they could take turns driving, while Wyatt stood by the open tailgate to lift her and Josey up into the back.

"It's a great day for a hayride," he said with a grin. "Of course, I wouldn't complain if it was night and we had a full moon, but that's a different kind of hayride. Up you go, Josey." With no effort at all, he helped her up, then turned to Cilla. "Ready?"

Cilla took one look at his roguish grin and knew she should run, not walk, for safety. He was up to something, and if she got into that wagonload of hay with him, she was just asking for trouble. But the whole family was waiting on her, and she couldn't back out now without a darn good excuse, which she didn't have.

Her pulse pounding, she forced a smile and held out a hand, expecting him to steady her as she stepped up into the wagon. But instead of taking her hand, he grabbed her around the waist and swung her up into the hay before she could do anything but gasp and latch on to his arms.

"Dammit, Wyatt, stop that!" she hissed in a low voice that didn't carry to the others.

"What?" he asked innocently, releasing her. Holding his hands away from her, he looked pointedly at where her fingers still curled into his arms. "You're the one holding on to me, sweetheart."

Heat stinging her cheeks, she snatched her hands back and glared at him, but he only laughed and vaulted up into the wagon beside her. Cilla wanted to hit him, but she had no intention of touching him again. Edging away from him, she moved to the opposite side of the wagon and sat cross-legged in the hay.

"Everybody in?" Gable called over his shoulder.

"Yeah," Wyatt said. "Let's get this baby in gear."

"All right!" the kids yelled.

Laughing, Gable clicked his tongue, gave the reins a light flip and set the wagon in motion. Wyatt, to the delight of the children, pretended to lose his balance, stumbled, then toppled over into the hay...and landed face-first in the hay mere inches from Cilla's hip.

Cilla's heart jumped into her throat, then seemed

to lodge there permanently when his hand brushed against her jean-covered thigh as he moved to push himself up out of the hay. Swallowing a gasp, she tried to tell herself that it was just an accident. But then he looked up at her and winked.

If he hadn't looked so funny, she might have given him a disapproving frown and pushed his hand off her knee, where it had casually slipped. But his hair was a mess, with hay poking out of it in every direction, and he scratched at his chest like a monkey to make the kids laugh. Before she knew how it happened, Cilla found herself laughing. Damn the man, what was she going to do with him?

"Hey, how about some Christmas carols?" Josey suggested. The boys broke into "Jingle Bells," and soon the whole family was singing...everybody but Cilla. Settling next to her, his own deep baritone carrying easily over the children's sweet tones, Wyatt waited for her to join in. When she didn't, he leaned over to whisper in her ear, "You got a frog in your throat or what? You're not singing."

At the first touch of his warm breath against her ear and neck, Cilla shivered. Lord, why hadn't she moved once he sat next to her? Hugging herself, she whispered back, "Believe me, it's better that way. My singing has been known to make grown men cry."

He chuckled, his green eyes crinkling attractively with amusement. "Can't carry a tune in a bucket, huh?"

"Make it a wheelbarrow and you're closer to the mark," she retorted as his nearness seeped through her like a tropical breeze, heating her blood all the way to her toes and back. Fighting the sudden unexpected urge to melt against him, she tore her gaze from his and held herself stiffly erect, but it took more than that to discourage the infuriating man. He didn't touch her, but he didn't have to. Aware of every breath he drew, she could feel the touch of his eyes on her, stroking her.

"And here I thought you had the voice of an angel to go along with that face of yours," he murmured teasingly. "You've grown into a beautiful woman, Cilla Rawlings."

She gave him a withering look and prayed he couldn't hear the pounding of her heart. "I don't know what you think you're doing, *cousin,* but it's not going to work," she said in a voice that was pitched too low to carry to the others. "Go find yourself someone else to sweet talk."

His dimples flashed, drawing her gaze to his mouth. "Now why would I do that when you're right here and so easy to tease? Do you know you're blushing?"

"I am not!"

"You are, too. Right here."

He reached out and traced a finger over the curve of her cheek, instantly intensifying the heat that stung her cheeks. Instinctively, Cilla grabbed at his hand, and the second she touched him, his smile faded. Something flared in his eyes, something that made her throat go dry and heartbeat quicken. "Don't—"

A sharp wind suddenly swirled around the wagon as they entered the rocky canyon that formed the western boundary of the ranch, tugging at hats and scarves and hay and abruptly dragging them both back to their surroundings. Gable's and Wyatt's cowboy hats went sailing through the air into the trees that crowded the canyon, Cilla's and Josey's hair flew into their eyes, and the kids laughed as the loose hay flew up around their heads.

"I guess this is where we'll get the tree," Gable laughed as he reined in the horses and set the wagon's hand brake. "Remember, everybody, this year we're getting a tree that fits in the house. Okay? No giants!"

"Ah, Dad, that's no fun!"

"You always say that."

"And we always get one we have to practically cut in half to get in the living room," Josey said, grinning. "Face it, honey, you're as bad as the kids when it comes to getting a big tree."

Laughing, he didn't deny it. "Guilty as charged."

"You've got to have one big enough to put all the presents under," Wyatt pointed out with a broad grin. "Come on, kids. Let's see what we can find."

They didn't need a second urging. Yelling excitedly, the kids tumbled over the side and took off into the trees with Wyatt right behind them. Watching them, Gable shook his head. "I'd better go with them. I've got a feeling Wyatt's going to be as bad as they are."

"He's changed, you know," Josey confided as Gable, too, was swallowed up by the thick patch of juniper that covered the entrance to the canyon. "I can't believe how much."

Cilla lifted a brow. "Gable?"

"No, silly. Wyatt. Don't tell me you haven't noticed."

What Cilla had noticed was that he was just as much of a flirt as he had always been. He had hurt her in the past and he would do so again if she made the mistake of trusting him. But that wasn't something she could obviously tell Josey. "No, I guess I haven't," she admitted cautiously. "But then again, I haven't seen much of him. He's been pretty busy coming up with the plans for Kat's cabin, and I've been on the move visiting with everyone."

"That's what I mean," Josey explained. "I wasn't surprised that he offered to design a room for Kat and Lucas, but I don't think anyone expected him to spend so much time on the plans. He's really given it a lot of thought and come up with a wonderful design for the babies. And he's been here a week and hasn't been to the Crossroads once. The last time that happened during one of his visits, he was sick with a stomach virus the entire time he was here."

"Yeah, but that was when everyone was footloose and fancy-free," Cilla pointed out. "Flynn even had his own stool at the bar, didn't he? Things are different now that everyone's married. Maybe he doesn't want to go by himself."

"And maybe he's growing tired of the bars and single scene and thinking about settling down. He's in his thirties now. He wouldn't be the first man his age who decided bachelorhood wasn't what it was cracked up to be."

It sounded good, but so did winning the lottery. The chances of either were slim to none. "Maybe," she said with a shrug. But she didn't think so.

The new, improved version of Wyatt Chandler might have fooled Josey, but Cilla knew better. The man she'd fallen in love with at seventeen hadn't cared about holidays or family traditions or anything remotely connected with sentiment. She was the sap for those types of things, and he'd always kidded her about being a Pollyanna in search of a white picket fence and the man and babies that went with it. If he appeared to have had a change of heart, it was only to get past her defenses. A skunk didn't change its stripes.

"Hey, this is it! I found it, everybody! Come look!"

Joey's triumphant shout brought them all running. Arriving on the scene two steps behind Josey, Cilla couldn't help but grin at the sight of Gable standing with his arms around his two sons and his daughter as the four of them turned expectantly to Josey. "Please, Mom," they all begged. "Ple-e-a-ase?"

"C'mon, Mom," Wyatt joined in teasingly. "It's not that big. Only twenty feet or so."

Cilla followed his gaze to the tree and almost choked on a laugh. Twenty feet wasn't much of an exaggeration. The thing wouldn't fit in the barn, let alone the house. "Uh, yeah, Mom," she chuckled, turning to Josey in anticipation. "It's not that big. All we have to do is trim it up a little."

"Trim?" Josey snorted. "You trim your toenails.

We'll have to take the chain saw to that thing just to tie it to the back of the wagon. Are you guys sure this is what you want?"

As bad as the kids, Gable nodded and spoke for the group. "C'mon, honey. We can put every decoration we've got on this sucker. Whatdaya say?"

"What I say is Alice is going to kill us, but what the heck," she laughed. "I don't imagine she'll be too surprised."

"All right!"

"Quick, Wyatt, get the chain saw before she changes her mind!"

"Does this mean Santa's going to bring us more presents because we've got a bigger tree to put them under?"

Mandy, in the process of hustling her little brothers out of the way, looked down at Joey and grinned. "Only if you're a big sister, which you're not."

"Mom!"

The adults laughed and assured the boys that nobody knew for sure what Santa was going to bring, and then the chain saw was started, drowning out the kids' moans. Cilla and Josey circled the tree, pointing out spots that needed to be trimmed and shaped while Gable applied the saw where they directed. Minutes later, the huge juniper crashed to the ground like a freshly shaved but drunken cowboy.

"Now comes the hard part," Josey said once Gable hit the kill switch on the saw. "Getting it on the wagon. It's going to take up most of the back. Where are we all going to sit?"

"You can have our seat, Mom," the boys said quickly. "We want to walk."

"Me, too," Mandy chimed in. "It's not that far back to the house."

That left the front seat of the wagon for the adults, but there was no way it could hold all four of them. Voicing the thought, Gable's eyes began to dance. "We'll just have to double up. Josey can sit on my lap—"

"And Cilla can sit on mine," Wyatt finished for him, grinning like a cat with the canary feathers still sticking out of his mouth.

"Oh, no you don't," Cilla snapped, her brown eyes flashing. "I'll walk, thank you very much. Like the kids said, it's not very far."

Amused, he arched a brow at her. "What's the matter, Prissy? Scared?"

"Of you?" she tossed back. "Fat chance."

"Then there's no problem, is there? You can ride with the rest of us."

Too late, Cilla realized she'd walked right into a trap. And before she could find a way out, Gable and Wyatt were lifting the tree into the back of the wagon and tying it down. Minutes later, Gable was back in the driver's seat with Josey perched on his knee, and a grinning Wyatt, seated next to him, was leaning down to offer her a hand up.

Standing on the ground and staring up at him, her gaze caught on his mischievous grin, Cilla fought the need to step up into the wagon and into his arms. He was the only man who had ever been able to push her buttons and make her want him at one and the same time, and she'd missed him in her life. She hadn't realized how much until just now.

Staggered by the thought, she stared blindly at his broad, strong hand, her heart jumping crazily in her breast. How could he still have the power to do this to her? she wondered in confusion. She'd thought she was over him, through with him. Why, then, did just the thought of placing her hand in his and sitting on his lap make her go weak at the knees?

She should run, get out of here, and not stop until half the country was between them. It was the only way she knew for sure to protect her heart from him. But she was a woman now, not a seventeen-year-old child who wore her heart on her sleeve, and she didn't run from her emotions anymore. She stayed and faced them head-on, then put them behind her where they couldn't hurt her. And that, she promised herself, was what she was going to do with Wyatt.

Her chin lifting to a determined angle, she placed her hand in Wyatt's and had the satisfaction of seeing surprise flicker in his eyes. A slow smile curled the corners of her mouth. So he'd expected her to chicken out, had he? Maybe it was time she showed him that the Cilla Rawlings who had followed him around like a puppy during that long-lost summer could now hold her own with him or any other man. He wanted to flirt—she'd be more than happy to oblige him.

"Are you sure you want to do this?" she asked with a grin as he tugged her up in front of him and she settled gingerly on his knee. "People will talk."

"What people? There's nobody around but Gable and Josey and the kids."

Her lips twitching, Josey said solemnly, "And we won't say a word. Will we, honey?"

"Sure we will," he retorted teasingly. "As soon as we get back, I'm going to call Sydney and have the story put on the front page of the *Gazette*. By this time tomorrow, the whole county will know there's another hot romance brewing out at the Double R."

His eyes only inches from Cilla's, Wyatt flashed his dimples at her. "Is that what we've got going here, cousin? Another hot romance?"

She wanted to flat out deny it, but her heart was knocking so loudly against her ribs as he settled her more comfortably against him that she couldn't quite manage the lie. Instead, she leaned back as if she didn't have a care in the world and laughed with an ease that cost her more than he could possibly know. "In your dreams, Chandler. In your dreams."

CHAPTER FIVE

HOW SHE RODE all the way back to the house without going quietly out of her mind, Cilla never knew. All her senses were on red alert and throbbing with awareness. And it was all Wyatt's fault. His arms and scent surrounded her, and every time the wagon hit a rut in the rough track, she was thrown back against the hard wall of his chest. She laughed along with the others, but inside, her heart was flip-flopping like a salmon at low tide.

This close, she could feel the power in him, the strength that left her breathless. He laughed at something Gable said, and she could almost trace the sound as it rippled through him like a summer wind through the desert grasses. It was unnerving, exhilarating. Her mouth suddenly dry, she couldn't stop herself from closing her eyes and savoring the feeling.

"She's gone off into the ozone again. Look—she's nodding off." Snapping his fingers in front of her face, Wyatt grinned. "Earth to Prissy. You with us, sweetheart? What planet are you on?"

Cilla blinked and came back to earth to find herself nose to nose with him. And from the glint in his eyes, she had a horrible feeling he knew exactly what she'd been doing. Mortified, she felt hot color surge into her cheeks and snapped, "Don't call me that!"

"What?" he quipped. "Prissy or sweetheart?"

"Both!"

"Don't tease her, Wyatt," Josey scolded, her lips twitching. "You know she hates to be called Prissy."

"That's why he does it," Cilla retorted, glaring at him. "Small minds are easily amused."

Unrepentant, his eyes laughed into hers. "Are you calling me a pea-brain?"

Despite her best efforts, Cilla felt her own lips twitch. "If the shoe fits…"

"Now, children, don't fight," Gable said with a chuckle. "Santa won't bring you any presents if you're bad."

His arms tightening playfully around Cilla, Wyatt drawled suggestively, "Then I guess I'll have to be very, very good. What do you say, sweetheart? Do you think I can be good?"

Unbidden, images of a long ago loving flashed before her eyes, taunting her. Good? she thought wildly. That didn't begin to describe what he could be when he set his mind to it. But she had no intention of telling him that. Looking down her nose at him, she drawled, "Not in a million years, Chandler."

The rest of the ride home passed in a blur for Cilla. Sitting stiff and straight on Wyatt's lap, she stared straight ahead, tension crawling through her like a troop of ants. Then the house came into view, and she felt they couldn't reach it fast enough. She needed some time to herself. Now! The second Gable brought the horses to a stop at the porch steps, she jumped up from Wyatt's lap.

"Cilla, wait—"

He reached to help her, but she was too quick for him. Scrambling over the side, she ignored his muttered curse and turned to Josey as she joined her on the porch. "Why don't I get the decorations out while the guys are getting the tree?"

Her eyes knowing, Josey nodded. "They're in the attic, but you won't be able to carry them all down by yourself—there are enough boxes of lights alone to fill a small truck. Let me supervise getting this monster onto its stand and into the house, and then I'll be up to help you."

The minute she stepped into the attic, Cilla saw it had changed little over the last ten years. Tucked up under the eaves and isolated from the rest of the house, it was filled with shadows and old furniture and musty smells of the past. It was here, as children, that she and Kat had spent hours playing dress-up in the vintage clothes they'd pulled from the dusty trunks that had belonged to long-forgotten Rawlingses. Then later, when they'd outgrown such childish games, the two of them had claimed the attic as their own special hideout from the boys. Here, they'd talked about school and boys and dances and first loves. They'd confided secret crushes to each other and dreams of the future and fantasized about the men they would marry.

Until that last summer Cilla had spent at the ranch. Then she'd never once mentioned Wyatt to her cousin or anyone else.

Stepping into the thick shadows that rose to the rafters, Cilla stared blindly at the cardboard boxes and discarded antiques and saw instead the past and a perfect summer—up until the end—stolen out of time. Long hot days. Secret kisses. Touches that nobody saw.

She'd been so young, so naive, so much in love that she'd thought no one else but Wyatt had suspected a thing. But looking back on it now, she knew she and Wyatt had been anything but discreet, and even the lowest ranch hand must have known what was going on. Now that horrified her. Then, she'd wanted him so badly that she wouldn't have batted an eye if the whole world had known.

Regrets and a sweet melancholy for what might have been stirred in her. Stepping over to an ornate dresser that had belonged to some nameless Rawlings woman near the turn of the century, she drew a heart in the thick coating of dust on the top with her index finger, then added C + W in the middle. A children's rhyme about a boy and girl sitting in a tree played softly in her head, bringing the sting of foolish tears to her eyes.

The sound of footsteps on the stairs behind her cut through her musings, jerking her roughly back to the present. Hastily swiping at her cheeks, she dragged

up a shaky smile as she turned to face Josey. "I'd forgotten how much junk there was up here—"

But it wasn't Josey standing on the threshold
watching her every move—it was Wyatt. And his
sharp eyes had already picked up the tracks of her
tears in the poor light. "Josey said you could use
some help. What's wrong?"

"Nothing."

"Then why are you crying?"

"I'm not," she lied, turning away. "I just…"
Frantically searching for an excuse, she froze as her
gaze dropped to the dresser top where she'd traced
their initials in the dust.

C + W

Lord, what was she going to do now? If he saw
that childish message, he'd never let her live it down.
She had to do something…erase it. But even as she
glanced around for a rag to wipe it away, a voice in
her head mocked, *You came up here for Christmas
decorations, not to clean house. He'll think you've
lost your mind.*

"You just what?" he prodded, stepping up behind her.

Panicking, she snatched an old straw hat from its
hook on the wall. "I was just looking at all this old
stuff and dust must have gotten in my eye," she said
with a shrug. Pretending to examine the hat, she
tossed it casually over the dust tracings on the
dresser. "I guess Alice hasn't cleaned up here in
awhile."

It was a logical explanation, but something about it

didn't quite ring true. Frowning, Wyatt reached up to brush at the cobwebs that had caught in her hair. "You go downstairs looking like that, and everyone's going to be wondering what we've been doing up here."

It was a mistake, of course, touching her and thinking about what they could do together in the intimate, shadowy confines of the attic—he knew it the second his fingers brushed her forehead and the words left his mouth. He felt her stiffen, saw her eyes widen slightly, and should have let her go immediately. But suddenly images from the past— *need*—was there between them, as strong as the pull of the moon on the tides, and he could no more walk away from her than he could cut off his own arm.

His hand moved from the wisp of her bangs to the back of her neck. "Oh, God, Cilla, I've got to do this."

He didn't know if he was apologizing or warning her, he just knew that he had to kiss her. Now. Lowering his head, he swooped down and covered her mouth with his.

Like a chocoholic in desperate need of a fix, he promised himself that all it would take to satisfy him was one simple kiss. Nothing more. After all, the family was waiting downstairs—there wasn't time for anything else. If they didn't get down there soon with the decorations, someone would come looking for them. And while he didn't care who caught him kissing Cilla, he had a feeling Cilla wouldn't be too thrilled with the idea.

But the minute his lips touched hers, every logical thought he had slipped right out of his head. It seemed he'd been waiting days to hold her again, taste her again, lose himself in the heat and scent of her. Growling low in his throat, he gathered her close and nearly lost it right there and then. God, she felt good against him. So damn good. She fit in his arms as if she was made for him, the crush of her full breasts against his chest burning him from the inside out, her slender hips enticingly flush with his, trapping his arousal between them.

And then there was her mouth. No woman with such a seductive mouth had a right to be walking around free. He nipped at her full, sexy lower lip and something in her seemed to shatter. His name a hoarse, lost cry on her tongue, she kissed him back like a woman who had been alone too long, lonely too long. With heart and soul and all the scorching heat she had in her, she clung to him as if she would never let him go.

His arms tightened around her, madness pulling at him. He could have her…here, now, as he'd dreamed of having her ever since that first day when she'd stepped up on the porch and just the sight of her had nearly knocked him out of his shoes. She was as hot, as eager, as hungry as he was. And they were finally alone. All he had to do was sink down to the floor with her and give into—

"Hey, Wyatt! Cilla!" Gable suddenly called up the stairs teasingly. "What are you guys doing up there? Making the decorations from scratch?"

Lost to everything but the ache of desire that she had been denying for days, Cilla heard nothing but the rush of her blood in her ears. This was what her body had cried out for in the dark of the night for too long. Aching, yearning, she crowded closer, then Gable's words abruptly penetrated the sensuous fog that enveloped her brain and she thought she heard footsteps on the stairs. Jerking back with a gasp, she stared up at Wyatt in horror.

Quickly calling out to Gable that they'd be right down, he murmured, "Now don't get all bent out of shape on me, sweetheart. Gable doesn't suspect a thing. And it was just a kiss—"

"Just a kiss!" she squeaked, hurt squeezing her heart. God, if that wasn't just like him. He'd always dismissed what they'd shared as just a kiss, just a summer romance, just a fling. It—*she*—had never meant anything to him and never would. How many times did he have to hurt her before she got the message?

Angry tears stinging her eyes, she glared at him accusingly. "You haven't changed at all. Oh, you may have fooled the rest of the family, but I know better."

"Then you know more than I do. What the hell are you talking about?"

If she hadn't known him so well, she might have been fooled by his very real-looking confusion. But she knew better. "This perfect-family-man act of yours," she snapped in growing frustration. "Designing a room for Kat's babies, offering to help build it, getting the Christmas tree when you know you don't care two cents about the holidays—none of it fits. Josey thinks you've mellowed, that you might be ready to settle down—"

"But you don't think so," he said in a gravelly voice, his narrowed eyes locked with hers. "Do you?"

"No." She couldn't, because if she did, she'd lose her heart to him all over again, and that was a chance she couldn't take. Not again. "I've got to get out of here!" Turning her back on him, she looked distractedly around. "The decorations…God, I forgot all about them."

"They're over in the corner. Dammit, Cilla, if you'll just wait, I'll help you!"

But she had no intention of letting him get close enough to help. Hurrying over to the corner and the pile of boxes labeled Christmas Decorations, she snatched up as many as she could carry, then stepped around Wyatt as if he were a snake that could reach out and bite her any second. Uncaring that she was practically running from him, she hurried down the stairs.

His blood still hot, Wyatt stared after her and wondered what the hell had just happened. Except for earlier in the wagon, he had, much to his satisfaction, been careful to keep his distance all week. He hadn't touched her, flirted with her, or even made eye contact with her. He'd been damn proud of himself, and as the week had passed, he'd convinced himself that whatever feelings the lady still stirred in him, he could handle them with one hand tied behind his back. So sure of himself was he that when he'd come upstairs to help her, he'd have sworn kissing her was the last thing on his mind.

Dammit, he didn't even remember reaching for her!

Feeling like a man who had just fallen down a flight of stairs, he tried to tell himself that it was just chemistry. She'd grown into a beautiful woman, and his body had responded to her just as it would to any other gorgeous female. It was nothing personal.

Yeah, right. That's why you can't close your eyes at night without dreaming about the lady. Face it, man. You're lying through your teeth. All this time you thought you'd gone on with your life, you were really marking time, just waiting for the chance to see her again. You never got over her and you know it.

The truth hit him right between the eyes, stunning him. No, dammit! he thought, scowling. That was bull. He'd gone on with his life and left whatever he'd once felt for her far behind. But even as he tried to deny it, he couldn't forget the feel of her in his arms. She'd felt right, in a way no other woman ever had.

The sound of footsteps on the stairs intruded on his thoughts and he looked up to see Gable standing in the doorway, a puzzled look on his rugged face. "I thought you were getting the rest of the decorations. You need some help?"

"Yeah," he muttered grimly. "What I need is my head examined, but I don't think you can do much about that. You want to carry the little boxes or the big one?"

Blinking at the swift change of subject, Gable raised a brow in amusement. "The big one. Why do I feel as if I missed something here?"

"Because you did," Wyatt retorted, passing the largest of the boxes to him. "And that's all I'm going to say on the matter." Scooping up the last of the decorations, he headed for the stairs, only to give his cousin a fierce glare when he grinned knowingly at him. "What the devil are you grinning at?"

"Oh, nothing." Gable laughed, not the least offended. "You just look like you're coming down with something, and it hasn't been that long since I suffered the same symptoms. All I can tell you is that it's not nearly as fatal as it seems right now."

"What the hell is that supposed to mean?"

Gable chuckled again, enjoying himself. "You'll figure it out soon enough. C'mon. We've got a tree to decorate."

Wyatt followed him downstairs, half tempted to find some excuse to go off somewhere by himself rather than inflict his foul mood on the rest of the family. But the second he reached the living room, the kids surrounded him, chattering like magpies as they tore the boxes open and showed him their favorite ornaments.

"Look, Wyatt," Mandy said eagerly. "Uncle Cooper gave me this for my first Christmas. I've had it for years and years and years. Isn't it pretty?"

"It's just an old pony," one of the boys said dismissingly, crowding her out of the way. "My dinosaur is a lot better. Look, Wyatt. It's a T-rex. Isn't it great?"

Unable to spoil their fun, he grinned and ruffled the five-year-old's hair. "Yeah, great. I don't think I've ever seen something that fierce on a Christmas tree before, though. This is gonna be some tree."

"You ain't seen nothing yet," Josey replied, chuckling. "Their uncles have this competition between them to see who can buy them the most outrageous ornament. So far, the T-rex seems to be the winner."

"Are you guys going to stand there talking all day?" Gable drawled from across the room. "Cilla and I could use some help with these lights. It looks like whoever put them up last year just threw them in the box for a rat to nest in."

At his pointed look, a slow smile spread across Josey's face. "You took the tree down last year, honey," she reminded him gently. "Remember?"

Nonplussed, he just looked at her, then had the grace to laugh. "Like I said, someone just threw them in the box and I don't want to hear another word about it."

"Are you kidding?" Wyatt retorted teasingly as he and Josey both moved to help. "What else have you been blaming Josey for? Or don't you remember?"

Josey was quick to name a few things, and that started them all laughing as they untangled the lights and began the daunting job of decorating the huge tree. With the kids helping and everyone talking, no one but Wyatt seemed to notice that Cilla not only didn't once speak to him, but also managed not to get anywhere near him the entire time they were decorating the tree. Her conversation was directed to Gable or Josey, her laughter to the children. And when they were hanging bulbs and she looked up to find herself on the same side of the tree, she shied away from him and gave the ornament she held to one of the kids to hang. Seconds later, she disappeared to the other side of the tree.

Unable to take his eyes off her, Wyatt knew he couldn't put it off any longer. He had to give serious thought to what he was going to do about her. She thought he was the same man who had betrayed her ten years ago and she wasn't prepared to believe that he was anything but what she'd thought he was back then—an unprincipled bastard. She wanted to believe she hated his guts, but that hadn't stopped her from responding to him. He could, he knew, talk her into an affair, but that wasn't what he wanted, dammit! He wanted...hell, he didn't know what he wanted!

Disgusted with himself, blaming Cilla for the sudden restlessness that was like an itch under his skin, he had withdrawn to the far side of the room to scowl at her when Flynn and Tate arrived. Tate immediately laughed over the size of the tree and waded through the boxes to help while Flynn, claiming he was going to supervise, joined Wyatt on the couch.

Taking one look at his cousin's set face, Flynn raised his eyebrows, his sapphire eyes dancing. "Something's got your tail in a snit. You want to talk about it?"

"No."

His answer was curt and tight and had Back Off written all over it. Not the least discouraged, Flynn followed Wyatt's gaze to Cilla and back again, the laughter in his eyes spreading to a broad grin. "Cilla's getting to you again, isn't she?"

"The hell she is!"

Stretching his legs out, Flynn nodded as if he hadn't spoken. "Yep, that's what it is. And it's damned uncomfortable, isn't it? Believe me, I know. When I found myself falling for Tate, it really shook me up. But nobody falls harder than a flirt, and now I wonder why I even tried to fight what was so right."

His jaw set in granite, Wyatt said through his teeth, "I never said I was falling for anyone."

"You didn't have to—it's written all over you." Flynn laughed. "And it couldn't happen to a more deserving guy. Come on, cousin, jump right in. Trust me. The water's fine."

CHAPTER SIX

HALF-EXPECTING Wyatt to ambush her again the first chance he got, Cilla spent the next week looking over her shoulder. But he spent most of each day at Kat's with the rest of the men, working on the room addition, and she didn't know if she was relieved or disappointed. When they did chance to run into each other, he was always the one to end the conversation as soon as possible. And in his eyes was a wariness that hadn't been there before. A wariness that cut her to the bone.

Hurt, she tried to convince herself it was for the best. But still, she found herself looking for him, waiting for him, dreaming of him...and longing for the teasing banter they had once shared. It was gone, however, apparently forever, and Christmas was quickly approaching. She didn't see any way it was going to be a festive one.

If the family didn't notice that they were hardly speaking, they had good reason. For the second time in a week, Gable announced over supper, "Someone decorated another cactus."

That got everyone's attention. Over the course of the last seven days, someone had been decorating cactuses around the ranch with garlands and paper decorations. Flynn had discovered the first one near the ranch entrance the day after the Christmas tree was put up and everyone on the ranch had been questioned about it. No one had claimed responsibility, however, and since then, three more cactuses, including the latest, had been decked out for the holidays. The whole ranch was abuzz with the mystery.

"Where?" Mandy asked excitedly, her mouth full of Alice's chicken enchiladas.

"Just south of the clinic," her father said. "Wyatt and I saw it when we went over to Flynn's this afternoon."

"Is it like the last one?"

"Can we go see it after supper?"

"Were there any tracks?" Josey asked over the excited questions of the kids. "Whoever's doing this is bound to leave some kind of clue to his identity eventually."

"You'd think so," Wyatt agreed. "But we scouted the whole area and didn't find so much as a footprint. Whoever's doing this is darn clever."

"Maybe Santa sent one of his elves," Brian said hopefully, his supper forgotten at the thought.

Joey, wide-eyed as only a five-year-old can be, nodded. "Elves don't leave footprints, you know. They can come and go and no one ever sees them."

Cilla, struggling to hold back a smile along with the rest of the adults, nodded solemnly. "I've heard that, too, sweetie. You just may be right. Those elves can be pretty sneaky."

The children were more than willing to accept that explanation, but when small presents were left for all the kids on the front porch the following morning, the grown-ups started looking at each other with suspicious grins. Cilla knew she was innocent, though she wished she'd thought of the idea. Secrets were part of the fun of the holidays, and someone was making sure that this was a Christmas the Rawlings kids would never forget. The question was…who?

"Don't look at me," Josey said when Cilla confronted her as the two of them cleared the table after supper. "With the flu that's been going around and the clinic packed to the rafters from dawn until after dark, I haven't had time to turn around, let alone decorate cactuses or shop for extra presents. I thought you were doing it. Or Wyatt."

"Wyatt?" Cilla echoed, surprised. "I don't think so. Not that he hasn't been great with the kids and shown them a lot of attention, but frankly, I just can't see him playing one of Santa's helpers in the middle of the night. Flynn, maybe, but not Wyatt."

Josey shrugged. "You could be right about that. Flynn's just like one of the kids when it comes to surprises. When I see Tate at the clinic tomorrow, I'll ask her if he's been slipping out in the middle of the night." Cocking her head, she listened to the thunder of little feet running down the upstairs hall. "Speaking of kids, it sounds like mine are playing football in the hall again with their daddy instead of taking their baths. I'd better get up there. Save the dishes and I'll do them after I get the tribe in bed."

Cilla nodded, but she had no intention of acting like a pampered guest while everyone else worked. Alice had taken some food to a friend who was down with the flu and would be gone the rest of the evening, and Josey had had a long hard day at the clinic. The least she could do to help her, Cilla thought, was the dishes. So as soon as she was out of sight, she started loading the dishwasher.

With the water running and the clatter of dishes drowning out most of the sounds from the rest of the house, she never heard Wyatt step into the kitchen doorway from the dining room. Her attention focused on what she was doing, she rinsed out the pan that the enchiladas had been cooked in, then turned to load it in the dishwasher, only to jerk to a stop at the sight of Wyatt leaning against the doorjamb silently watching her every move.

Her heart stumbled to an abrupt stop in her chest, then jumped into an uneven rhythm that suddenly made breathing difficult. Dragging her attention back to the task at hand, she quickly placed the pan in the bottom rack, then turned off the water. In the sudden silence, the only sound was that of the kids upstairs calling to Gable for a bedtime story.

When she glanced back to the doorway, he was still there, his gaze steady and unblinking. He stared at her as if he was seeing her for the first time in years, and something about his very stillness caused her throat to tighten in apprehension. "What?" she demanded with a quizzical smile as she glanced down at herself, then back up again. "What is it? Do I have on two left shoes or what? Why are you looking at me that way?"

He straightened but never moved away from the doorway. "I've been thinking about the other day in the attic."

Caught off guard, she frowned. "We've already discussed this, Wyatt. There's nothing left to say."

She started to turn back to the dishes, but he stopped her without even touching her. "You think so? Then try this on for size. I've been giving it a lot of thought, and I realize that I never really got over you."

Wide-eyed, Cilla stared at him as if he'd lost his mind. "This is a joke, isn't it? You're just pushing my buttons again, the way you always do."

He should have laughed, or at the very least, gotten that wicked glint in his eyes that always made her want to smile. But he merely looked at her, his expression dead serious. "Do I look like I'm joking?"

No, God help her, he didn't. Her heart pounding out a frenzied jungle beat in her breast, she paled. "Then I'd say you've got a problem," she retorted. "Because you may think you never got over me, but I *know* I got over you. So this conversation is pointless."

For the first time, the glimmer of a smile flirted with the corners of his mouth. "Somehow I had a feeling you'd say that. But in case you've forgotten, there's the matter of a couple of kisses—"

"I haven't forgotten anything!" she retorted. "Not

a single moment of that day when I walked in the barn and found you with another woman. So don't talk to me about a couple of kisses. I lost my head— that's all. It won't happen again."

Undaunted by her sudden fury, he said, "For someone who claims to hate my guts, you've got an awful lot of passion in you, sweetheart. And I can think of only one reason for that—you feel the same way about me that I feel about you—"

"No!"

"Yes," he insisted. "I thought I'd gone on with my life and forgotten all about you, but the minute I saw you again, I knew I'd just been killing time for the last ten years, waiting until our paths crossed again. And I'm willing to bet you've been doing the same thing. Face it, honey. We were made for each other, like it or not."

Caught in the trap of his steady gaze, she wanted to laugh, to scoff at the very idea that she could still be carrying a torch for him after all these years. But somewhere deep inside her, his words struck a nerve, scaring her to death. Suddenly terribly afraid he might be right, she lifted her chin. "The only thing I'm facing right now is these dishes." Turning her back on him, she deliberately reached for another pot.

She appeared totally focused on the task at hand, but all her senses were tuned to where Wyatt stood frowning in the doorway silently watching her. She didn't need to look over her shoulder to know that he was still there—she could feel his eyes on her, touching her, watching her, studying her. Then, in a voice

as rough as the gravel road that led from the highway to the main house, he growled, "Fine, if that's
the way you want it. But I'm giving you fair warning, Cilla. I'm not giving up on you. One way or the
other, I'm going to win you back."

Cilla didn't hear him walk out, but she knew the
second he was gone. Suddenly the kitchen was empty
and quiet, and she was alone, just as she had been for
the last ten years. The pride that had refused to let her
tremble before him vanished. Shaking, she dropped
the pot she'd been holding and hugged herself.

She didn't care what he said, he wasn't serious,
she told herself fiercely. At least not about pursuing
what they had once had. A rattler didn't change its
spots and he'd proven a long time ago that he was
nothing but a snake in the grass. He talked about
winning her back, but all he really wanted was her
back in his bed. That's all he'd ever wanted from her,
and once she'd given him her heart and soul, the
thrill had gone out of the chase and he'd turned to
someone else. History was not going to repeat itself,
she vowed grimly. A man who had done that to a
woman once would do it again, and there was no way
on earth she was going to let herself fall for him a
second time. She didn't care how desperately he
made her want him.

Her spine stiff with resolve, she heard Gable and
Josey coming down the stairs and quickly finished
the dishes, then joined them in the family room,
where they usually relaxed over cups of hot chocolate after the kids were in bed. Wyatt was already

there and looked up the minute she entered. Her eyes locked with his, the thumping of her heart loud in his ears. She was half-afraid he would say something about their conversation in the kitchen, but he only asked Gable about a renegade bull that kept making a break for it every chance he got. From there, the conversation shifted to the newest pepper hybrid the family planned to plant in the spring to speculation on when and where the mysterious cactus decorator would strike again.

Not once over the course of the next few hours did Wyatt say or do anything that could be considered the least bit flirtatious. He rarely even looked at her. Still, Cilla was a nervous wreck. Seated as far from him as possible, her heart tripping over itself every time he opened his mouth, she kept waiting for something that never happened. By the time ten o'clock rolled around, she was exhausted.

"I hate to break up the party, guys, but I've got to call it a night," she said the second there was a lull in the conversation. "I'm bushed."

"Ah, c'mon," Josey protested. "It's early yet."

Uncomfortably aware of Wyatt's eyes following her every move, she set her barely touched hot chocolate on the serving tray Josey had carried from the kitchen earlier and rose to her feet. "Blame it on the hot chocolate," she said, forcing a smile. "I can hardly keep my eyes open."

"Party pooper," Gable teased. "Admit it, it was the shoptalk about the peppers that did it, wasn't it? You're not sleepy. You're just bored out of your mind."

"If I was bored, I would have been snoring by now," she retorted, grinning. "'Night, guys. See you in the morning."

She turned, only to have her gaze clash with Wyatt's. Her smile faltered, but Josey was already rising to her feet and talking about going up, too, and nobody else saw. Feeling as if she'd just escaped a close brush with something she didn't even want to put a name to, she hurried up the stairs.

Midnight had come and gone when Wyatt soundlessly opened Cilla's bedroom door and slipped inside. Silence engulfed him, thick and warm and hushed, making the drumming of his heart loud in his ears. Giving his eyes a few seconds to adjust to the change in light, he leaned back against the closed door and waited until the shadows that filled the room sharpened into recognizable shapes. With the glow of a full moon streaming through the open curtains at the wide windows that took up half of the far wall, it didn't take long.

The room, he saw in a single, all-encompassing glance, was pretty much the same as his. Large and airy, with nine-foot ceilings and old cedar-plank flooring, it was furnished with a massive, intricately carved antique walnut bedroom set that would have overpowered a room in a more modern house but hardly made a dent here. The bed was tall, with posters, and at least two feet off the floor. And lying in the middle of the huge mattress, covered by a patchwork quilt that was at least a hundred years old, was Cilla.

With her face half-buried in the pillow she clutched to her breast, and her hair a tangle of dark curls around her head, she looked like a little girl who had simply run out of gas at the end of the day. Soft and vulnerable, her lips parted softly in sleep, she was dead to the world.

Transfixed, Wyatt couldn't drag his eyes away from her. He'd never seen her like this. All those years ago, when they hadn't been able to keep their hands off each other, they'd snatched every stolen moment they could together, but they'd never actually slept together. Not once. And he hadn't noticed the loss until now.

Unable to resist her, he pushed away from the door and quietly moved to the side of the bed. Itching to touch her, to crawl under the covers with her and slowly bring her to wakefulness, he clenched his hands into fists and had to be content with stroking her with his eyes instead. Because if he made the mistake of giving in to the need to touch her, he'd never be able to stop with just that.

God, she was beautiful! Now that he was closer, he could see the flush of sleep that stained her cheeks, the way her lashes lay like sooty smudges against her skin. She murmured something, then sighed and drifted deeper, and never had a clue that he was there. Was it him she dreamed of? he wondered, then had to grin. Fat chance. If she did, she'd probably cast him as the main monster in a nightmare.

But his time was coming, he promised himself confidently. She could ignore him, run from him, look him right in the eye and lie through her teeth about her feelings for him, but they both knew that what they'd once felt for each other was as strong as ever. And it was only a matter of time before he made her admit it. Where they went from there, God only knew.

For now, though, he had another problem. He had to find a way to wake her without giving in to the yearning that burned low in his gut.

"Cilla?"

His voice sounded loud in the darkness in spite of the fact that he kept it pitched deliberately low so that he wouldn't scare her. But she didn't move by so much as a flicker of an eyelash. Frowning, he stepped closer to the bed, stopping a good two feet away. "Priscilla? Wake up. Do you hear me? I need to talk to you."

His only answer was a soft snore.

He was, he promised himself, going to kill her. But first he had to wake her up. His jaw clenched on an oath, and he eliminated the distance between the bed and himself with a single step and reached for her. "Dammit, Prissy, why didn't anybody tell me you were such a deadhead? What do I have to do to wake you up? Throw a glass of water in your face?"

From the dark depths of sleep, Cilla thought she heard Wyatt call to her from a long way off. Stirring slightly, she turned her face more fully into her pillow, a frown skimming across her brow. He'd followed her into her dreams, she told herself groggily. Again. And this time she didn't have the strength to wake up and make him leave her alone. Later, she promised herself. When she wasn't so tired.

"Dammit, woman, don't make me crawl into bed with you. Wake up!"

What did he mean…*crawl into bed with her?* He was a dream, so he was already in bed with her, she thought drowsily. Then he touched her, his hand settling at her shoulder to give her a quick shake, and a frown furrowed her brow. He felt so real! But that was impossible, she silently argued as she swam up from the depths of sleep. He might dare just about anything, but not even Wyatt would sneak into her room in the middle of the night when Gable and Josey and the kids were sleeping just down the hall.

"I can't believe this," he muttered. "The one time I'm trying to do the right thing—"

She felt the bed dip, his breath against her face, and suddenly she was wide awake. Her eyes flew open and she looked up to see Wyatt bending over her in the dark, his jaw set with determination. Startled, she gasped. "What do you think you're doing?"

"Now, don't get all bent out of shape," he began quickly. "I can explain—"

"Explain?" she echoed in growing outrage as she scrambled to sit up and jerk the covers up to her chin. "What's there to explain? I caught you red-handed, crawling into my bed!"

His mouth twitched at that. "Believe me, sweetheart, if I really was crawling into your bed, I wouldn't have to sneak around to do it—you'd invite me in. And you wouldn't be complaining about it, either—I'd make sure of it. I was trying to wake you up, dammit!"

"Sure you were. Tell me another one, Chandler. I didn't just fall off the hay wagon yesterday, you know. I know what you're up to."

"You don't know squat, sweetheart. The only reason I'm in here is to tell you Kat's gone into labor."

"What? Don't be ridiculous. The babies aren't due for another couple of months."

"You can tell them that when they get here later in the morning," he tossed back, grinning. "In the meantime, Cooper and Flynn are bringing their tribes over here so the two of us can baby-sit while everyone else goes to the hospital. So get your pretty little butt out of that bed, honey. We've got work to do."

CHAPTER SEVEN

IT WAS three o'clock in the morning and the family room at the back of the house was wall-to-wall kids in their pajamas. Gable's three should have been asleep in their beds, but somehow they'd instinctively known the second their cousins arrived, and within minutes, they were downstairs and ready to play. Cilla had tried to talk them all into going back to bed, but her pleas had fallen on deaf ears. The boys had dragged out their toy trucks, Mandy and Haily had pulled out building blocks for the toddlers, and before Cilla quite knew how it happened, they had a day care up and running in the middle of the night.

"C'mon, guys, I know you're not used to being up at this time of the night. Why don't you put up the toys and go on up to bed? It's way past your bedtime."

She might as well have been talking to herself. The only one who paid the slightest bit of attention to her was sixteen-year-old Haily, who was building a castle for the younger kids. "It's okay, Cilla. Mandy and I are the only ones who have to go to school to-

morrow, and it's our last day before Christmas vacation starts. No one will care if we're a little sleepy.
We're not going to do anything, anyway."

"But—"

"You're wasting your time, sweetheart," Wyatt
drawled in her ear as he came up behind her from the
kitchen with a bowlful of popcorn. "You don't try to
reason with rug rats—you bribe 'em." The smell of
the popcorn preceding him into the family room, he
walked over to the couch and immediately had everyone's attention.

"Popcorn! All right! Can we have some?"

They rushed him like a bunch of young puppies
that had just spotted dinner, all of them chattering at
once. Laughing, he held the huge bowl of popcorn
out of reach. "Hold it! Nothing's free in this world,
you greedy little beggars. We're going to make a deal
first. You get popcorn and a story and then everyone
goes to bed. Okay? And that means no arguments.
Got it?"

Six heads nodded solemnly. Holly, Cooper and
Susannah's toddler who would be two on Christmas
Eve, couldn't have cared less about making a deal.
Climbing up on Wyatt like he was some type of jungle gym, she scrambled up his chest and balanced
herself by grabbing his hair. "Gimme," she said with
a big baby grin. "Now."

Laughing, he dropped two pieces into her free
hand, then arched a brow at the others. "Well? What's
it gonna be?"

"Aw, Wyatt, do we have to?"

"We get two new cousins tonight. Can't we at least wait up to see if they're going to be boys or girls or one of each?"

"Nope," he said emphatically. "Popcorn, a story, then bed. Take it or leave it."

Grumbling, they gave in, but only after Mandy warned with a cheeky grin, "We're talking about a really cool story, right? Not Goldilocks or something silly like that?"

His lips twitched, but he held back the smile that threatened and nodded. "No Goldilocks. Scout's honor." Scooping Holly down into his lap, he plopped the bowl of popcorn down in front of her so the rest of the kids could reach it. "Okay, who wants to hear about the night Santa forgot his glasses and got lost when he was delivering presents?"

"I do! I do! Where did he get lost?"

"Right here in New Mexico," he said promptly. "Just down the road, in fact. It was a cold and rainy night…."

Silently slipping into a chair across the room, Cilla watched the children's rapt faces as they quickly settled in a circle around Wyatt, spellbound as he began a story about the year Santa ended up just miles from the Double R because he didn't have his glasses and couldn't read his map. According to him, it was Cooper, Flynn and Gable who found him, acted as his navigators, and helped him deliver presents all over the world.

He was doing this for her benefit, Cilla desperately tried to tell herself. This was just another trick to make her think he was no longer the irresponsible flirt who flitted from one girl to the next without a thought to the one he left behind. If she was gullible enough to fall for it, he would be all over her like candy on a candied apple the first chance he got. Then when Christmas was over and they both went home to their own lives, she would once again be the one with the broken heart because he would walk away without a backward glance. All this talk about having changed was just that...talk. And talk was cheap.

But even as she tried to convince herself that she couldn't trust him as far as she could throw him, her eyes kept drifting to the children's faces. As he got to the part about their parents helping Santa when they were kids, the popcorn was forgotten. They stared up at him in hushed silence, hardly daring to breathe and chance missing a word, totally capti-vated. Cilla wanted to believe that it was just the part about Santa and their parents that fascinated the kids, but her conscience balked at that. Kids were pretty smart and it wasn't easy to fool them. They could see through a phony in the blink of an eye. If they thought Wyatt was stringing them along, they wouldn't just sit there and let him weave a spell around them. They trusted him and were just as charmed by him as they were by the story.

If this was the type of father he would make, his kids would adore him.

The thought slipped past her guard as silently as Santa slipped from one house to the other every Christmas Eve, catching her unaware, intriguing her before she could dismiss such a foolish notion. Too late, she found herself looking at him with different eyes, and it was all too easy to imagine that at least some of the kids surrounding him were his own. And hers.

Alarm bells went off in her head so loudly she was sure he must have been able to hear them from where he sat. But when he glanced up at her, he only grinned and winked, then went back to the story without ever noticing that she was staring at him like a woman who had just been run over by a Mack truck. No! she cried silently. Dear God, what was she doing? She didn't want to think about him that way. She didn't want to imagine what their children would look like or see his face and hers in the features of babies that didn't even exist. It was too painful, too intriguing, too late.

Caught up in her imaginings, she never noticed that the story had ended or that most of the younger children had quietly fallen asleep. Then he looked over at Cilla and grinned, his green eyes sparkling with satisfaction. "Looks like it worked," he said softly. "Think we should leave them down here or carry them up to bed?"

Cilla blinked at the sight of Holly and Christopher, Flynn's three-year-old, asleep in his lap. Lainey and Gable's boys were yawning and fighting a losing battle to keep their eyes open, and Mandy and Haily weren't far behind. Warmed by the glint in his eyes, she flushed and quickly bolted to her feet. "They're probably going to be here for the rest of the night, so we might as well take them up. They'll sleep better. Haily, sweetie, can you help us get everybody upstairs?"

A sixteen-year-old version of her mother, Tate, Haily nodded sleepily and reached for Christopher. "Sure. Gosh, it's really late, isn't it? You think Aunt Kat's had the babies yet?"

"Probably not," Wyatt said as he struggled to his feet with a limp Holly in his arms. "We would have heard something, and babies like to take their own good time getting here, especially when there's two of them."

Putting an arm around Mandy's shoulders when she stared blankly at the stairs as if she had never seen them before, Cilla chuckled and said, "Come on, Mandy, girl. Up to bed, sweetheart, before you fall on your face."

"I'm okay. Really."

The eight-year-old was weaving on her feet and would never be able to navigate the stairs alone, but Cilla only fought back a grin and suggested, "Then maybe you could help me up. It's been a long night and I'm bushed."

"Oh...sure," she said, shuffling in the general direction of the stairs. "I'm kinda tired, too."

With Haily's help, they finally got everyone into bed and tucked in, all without a single word of protest out of anyone. The upstairs was hushed and dark, with only a small table lamp left on in the hall in case anyone woke up and was scared. Hesitating at the top of the stairs after Wyatt had gone back downstairs and Haily had quietly wished her a good-night and gone off to her own bed, Cilla knew she should do the same. But she was wide awake, and something in her rebelled at the thought of scurrying off to her room just because she didn't want to go downstairs and be alone with Wyatt. After all, Kat was her cousin, too. If she wanted to stay up and wait for word from the hospital, she could.

Defiantly, she went down to the family room, only to find it empty. Surprised, she went looking for Wyatt and found him pouring himself a cup of coffee in the kitchen. At her entrance, he arched a brow. "I thought you went to bed."

"I wouldn't be able to sleep, worrying about Kat," she said simply. "I was hoping we would have heard something by now."

"We would have if something was wrong," he assured her. Pouring her a cup, he pushed it across the breakfast bar. "Here. Have some coffee."

She hesitated. She really didn't want any caffeine this late at night, but she couldn't just stand there and stare at him. Moving to the breakfast bar, she took a seat, then spent the next thirty seconds stirring creamer into her coffee. When she looked up, Wyatt was openly staring at her and making no apologies for it.

Her heart suddenly skipping a beat, she frowned at him. "What are you doing?"

He grinned. "Looking at you. You know, Prissy, you grew up into a darn good-looking woman. Any of the men in your life take the time to tell you that?"

"If they did, it's none of your business," she retorted, fighting the smile he pulled from her so easily. "Dammit, Wyatt, stop that! I know what you're doing and it's not going to work."

"Oh, I don't know about that," he drawled, his dancing eyes crinkling with amusement at her over the rim of his coffee cup as he took a sip. "Looks like it's working to me. You wear a blush better than any woman I know."

"And you know a lot, don't you?" she replied sweetly.

If she'd hoped to put him in his place, she might as well have saved herself the trouble. Not the least offended, he only grinned in pleased delight. "Jealousy rears its ugly head. And here I thought you didn't care."

That struck too close to the bone. Irritated with herself for letting him get to her, she set her coffee cup down with a snap. "I think I'll play some cards to pass the time. Solitaire," she said pointedly.

Not giving him time to comment, she strode out of the kitchen into the den and found a pack of cards in the built-in cabinet by the fireplace. She heard Wyatt moving around in the kitchen, but she studiously ignored him and sat down on the floor at the coffee table to shuffle the cards.

Her concentration was shot, but she laid the cards out and frowned down at them as if her only care in the world was matching a red queen to a black king. She never looked up, but all her senses were attuned to Wyatt as he followed her into the den and laid a couple more logs on the fire. Seconds later, a light on the far side of the room was switched off, then another one by the TV. Just that easily, the atmosphere was warm and intimate.

But it wasn't until he sat down on the couch, though, his feet just inches behind where she sat on the carpeted floor, that her nerve endings vibrated in warning. He was close. Too close. She only had to lean back mere inches to find herself resting intimately against his knee and thigh. Her hands suddenly trembling, she turned up a card and automatically moved it to an open spot without sparing it a glance.

"You can't put that there. A red seven has to go on a black eight."

Startled by his soft, husky growl, she jumped. "What?"

"The red seven," he repeated patiently. "You laid it on a red eight. You can't do that. It has to be a black one."

Lost, hardly hearing him for the thumping of her heart in her breast, Cilla frowned down at the cards spread out before her. "What red seven?"

"This one." Leaning over, he reached around her, his arm brushing hers and nearly circling her shoulders as he pointed out her mistake. "See?"

Her mouth dry, Cilla couldn't have answered if her life had depended on it. Unable to drag her eyes from the strong masculine hand that hovered mere inches from hers, she nodded dazedly. When had he moved so close? He wasn't touching her, not really, yet she would have sworn she could feel his hard chest against her shoulders and the heat of him seeping into her, warming her, melting her bones.

And his scent...God, it was just as she remembered it. Clean and spicy and all man. She'd tried her best to forget him over the years, but nothing had driven the scent of him from her head. She'd lost track of the number of times over the years when she'd stepped into a crowded elevator or restaurant and found her senses assaulted by a whiff of a cologne that was all too familiar. And every time, her heart took off at a gallop and her eyes looked for him before she could stop herself.

There'd been so many things about him that she'd missed, and she hadn't even realized it until now. The size and strength and sheer magnetism of him, not to mention what it felt like to have him hold her. How could she have forgotten? Other men had held her, but no one had ever made her feel the way he did when he put his arms around her. Safe and treasured. Needed. If she leaned back a few centimeters, she could feel that way again....

Don't you dare, Cilla Rawlings! a voice snapped in her ear. *You let that man touch you now, and you're a goner for sure. Wake up and smell the coffee, for God's sake. He's already warned you he wants to take up where you left off. That means bed, Cilla. B-e-d. A roll in the sack, nothing more. Is that what you want?*

She never remembered moving, but suddenly she was across the room and switching on the TV. She wanted noise, and lots of it. Enough to drown out the frantic cadence of her heart and her jumbled thoughts. "I was never very good at card games anyway," she said in a shaky voice she hardly recognized as her own. "I'd rather watch an old movie on TV."

Not bothering to hide a grin, Wyatt gathered up the cards and propped his feet on the coffee table. His arms stretched out on either side of him along the back of the couch, he drawled, "Oh, good. Why don't you turn the rest of the lights out and we'll neck."

Damn him, he would not make her laugh! Struggling to keep her expression impassive, she said, "I'd rather kiss a randy goat."

"B-a-a-a-a."

"Dammit, Wyatt—"

Grinning, he clicked his tongue at her. "No cussing, sweetheart. The children are just upstairs."

She laughed. She couldn't help it. What was she supposed to do with such an impossible man? "Then don't push your luck, Chandler. And don't call me sweetheart." Choosing a seat at the far end of the couch, she stared pointedly at the television and silently promised herself she wasn't going to say another word to him. Then the opening credits for *White Christmas* rolled onto the screen.

Stifling a groan, Cilla couldn't believe her miserable luck. First *It's a Wonderful Life* the night she arrived, now this. Why did they have to show all the sentimental movies at Christmas, for heaven's sake? Didn't they know that some people just couldn't take it? She knew the whole movie by heart and could quote the dialogue word for word, but she still got misty-eyed at the end. And it wasn't a movie she watched with a man. Especially one like Wyatt. He would make fun of the singing and the hokiness of the story and all the parts she loved, then tease her about crying over a movie that wasn't even a tearjerker.

She couldn't take it, she decided. Not tonight, when they were alone together and the house was dark and quiet and she only had to reach out to touch him. She was too vulnerable, too aware of him, too emotional. Leaning forward, she reached for the remote control on the coffee table.

"Hey, what are you doing that for? I thought you liked that movie!"

"I do, but I've seen it a zillion times. There's bound to be something else on."

"But you love all that syrupy holiday stuff. Turn it back on."

"I'd rather watch a spaghetti western," she retorted, deliberately switching channels and scanning the airwaves. "There's bound to be one on somewhere. There always is this time of night."

"But I want to watch Bing!"

"You do not. You just want to make fun—hey, give that back!"

He snatched the remote out of her hand before she could do anything but gasp, switched the channel back to *White Christmas,* then shoved the remote into the back pocket of his jeans. His grin wicked, he taunted softly, "You want it? Go for it, sweetheart. I dare you."

He didn't think she would—she could see the cockiness in his eyes, but it was the middle of the night and she was too tired to think clearly. Impulsively rising to the bait, she threw herself across his lap and reached around behind him for the remote.

Like a well-oiled trap that was sprung by a whisper of movement, his arms instantly closed around her. Grinning down into her startled eyes, he growled, "Gotcha."

Her heart stopped in mid-beat, then stumbled into a frenzied flutter as he tangled his hand in her hair and slowly started to lower his mouth to hers. Stiffening, she wedged a hand against his chest and glared at him. "Is this the latest Chandler technique? You have to trick a woman in order to kiss her?"

"Only you, sweet pea," he admitted with a chuckle. "And I wouldn't have to do that if you gave me any other choice. Every time I think I've got you to myself, you take off running the other way. Kiss me, honey. You wouldn't believe how long I've been starving for another taste of you."

"No—"

His mouth smothered hers, cutting off her protests, scrambling her brain. Every time he held her, kissed her, it was like the first time. She didn't understand it, couldn't explain it. She just knew she couldn't resist the need he stirred in her so effortlessly. With a murmur that could have been his name, she wrapped her arms around him, hugging him as if she would never let him go. But still, she wasn't close enough. Shifting restlessly, she kissed him back hungrily, wanting, needing, more.

Wyatt groaned low in his throat as she moved against him, the feel of her breasts against his chest setting him afire. God, she was sweet. And so hot she made him ache. She could have made him beg if she'd only known it, and that was something he could say about no other woman.

And he had to have her. Now! Muttering a curse, need clawing at him, he pulled her completely across his lap and rolled with her on the overstuffed couch. A split second later, he had her right where he wanted her...under him.

CHAPTER EIGHT

THE SUDDEN RINGING of the phone was like the scream of a fire alarm in the heated silence. His hand already sliding under the hem of Cilla's T-shirt, Wyatt froze, the string of rough, muttered curses that fell from his tongue turning the air blue. "I don't believe this! Ignore it, dammit!"

But even as he said it, he knew they couldn't. At this hour of the night, it couldn't be anyone but one of the cousins at the hospital with Kat. "Forget I said that," he said through his teeth as he rolled off her and pushed to his feet. "It's probably Gable."

Stepping into the kitchen, he jerked up the receiver of the wall phone and growled, "Yeah?"

For a moment, there was nothing but silence, then Gable said wryly, "I'm not going to ask if I interrupted anything—obviously, I did."

"Stuff it, Rawlings," Wyatt grumbled, reluctant amusement easing the tight set of his jaw. "How's Kat?"

"Beaming like a proud mama. She came through it like a champ, but she's a whipped puppy. We're going to get out of here in a couple of seconds and let her get some sleep."

"And the babies? Everything okay there?"

"Yeah, thank God. She had two boys—Nathan and Alex—and they barely topped out at four pounds apiece. Right now their names are bigger than they are, but the doctors say they're healthy. They won't be able to go home for a couple of weeks, but that seems to be par for the course with preemies."

"Good. Tell her congratulations for Cilla and me. Lucas holding up okay?"

Gable laughed softly. "I don't think he's going to want to repeat the experience anytime soon, but right now, he's ten feet off the ground. Did the kids give you two any trouble?"

"Not after they got popcorn and a story," he said with a chuckle. "Everybody crashed after that, and we haven't heard a peep out of any of them in the last hour."

"Good. Since it's so late, we thought we'd all just stay in town for the rest of the night—if that's all right with you and Cilla," he quickly added. "It's already going on four and even if we left right now, we wouldn't get in till close to dawn."

"Don't sweat it," Wyatt assured him. "There's no need for you to rush back when everybody's asleep. We'll just go on to bed and see you in the morning."

"Good idea," Gable agreed. "If you need to get in touch with us, we'll be at the Town and Country Motor Lodge. The number's in the book."

Standing in the kitchen doorway listening to Wyatt's side of the conversation, Cilla watched him hang up the phone and assured herself that he couldn't have possibly just told Gable that they were going to bed together. He still had her on her heels from that kiss, that was all. She'd just misunderstood. Frowning, she said carefully, "Kat had the babies? Are they okay? What did you mean we'd see Gable in the morning? Is there a problem? Is that why no one's coming home tonight?"

"Yes, Kat had two little boys, and no, there's not a problem." Giving her a quick rundown of the situation, he added, "I didn't think you'd mind if I told them to go ahead and stay in town for the rest of the night. The kids are out for the count. Considering how late they went to bed, they probably won't start straggling downstairs in the morning until at least ten, and by then, their parents will be back."

Mind? she almost echoed shakily. Of course she minded! But not because she didn't want to baby-sit. Things had already nearly gotten out of hand and that was when they both knew that Gable and the others could have returned at any moment. Now they were going to be alone for the rest of the night, and the only chaperons were seven sleeping kids upstairs. God, what was she going to do?

Nothing, she decided, squaring her shoulders. If she showed the least nervousness, he would tease her unmercifully and take the first opportunity to get her back in his arms. And if he touched her again tonight, she didn't think she'd be able to summon up the strength to push him away. Not when she still ached for him deep inside.

"Of course I don't mind," she lied easily. "I would have suggested the same thing if I'd talked to Gable. Everyone's had a long night and there's no use anyone getting on the highway at this time of night unless it's an emergency, which it isn't. Why don't you lock up down here and get the lights while I check on the kids?"

"No problem," he said just as easily. "I'll be up in a few seconds."

Cilla planned to be safely in her own room by then, but she didn't tell him that. Quickly hurrying up the stairs, she started at the first room on the left, where the lights of Flynn and Tate's eyes—Haily and Christopher—were sleeping. Checking on them should have been as simple as opening the door and taking a quick peak inside, but Christopher was out from under the covers and already curled up like a puppy. By morning, he'd be chilled. Rushing over to him, she pulled the quilt up, waited a second to make sure she hadn't disturbed him, then stepped back out into the hall.

The whole procedure took all of twenty seconds and shouldn't have slowed her down. But at every other room she came to, there was something that wasn't quite right that drew her inside. Holly, who still slept with a pacifier, had lost it in the dark and was whimpering in her sleep as she searched for it. And then there was Joey, who had a reputation for being a restless sleeper. He'd kicked all the covers off his bed and hung half off the mattress himself. One wrong move and he'd go tumbling to the floor and no doubt wake the whole house with his howls.

"What are you doing?"

In the process of trying to lift the five-year-old back onto the bed without waking him, she didn't hear Wyatt soundlessly step into the room. Startled, she gasped and nearly dropped Joey, who was rock-solid and limp as a dishrag. "I was afraid he was going to roll off the bed," she gasped in a hushed whisper.

"Here, let me help you."

Lightning quick, he was at her side and taking most of the boy's weight as they lifted him back onto his pillow. Sighing in contentment, he snuggled down, hunched his little bottom in the air, then didn't move so much as an eyelash again.

Cilla couldn't help but grin at him, but when she quietly stepped out into the hallway with Wyatt right on her heels, her heart was thundering with expectations she didn't dare analyze too closely. "Well, that seems to have been the last of them," she said with a cheerfulness that sounded more than a little forced. "Guess we might as well turn in."

"Good idea," Wyatt agreed. Grinning broadly, he reached for her. "Now, where were we?"

She moved, but not quickly enough. Scowling at him, she tried not to laugh. "*We* weren't anywhere."

"Oh, yes we were. If I remember correctly, we were right here." Pulling her into his arms, he smiled down into her eyes. "Now all we have to do is get horizontal."

When he looked at her like that, it was all she could do not to go boneless in his arms. Feeling herself weakening, she warned, "I'm not going to bed with you just because we've got the place to ourselves except for the kids."

"Of course you're not," he said promptly, lowering his head to nip playfully at her ear. "You're going to bed with me because it's what we both want."

"No!"

"Yes," he murmured against her neck. "Admit it, honey. You know it's true. We've both been waiting for this moment ever since you got here."

She wanted to deny it. She would, in fact, have given anything to tell him that the only thing she'd been waiting for was for him to realize that whatever feelings she'd once felt for him had long since been left behind with ankle socks and her high-school pompoms. But the words just wouldn't come. Because, God help her, he was right. There'd always been a sense of inevitability about her relationship with him. From the first moment she'd met him all those years ago, she'd known he was the only man for her. And nothing had changed. She wanted him, heart and soul. In spite of the past. In spite of the fact that he didn't seem to be interested in anything but a steamy holiday affair. He would hurt her again; she knew that as well as she knew just where to touch him to make him groan. But when he held her and kissed her like there was no tomorrow, none of that seemed to matter.

"I used to wait up for Santa on Christmas Eve, too," she told him huskily, holding him off even as she fought the need to melt against him, "but I always woke up disappointed in the morning."

He laughed softly, the sound a moist, erotic caress against her throat. "I can't promise that you'll see Santa, but I'm not bragging when I guarantee that you won't wake up disappointed. Where are you going?"

"To my room." Slipping out of his arms before he could stop her, she almost made it. But two steps from her door, he quickly sidestepped around her and she plowed right into his chest. Chuckling, he gathered her close. "Sweetheart, you don't have to throw yourself at me. I'm not going anywhere without you."

"Dammit, Wyatt, I am *not* going to bed with you!"

Even to her own ears, the protest sounded pitifully weak, but instead of pressing her, he said simply, "Fine. Then how about a kiss? C'mon, Cilla, honey, what's one little kiss between old lovers?"

"More than you're going to get," she tossed back, struggling to hold back a smile. "Let me go."

"In a minute," he promised.

"Wyatt!"

"Hear me out first. All I'm asking is one kiss. You set the rules."

That got her attention. Studying him speculatively, she said, "Let me get this straight. You get one kiss, and I start it and end it whenever I want? With no argument from you?"

He nodded. "You got it. Take your best shot, honey. I'm ready when you are."

She could see by the glint in his eye that he expected her to make it short and sweet, but she had no intention of doing any such thing. He would only protest that it wasn't a real kiss and expect another. No, she was going to kiss him, all right, and knock his socks off in the process. To do that, she was going to have to put more than a little effort into it.

Blatant seduction was what she was going for, and for a while there, she almost pulled it off. Linking her arms around his neck, she pulled his mouth down to hers and kissed him with a wantonness she hadn't known she was capable of. Focusing all her attention on his reaction, she nibbled and nipped and took his mouth with a pent-up hunger that came from the very depths of her being. And he loved it. His arms snapped around her, crushing her close, his heart pounded out a frantic rhythm against hers, and with nothing more than the teasing trail of her tongue along his bottom lip, his breathing grew short and ragged. Muttering a curse, he backed her up against her bedroom door and kissed her back with a wildness that delighted her.

Somewhere in the back of her brain, the thought registered that she should end this madness now—while she still could. But it was already too late. Instead of running, she was rubbing up against him with a daring that would shock her in the light of day. And then there was this crazy need to kiss him…everywhere. With a will of its own, her mouth wandered to his ear, his brow, the V-neck of his T-shirt, the hard line of his jaw and the sandpaper roughness caused by a night's growth of beard. She loved the feel of him against her, his hardness against her softness, the sinewy strength of him, the arousal he made no attempt to hide. Desperate for another taste of him, she went up on her toes and fitted her mouth hungrily to his.

With that single kiss, she told him things that nearly brought him to his knees. Like how she had forgotten that she intended to stop with just one kiss, that *he* was the reason that she'd forgotten, that the need that had once burned so hot between them was nothing compared to the inferno they lit in each other's blood now.

God, he wanted her. Every time he held her like this, it was harder to let her go. And while she may have forgotten that she'd only bargained for one kiss, he hadn't. Before they went any further, she had to know what she was getting into. They weren't kids anymore who got caught up in the heat of passion and could claim later that they didn't know what they were doing. If they made love now, it would be a joint decision or nothing.

Tearing his mouth from hers, he held her tight and buried his face in the dark cloud of her hair, his breathing loud and ragged in the quiet stillness of the night. "You're not making this easy for me, sweetheart," he said thickly. "I thought you just wanted one kiss."

Blindly nuzzling against him, she tightened her arms around his waist. "So did I," she murmured. "I don't know what happened."

She sounded so bewildered, he almost smiled. He knew exactly how she felt. Just when he thought he could control his response to her, she turned around and did something that cut him off at the knees.

Drawing back slightly, he captured her face in his hands and stared down at her, his thumb lightly rubbing her bottom lip in a caress he could have no more denied himself that he could have stopped the beating of his heart. "This is your call, honey. You know I want you. There's not a night that goes by that I don't dream about making love to you. But you've got to want it, too—here, tonight, right now—or we're not going any further until you're ready."

Caught in the heat of his tender gaze, she couldn't believe what she was hearing. The brash, young Wyatt she'd known in the past had been just as caught up in the uncontrollable passion that had sparked between them as she had. Even if he'd thought to make such a suggestion, he would have never been able to carry it off. But the Wyatt who held her before him was a man, not a twenty-two-year-old kid. And he meant what he said. One word from her, and he'd leave her to her lonely bed.

But she couldn't say it. She might regret it in the morning, but she couldn't send him away and deny what they both wanted so badly. "I do want it," she said huskily. "I want *you*. Please...don't go."

She didn't have to say it twice. He swept her off her feet and up into his arms before she could do anything but gasp. "God, sweetheart, you don't know how glad I am you said that," he groaned, kissing her fiercely. "If you'd really wanted me to leave you alone, I would have, but don't ask me how. Open the door, honey. I've got my hands full and it's going to be a long time before I'm ready to let you go."

With his words alone, he warmed her inside and out. Touched, unable to stop smiling, she kissed him softly while she reached behind her for the door handle. A split second later they were in her room with the door closed, shutting out the world, and there was nothing but the two of them and the dark.

She expected him to set her on her feet then, but he carried her to the bed and laid her on it, his mouth smothering hers as he followed her down. Feeling like a kid again, urgency firing her blood, she reached for the hem of his T-shirt. But his hands were there before hers, closing around her fingers to draw them up and press them into the mattress by her shoulders. "No," he murmured, giving her a slow, languid kiss that liquified her bones. "I've dreamed of taking this slow and easy and driving you right out of your mind, sweet girl. Let me."

She stared up at him in the darkness and felt her heart turn over in her chest at the sight of the need glinting in his eyes. Emotion, sweet and hot, clogged her throat, making it impossible for her to tell him that that was what she'd dreamed of, too, for longer than she could remember—Wyatt in her bed and loving her the whole night through. Her hands still trapped in his, she squeezed his fingers and gave him the only answer she could manage.

She thought she knew what to expect…of herself and him. It had been ten years, but there were some things a woman didn't forget. Like every touch, every kiss, every heated moment of the times they'd been together over the course of that long-ago, magical summer. Since then, she'd cursed him and tried to hate him for clinging to her memory so vividly, but she hadn't been able to push a single second from her mind. But the loving they shared now was like nothing out of the past.

He loved her as if she was the most precious thing in the world to him, a treasure that had been lost and was now found, a piece of his heart that he'd carelessly misplaced and never intended to let get away from him now that he'd finally found her again. Without saying a word, he told her with long, heated kisses how much he'd missed her, how much he needed her, how impossibly lonely the nights had been without her. Then he showed her.

She never knew when her clothes or his melted away or when he moved them both under the covers. She couldn't think, couldn't feel anything but his hard body against hers, his hands and mouth moving over her, seducing her, loving her, enchanting her. He touched her and she shuddered, then kissed her and she moaned. He'd released her hands, but she couldn't have said when. Dazed, mindless, every nerve ending in her body tight with need, she reached for him with a hoarse cry, lost to everything but the fire he'd slowly built in her blood.

"Easy, sweetheart," he growled against her breast, curling his tongue around a sensitive nipple. "I'm right here."

But his lady was no longer satisfied with slow and easy. She surged toward him, her mouth hot and eager, nipping at him, her hands demanding as they swept over him, seeking, searching, rubbing, determined to crack the iron control he'd imposed on himself. He could have told her all it took was one touch from her, but she didn't give him the chance. With a push of her hand, she sent him rolling over onto his back, and then she was covering him like a dream, delighting him, dropping kisses wherever she could reach, straddling him and loving him with a fierce sweetness that burned hotter than a forest fire. Control, what little he had left, was lost in the flames.

Seizing her hips, he brought her down to him and took her like a man possessed. He should have been gentler, he should have at least tried to slow the pace, but she was as caught up in the madness as he was and would have none of it. Her wet, hot heat surrounding him, she caught his rhythm and urged him on, riding him, racing with him in the dark to a destination that was theirs and theirs alone. And when they reached the edge and plunged headlong into ecstasy, it was his name she called in the night, his arms she trusted to catch her as the mindless pleasure took them both, his heart she claimed as her own.

CHAPTER NINE

BRIGHT winter sunlight was streaming through the bedroom window when Cilla opened her eyes hours later. Lying on her stomach on the side of the bed nearest the window, she didn't have to check the mattress next to her to know that she was alone. Sometime near dawn, she had a vague, shadowed memory of Wyatt easing away from her and stopping to kiss her softly on the cheek before silently making his way back to his own room. If she hadn't been so tired, she would have reached for him and pulled him back to her, but now she was glad that she hadn't. He knew her too well. One look at her face and he would know that she'd done the one thing she'd sworn she'd never do again. She'd fallen in love with him for the second time in a lifetime.

Denial rose up in her like a tidal wave, threatening to choke her. No! She had to be mistaken. No one had ever hurt her like he had; there was no way she'd be stupid enough to let him do it again. She was just being fanciful because of the holidays. That had to be it. She always got sappy at this time of the year, this year especially with the unexpectedly early arrival of Kat's babies. No wonder she couldn't think straight—her emotions were up and down the scale.

Nice try, Cilla, a voice drawled sarcastically in her head. *But it's not going to wash. You love him. You always have. Deal with it.*

Panic seized her, urging her to run. To pack her bags and get the heck out of there. Now, while she still could. But where would she go? Back to Denver? To a job she no longer had? To a life that no longer seemed hers? Her whole world was in an upheaval; she didn't even know where she belonged anymore.

Trembling, she hugged herself and readily admitted she was scared. What she'd felt for Wyatt at seventeen was nothing compared to what she felt now. And he wasn't the marrying kind. Dear God, what was she going to do?

Staring with unfocused eyes out the bedroom window, she toyed with the idea of going back to bed and just pulling the covers over her head for the rest of the day. But that would only bring Josey and Tate running with their medical bags to see what was wrong. And there were two new babies to meet and love and fuss over. Only a self-centered, whiney baby would hide in her room like a spoiled brat while the whole family celebrated. Reluctantly pushing back the covers, she reached for her clothes.

"Well, looky here," Flynn greeted her with a wicked grin as she stepped into the dining room thirty minutes later and found everyone but the new parents gathered there. "Sleeping Beauty arises. And I just bet Cooper we wouldn't see hide nor hair of you until at least noon. I'm out ten bucks, cousin."

Every eye turned her way, but it was Wyatt's narrowed gaze that she was achingly aware of. Cursing the sting of a blush that rose to her cheeks, she avoided looking directly at the entire end of the table where he sat and turned thankfully to Flynn with an impudent flash of her dimples. "That's what you get for betting against your favorite cousin."

"You tell him, Cilla," Tate laughed. "I told him he was throwing his money away, but he wouldn't listen. You ready for breakfast or you want to wait awhile? Alice saved you some biscuits and gravy. They're warming on the stove."

Cilla's stomach curdled at the mere thought of food. "No, thanks. I just need a shot of coffee to get my motor running this morning."

"Don't you mean this afternoon?" Cooper teased.

"Don't you start, too, string bean," she tossed back, using the nickname she'd tacked on him as a kid. "Not until I get some caffeine in my bloodstream." Grabbing a cup from the sideboard, she filled it to the rim, then turned back to the table and took the seat that was farthest from Wyatt. Her smile as bright and phony as a ten-dollar Rolex, she said, "Okay, who's going to tell me about the new babies? Are they as gorgeous as the rest of the Rawlings men?"

That, thankfully, started everyone talking at once, and no one noticed that she said very little after that and Wyatt said nothing at all. The conversation naturally revolved around the new additions to the family and the type of mother Kat would be, which everyone agreed would be wild and wonderful. There was a lot of laughter and reminiscing, then the discussion turned to the work that had to be done to the new room addition before the babies came home. By the time breakfast broke up, the fact that Cilla had overslept had long since been forgotten.

By everyone, that is, except Wyatt.

She only glanced at him in passing, but she could feel his eyes on her, dark and brooding, surreptitiously watching her every move. He didn't do anything to draw her attention to himself—he didn't even force her to speak to him, which he very well could have done just by asking her a question. But Cilla wasn't fooled. He was biding his time, waiting for the chance to get her alone, which was the last thing she wanted.

So as soon as breakfast started to break up, she was on her feet. She intended to follow Josey into the kitchen and ask her what Kat needed for the babies, but before she could take a step away from the table, Wyatt was right behind her. "We need to talk," he growled in a low voice that didn't carry to anyone's ears but her own.

Startled, she glanced over his shoulder and found him just inches behind her. Her heart thumping crazily, she quickly turned away. "I can't," she said stiffly. "Not now. I'm going shopping in Tucson."

"I didn't mean now—I've got an errand to run anyway. Later—"

"I'm going to be busy most of the day."

"Dammit, Cilla—"

Ignoring his muttered curse, she hurried to catch up with Josey in the kitchen. "Josey? Have you got any idea what Kat needs for the babies? I wanted to buy them something special, but I don't know what Kat's already got."

In the process of returning a jar of Alice's home-made jelly to the refrigerator, Josey frowned. "I think she still needs a stroller, but she and Lucas may have already bought one...."

Wyatt didn't follow them into the kitchen, but Cilla could feel him scowling daggers at her from the hall. He was more than a little miffed at her, but he didn't force the issue. For what seemed like an eternity, he just stood there, waiting. Then, without a word, he turned and stormed off.

Releasing the breath she hadn't even realized she was holding, Cilla almost wilted in relief. She'd wasn't foolish enough to think she'd put him off indefinitely, but she'd bought herself some time...at least for now. With luck, by the time she did have to face him one-on-one, she'd be more in control of her emotions.

When she walked into Kat's hospital room six hours later, she was pushing a twin stroller that was loaded down with flowers and presents. Kat, in the process of giving one of the babies a bottle, laughed in delight. "A stroller! How did you know we needed one?"

"Josey suggested it." Grinning, Cilla hugged her,

making sure not to squash the baby. "Congratulations, Mama! Who do we have here?"

Fairly beaming with pride, Kat eased back the receiving blanket from the infant's face and head and said, "This is your new cousin Nathan. Nathan, open your eyes, sweetheart, and meet Cilla. She's brought you and your brother some presents."

"And you," Cilla added. "Since you weren't planning on this little one and his twin showing up so early, I figured you weren't quite prepared to spend a night or two in the hospital, so I bought you a gown and robe." Dropping her gaze to the baby, she felt her heart melt. "Oh, Kat, he's beautiful! Look at that hair! Where's Alex?"

"In the nursery. They're both on oxygen except when I'm feeding them. It's just a precautionary measure since they decided to check in so early."

"Are they identical?"

"Carbon copies," her cousin confirmed with a rueful grin. "God knows how we're going to tell them apart. Lucas is terrified we'll get them mixed up and warp them for life."

"No, you'll do fine," Cilla laughed. "If worse comes to worst, you can always do like Gable and Josey did with the boys and leave their hospital bracelets on them until they outgrow them. If you can't tell them apart by then, you never will." Looking her cousin over, she shook her head. "I don't know how you can look so rested when you just spent most of the night in hard labor. When are they letting you out of here?"

"Tomorrow morning, but I really won't be going anywhere. Tate wants the babies to stay another week or so, just to make sure their lungs are developed properly, so I'll be here most of the time." Shifting the baby to her shoulder so she could burp him, she sent Cilla a teasing look. "Enough about me. I want to hear all about you and Wyatt alone at the ranch last night with the kids. How'd you manage it without killing each other?"

Cilla knew she should have come back with a teasing retort and found a way to change the subject, but her cheeks were already hot. Turning away to wander aimlessly around the small private room, she said, "The kids kept us busy for awhile. Wyatt finally bribed them into going back to bed with popcorn and a story."

At her stiff tone, the teasing smile faded from Kat's face. "Cilla? Why do I feel like I just put my foot in my mouth? Are you okay? What happened last night?"

"Nothing," she said quickly, but the lie stuck in her throat, and before she could stop herself, the truth— or at least all she was willing to talk about—came spilling out. "No, that's not true. Wyatt wants to pick up where we left off, and he's not going to take no for an answer. I don't even know if I want him to. I don't know what I want. I just know I can't go through losing him again. It hurt too much the first time."

Leaning back against her raised pillow, Kat let out her breath in a huff. "Well! This is certainly a surprise. I thought you were over him a long time ago."

"So did I," Cilla replied, her shaky laugh holding little humor. "Surprise, surprise. The joke's on me. All he had to do was kiss me again and I knew why I couldn't marry Tom."

"You still love him."

It was a statement, not a question, one that Cilla couldn't deny. Hugging herself, she nodded miserably. "Yeah. I guess I'm just a glutton for punishment."

"Not necessarily. If you love him and he loves you—"

"But he doesn't. At least he never mentioned the *L* word. To be perfectly honest, I don't think it's even in his vocabulary. He *wants* me," she said flatly. "He wants to pick up where we left off. I don't know about you, but that doesn't sound like a declaration of undying love to me, not when all we had before was a hot summer romance."

She thought she had her emotions firmly in check, but suddenly tears were welling in her eyes and spilling over her lashes. Giving Kat a watery smile, she felt her heart squeeze at the sight of her and the baby. "I want what you have, Kat. You and Cooper and Flynn and Gable. I want the ring and the babies and going to sleep and waking up with the same man every day for the next fifty years. But I don't think that's ever going to happen—not with Wyatt. He likes his freedom and other women too much."

"But just because he hasn't mentioned anything permanent doesn't mean he's going to let you just walk away after Christmas," Kat pointed out quietly. "He's changed, Cilla. Haven't you noticed? He's not the same man he was ten years ago. He's more settled, more...I don't know—family oriented, I guess."

"That's what Josey said," Cilla replied. "Personally, I haven't seen it. He's just as much a flirt as he always was."

"With *you,* silly. But not with anyone else, at least not that I've noticed. Has he been going out? Hanging out at the Crossroads looking for babes?"

"No, but—"

"No, but nothing. That doesn't sound like a man who's on the prowl. Face it, cuz. The guy's nuts about you—everybody but the two of you seem to know it. He can't take his eyes off you whenever you're in the same room together."

Cilla wanted desperately to believe her, but she'd learned the hard way that she couldn't put much stock in what she *thought* Wyatt's feelings for her were. Ten years ago, she would have sworn on all that was holy that he loved her with all his heart. Then she'd found him with another woman. "I don't know. God knows I want to believe it, but right now I'm so confused, I can't be sure of anything."

"Then ask him what his intentions are," Kat said bluntly. "It's the 1990s, not the Gay Nineties. You've got a right to know if he's planning just a roll in the hay or a walk down the aisle. Of course, he may not know yet himself, but you've got a right to know that, too. Then you can make up your mind about what you want to do about it."

It was good advice, and long after she'd left Kat and the babies at the hospital and headed back to the

Double R, Cilla chewed over the idea, liking it more and more the closer she got the ranch. Why shouldn't she ask him his intentions? She wasn't some Victorian maiden who had to sit around twisting her hands waiting for a man to take the initiative that would affect the rest of her life. She'd find him, demand some answers…and pray they were the right ones.

Her chin set at a determined angle, the light of battle in her eyes, she pulled up in front of the house and marched inside, all set for a confrontation. But there wasn't a soul in sight and the place was as quiet as a tomb. Surprised—with three kids in the house, the only time you ran into silence was in the middle of the night—she yelled, "Hey, anybody home?"

"In here," Alice called in a muffled voice from the nether regions at the back of the house. "I'm in the pantry."

Following her voice into the kitchen, she found the housekeeper up to her ears in jars of homemade canned goods that she was transferring from the large walk-in pantry to the kitchen table. Eyeing her flushed face in amusement, Cilla hurried forward to help her with the armload of pint jars she was struggling not to drop. "Lord, Alice, what are you doing?"

"Getting out all my Christmas presents for the neighbors," she huffed as she set the last of the lot on the table. "I usually make homemade jam for everybody, but this year I tried making my own picante sauce." Behind the lenses of her bifocals, her faded eyes twinkled. "It'll strip the hair right off a man's tongue."

"Alice, I've never seen hair on a man's tongue and hope I never do," Cilla said with a laugh.

"You won't if you feed him my picante sauce," she retorted, grinning. Suddenly realizing that Cilla was home long before she expected her, she said, "What are you doing back so early, anyway? I figured you and Kat would talk the afternoon away about those new babies."

"I didn't want to tire her out," she explained. "And I need to talk to Wyatt. Have you seen him? Where is everybody?"

"God only knows. They've all been going every which way since breakfast, with everybody keeping secrets—you know how it is at Christmas. And then the phone's been ringing off the wall with everyone calling about Kat's babies, and sales people, and someone doing a survey, and everything in between—"

Wound up, she would have gone on, but Cilla stopped her with a gentle reminder. "What about Wyatt? Did he say where he's going? His truck's not out front."

"Last I saw him, he was headed for Kat's. That was over two hours ago, though. He could have gone anywhere since then. That's what I told that—hey, where're you going?"

"To see if he's still there," she called over her shoulder as she hurried out the door. "I need to talk to him. See you later."

She was gone before Alice could stop her, before she could finish what she'd started to say—that she'd told the unknown woman who had shown up on the doorstep looking for him the same thing only moments before. Worried, she started after her. Maybe she could catch her before she pulled out of the driveway. But then the phone rang—again!—and the opportunity was lost.

Kicking up a cloud of dirt, Cilla raced toward the rocky canyon where Kat's cabin was, unable to hold back the smile that kept insisting on tugging at the corners of her mouth. Right or wrong, she was taking the bull by the horns and she felt good about it. Kat was right. She loved Wyatt—why shouldn't she tell him so, and ask him if he felt the same way?

He did, she told herself. He had to. Anything else was unacceptable. Her hands unconsciously tightening on the steering wheel, she pressed down on the accelerator and fairly flew across the desert, the inexplicable need to hurry pushing her on.

She would have sworn nothing on earth could have made her check her speed until she reached him, but at the rocky entrance to the canyon, she slammed on her breaks, unable to believe her eyes. The trees and the cactuses lining the road all the way to Kat and Lucas's cabin were decorated with ribbons and bows and garlands.

Stunned, her smile broadening into a grin, Cilla could do nothing but stare. Wyatt had done this. And the other cactuses near the house. It had to be him. He'd said this morning that he had an errand to run, and Alice had seen him heading this way. And he had no other reason to come to the canyon by himself since Kat was still in the hospital at Silver City and when Lucas wasn't with her, he was catching up on his sleep at a nearby hotel.

Foolish tears stinging her eyes, Cilla laughed shakily and blinked them away. Kat and Josey were right—he *had* changed. Afraid he'd break her heart again, she hadn't wanted to see it, but suddenly all the pieces fell into place. The evenings with the family, the play time with the kids, the total lack of interest in carousing with the ranch hands the way he usually did—he hadn't hung around the house all those nights just to make an impression on her. He really had changed.

Suddenly anxious to see him, to tell him how she felt and to feel his arms around her, she hit the gas, her heart knocking crazily as she imagined his reaction to her announcement that she still loved him, had always loved him. God, the time they had wasted! Just thinking about it made her want to cry, but they'd both needed to grow up and mature and find each other again. Now that they had, they had nothing but clear sailing in front of them.

Driving as fast as she dared through the brightly decorated trees, she burst into the clearing where Kat's cabin sat, her face lighting up like a star on top of one of the Christmas trees when she spied Wyatt's sports car parked at the side of the house. Only when she braked to a stop behind his Corvette, though, did she see the dusty red Mercedes with California plates parked next to it.

Surprised, she looked around and started to call

out for him when she suddenly spied him in the trees at the edge of the clearing. And he wasn't alone. There was a tall blonde with him, and he was kissing her for all he was worth.

CHAPTER TEN

FEELING that she'd just been swept back into a nightmare from the past, Cilla stood as if turned to stone while a scream of pain and outrage echoed in her head. *No!* This couldn't be happening! Not again. She couldn't have fallen in love with the same man twice in a lifetime only to have him betray her twice in that same lifetime. How could she have been such a fool? Like a naive schoolgirl caught up in the thrill and rush of first love, she'd wanted to believe so badly that he'd changed that she'd let her guard down and convinced herself he loved her. God, what a crock! Wyatt Chandler didn't love anyone but himself. How many times did he have to stab her in the back before she realized that?

No more, she thought, swallowing the hot tears that threatened to choke her. This was it, the last time he hurt her, the last time she let him hurt her. Some things just weren't meant to be, and she and Wyatt were evidently one of them. Trying to force the issue wasn't doing anything but torturing her and she couldn't take it anymore.

Fury hit her then, hot and quick and cleansing. How dare he do this to her! It was just last night that they…that the two of them… Shying away from that thought and the heated images it dragged up, she seriously considered storming over there, jerking him away from the hussy who was plastered all over him, and tell him exactly what she thought of him. It was the least he deserved, the rat! But she didn't even want to look at him, let alone tell him off. Whirling, she headed for her car.

Glaring, nose-to-nose, at the woman who had snuck up on him while he was decorating the last cedar and laid a kiss on him before he even knew she was on the property, Wyatt stood unmoved, unresponsive and re-volted, his lips as cold as a dead fish and his arms at his side. He could have pushed her from him, but the lady had more moves than an octopus and he'd have had to hurt her to do it. As much as she infuriated him, he had to draw the line at that. So he waited her out, not giving her the least encouragement. He didn't know how the hell she had found him, but she'd made a wasted trip. And he was going to tell her that just as soon as she finished making a fool of herself.

But the lady was nothing if not persistent. His pa-tience growing thin, he was on the verge of telling her to give it up when he suddenly heard the sound of tires spinning in the drive and kicking up gravel. Jerking his head back, he looked up just in time to see Cilla's Honda racing wildly down the road that led back to the main ranch house.

"Ah, hell!" Curses rolling off his tongue, he pushed Eleanor to arm's length, furiously untangling himself from her. "Damn you, woman, *let go!*"

Undaunted, Eleanor only smiled and tried to rewind her arms around his neck. "You know you don't mean that, Wyatt, honey. C'mon, give me a kiss. You know you're dying to."

What he was dying to do was go after Cilla— God, he had to explain! but first he had to deal with this little witch once and for all. A muscle jumping along his rock hard jaw, he laid his hands on her shoulders and looked her dead in the eye. "Listen to me, Eleanor, because I'm only going to say this once. You're an attractive woman. I'm sure there're a lot of men out there who would like to get to know you better if you'd give them the chance, but I'm not one of them. I'm never going to be one of them."

"Don't say that, sweetie. If you'd just—"

"I'm in love with someone else," he said with brutal honesty.

"Don't be ridiculous!" She laughed, the sound more than a little desperate. "You love me."

"No, I don't. I never loved you. I never even gave you any encouragement. Not once. Hell, I even left the damn state so you would finally realize that I wasn't interested, but you found a way to track me down—"

"I hired a private investigator," she said simply. "I thought you were playing some kind of a game."

"I don't play games. Not those kind, anyway." Unwrapping her arms from around his neck, he stepped back and this time she let him go. "I don't want to hurt you," he said quietly, "but the truth is that you don't love me. No, you don't," he said quickly when she opened her mouth to protest. "You love the thrill of the chase. The hunt. So find yourself somebody else to chase, because I'm out of the race. I love somebody else and I plan to spend the next fifty or sixty years proving it to her. So if you'll excuse me, I've got to go. I've got a lot of explaining to do. Just go back the way you came and you won't have any trouble finding your way back home."

Stepping around her, he strode quickly toward his Corvette, his thoughts already jumping ahead to Cilla. Of all the rotten, miserable luck! Dammit, how could he have let this happen? He knew how resourceful Eleanor was. She left no stone unturned when she wanted something and for some crazy reason that only she could understand, she thought she wanted him. God, what must Cilla be thinking? He'd never thought to tell her about Eleanor because she never had been and never would be a part of his life, but there was no way he was going to be able to convince Cilla of that now. Not after she'd witnessed that one-sided kiss. She'd think that he'd invited the woman here on purpose, that history was once again repeating itself, when nothing could have been further from the truth. He had to find her, had to make her understand!

But when he raced back to the house, there was no sign of Cilla's Honda. Swearing, he braked to a screeching stop in the front drive and just sat there with the motor running, trying to figure out where the hell she could have gone. She wouldn't have left without her things, and she hadn't had time to pack. Dammit, where was she?

But even as he hit the steering wheel in frustration, he knew. Praying he was right, he wheeled around and headed back to the canyon.

The line cabin was located miles from Kat's place, at the opposite end of the canyon. A simple structure that consisted of four bare walls and a roof, its weathered logs had never seen a coat of paint, and electricity was just a dream. The only running water was the nearby creek, which ran the entire length of the canyon, the only furniture a roughly built bunk and a crude table and chairs. It hadn't been designed for comfort but as a refuge for cowboys who had wandered too far from the ranch headquarters and suddenly found themselves caught up in a storm.

Braking to a stop in front of it, Cilla cut the engine and just sat there for a long time, staring at the rough-hewn cedar walls with eyes that were stark with despair. She shouldn't have come here. Not now. She was too hurt, too vulnerable. And there were too many memories here. Memories of her and Wyatt, here, together, swimming in the creek, exploring the canyon, teasing and playing and falling in love.

Well, at least one of them had fallen in love…then and now, she thought bitterly. God, she had to get out of here! But instead of starting the motor and heading back to the house, she reached for the door handle and stepped out of the car.

The wind that always swirled through the canyon immediately grabbed at her hair, blowing it into her face with a playfulness she would have normally laughed at. But not today. Then she heard the creek. As the clear, cold water tumbled over the rocks that lined the creek, it murmured and bubbled and whispered secrets to the wind.

Stopping in her tracks, Cilla cocked her head to listen, her lips twitching into the barest semblance of a smile, and suddenly she knew why she'd come here. The water. How could she have forgotten it? She's always loved the sound of it, the soothing murmur that never stopped. It called to her soul, seeped into her bones, calmed her as nothing else could.

That long-ago summer, she'd spent more hours here than she could remember. Most of the time, she'd been with Wyatt, but she'd also come here by herself, drawn to the peace of the place, the privacy, the solitude. Here, she'd fantasized and dreamed and built castles in the sky. And when all that had come tumbling down around her ears, it was here she'd come to cry her eyes out.

Nothing, it seemed, had changed.

Emptiness spread through her like a cold, creeping fog, chilling her to the bone. Shivering, she hugged herself, but it didn't help. She'd never felt so alone in her life. She wanted to believe that she'd get over this, but if this time with Wyatt had proven anything, it was that she was and always would be a one-man woman. And an idiot. How many times did she have to catch him with other women before she got the message that he didn't have a faithful bone in his body?

Anger, sharp and biting, coiled in her gut. The man was a skunk, lower than dirt, she decided as she wandered through the trees to the creek. He'd used up all his chances and hurt her for the last time. Reaching down for a small rock, she tossed it into the water and watched it sink to the bottom. She didn't pretend that she didn't still love him—evidently that was to be her lot in life, like it or not—but she wasn't a masochist. She could love him and not let him be a part of her life. After all, wasn't that what she'd been doing for the last ten years?

Lost in her misery, trying to figure out what she was going to do with the rest of her life, she didn't hear the sports car that quietly rumbled into the canyon and drew up next to her Honda. But then the sound of a vehicle door being slammed carried easily to her over the gurgle of the creek, and she whirled to see Wyatt striding toward her, the angles of his lean face set in somber lines.

Her heart kicked into gear at the sight of him, irritating her no end. Lifting her chin, she glared at him from twenty feet away. "I don't know why you followed me, but I came here to be alone. So go back to your hot-to-trot little blonde from California. We've got nothing to say to each other."

"The hell we don't," he growled, stalking toward her. "She's not my hot-to-trot little anything!"

"Oh, really?" she taunted, standing her ground. "That's not the way it looked to me. She was plastered all over you like a heat rash—"

"You're damn right," he agreed. "*She* was plastered all over me. And *she* was kissing me, not the other way around."

She laughed at that, but there wasn't a trace of humor in the painful sound. "And you were fighting her off with a stick, right? Tell me another one, Wyatt."

"Dammit, Cilla, if you'll just let me explain! That wasn't what you thought it was—"

"Oh, yes it was," she retorted. "So save the fairy tale for someone who's interested. I'm not." Presenting him her back, she headed for the cabin.

The tears she was so sure she wasn't going to shed thankfully held off as she stepped inside and slammed the door behind her. But once the silence closed around her, once she was well and truly alone, her eyes burned and suddenly she was shuddering with sobs she couldn't control. With a muffled cry, she threw herself onto the bunk that was built against one wall and cried her eyes out.

When Wyatt soundlessly opened the cabin door, his heart twisted in his chest at the sight of her misery. In two strides, he reached the bunk and went down on one knee beside Cilla. "Ah, honey, don't do this to yourself," he said thickly. "You're crying over nothing."

"G-go away," she choked, burying her face in the bare mattress. "J-just g-go a-waaay."

"Not on your life," he growled. "I'm not going anywhere until we get this straightened out."

He didn't give her a chance to argue, but simply scooped her up and settled her in his lap as he sank down onto the bunk with his back against the wall. She cursed him and tried to wiggle free, but he was ready for her. Wrapping his arms around her, he crushed her against his chest and just held her. "I'm not letting you go, honey. Not now. Not ever. So you might as well get used to it."

She stiffened, her slender body as rigid as a broom handle in his arms, and for a second, he thought she was going to haul off and belt him one—she was that upset. He couldn't have said he'd have blamed her, not after she'd found him with another woman just hours after they'd made love. As far as she knew, he was guilty as sin and deserved anything she could dish out. But instead of letting him have it with both barrels, all the fight just seemed to go out of her. A sob caught in her throat, and suddenly she pressed her face against his throat and cried as if she was never going to stop.

His arms tight around her, Wyatt just held her, emotion clogging his throat. He couldn't lose her, not again. He loved her too much even to consider the possibility. The words rose to his tongue, the need to tell her almost more than he could bear, but first he had to explain about Eleanor and make her understand that the woman had never been anything to him but an aggravating problem that he'd tried his damndest to avoid.

"I wasn't lying to you, honey," he said gruffly as her sobs gradually quieted and she lay spent against him. "I never gave Eleanor the time of day, but somehow she got it in her head that she was in love with me." He told her everything then, how Eleanor showed up uninvited at work, how she followed him whenever he went out, even when it was just with friends, the telephone calls in the middle of the night to make sure he wasn't with someone. "I'm telling you, she's nuts. Certifiable. She stalked me everywhere I went and even announced our engagement in the paper. And I don't even really know her! That's why I came here for Christmas. I thought if I got out of California for awhile and didn't tell anybody where I was going, she would become fixated on somebody else and leave me alone. I should have known better. The lady is nothing if not stubborn."

At his bitter tone, Cilla pushed back just far enough so that she could see his face. "Are you serious?"

"Do I look like I'm kidding?"

No, she had to admit he didn't. She'd never seen him more somber. "How did she find you?"

"Apparently she hired a private investigator. I never thought she'd go that far, which shows how stupid I am. The lady's rolling in it and used to getting anything and everything she wants. When I first told her I wasn't interested, I guess she saw me as a challenge."

Even to his own ears, it sounded like a half-baked story that was an insult to any woman's intelligence, and Cilla was no exception. He saw the doubt in her eyes and it hurt, dammit! He was telling the truth and somehow he had to make her believe him. "If I was going to lie, I'd come up with a hell of a more believable story than this," he said flatly. "I know it sounds farfetched, but if you don't believe me, ask Gable. When we talked at Thanksgiving, I told him all about Eleanor and how she was driving me crazy. He was the one who suggested I get out of L.A. for awhile and come here for the holidays."

Her eyes searching his, Cilla wanted desperately to believe him, but she was afraid to take the chance and let him shatter her heart again. "Why would she think she's in love with you if you didn't encourage her? Did you ever go out with her?"

"Not once. I swear it!"

"Oh, come on, Wyatt," she scoffed. "I know what a flirt you are. The family's been keeping me apprised of the women in your life for years. You had to have done something to make this woman think you were interested in her."

Grinning at the sudden temper that flashed in her eyes, he caught her hands and held them firmly against his chest. "So you've been keeping tabs on me, have you? I'm glad to hear it. Yeah, there were women, but not that many and I wasn't serious about any of them. As for Eleanor, all she ever got from me was a smile, and I've been regretting even that ever since. That's the truth. I can't prove it—you'll just have to take it on faith."

She could have told him that was a lot to ask of her, considering the number of times she'd found him with another woman, but when she stared into his eyes, she couldn't doubt the sincerity she saw in his steady gaze when he spoke about Eleanor. If he was lying, he was much better at it now than he had been in the past when he couldn't fib and look her in the eye at the same time. As for his heartthrobs over the years since she'd last seen him, that was another matter.

"You don't have to prove it," she said quietly. "I believe you…at least about Eleanor. But you're really pushing it if you expect me to believe you've been a monk all these years. I know better."

His smile faded. "I meant for you to. A man's got his pride, you know. I exaggerated things because I knew the news would get back to you through the family, and I didn't want you to think that I missed you or anything. But I did. I just didn't realize how much until I saw you again."

His words echoed her own feelings so exactly that she felt as if he'd reached out and squeezed her heart. All the lonely years rose up in her throat, thick and hot, threatening to choke her. "Don't."

"Don't what?" Frowning at the tears that once again sparkled in her eyes, he released one of her hands to cup her cheek in his palm. "Sweetheart, what is it? What did I say? Please don't cry again. I love you, dammit! You've got to believe me!"

God, how long had she waited to hear those words? It seemed like a lifetime. Hope lightening her heart, she could only stare at him. "You love me?"

"Well, of course I do! I've only fallen in love twice in this lifetime and both times were with you."

"But—"

"I know what you're thinking. If I loved you, how could I have fooled around on you ten years ago? I didn't. That was all a setup, honey, staged for your benefit."

"A setup? What are you talking about? Are you saying you weren't involved with that girl I caught you kissing?"

"She was my roommate's girlfriend. I had to do something, Cilla. You were only seventeen, for God's sake! You were already planning a wedding and picking out china, and I knew you wouldn't believe me if I just told you I didn't love you. So I talked to Kurt and Sharon and we came up with this plan." His eyes dark with entreaty, he said gruffly, "I had to let you go so you could grow up, sweetheart. If you want to hate me for it now, I can't stop you. But it was just as hard on me as it was on you. All these years, I thought I'd lost you for good."

Shaken, Cilla couldn't believe what she was hearing. All this time, she'd thought she knew him, the type of man he was, what being loved by him meant. But she hadn't had a clue. He'd nearly sacrificed them for what was best for her, and she didn't know many men who would have done that. She wanted to rail at him for putting them both through such pain, but she knew he was right about one thing. At seventeen, she never would have believed he simply didn't love her, not without the "proof" that Sharon provided.

Cocking her head at him, she smiled. "You decorated the cactuses for the family, did you? Don't try to deny it. I'd already figured it out when I saw Eleanor giving you a tonsillectomy."

The abrupt change of subject caught him off guard, but only for a second. Shrugging, he grinned. "Maybe I did, and maybe I didn't. Why?"

"Because I've got a feeling the man I love did," she said simply. "I didn't know it before, but I think that's just the type of thing he'd do."

Tightening his arms around her, he lifted a teasing brow at her, his green eyes alight with love. "The man you love, huh? You sure about that?"

"Surer than I've ever been about anything in my life," she replied confidently, and kissed him.

It was a kiss of promise, of renewal, of a love that had withstood the test of time and was better for it. Without saying a word, forgiveness was given, the past forgotten, trust shared. And when they both came up for air, there was nothing but the future in front of them.

"I was going to wait until Christmas Eve to propose, but I can't wait," he said thickly. "I love you more than you'll ever know, Cilla Rawlings. Will you marry me?"

All her dreams coming true, she laughed with joy. "Well, it's about time! I thought you'd never ask!"

"Can I take that as a yes?"

"You'd better," she retorted, hugging him fiercely. "You're mine, cousin. Now that I've found you again, I'm not ever letting you go."

"Good. Because I'm not going anywhere." His grin broadening, he shifted on the bunk and drew her down beside him. "Now, what was that you were saying about the man you love?"

All the magic you'll need this Christmas…

Angels in the Snow

Do fairy lights and family make the perfect Christmas?

Sarah Morgan

When **Daniel** is left with his brother's kids, only one person can help. But it'll take more than mistletoe before **Stella** helps him…

Patrick hadn't advertised for a housekeeper. But when **Hayley** appears, she's the gift he didn't even realise he needed.

Alfie and his little sister know a lot about the magic of Christmas – and they're about to teach the grown-ups a much-needed lesson!

Available 1st October 2010

www.millsandboon.co.uk

M&B

Spend Christmas with
NORA ROBERTS

Daniel MacGregor is the clan patriarch. He's
powerful, rich – and determined to see his three
career-minded granddaughters married. So he
chooses three unsuspecting men he considers
worthy and sets his plans in motion!

As Christmas approaches, will his independent
granddaughters escape his schemes? Or can the
magic of the season melt their hearts – and
allow Daniel's plans to succeed?

Available 1st October 2010

www.millsandboon.co.uk

THE *Balfour* LEGACY

EIGHT SISTERS, EIGHT SCANDALS

VOLUME 5 – OCTOBER 2010
Zoe's Lesson
by Kate Hewitt

VOLUME 6 – NOVEMBER 2010
Annie's Secret
by Carole Mortimer

VOLUME 7 – DECEMBER 2010
Bella's Disgrace
by Sarah Morgan

VOLUME 8 – JANUARY 2011
Olivia's Awakening
by Margaret Way

8 VOLUMES IN ALL TO COLLECT!

www.millsandboon.co.uk

M&B